KISS
for a
Killer

THE
NORTHERN
SINS SAGA

Book 2

NIK TERRY

Copyright Statement

Published on 1st March 2022 by Nik Terry.

The author can be reached by email on
nikterryauthor@gmail.com

Or Facebook https://www.facebook.com/NikTerryAuthor

Or Instagram https://www.instagram.com/nik_terry_author_/

If you enjoyed this book, please encourage your friends and family to download their own copy from Amazon and I would also love it if you could leave a review.

Character Pronunciations

Cian (Kee-An)

Oisín (O-sheen)

Fiadh (Fee-a)

Lorcan (Lorr-can)

Lukyan (Look – ee – yan)

Chapters

Chapter One

ஐ Cian ௸

The burn of whisky against the back of my throat distracted me from the sting of the expensive cologne I'd just soaked my jaw with. I smoothed my hair into place before shrugging on a crisp white shirt, finishing it with a black bow tie and looking as stuffy as a penguin with a stick up its arse.

The fundraiser was the other side of the City and my car would be here any second. Clocking the time on the display of my mobile, I pushed my arms into the black jacket, secured the cuff links in place, and dropped my phone into my breast pocket. Party time.

We were halfway across Manhattan when my phone vibrated against my chest. I slid the green button across the display and held it to my ear.

"Yes?"

"It's Eddie Two Blows. He's our skimmer," said the American voice with a hint of Irish.

"Fuck."

"You need to deal with this tonight."

1

"Fucking figures."

This was not what I fucking needed right now.

"Conor, we're detouring to Monty's gym," I called to my driver.

"What? Now, boss?"

"Aye. Now."

The gym was an old-fashioned place operating out of the one of the most deprived neighbourhoods in New York. Old Monty had passed on years ago, but the gym still stood in his honour. The building was drab; crumbling walls decorated with a scrawl of graffiti and the red the sign that was painted vertically down the wall, peeling and fading. As the car rolled to a stop next to the sidewalk, I fumbled around under my seat, popping the lid on the storage box underneath and pulling out a gun. Taking off the black dinner jacket, I dropped the diamond studded cuff-links into my inside pocket and rolled my shirt sleeves up, shrugging my arms into my holster and tucking my Glock snugly in place.

I glanced at my watch before stepping inside. It was already 7pm. This had to be sorted quickly. Conor locked the car, taking a last worried glance around as the black town car stuck out like a sore thumb on a street of boarded properties and chain-link fences full of holes. It didn't matter who we were. In New York's capital of depravation, murder and drug-users, there was a still a pretty good chance the car might not be here when we got back.

2

The gym was alive with the swish of gloved fists hitting a myriad of punch bags, rhythm varying from punter to punter. I stepped around a couple of men lightly sparring in an empty space and continued towards the ring at the back.

A man in a red padded helmet ducked and dived, coolly moving away from the padded fists flying at him until a sharp right hook caught him off guard and he staggered backwards. The other man, shorter and older, but out-matching his opponent in weight, muscle and technique, advanced quickly, delivering a combination of quick jabs until a strong back-hand blow sent the red-helmeted opponent to the floor.

I leaned casually against the ropes, watching the scene play out in front of me. Red helmet lay on the floor momentarily dazed before pushing up on to weak arms and collapsing back down again. He was done. The older guy yanked off his gloves as he walked towards him and helped him back to his feet, pulling him into a sweaty, manly hug as they retired to the far side of the ring.

"Yo, Eddie, not bad," I called as I wandered round the other side of the ring, Conor falling in behind me.

He looked at me, a flicker of reaction across his eyes.

"Good to see ya, Cian," he answered, unwrapping the fabric wraps from around his wrists and hands.

"Is it?"

3

Eddie looked over my shoulder to Conor, glancing around the gym and back to me.

"What do you need?" he asked, and I sensed a tension in his voice.

"A word. Wanna clear this place out?"

He hesitated for a moment but then popped his head up, raising his voice, "Yo. We're closing now."

There was a mutter of low voices and with no urgency, jackets and sweatshirts were put back on, people filtering out until there were only a few bodies left. Two men strolled over, coming to a stand just behind Eddie. One was huge, nearly as wide as he was tall. Tree-branch like arms bulging as he crossed them over his chest. He was the sort of man who would make most people piss themselves. I paid him no consideration.

Propping my arse on the side of the ring, I turned my attention back to the boxer in front of me.

"Your friends staying?"

"Jonno and Stubbs will stay."

I shrugged. No matter.

"Now, the thing is, it's come to our attention we're missing some money."

I paused, watching his reaction. His jaw tightened.

"Don't suppose you know anything about that, do you?"

"Nah."

4

"Hmmm. You see, it's been going on for a few months now and, well, we're really fucking out of pocket."

He looked at me blankly.

"And we don't like that. Not. At. All. Someone's been skimming. Stealing. From us."

I paused again. His jaw clenched tighter. I picked at a bit of dirt from under my fingernails and checked my watch. Nope, no time for this.

"So here's the thing. You're gonna send your boys here to fetch that money. All $750,000 of it."

"It was only $500,000!" he blurted out suddenly.

Dumb fuck. He'd clearly taken one too many punches to the head.

"So it *was* you?"

He went quiet again.

"Get me my money," I stated flatly, "I've added the interest. It's $750,000."

"I don't have that much!"

I cocked my head to the side.

"I, I, I, can get it Cian. It was a mistake. I'm sorry."

"A mistake? Oops, I just took off a few 'K' before I handed the profits to the Murphys? Huge fucking mistake."

I watched him swallow, then he looked behind him and motioned sideways with his head.

5

The shorter of the two men turned and walked away. It would have been easier if the big one had gone. Never mind. I stepped forward quickly, driving my fist into Eddie's nose, feeling the crunch of bone and the squeal erupt from his lips. Eddie Two Blows cradled his face in hands, blood dripping between his fingers. The big guy stepped forwards.

"I wouldn't," I said, shaking my head.

He stopped where he was. This one clearly had some brain cells left. Then I delivered a few quick blows to the already bloodied face of Eddie, pummelling into him with my fists, his skin ripping with each blow, until he collapsed to the floor, face down.

I bent down, pushing my knee between his shoulder blades and pulled his right hand from underneath him. Opening his fingers up so I splayed them on the floor in front of him, I unsheathed my knife from its place on my holster and hovered it over his hand.

"You steal from us again and it'll be more than your finger I take."

I sliced the blade over his index finger, skin and flesh giving way, snagging on the hardness of bone. He shrieked and writhed underneath me like a tortured animal, blood spilling onto the gym floor. Removing my knee from the boxer, I stood up as the shorter guy returned with a holdall and stopped, the colour draining from his face. He placed the bag in my outstretched hand and in return, I tossed Eddie's finger at him.

6

"Have a good evening," I said, turning and stepping over the man lying at my feet, groaning into his own blood.

My reflection stared back at me from the tinted glass of the town car windows. My white shirt was soaked in red, sticking to my chest in places where the blood had drenched right through. I glanced at Conor, looking him up and down.

"What's up, Boss?" he asked.

"Take your clothes off," I instructed, watching the confusion on his face turn to realisation.

He shrugged out of his jacket, his fingers plucking the buttons of the white shirt underneath free and pulled it off over his shoulders and holding it out to me. The shirt was tight, straining across my chest and pinching at my biceps, but it fit, just. I tossed the blood-soaked shirt under the seat with my guns and tied the black bow tie across my throat.

"Just pull up on the side-walk," I instructed Conor, opting to walk the short distance to the boutique hotel where the fundraiser was being held.

I didn't need any unnecessary attention on my near-naked driver.

"Chuck those clothes in the incinerator, Conor," I directed as I climbed out, "I'll get a cab back."

I spent the next few hours talking to various politicians, businessmen and big-influencers, feigning interest in their projects, sipping back the best whiskies the hotel offered and sneaking glances at the many beautiful women cruising the room on the arms of older men. Half way through the night I'd made it round everyone I needed to, ensuring continued support for the Murphys as well as reminding others what would happen if they stepped out of line. All but one.

He was a middle-aged ex-banker with an agenda to make it as the next Mayor. He'd climbed the ranks at some speed the last few years, but he was a loose cannon and needed to be bought, somehow. The only problem was we had nothing on him yet.

I approached, pasting on a charming smile, touching his arm lightly.

"Cian O'Sullivan," I introduced myself, my hand outstretched, watching the middle aged man's eyes search my face, trying to place me but failing.

"Jonas Artruro," he replied, turning to the dark-haired curvy, beauty beside him, "my wife."

I smiled, grasping her slim hand gently, my eyes catching the sparkle of the heavily encrusted diamond rings like a magpie. Her eyes lingered on me, a very slight dilation of her pupils, the tiniest shift of her lips.

"Have we met?" he asked, suspiciously.

"No. But I understand you're acquainted with my Uncle. You've helped him with funding for various property investment projects over the last few years."

"I remember," he answered.

He didn't. But he would soon enough.

We talked about the usual boring shit; the stock markets, his run for mayor, his thoughts on the newest planning restrictions, until I was bored of the sound of my own voice. I patted him on the shoulder as I moved on, my hand swiping over his breast pocket and inserting the tiny listening device.

Time for another drink. I pushed through the crowd at the bar, aiming for the tall brunette, who'd been standing there for at least two drinks. My hand brushed her bare arm. She looked at me through dark lashes in the mirror in front of us, her gaze dropping from my face and down my body.

"Can I get you another drink?" I asked, turning sideways towards her.

Her cocktail glass was empty, the cocktail stick of olives left untouched in the bottom.

She nodded, "Thank you. That's very kind."

I waved the barman back and ordered her another and as the new cocktail was pushed onto the bar in front of her, I reached across, plucking the abandoned cocktail stick out of the empty glass and picking the olives off with my teeth. Her eyes dropped to my lips, her own parting slightly. I chewed at the cocktail stick, watching her reaction, the look of excitement across her face, the lust for attention and the dilation of her pupils. I'd seen how she had stared from across the room the whole night, bored with her husband's conversation, looking for that little spark of excitement, of exhilaration, amidst the talk of banking deals and interest rates, of bills and pieces of legislature and shallow gestures of interest in her own affairs.

I let my eyes wander purposefully over her body. She was stunning for an older woman. Her dress clung to her, pushing her big tits together as it dipped low over her chest. It fell all the way to the floor, but I could see well-shaped legs from the thigh high split.

"Having a good night?" I asked, leaning into her ever more closely.

"Yes, if you like talking politics with old men."

"No, I don't. I could think of faster ways to die," I answered, watching her stroke a strand of dark hair behind her ear.

She giggled; a light airy laugh.

"What do you do?" I asked.

"I'm a jewellery designer."

I reached out and stroked my fingers under her ear, gently pulling at the diamonds that twinkled as they hung from the platinum tear drop in the middle of her earlobe.

"Did you design these?"

"Yes."

"They are beautiful," I answered, looking directly at her, my fingers still closed around the delicate metal.

I dropped my hand, brushing her neck with my fingers.

"So, what are you doing here at the bar by yourself?" I asked.

"Having a more exhilarating conversation talking to an empty cocktail glass than with stuffy middle-aged men," she mumbled, her eyes dropping to the clear liquid in the glass in front of her

"I can make it more exciting," I said, dipping my face towards her, inhaling the strong feminine scent from her expensive perfume.

She looked at me for a moment, studying me, holding my gaze, her dark eyes burning into mine.

*****

It was 11am before I'd rallied round and got myself over to the Murphy mansion. Conor had been waiting for me out on the street for an hour as I sluggishly showered away the hang-over, and the lingering scent of perfume on my skin. The drive to the mansion took just over an hour from my condo and the fresh air was a relief when we eventually pulled up in front of the double-fronted house.

Everyone had congregated in the huge kitchen and I wandered in, grunted at them and advanced on the coffee machine. Taking a very needy gulp of the strong liquid, I turned around.

"How'd it go last night?" my uncle asked.

He was my mother's older brother. I had joined the Murphys out here in New York five years ago, after my mother's death. Ireland had been too harsh a reminder and my attempts at self-destruction by stoking the fire that burned between us and our rivals, the O'Malleys, was breaking apart an already fragile peace between us. My father packed me off across the Atlantic Ocean to quell my destructiveness and learn some discipline then married my older brother, Torin, to an O'Malley girl to stop years of further bloodshed and revenge. Now I was the Murphys' enforcer; cold and calculating and I loved every minute. Life was simple: sort the family's problems, ensure everyone towed the line and punish those who didn't, whilst fucking and drinking my way through New York.

"Got the cash back, well some of it," I answered him after another long gulp of coffee, "Eddie Two Blows will have the rest next week."

"And if he doesn't?"

"He'll lose another finger. And another, until it's paid in full."

"And what about Jonas?"

"That's sorted too. Bugs are all planted. We should get some dirt on him soon."

My Uncle smiled, "good work. How many did you plant?"

"Five. One in his mobile and his wife's mobile. I swapped out his favourite tie pin and there's one in his briefcase and his jacket pocket."

"Christ, how'd you manage all that?"

"I fucked his wife."

A phone rang and my uncle answered it. His eyebrows knitted together and he walked out of the kitchen.

Tully, my older cousin, slapped me on the back, smiling.

"Ah, we've taught you well, young-un," he said with a huge smile.

I shrugged.

"Got the job done, didn't it?"

"Sure, and a nice piece of pussy to go with it. She's a real stunner. Boy got himself a cougar!" he turned and addressed the room and a reception of chuckles broke out.

My uncle stepped back in, his face dark and serious and beckoned for everyone to move out. That was never a good sign, particularly when it left just the three of us; me, Tully, and my uncle.

"Son," he said, approaching me, his voice soft.

Hairs tingled on my arms and stood up at the back of my neck.

"That was Ireland. Your father and your brother are dead. Murdered."

My mouth went dry. My heart beat faster.

"They were taken a couple of days ago. Their bodies have just been found. One between the eyes."

Fuck. But there was more. I could see it in his eyes.

"What else is it, Mack?"

"I'm sorry. They got your sister too."

White-hot, searing anger hit me square in the chest. My stomach coiled and tightened. With a roar, I launched the cup across the room. I took out my Glock, checked the chamber and the sights and returned it to the holster. I needed to kill someone. Anyone.

Chapter Two

❧ Charlie ❧

Wind rushed against my face, whipping the tears from my eyes, adrenaline coursing through my veins. My heart thumped against my ribcage as hooves pounded underneath me. I checked the filly on the bend, feeling another horse just to my right. Distance fell away as a row of metre high hurdles approached fast. I checked again, nipped my knees to the saddle, and the filly flew over without a fault in her stride.

We reached the second hurdle, sailing over with barely a change in pace, and then we were on to the next. The rest of the field had fallen away behind us as we'd pushed out a few horse's lengths in front. We neared the next fence, the biggest on the gallops. I sat back a little, felt down the reins, connecting myself with her mouth and then she was up and over. Touching down safely on the other side, I glanced behind, noticing the gap had widened further and I kicked on up the hill, feeling the horse stretching through her body, taking me forwards with her.

As we reached the top of the hill, I started to gently pull her up, patting her neck until she'd dropped to a trot and the others caught up.

"Shit, Charlie, she's a real goer," one of the riders said breathlessly from behind me.

"She sure is. Think she's ready for the weekend."

I patted the filly again and her ears flicked forward.

"That was damn fast," old Bobby said excitedly as we passed his vantage point at the top of the hill.

Back down at the yard I jumped off the bay horse, scratching her neck before handing the reins to one of the stable boys who was waiting to take her away and wash her down. The filly was one of my favourites, not just because she was one that I had bred here at the yard, but mostly because she was brave and tenacious and always willing. Not like my next ride.

The black horse came out of his stable almost vertical; up on his two hind legs, punching the air with his hooves, the gleam of late winter sunlight catching the metal shoes on his feet. The stable boy held on, alarm etched across his face, watching carefully where the angry horse's legs came down.

"You sure you want to get on this one today?" Bobby asked, concern in his voice.

"He'll be fine when I'm on."

The stable lad turned the horse in a circle around him as I skipped along beside and another jockey grabbed my leg and hoisted me upwards. I hit the saddle and scrambled up the reins, getting some semblance of control as quickly as possible. The rest of the riders mounted quickly and we turned to make our way back up to the gallop track.

The black horse jumped around angrily beneath me, snorting and bucking, his metal shoes ringing on the concrete path as sparks flew out in all directions. Up in the middle of the field of horses I kept him; a tail in front for him to follow and a horse behind to drive him forwards. He was sweating already, over excited and tightly coiled; a spring ready to break free at any second. I just had to keep a lid on him until we hit the track.

The minute his feet touched the rubber and sand of the surface, he was up off all fours, the snorting beast having returned. I scratched his neck as I glanced from rider to rider and then I nodded and we sent the horses onwards. The black horse leaped forwards, flying through the air and then hitting the ground at a gallop. He was fast and sharp but strong too, pulling the reins from me. I checked him slightly, dropping my weight back on to the saddle and rubbing at his neck with my knuckles. Clamping my legs around him as much as I could, I held him there, breathing steadily and letting any stiffness drop from my limbs, hoping he would react to me. Soon he relaxed, his stride lengthening and the tension falling from him.

He cruised around the gallops in the middle of the pack, settling into his own rhythm, focusing on the hurdles coming towards him. He faltered over the first, hesitating slightly just before take-off making him land awkwardly the other side, but he picked up his tempo again. As the next fence approached I squeezed slightly on the reins, nudging him with my heels when I could barely see the brush of the hurdle before us anymore. His black ears pricked and he tucked his front end up neatly, landing effortlessly the other side, not missing a step.

Eventually, at the top of the hill, the group of horses slowed.

"Good lad, Brian", I whispered to the stallion, scuffing at his neck with my fingertips.

"Told you he'd settle," I called as we rode past Bobby and back down to the yard.

The old man's smile seemed strained, his usual unimpressed eye-roll not following my quip. His shoulders were set tense against the wind at the crest of the hill and for a split second he looked sad.

*****

I walked along the road in the dark, swinging my torch back and forth in front of me. It wasn't so bad on the way to Bobby's house, but after a couple of glasses of wine with dinner I would stagger back to my flat above the stables, precarious in the pitch black.

Old Bobby's house was at the back of the property, on top of a small hill which looked down onto the stable block and groom's accommodation about a third of a mile away. The land which the yard and facilities sat on was undulating, normal for Durham's countryside. There was virtually nowhere flat and anywhere that was, wasn't level for long. The property was extensive and sprawling, which seemed a waste as the old man lived there alone, no family to his name. It had been a barn in a past life, converted years ago. The older part of the building was single storey but with high ceilings, original beams exposed against the white-wash of the walls and old sash windows set in heavy lintels.

On the west side it had been extended, and a two storey, modernised wing had been added which now housed the front door. I kicked my boots off at the doorstep and nudged the door open, the smell of dinner and sudden warmth greeting me, a contrast against the freezing February air. I padded into the kitchen, thick socks pulled over my jeans and three layers of jumpers under my coat, discarding a few after the first glass of wine seeped into my blood.

Bobby had been quiet over dinner, lost in probably the same thoughts I'd been seeing him grapple with over the last few months. Once the dishes were cleared, we sat in front of the log burner, kindle popping gently in the heat of the flames. Bobby picked at the blanket he'd thrown over his knees, distracted.

I sipped on another glass of wine.

"What's up, Bobby?" I asked.

The old man paused, silence hanging heavy in the air between us, his eyes glassy with a look I hadn't seen on him before.

"Charlie, there's something I need to tell you," he started eventually, his voice strained.

I sat quietly, those words echoing in my head. The same words my father said to me as a four-year old. The same words my sister said to me only a year ago.

"Some years ago I got into difficulty with this place," Bobby started again, before pausing and glancing around the room pointedly before continuing.

"I lost control of my gambling, got in a lot of debt. A *lot* of debt. I was going to lose everything. All this. A jockey I knew offered me a way out, introduced me to some people. They loaned me some money to pay off my debts. It sorted things out for a time and then you came along. You got the yard back in the limelight again, got winners back on our books and, with that, attracted some real good owners. It was good for a while. Really good."

A knot was forming in my stomach. An uneasy sweat prickling uncomfortably on my palms.

"Then I started betting again, putting more and more down till I was back there again; in debt. I went back to them and asked them to bail me out, again, and they did. There was money left

20

over, so we ploughed it into the breeding side of the business."

Bobby had taken a leap of faith breeding his own racehorses and over the last two years we had seen them notch up some big wins. I'd ridden a load of winners too and that had led to some wealthy owners who had put their horses with us. I swallowed. I really didn't like where this was headed.

"But I never really kicked the habit," he said sadly, his eyes searching the bottom of his wine glass for something, "it's got out of hand again and the debt's mounting. I asked for another loan, for more time, but they won't help."

"So, do we need to find some finance somewhere else? I can see what the bank can do for me?"

"No, Charlie. I missed a load of repayments too. The people I borrowed the money from, they're calling in the debt."

I stared at him blankly, my thoughts whirring round in my head.

"What are you saying, Bobby?" I whispered, not sure I really wanted to know the answer.

"I've lost it. The yard, the house, the business. All of it. I have to hand it over to the people I took the loans from. And walk away."

I could see the heartbreak in his eyes; I could feel it emanating from him. But I was angry. Really angry. This was my home. My life.

My everything. I couldn't just let it all be taken away.

"I'm so sorry, Charlie," he muttered.

Rage simmered in me. I stood up. Bobby stood too, his blanket falling in a heap at his feet. I put my hand out, halting him.

"No," I said, not hiding the anger in my voice, "I've got the horses to check."

I turned and walked out, feeling his eyes bore into my back as I left.

Chapter Three

ஐ Cian ᘇ

I buried my father, older brother and little sister on a cold, grey Friday in Ireland. The weather was typically shit; sleet driven at you by wind and a dull greyness that had lasted for days.

Their Wake had been a raucous affair, as was tradition, but I'd sat in a corner avoiding as many people as possible with their shallow words of commiseration. I'd watched the families that had joined us, looking for anything out of place.

We assumed the O'Malleys had arranged the hit, although there was no evidence yet that was the case. If it was, it meant the peace was broken and I would launch an all-out war on them. But I needed to be certain before I took action. I was cruel, and I was thorough, but I wasn't reckless and I had learned some things whilst I'd been with the Murphys in America. I'd learnt restraint, I'd learnt to bide my time, and I'd learnt that revenge should be drawn out, that when you destroy someone you make sure they can never come back from it. And so, when I was sure who was responsible for my family's deaths,

I would take everything from them, more than just their lives, more than their legacy, everything.

My father had been head of the family, my older brother Torin next in line. Torin's marriage to the O'Malley girl had united the families for a while, but they had grown greedy again, pushing the boundaries, always asking for more. Now she sat in a far-off corner dressed in a black dress, her strawberry-blonde hair pinned to her head. She looked genuinely miserable and uncomfortable. Her eyes flicking across the room, watching my men and their rowdy toasts, recoiling at the odd brawl that would break out from time to time and staring off into the distance as conversation at the table of O'Malleys carried on around her. She would have known enough to figure out where Torin would be, where he could be picked up from, and she was weak enough to give in to O'Malley pressure.

I doubted she'd ever had any real loyalty to Torin. The marriage was for one purpose and to date there was no heir, nothing keeping her loyal to us. It was loveless, and I suspected she had suffered at the hands of my brother. If I was cruel, Torin was a monster, a thing of nightmares. I'd come off on the wrong side of his temper many a time and I'd wager so had she. She would have had reason to be turned against him, to free herself of him.

Those parts were still unclear. Our intel had told us my father and brother had been intercepted on the way to a business meeting. The car was found later, the driver's body still in the

24

driver's seat with a hole in his temple. My sister, Fiadh, had been taken separately. A familiar anger stirred in my chest. She was the baby of the family, sweet and loving and loyal. It was only Oisín who had been left alive, and only because he was out whoring and not where he was supposed to be. Fucking typical.

Osh was younger than me by four years, which, at age 36, meant I was the oldest surviving male and so the title of head of the O'Sullivan family had passed to me. Not what I had fucking wanted. I was happy in New York with the Murphys. Away from the memories of my mother, providing connections with my family by working with our American cousins. Now I'd inherited the whole fucking thing. In fucking Ireland.

I'd spent the next few days in the O'Sullivan family home. It was dated, lacking a woman's touch despite Faidh living there, and in real need of redecorating. I sat in the office at the far end of the property at my father's desk. The leather chair was uncomfortable. I didn't fit the imprint of his larger arse, and it didn't feel right under me. The room was scattered with various people.

"The protection businesses are fine, Cian," an older man, the family's accountant, told me. "Everyone pays as they should and it's not taking up much resource."

I nodded in reply.

"Street operations?" I asked.

"There's been some problems recently," Riley, my oldest friend, answered, "couple of dealers had their patches taken over. Not sure by who though. We're working on that."

"Connected to the shootings?"

"We don't know. Could be."

We moved on.

"Then there's this," the accountant continued, "Reynold's Racing. We've loaned the old man money for years. He's a gambler. A shit one. But the last few months he hasn't been paying."

"Spoken to him?" I asked.

The man nodded, "seems he's gambled himself into debt again. It happens frequently, but the business profits and winnings aren't covering the repayments. I suggest calling it in."

"Can't we just send some boys to sort it out?" Oisín asked.

"There's no point. He doesn't have the money. The Yard is decent. They've had loads of winners and some really good owners. If we take it over, it'll turn a good profit."

I rubbed at the stubble on my jaw.

"Suppose it'll be good for cleaning money, too."

The accountant nodded.

"Looks like we're going racing then."

*****

The racecourse was packed out for a misty February day. Revellers slugged back champagne, splashing cash on ludicrous bets, all the while dressed in their best. I stayed out of the rain in the owners' lounge watching out the panoramic windows, the parade ring and winners enclosure below me. I sipped on whisky, listening to my men in the background laughing and jesting and clearly enjoying our business trip.

Newcastle had the same shitty weather as Ireland, perhaps a little less volatile, but wet, grey and miserable all the same. The going was good to soft today, the commentator had said over the tannoy as the races got underway.

"Mr O'Sullivan?" a voice asked tentatively from behind me.

I turned, my eyes settling on the old man before me. He was in his sixties, if I had to guess, sporting a halo of grey hair around the sides of his head, bald and shiny on the top. He clutched a flat cap nervously in his hands.

"Reynolds?"

He nodded.

"Come," I beckoned, "talk me through your horses today."

He wandered over, his steps slow and shuffling, stopping in front of the window.

"I've got four running today. One is a home bred filly in her first hurdles. She's an exciting prospect."

Horses spilled out into the parade ring, led by handlers as jockeys sprung up onto their backs, light and agile.

"My first is down there."

He pointed to a chestnut. The jockey, wearing black and white silks with red chevrons had just been hoisted on, vaulting into the saddle with finesse, the horse relaxed under him.

"It's owned by Lord and Lady Denholm. Really strong mare this one. We've been training it for the last three seasons."

Soon, all the jockeys were on board and the horses made their way to the starting line. Some were calm and collected, others jogged and danced as they milled into a mass of squirming equine bodies. Then with a leap they were off, hurtling along the first furlong. The chestnut mare stayed towards the front of the pack, cruising around the course in long strides and gliding over the big fences with the most grace I had ever seen. It was an impressive animal. A number were caught out, falling on landing after jumping, but the chestnut never faltered, never broke pace and never misjudged a jump.

Two jumps from the finish and it was still tucked behind the lead and second horse then, as the horses jumped the last, the jockey nudged it with his heels, sending it careering forwards, its legs moving with a sudden ferocity as it swallowed the space to the finish line, a good few horse's lengths ahead.

"Amazon Flower and Charlie Porter take the win," the tannoy announced as spectators cheered.

I turned back to Reynolds and he smiled at me.

"Good little horse, that one, but it does have my best jockey on it."

As the second race was announced and commentators urged punters to place their bets, Osh wandered towards me, his fingers curled round another glass of whisky, coming to stand in front of the old race horse trainer.

"So where'd you suggest I put my money?" he asked.

The man nodded towards the parade ring.

"Number five. The bay filly over there. That's one I bred. 'Good Time Girl' we call her."

Osh snorted into his drink.

"Love spending money on a good time girl."

He wasn't wrong there. I watched the scene in the parade ring. The bay horse was tense. I could see it as it jogged and pranced as the handler led it round rider-less, until eventually the jockeys trickled into the ring. The minute the jockey touched the saddle the horse calmed, striding out confidently around the ring before it left and cantered sedately up to the start line.

The horses were led into the stalls; some walking in sensibly and others being pushed and tugged, squeezed into the small spaces, hooves tapping a jig in anticipation. Then with a pop the doors sprang open and ten thoroughbreds emerged already at a gallop. The bay mare stayed near the back, the front runners breaking away quickly. I watched the monitors in the lounge with interest, noticing its ears flick back and forth, listening to its rider. Its pace was consistent; firm long strides as it tackled the fences with a cool confidence. As the race hit the midway point the horse started to pull forwards, gliding with ease. The last fence approached, and it flew over nose to tail with the horse in front. The leading jockey glanced behind him and started pushing his horse on, but it was no use. The filly breezed past effortlessly; its jockey sitting there, just enjoying the ride.

"And that's another win for Charlie Porter on Good Time Girl," the tannoy announced.

"Yes!" Osh shouted a little way away.

I glanced back at the old man, who was smiling.

"Bring me the jockey," I instructed, "I want to meet him."

The old man raised his eyebrows.

"As you wish," he said and turned and walked away.

I joined my men after another trip to the bar, Oisín slapping me on the shoulder as he continued to celebrate his win.

"Not bad for an impromptu visit to the races," he said, slugging the rest of his drink back.

"How much did you put on?"

"Just a grand."

I dragged my hand across my face. He was a fucking liability my brother. Luckily, this time it had paid off.

"Mr O'Sullivan," the soft voice behind me spoke.

I turned to see Reynolds back, a jockey a little way behind him.

"You wanted to meet Charlie."

He stepped to the side, and the jockey moved closer. I looked at them, shock silencing me for a moment, my eyes failing to comprehend the woman stood in front of me. Blonde hair was scraped back in a ponytail, her face still flushed. She'd removed the racing colours and was stood there in a black base-layer which clung to her figure, bulging over small, shapely tits and clinging to a slim stomach.

Osh wolf-whistled beside me and she shot him a look that was entirely made of venom. I moved a little closer so I could see her better.

"My face is up here," she said coolly, a bite in her voice.

"That was a good ride out there," I stated, ignoring her

"Thank you," her tone was uninterested, cold.

"I didn't expect a woman to ride like that."

"Why not?"

Reynolds shifted uncomfortably beside her, his eyes flitting between us nervously.

"Because that's not what a woman's legs should be wrapped around," Osh piped up behind me.

Her head shot towards him, her glare turning icier, if that was even possible. I stepped sideways, cutting her off from him.

"I'm sorry. My brother seems to have left his manners at home."

"Didn't realise you Irish knew what manners were," she shot back, holding my gaze a few seconds; cool, light blue eyes searing in to mine.

"Charlie," Reynolds warned.

"I don't have time for this shit, Bobby. I've a race to win."

Then she turned and walked away.

"Mr O'Sullivan, I'm so sorry. She's very...."

"Spirited? Yes I noticed."

The old man loitered, pointing out horses in the parade ring. Telling me where they had raced and who owned and trained them. A short amount of time later, the next race was ready to start. Reynolds seemed a little quieter, and I sensed tension. The parade ring was filling up with horses, but one caught my eye. Tall and black, it took two handlers on either side of its head to lead it as it sprung off all fours, going airborne like a kite in a hurricane.

The jockey sprung onto its back, grabbing the reins as the horse tossed her around like a rag doll, rearing and bucking, yet she sat still and calm, patting it patiently on the neck.

"One of yours?" I asked incredulously.

Reynolds nodded, "Messiah Complex. One of Charlie's projects. It's a nutcase, but she sees something in it."

Soon they were all in the stalls, all calm except for the black horse. Twice its front legs went up in the air and I could hear the rest of the room ooh and ah as it crashed around, becoming more and more worked up. I was almost relieved when the stall doors shot open and the horse bounded out, the jockey still in the saddle. Yet out on the field it quickly settled.

Charlie tucked it in behind the front line of horses and let the horse find its own pace. It tackled each hurdle without a foot out of place and then, as they were three from the finish, she moved the horse forwards. It made quick work of third and second place, covering the ground with a powerful long stride. Then, just as they approached the last fence, they squeezed up on the outside of the leader. The jockey saw them coming, but had little time to react. Their approach to the fence was perfect, the black horse tucking his front feet high into its body and landing safely. But as they pushed forward, the other horse jumped crookedly, landing awkwardly and clipping the hind legs of the black stallion.

The stallion stumbled, sliding onto his knees. I watched, holding my breath as the jockey went flying up its neck, losing a stirrup and wobbling dangerously. But she pushed back into the saddle, keeping the horse's head up, and he found his feet. He pushed on again quickly, but he'd lost too much advantage. They crossed the finish line in fifth place.

I glanced at the trainer watching behind me.

He shrugged, "it happens. Would you like to come and meet the horses?"

I nodded, and we filed out, escorted down to the stables. As we got around the other side of the building and were let through into the restricted area, there was a commotion up ahead. Charlie strode towards the winning jockey who was returning with his saddle. Voices were raised angrily and then the blonde jockey launched herself at him, other jockeys catching her just before her fist connected with his face. Fuck, the girl had an impressive right hook, even if it hadn't been given the chance to reach its target.

"I'm sorry, I need to go sort this," the old man said before rushing towards them as quick as he could.

Chapter Four

og Charlie ෨

I'd been in a foul mood for days. The only thing that eased it was being around the horses. They always had a way of calming me, grounding me. My mind kept going back to my last conversation with Bobby and every time it did, I felt a pang of nausea.

I hadn't even spoken to him at the race yesterday, not properly, uttering only enough words to get the job done. It hadn't sat well with me, though. I'd known him for years, worked for and with him for years. He meant as much to me as my own family. He *was* my family, seeing something in me all those years ago when I rocked up to his racing yard to shovel shit as punishment for my misdemeanours.

Again, my stomach filled with dread and uncertainty and anger. I turned the music up higher, pushing myself harder, running faster, my legs pounding the country roads just as daylight was breaking. As I returned to the yard gates, I dropped to a jog, slowing my pace as I ran back up the drive.

The stable yard was a hive of activity. Horses were being led out to the horse walker, stable hands moving between stables, mucking each one out and making sure each horse had fresh hay and water. I bounded up to my apartment above one of the stable blocks, changing quickly. We had horses to ride out this morning, and everyone who had run yesterday needed gentle exercise so they could recover.

I grabbed a set of tack and walked over to a stable. The black horse stuck his head over the door, ears flat back, ready to take a chunk out of anyone too close.

"Behave, Brian," I called out to him.

His ears pricked and he relaxed, stepping away from his door to let me in.

"You're a grumpy bugger today, mate," I said gently to the big horse as I ran a brush over him, his coat glistening effortlessly underneath each stroke.

Brian was an odd character. I called him misunderstood. Everyone else would say a nutter. We had bonded, but he could still be a handful, and I was the only one who could stay on him. He'd sent every other rider flying; on and off the track. And today he was wound like a coiled spring; up off all fours the minute my arse hit the saddle, tossing his head about and jumping around. I can't say I blamed him. I was still pissed that we'd been nobbled yesterday, too.

"What happened yesterday in the two o'clock?" Ryan, one of our exercise riders, asked on our way out of the yard.

"Dickie was a dick, as usual. He checked us on the last fence, nearly sent Brian down. Fucking bastard."

I held back the anger at recalling the scene. The arsehole could have injured one or both of us and all because he didn't like being beaten by a woman. It had been the same with Dickie Hargreaves since I started my racing career and only got worse when I dumped him and then beat him. I wasn't sure which one had pissed him off more.

"Come on," I instructed, and we pushed on up the hill in a steady canter.

The black stallion was calmer when we arrived back at the yard, as a worried looking stable hand rushed over to take him away and wash him off.

"Don't worry," I said to the young lad gently, "Brian has promised to be on his best behaviour."

The lad smiled back at me.

"Who are they?" he asked suddenly, peering over my shoulder.

I turned in the direction he was looking as two big black cars pulled into the yard, Irish number plates on the front.

"My next fucking problem," I groaned, tipping my head and hinting to him to take the horse away.

The tall man I met yesterday sauntered across the yard, the arsehole brother following close behind.

I folded my arms across my chest and stood waiting for him to approach. He was around six foot I guessed, and had an imposing presence, one that only served to get my back up. I couldn't tell his age. His hazel eyes hinted he'd seen a lot in life, yet his skin was smooth, the only wrinkles were the faint lines at the corner of his eyes. Seemed he must be able to smile occasionally.

He smoothed down the cuffs of his suit jacket as he approached, fastening it around him across a broad chest. His tie was fastened loosely, hanging down from his shirt collar, the top buttons of which were undone. I stood defiantly in front of him, having to tilt my head up to look at him as he got closer, noticing the way his brown hair was carelessly styled, sweeping across to the right slightly, the sides cropped short.

"Morning, Charlie," he said like he knew me, his words accented in the soft Irish grumble but with a hint of something else that I couldn't quite grasp.

I nodded, pouring as much disrespect into the curt movement of my head as I could.

"I'm looking for the boss," he said, glancing around the yard.

"You're looking at her."

The arsehole brother snorted from behind him and I resisted the urge to show him a couple of fingers.

O'Sullivan sighed.

"I mean, Bobby. I'm looking for Bobby."

"Up at the house," I answered shortly, tipping my head.

He raised his eyebrows at me, giving me an exasperated expression and I shot him one back, shrugging my shoulders.

He sighed again.

"Where's the house?" he asked again, a faint growl to his voice.

I cocked my head sideways.

"Follow the road further up. Can't miss it."

"Can you take me?"

I heard the quiet instruction in his voice. Fuck that.

"No. I've got work to do here."

"I'll stay down here," the arsehole brother interrupted, stepping towards me, "you can show me what happens around here, doll," he continued, wrapping an arm across my shoulder.

"Take *that* off me, unless you want to become an amputee."

He looked at me dumbfounded, opening his stupid mouth like a fish and then thinking better of it and closing it again. I glanced back at the taller O'Sullivan, catching the amused smirk across his face before he turned and walked back to the car, leaving me with 'stupid' who was clearly going to follow me around like a frigging shadow.

I stalked off, hoping to put as much space between us, but he found it pretty easy to keep up, not being much shorter than his brother. I walked into the kitchen, a small room in the corner of one of the stable blocks, and flicked the kettle on.

"Cuppa?" I asked, flippantly.

"Aye, lass, that would be good."

"Great. Cups are in there, tea is there and well, I guess you know where milk will be."

I dumped a spoon of coffee in a mug, lifted the kettle off the stand as the water started to bubble, then walked out with my coffee, sipping carefully. I gave out some instructions telling the stable hands which horses to take to the field and which needed to go on the walker. Brian was already bouncing around like an imbecile as one of them tried to get him to his paddock. I swapped the mug for a horse, uttered a word of caution into the black horse's big lugs and took him myself.

Once back up from the field, I reclaimed my coffee and got to work mucking the last of the stables out. I was sifting the clean from dirty straw when I got the feeling I was being watched.

"If your eyes are lingering on my arse, I'll poke them out with this pitch fork," I shot over my shoulder, "if they're not, pass me the shovel over there."

"Shovel," the voice behind me answered gruffly.

I turned. It wasn't the brother I had been expecting. He was stood in the doorway blocking my light, casting shadows from his tall stature as he leaned against the doorframe. The metal of the shovel scratched harshly on the ground as I scooped up a pile of straw mixed with horse poo and the pungent reek of urine. Even with my love of horses, I never got used to the smell of their wee. It stung your eyes and burned the soles off your boots.

"Can you join us out here? I'd like to introduce myself to the staff."

"Two minutes while I finish this."

"No. Now," he commanded.

I caught his gaze, scooped the next pile of shit and piss soaked straw and moved it towards the wheel barrow just in front of him. I gave the shovel a little nudge, too hard a nudge, and dropped the pile down his leg and onto the polished leather dress shoes he wore.

His jaw tightened and I stared into his eyes as I moved to the front of the stable where he stood. His hazel eyes were dark and stormy, his lips pressed together tightly but were deliciously plump, surrounded by short dark stubble, that they looked almost like he was pouting.

"Lead the way then," I stated, gesturing with my hand.

In the middle of the courtyard surrounded by the stable blocks, the entire staff had gathered; a muddle of stable hands, exercise riders and jockeys, with Bobby just a little way off to the side, looking defeated.

"Thank you for your time," the taller O'Sullivan started, "I'm Cian and this is my brother, Oisín."

Oisín nodded at the people in front of him before resting his eyes on me.

"The ownership of the racing yard and the business is transferring to us."

Hushed muttering surrounded me as I kept my eyes on the tall man with the mid-brown hair, wondering whether he could feel the intensity of my stare, feel the hatred that I radiated towards him.

"We will be sending each of you a new contract to be employed under us. We will not be looking to make any changes to the current staffing structure, at least not at the stable hand or exercise rider level."

Then he turned his hazel eyes on me, the same annoyance and hatred reflecting back at me. I folded my arms across my chest in response.

"The yard will be renamed O'Sullivan racing. Thank you for your time. I look forward to working with you."

I walked off, not waiting to be dismissed. Hurried footsteps rang out behind me, growing louder as they got closer. I didn't turn around. I ground the anger between my teeth and kept walking. I wanted to scream. I wanted to shout and I really wanted to punch something. A hand touched my arm, and I whirled round, a paragraph's worth of expletives ready to roll off my tongue.

"What's going on Charlie?" the jockey asked, recoiling slightly from me, "did you know about this?"

"Yes, some of it."

He looked at me quizzically.

I sighed, calming slightly and continued, "Bobby told me the people he took a loan from were calling it in. I knew the business was being taken over."

The jockey looked pale.

"Bobby took a loan out with the O'Sullivans?"

"That's what he said."

"No. I mean the *O'Sullivans*."

He searched my eyes for something; some little grain of understanding.

"What, George? What's so special about the O'Sullivans?"

He glanced over my shoulder and then guided me into a stable. I stared at his hand on my elbow and then at him and he dropped it quickly, looking a little paler.

"They're mafia, Charlie," he whispered, "Irish mafia."

"What do you mean they're mafia?"

"You know? Like the Godfather? Horses' heads in beds, that sort of thing. Just Irish ones."

"Don't be stupid," I scoffed, shaking my head and storming off. I was pissed off enough already without stupid conspiracy theories of the frigging underworld.

Chapter Five

๑ Cian ๏

I'd spent the rest of the day watching the stable yard being run, horses being exercised, groomed and well taken care of. I'd watched the blonde jockey giving orders, riders and stable boys obeying her instantly, and admittedly, she ran a tight ship. Osh spent the rest of the afternoon with his tongue drooping on the floor, unable to take his eyes off her, and his trousers bulging tightly over his groin.

She was pretty. I couldn't deny it. Cool, light blue eyes and ash blonde hair. It was hard not to admire her round, pert arse as she marched backwards and forwards in tight breeches.

And spirited was an understatement. She was a ball-buster to be sure and had given both Osh and I a hard time in equal measures throughout the day. She was prickly and insolent and undisciplined, and if she had belonged to me, I would have taken my hand to her backside and made it red raw. Not that I hit women. But there was something about her that seemed to rub me up the wrong way.

My men had returned to our hotel, but we had stayed up at the house, sitting in front of the big open fire.

"What are we going to do with this place?" Osh asked as he sipped at a glass of whisky.

"Dunno yet. We'll have to get the old man out first."

The old man who was currently cooking us dinner. We'd been invited to stay for the evening and there was certainly more to talk about.

"And what are we going to do about her?"

"I don't know. She's fucking hard work. But seems to know her way around a horse."

"Does she though? Aye, she looks the part. I would look at that all day, but is she all fur jacket and no knickers? Wouldn't mind that either, though," Oisín was grinning inanely.

I rolled my eyes, but the image had been placed in my head now. Osh was right, I wouldn't mind that either.

"And why do you smell of horse piss, brother?" Osh asked suddenly.

I groaned, clenching my teeth at the memory, irritation nibbling away at me and then choosing to ignore all of it before it snowballed into a rage towards the blonde jockey that I couldn't control. Or the image of her naked. Neither was good.

"I'm thinking of bringing Jonjo over. He's a fucking good jockey and knows who pays his wages," I changed the subject.

Jonjo was racing at home in Ireland. He was a good rider, on the heavier side of the spectrum, but strong enough to sort that black thing out. Although I was beginning to think it was better off with a bullet. Jonjo followed orders, whatever the family asked him to do. He would make us a lot of money here.

"Can I get you gentleman another drink?" old man Reynolds asked from the doorway, holding his own glass in one hand and the whisky bottle in another.

"Join us," I offered, and he plonked himself in a worn armchair close to the fire.

"Don't be too hard on Charlie," he said suddenly, "she's a tough cookie, but she's loyal and hardworking and she has an amazing ability with the horses."

"How the hell did you find her?" I asked.

I couldn't see her being persuasive at interview. The man smiled and took a sip of his drink.

"I met her when she came to me as a sixteen-year-old. I used to let juvenile delinquents come and shovel muck for me as part of the Community Service programme. It was free labour, and they needed to be punished. Most teenagers hated the smell and the mess and the physical side of it.

"Charlie had got herself into trouble with the police. Minor things; anti-social behaviour, disturbing the peace, there was a small assault too."

"Figures," I muttered.

"She was a nightmare. I couldn't wait for her to serve the time and leave after the first day. But then I started noticing how she was with the horses. She would stand for ages, when she was supposed to be working, stroking and talking to them. She calmed them and they calmed her.

"Then one morning I came down to the yard to find a stable door open and a horse missing. I thought it had been stolen. I drove back up to the house to ring the police and report it, but as I looked over towards the gallops, I saw it there. With Charlie on it.

"They were racing round the gallops at an incredible speed. No hat. No saddle. No bridle. The horse in question had been proving difficult and none of my jockeys could keep the damn thing contained long enough to get it to perform. Yet here was a sixteen-year-old girl riding it in just a head collar and lead rope."

"You sure she's not Irish?" Osh piped up.

"No, she's a Geordie," he answered flatly, "I bollocked her, of course. She could have killed herself. Once she finished her community service, I told her to go get some riding lessons then come back to me after she left school."

Reynolds rose to his feet, slowly.

"She's the daughter I never had. If I hadn't messed this all up, she would have been left it all when I die. Guess old habits aren't that easy to kick. I'll go check on dinner."

The old man shuffled away.

"Looks like the old man's got a soft spot for her," Oisín broke the silence as I sat watching him hobble away.

"She's a fucking handful," I groaned.

I should be getting rid of her. She was a liability; a ball ache. But something about her held my interest; she was different.

"I'm pretty sure I can break her in."

Osh grinned at me over his glass and for some reason that really pissed me off.

A short time later, I could hear the old man's voice in the kitchen talking to someone. The voices moved closer and he came shuffling in, the blonde-haired girl following behind him. She stopped suddenly when she saw us, her eyes narrowing.

Charlie was dressed in jeans, tight jeans, socks still up to her knees, and a thin black jumper clung to her body. Her hair was loose, not scraped back in a ponytail as I had seen her before. The ash blonde locks fell over her shoulders far longer than I would ever have imagined. She was slim and toned and.... stunning.

"The lass scrubs up well," Osh stated loudly from behind me, and she shot him a warning look.

I could almost see her hackles standing up. She'd gone from relaxed to on her guard the minute she had set eyes on us. If those baby blues could have turned navy, I'm sure that's what they would have done. She made no effort to hide the anger in those eyes, or on her face, or in the fists that were now screwed into tight balls at her sides.

"You didn't tell me you had company, Bobby," she said with that familiar iciness to her voice.

"Come on, Charlie. Be nice," the old man said to her pleadingly.

"Yes, come on now. Be a good girl," Osh taunted.

"Ignore my brother. Please, join us," I offered, trying to diffuse the hostility in the room.

"I'm not hungry," she stated, turning and walking away, the old man watching after her sadly.

I rolled my eyes and followed her, catching up with her in the kitchen at the far end of the house and grabbing her arm gently. She shot me that look again, her eyes cascading down to where my hand was wrapped around her slim biceps and then up to my face, anger flashing from behind the long eyelashes stubborn, petulant and challenging and that feeling returned, the need to punish her, to make her obey me, overwhelming like nothing I had felt before. It took all my effort to let go of her arm and not rag her round the kitchen until she cowered at my feet, or submitted to me on her knees.

"What the fuck is your problem?" I growled.

"You're my fucking problem."

She turned back to me, her eyes so full of venom and anger they seemed ablaze.

"You waltz in here with your fancy cars and your Irish attitude like you own the world and everyone in it."

"I do. I own this world. I own this yard, your horses, all this. I own it now," I flounced my hand in the air, my temper threatening to overwhelm me.

"Fucking parasites, the lot of you."

"I didn't get the old man into debt. That was all his doing. You deal with the devil, what do you think happens?"

"Christ. And I thought Brian had an ego. You're the devil now huh?" her voice was sharp, "now let me get the fuck out of here."

I looked around, realising that I was blocking the doorway. She gave me that look of petulance again as she went to pass me; the blue in her eyes as clear as the morning sky, the slight plumpness of her pink lips pushed into a sneer and well-shaped eyebrows knitted together in rage. Fuck, she was beautiful. And wild.

"Arse hole," she cursed at me as she went to pass.

Grabbing her by the arm again, I pulled her back into me, my fingers pushing into that lean toned muscle underneath.

I lowered my head so that my lips brushed her ear, "I don't think I'm the devil. I *am* the fucking devil. You'll find out exactly what that means if you don't behave."

She glared at me, furious, but made no smart ass comment for once and I held her there for a second, holding her gaze, feeling anger, or something bubbling in me. God, she was fucking beautiful, much more so when she wanted to kick me in the nuts. I let her go and she marched off; the door banging loudly behind her.

I stood for a moment calming myself, listening to the hammer of my heart and the unevenness of my breaths. I'd never met a woman who frustrated me the way she did. I needed a drink.

Chapter Six

ᴄᴈ Charlie ᴈᴑ

A couple of days had passed and the Irish seemed to have gone for now. I'd relaxed a little and my face had stopped tripping me up. The horses were looking great, muscled and fit and in good spirits; even Brian. The whole yard was preparing for the weekend's racing, loading the horsebox with every bit of kit imaginable for the horses we were taking.

Brian was staying at home this time. He'd become tense again over the hurdles after last weekend's race, and I needed time to rebuild his confidence. I'd enjoyed the quiet of the last few days, pretending the takeover of the racing business wasn't happening. Being free of the oppressive presence of the big handsome Irishman and the disapproving looks he shot me had definitely helped my mood.

But it hadn't relieved Bobby's mood. He was quieter than usual, tired and withdrawn. He'd maintained his watchful eye over the training, but without his usual excitement at seeing the horses run. There wasn't the typical colour in his cheeks or the sparkle in his eyes, and there was a nervousness about him.

The next morning we loaded the horses and made our way south to Doncaster. The day was clear and bright, echoing my mood.

Watching the first few races, I studied the way the ground seemed to ride, how the fences jumped, conditions perfect for our runners. As I returned to the stables to check the horses over, a tall man in a suit loitered, his brown hair and strong stubborn jaw familiar even a few metres away. My day had just gone downhill.

"Nice to see you again, Charlie," Cian spoke.

"Is it?"

His tone was forced, and he didn't offer me a smile. I was happy to keep it that way.

"I'd like to introduce you to someone," he said, looking over my shoulder.

I turned, following the direction of his gaze, fixing my eyes on the jockey coming towards us.

"This is Jonjo Moore," Cian said.

"I know who he is."

"Jonjo works for the O'Sullivans," he continued, "he'll be riding today."

I looked at the tall man, not quite realising what he was saying right at the moment.

"By riding you mean...."

"You're not."

54

His words hit me hard in the chest as if he himself had hit me and for a while I stood staring at him, deciding whether I would punch the smirk off his face and ruin my career in one easy right-hook or step aside, and pretend the whole thing didn't bother me. I clenched my fist, my arm hanging tense and ready at my side.

"I want you to brief him on the horses, then join me in the owner's area."

"I'll brief him on the horses," I said pointedly, and moved to step around Cian.

The sudden bite of strong fingers gripped my arm, and I stiffened, anger igniting and heat rising to my cheeks. I trailed my eyes from his fingers and up his arm, slowly stopping as I got to his face, my teeth pinching the inside of my cheek as every fibre of my being was telling me the right-hook was looking like a great option. Instead, I met his gaze, staring back at him, focusing my rage into the silent stare, the atmosphere between us fragile.

"Do not fuck with me," he growled into my ear, stubble grazing my cheek leaving a tingling sensation across my skin, "brief Jonjo and then come to me."

I shrugged my arm from his grasp and walked away, signalling at Jonjo to follow, cursing myself at the lack of witty or insolent retort I could muster. My mind reeled in anger and my skin tingled from where his hand had wrapped around my arm, hot electric pulses igniting something else within me. Fuck him.

It went against my nature to follow Cian's instructions. I didn't obey anyone, not least the arrogant Irish bastard that thought he could command my presence with the squeeze of my flesh and the deep, throaty growl of commands into my ear. I needed to be near to the horses to get them ready, to calm and coax them, to fuss over the plaits in their manes and scratch at their withers. And I hated the idea of not riding, of seeing my horses with that over-sized jockey on them. And right now, I hated Cian O'Sullivan. Yet here I was obeying him and I hated that, too.

I explained the characters of the horses to the other jockey, telling him how to handle them before the race, how to handle them during the race, when to push them and when to hold them and then I went back to the horsebox and changed into something smarter. The black pair of trousers felt alien, the fabric swishing against my legs, not hugging my skin like my breeches did, and the sky blue blouse made me feel like someone's secretary. I scowled at myself in the mirror.

The owner's lounge was busy. People dressed in beautiful clothes milling about, clutching drinks and talking excitedly. There were several trainers I recognised as I walked through, quizzical eyes falling upon me in the busy room. I felt out of my depth. Looking around, I eventually found the familiar shape of Cian at the huge panoramic windows which offered the best view of the race track. He was talking to Lord and Lady Denholm and they seemed to be captivated by whatever he was saying.

I stayed back a little, keeping out of the way, watching him as he talked to our most wealthy owners, watching how they fixated on him, in awe of him and whatever charm he had turned upon them. His face changed as he talked to them, full lips curling upwards with a smile, hazel eyes warm and animated. He glanced sideways, catching me looking at him, his smile chased away by the sudden sternness of his face. He tipped his head, signalling for me to join him.

Cian held out his arm as I approached, letting it rest on the small of my back and I stood in front of the Denholm's, stiff and uncomfortable, resisting the urge to bend his fingers back as far as I could.

"You've met Charlie?" he asked the couple.

"Good afternoon," I greeted them.

We had met; countless times. Every time I'd ridden their horses for a win for them, I'd met them. Cian would know that.

"Nice to see you, Charlie," Lord Denholm responded, "we're really excited to see what such a good jockey like Jonjo Moore will make of our horses. It was a fantastic idea of yours."

I forced a smile at them as anger seethed within me, the heat of rage radiating across my chest. I stepped away from Cian before I did something more stupid than normal. Finding a space in front of the windows, watching the race as fury and hatred created a devilish cocktail of emotions writhing through me. The chestnut mare won, clearly, Lord and Lady Denholm whooping with joy behind me. I glanced back at the

Irishman, watching his mouth pull into a smirk, the look of satisfaction on his face, and for a moment I imagined the feel of punching him in the mouth.

The next race would be more difficult for the tall jockey. The bay filly was brave and willing, but she was stubborn. If he listened to me, they would win. If he didn't, they would lose. It was as simple as that. I studied the filly from the windows, watching her ears flicker in confusion; the higher set head carriage of tension, the slight jog to her normal relaxed step. She would feel the weight difference. Jonjo was on the heavier side of race jockeys and stronger with his hands. I'd told him she would need a gentle hold, not too heavy as she would fight it and not too light, or she'd charge to the front and peak too early. He'd rolled his eyes at me, as if I was teaching my granny how to knit.

The horses sprang free from the starting line and at first Jonjo kept her in a good position, but I could see she was pulling on and gaining pace with the front runners. He checked her too harshly, and she swung her head into the air, faltering slightly and losing some pace. Nerves fluttered in my stomach, my nails pinching into my skin from the fists balled together in tension. He needed to settle her, give her confidence. She surged on and he checked her again. Too heavy. Too much. Her head flung upwards, but this time she pulled harder, trying to take the rein back from him.

The hurdles were coming up on them fast and every time Jonjo pulled on the reins; the filly was getting more and more agitated. She jumped the next hurdle a stride out, reaching out with her front legs to make it all the way over. It cost her a place. She rushed the next hurdle, throwing in a short stride before take-off and then jumping awkwardly. She lost another position. Jonjo pushed her forward, trying to make up what they'd lost, but it was too soon. She was tired and tense, unable to stretch through her back and eat up the space between her and the other horses. Her nostrils flared, bright red spheres against a dark muzzle, and sweat caked her chest. They finished in third place.

"Fuck's sake," I heard Oisín swear from just to the side of me.

He turned to me, pulling me round to face him, his face red with rage.

"You did that on purpose," he growled, his face only centimetres away from me.

"Done what exactly?"

"Gave Jonjo a whole load of dumb shit about that horse!"

"I told him how to ride her. He didn't listen. Go take it up with *your* jockey."

Oisín looked like he wanted to explode, his jaw twitching and his eyebrows almost touching as he screwed his face up into a ball of fury. A hush fell over the lounge, people in there staring. I folded my arms across my chest and stared back at him, adding fuel to an already blazing fire. A hand grasped his arm, pulling him to the side, and I watched Cian dip his head to his brother, speaking to him quietly. Osh looked across at me, his eyes burning with anger, but then he walked away.

"What happened?" Cian asked, coming to a stop in front of me, one half of his chest stopping me from moving around him, his stance commanding despite the uneasy quiet in his voice.

"You tell me, but I reckon your brother bet on the filly to win."

"I meant what happened with that race?" his tone was calm, too calm, and cold. The hairs on the back of my neck stood up a little.

"I told him to keep her relaxed, keep her focussed. Jonjo is a very strong handed jockey, far too strong for that horse. He needed to keep her mouth soft and not piss her off. He did the opposite. And lost."

Cian stared at me for a moment, probably trying to decide whether or not I was lying. And suddenly I was distracted by his lips. They were soft and full and the more he tried to stay in control the more he pushed them together and the plumper and poutier they became. He had an incredible shape to his face: heart-shaped with a narrow chin yet strong jaw line either side. His eyebrows seem perpetually arched, a small scar across the left one, breaking it into two.

But what I really noticed was the anger building in his eyes, contradicting the quiet calmness that surrounded him. It was like the eye of a storm, and I had a really funny feeling I didn't want to see the rest of it.

"Jonjo is a good jockey, successful," I continued a little more carefully, wary of snapping the last tendrils of control he was exerting over his rage, "but he's arrogant and needs to remember to listen to the people who know the horses the best. They aren't machines. They have brains and intelligence and characters just like you and me. Tell him to listen to me next time."

The Irishman's shoulders relaxed a little, the storm in his eyes settling.

"You'd do well to listen to your own words," he growled into my ear.

I pinched my lips together to prevent myself from saying anything else.

"I need to get back to my horses."

*****

"I'm sorry that happened to you today, Charlie," Bobby uttered as I was settling the horses back in to their stables for the evening once we were home.

"That Irishman's an arsehole, Bobby. I'm not sure I can deal with this."

"Give him a chance to see how good you are. It'll take time."

I fell silent, gritting my teeth, but the old man wasn't finished with me yet.

"Just be careful. Stop winding him up. These aren't the nicest of people."

"What do you mean, Bobby?"

"Just that. Try to be less abrasive. Please, Charlie."

Eventually, he'd convinced me to join them for dinner. He looked really old tonight and frail. I assumed the situation was getting to him. It was getting to me and I really didn't want to cause him any more stress than he was already under and so I'd agreed to come to the house and join them. And I had promised to be on my best behaviour.

I hurried up to the house later that night, escaping the bite of the cold, my thoughts on bracing myself to suffer the dinner in silence. The weather was throwing a last attempt at a freeze at us before spring arrived and the temperatures had dropped dramatically. The warmth from the house combined with the smell of garlic and onions of whatever Bobby had cooked greeted me, hunger seemed to ambush me the moment I walked through the door.

I should have gone into the kitchen and helped Bobby sort dinner out, but instead the familiar growly voice from the small room in the opposite direction distracted me. I crept towards the room, listening.

"I don't care who they are. If they steal from us, I want their fingers... What do you mean you don't understand? Cut. Their. Fucking. Fingers. Off."

The door handle turned, the mechanism scraping loudly and I started at the noise. Cian burst out of the room, nearly bowling me over. I teetered backwards but he caught me, his big hands on my shoulders, setting me back on my feet. But he didn't leave go of me immediately. Instead, he stared into my eyes, studying me.

"How long have you been there?" he asked, his voice a threatening purr.

"Long enough to hear you have a thing for fingers."

Chapter Seven

ജ Cian ഈ

"I need you to get back and sort some shit out in Ireland," I said to Oisín later that night after dinner, "profits are short and I reckon someone's skimming. You need to find out who it is."

"Shouldn't you do it? You need to make sure these idiots don't think we're weak. Would be better if the head of the family is directly involved."

Osh was right. It really should be me. But I wanted to stay here longer and get things in place. I didn't even know who I was going to get to run the place, yet. Charlie was so volatile, as much a liability as my brother. Yet earlier she'd surprised me. How much of my conversation she had overheard I wasn't sure, but her reaction, or lack thereof, was interesting. She hadn't feared me, hadn't turned and run for the hills, but I could see in her eyes she sensed danger and it excited her, challenged her. She was something else. Had she been easier to control she would make an excellent mafia wife. Instead, it made her dangerous.

64

"Away with the pixies tonight, bro?" Osh broke my thoughts, "what's going on?"

I rubbed my hand over my face.

"This place. It just seems like hard work," I sighed.

"The place or the woman in it?"

Oisín's keen eyes studied me with interest.

"Just fire her," Osh kept watching me, scrutinising my reaction.

"She overheard me on the phone earlier."

"Fuck. What are you going to do then?"

"I dunno, nothing yet."

Charlie wound me up. She'd joined us for dinner but was making her presence known by her silence and lack of sarcastic comments. I'd become so used to her mocking tone that anything else was abnormal. Was what she had overheard bothering her after all? I should get rid of her, probably permanently, but something seemed to stop me from doing that; I just didn't know what that something was.

By the next morning, Oisín had started to make his way home to Ireland, leaving me here to deal with things at the yard. The day was bright and crisp and I'd made an effort to get out on the yard early to really observe how the place was run. I'd switched the suit for jeans, boots and a jumper; and, of course, a big coat. I made myself a coffee from the communal kitchen, taking it with me to a vantage point on the mounting block.

The stable hands worked with a seamless and methodical discipline, taking horses to paddocks or on the horse walker. The first set of horses had gone out earlier than I'd even got out of bed and were returning from their wander around the Durham countryside, their hooves ringing out on the concrete as they strolled back into the yard. Charlie had been out on the gallops with another group, her horse jogging back along the lane enthusiastically, snorting and throwing its head as she sat relaxed in the saddle, loose reins in one hand, chatting to one of the jockeys with her.

Bobby was right. She was a natural in the saddle. Cool, confident and calm and totally different from when her feet touched the ground. The horses drew closer and I noticed for the first time the dimples in her cheeks when she smiled; her face lighting up, a twinkle in her blue eyes.

A four-wheel drive pulled up behind them and I knew the smile on her face would disappear as soon as the driver got out of the car. I left my coffee cup on the stone set of steps and wandered over to the parking area.

"Morning, Cian," Jonjo greeted me, relaxed.

He pulled his hat and whip out of the car and followed me across the yard.

"Tack up the black stallion," I instructed one of the stable lads, who looked at me like I was speaking a foreign language.

"Well? Go on then," I urged when he continued to gawp at me.

"But Charlie....."

"But Charlie what?" I barked and he rushed away.

"I want you to tack something up to ride round the gallops with Jonjo," I called over to Charlie as she walked past, laden with tack.

She scowled in my direction.

"Who's Jonjo riding?"

"What does it matter?"

She came towards me, not having put any of the equipment down, her face the picture of defiance.

"It helps to partner horses up together who don't rub each other up the wrong way. You know? Like me and you?"

I gritted my teeth in annoyance.

"The black stallion," I answered, studying her face.

A flicker of darkness crossed her eyes and her jaw tightened, but it was gone in a moment.

"See, that wasn't hard, was it?" she said before walking away.

Eventually, the black stallion was tacked up. He'd managed to bounce two stable hands off all the walls in his stable in the process and was as angry and as bad tempered as Charlie. She'd already mounted a big grey thoroughbred and watched from a short distance away as the animal came out of his box like an angry bull. Its metal shoes clanged on the concrete of the yard as Jonjo tried to get it to stand close enough to the steps of the mounting block. After it had stood on its back legs three times, he barked at one of the stable hands and the poor young lad hoisted Jonjo on, scrambling out of range of the stallion's legs as it thrashed about.

Jonjo grabbed up his reins, getting tight hold of the black beast, keeping it from getting its head between its front legs and resembling something more suited to a rodeo.

"Keep him moving," I heard Charlie instruct, "keep him going sideways and then forwards and then sideways again. You need to distract him."

"I know how to ride a fucking horse," the other jockey growled at her.

I felt a little pang of anger, the sudden need to defend her, but I bit my tongue.

"Not this one you don't. No, don't kick him," I heard her voice.

The horse sprang off all fours, exploding in mid-air before landing back down in a scrabble of hooves. Jonjo slapped the horse with his whip and it exploded again. Crack. I heard the sound again. Then the black horse was up on his back legs before lurching forward, arching its back, bouncing up the road and flinging the jockey around with such force that it threw him out of the saddle and into the air, landing heavily on his side.

"For fuck's sake," he muttered, still holding tight to the reins as he got to his feet.

He grabbed his whip off the floor and clattered the horse on the neck with it, sending it back to its favourite vertical position, hooves punching the air over his head.

Charlie was on the ground, waving her arms at the shocked stable lads who rushed to take the grey horse from her, and then she moved on Jonjo. I saw the look in her eyes before I got to him. Hatred and rage. Pure and unstable.

"Don't you fucking hit my horses," she shouted and he looked at her with shock.

One of the young lads took the black horse from him, moving out of the warpath as Charlie advanced.

"You need to teach the fucking thing some discipline," he spat, wiping his legs down.

I saw the fury break, Charlie's face darkening. She was next to him quicker than I could get in between them. Launching herself towards him, she hit him square in the chest with both heels of her hands, sending him staggering backwards, surprise all over his face.

"You want some fucking discipline," her words were all venom, "I'll give you some fucking discipline."

She yanked his whip from his hands, raising it above her head. I dived at her, grabbing the whip before it came down on Jonjo's head, stopping her assault on one of the best jockeys in the country.

"Enough," I growled, yanking it free from her hand, "you. Here with me. Now. Jonjo. Car. I'll speak to you later."

I gripped her wrist, dragging her roughly behind me. If she'd had somewhere to have dug her heels into like a petulant child, I was sure she would have done. Instead, I towed her across the yard and into an empty stable.

"What the fuck?" I asked as I spun her to face me.

"Get off me."

She wriggled, trying to get her arm free from my grasp. I grabbed the other wrist, locking her arms against her sides.

"I mean it, Cian. Get the fuck off me!"

"Or what?"

She pursed her lips together, tilting her head and looking at me defiantly. If looks could kill, that would have been a bullet between my eyes right then. Her eyes still held that rage I'd just seen. Beautiful, light baby-blue. Angelic, yet devilish. Her cheeks were flushed pink and the cupid's bow of her top lip looked much more pronounced than I'd seen it before. I took a step forward, pushing her backwards into the stable wall with my body, sure that I'd heard the tiniest exhalation come from her.

I was nearly a foot taller than her and easily overpowered her, but her gaze never faltered. She matched me in attitude for every inch of height and every bit of muscle I had. Her lips looked delicious. She smelled delicious; a mix of deodorant, soap, hay, and her own light scent. I dipped my head to her neck, inhaling her, letting her scent flow over my senses and whirl around my head. My cock twitched. For fuck's sake.

I took a deep breath, calming myself, ignoring the flow of blood to my groin.

"I'm going to let go of you and you're going to calm down," I instructed, more softly this time.

I released her wrists tentatively and took a half step away from her, watching for any flicker or sign she'd come at me or go on the rampage at Jonjo again.

"Those horses don't deserve that," she said, her voice quieter but still tense, "they work for us, win for us. They need to be understood not beaten up."

I studied her. Her eyes were calmer, the fight in her had subsided.

"It won't happen again, Charlie. I promise you that," I said, closing the gap between us once more.

When she looked up at me this time it was something else I saw in her eyes. The blue seemed to smoulder and she tilted her face sideways, studying me. I could feel the heat of our bodies entangling. I could hear the little hitch in the breaths she tried to keep steady, the slight parting of her lips, the dilation of her pupils.

A cough at the doorway startlcd me and I whipped round.

"What's going on? What have I missed?" the old man said, his voice hoarse.

"Nothing," Charlie bit, stepping sideways, brushing against me as she moved out of the stable.

Chapter Eight

∽ Charlie ∾

The next few days were uneventful. Cian had been busy with Bobby finalising paperwork for the takeover of the business, and I continued training horses. Old Bobby had been distant. I'd tried to talk to him about where he was going to live after all this was over, but he avoided any conversation that wasn't about training or racing.

"Morning, Charlie," Jonjo called from the yard kitchen, passing me a cup of coffee, "what's today's schedule?"

"We have a few to ride out but they're easy rides so I'm going to let the stable hands do that. I need to partner Brian up and get him over some hurdles."

Jonjo nodded at me. We'd come to some sort of understanding over the last few days. Mostly, I told him who needed riding and he pretty much did as I said. If I was to guess, I would have said he was on his best behaviour at the instruction of Cian. He was useful, though. There were a few horses that benefitted from his heavier weight on their backs and as long as he listened to me about how to ride them, everyone was getting along.

"I have to admit, Charlie, you've got some balls to get on that thing," Jonjo mused as we made our way to the gallops.

Brian was his usual self this morning and I'd mounted mid-buck, springing on to his back and grabbing the reins quickly. He spent the small walk up to the track cantering and leaping and snorting, sounding more like an angry dragon than an actual horse.

"He's just misunderstood," I replied.

"And do you understand him?"

"No. Not fully. Some days I think I've got him worked out and others he flings me a curveball and I have to rethink everything," I answered honestly.

There was someone else who seemed to do that to me too, recently. I pushed those thoughts to the back of my head.

"Ok. Brian likes to go full throttle as soon as his feet touch the track," I warned, "Are you ready?"

"Let's have it."

The horses shot forward at a pace and we held them at a fast canter till their lungs filled and released and their joints had warmed up. Then on the next lap we pushed for a gallop.

"Have you tried keeping him at the front of the field?" Jonjo asked me as we pulled the horses to a steady trot.

"No. I've always felt that he was better behind another horse till the last minute."

"I think you should try keeping him in the front. He's so stubborn and reactive he might be best with open field to concentrate on and not the other horses."

"Hmmmm. Might be worth a try."

By the time we got back to the yard, I'd relaxed. We had chatted all the way back, reminiscing about old races, talking about our favourite horses. Christ, we were almost braiding each other's hair we were getting on that well.

"Do you need a hand with that guy?" Jonjo asked as we both jumped off and Brian scowled at anyone who looked at him.

"No thanks. We'll be OK, won't we Bri?"

Bobby and Cian were on the yard as we returned and I felt the Irishman glaring at me as we came to a stop. He took a long gulp from his coffee cup, keeping his eyes fixed on me the entire time, and I wondered what I'd done to piss him off today.

Cian followed me to the stable. He was dressed casually again today, blue denim jeans clung to thick thighs and his tight shaped arse. He was stocky; far too much muscle for a jockey, but he suited the country look with the padded gilet over his jumper. It looked like he'd actually been doing some work, the sinewy muscle of his big forearms visible between the sleeves of the jumper pushed up to his elbow and the thick gloves covering his hands.

"You two seem to be getting along better," Cian said, his voice low.

"Jonjo has some good ideas of his own. We may make a decent team yet."

The Irishman should have been happy his jockeys were no longer trying to kill each other, but his eyes were dark and his plump lips pushed together in a grumpy pout.

"What?" I challenged.

"What do you mean, what?"

I rolled my eyes.

"You know you're the most contrary person I've ever met?" he snapped, "you're either a ball breaker or sweetness and fucking light. Just stick to one or the other?"

"Christ! Who pissed in your corn flakes this morning?" I retorted.

Cian shook his head and walked away, swinging the hammer he'd been carrying as if he was hitting someone with it. I assumed he was imagining my head underneath it.

Bobby sat watching from his seat on the mounting block and I joined him with a cup of coffee later.

"Good to see you and Jonjo working together," even his voice sounded frail, "he's a good jockey despite his brutishness. Be open to what he can teach you."

The old man looked exhausted and there was a great sadness in his eyes. His skin was pale and dark circles shadowed the puffy skin under his eyes.

"What's going on with all this?" I asked him, looking around me as he let out a sad sigh.

"I just need to find somewhere to move to and then it's all completed. Shouldn't be too long now. I've a few irons in the fire."

I felt the familiar heaviness of anxiety and nausea tug at my stomach. I'd not thought about it much the last few days, thankfully distracted by plenty to do here. And we'd not spoken about it for a while. We used to confide in each other, but after I'd learnt the yard would be taken over, I'd avoided Bobby, not bearing to have the conversations we really should have been having. I'd even avoided eating with him on a night time as I usually would; something the old man really enjoyed.

"What time's dinner tonight?" I asked, watching the old man's face brighten up.

"Normal time. Any requests?"

By the evening I was famished, my stomach grumbling so loudly it was vibrating. With all the horses fed and tucked up for the night, I walked up the road to the house. I'd not been there for a few days so I wasn't prepared to stumble over the packing boxes lining the hallway as I pushed through the door. The photos and pictures had been taken off the walls, discoloured décor, the only evidence they had been there at all and all his ornaments and trophies and racing paraphernalia had gone. The house looked bare and unwelcoming.

Stripped of its character, Bobby's home felt barren, hostile. A lump formed in my throat as I glanced around. He'd been here for years. It was everything to him. Pressure built in my chest, sadness and worry filling my ribcage as a dry burn tugged at my throat.

The only familiar sensation was the smell of Bobby's cooking. He was as good a chef as a racehorse trainer. My stomach growled angrily. I poked my head in the kitchen.

"Can I help you with anything?" I asked, watching the old man shuffle around the room.

He tipped his head to the bench.

"You can start taking the dinner through."

A short time later my stomach was full of roast lamb and red wine. I'd suffered Cian's presence, but I'd made a real effort to be pleasant and surprised myself that it had not been as difficult as I had expected. But I frequently found myself distracted by the old man. He'd eaten very little, pushing the food around his plate countless times before it made it to his mouth.

He was still pale, yet a small sheen of sweat was sitting on his face and head, glistening under the lights of the dining room. I kept glancing at him, watching him. His hand shook slightly as he brought the wine glass to his lips, taking the smallest of sips as though anymore might burn his throat.

"I'm going to have an early night. I've got a headache I can't shift," he said eventually, "Charlie, would you mind cleaning up?"

"Sure, Bobby. Get yourself some rest."

"I'll help too," Cian said from beside me.

"Sure you know how to do it?" I mocked after Bobby had shuffled off to bed.

"Think I can figure out how to wash a few dishes."

We stood next to each other at the sink; Cian washing as I dried. He was tall, making me look up every time I stole a glance at him. His brown hair was still in its messy short style, but he hadn't shaved for a couple of days, a light stubble covering his face. He'd stripped off down to a t-shirt in the warmth of the house, the muscle of his biceps bulging with each movement. A tattoo peaked out of the sleeve of his left arm and I resisted the urge to push the material up to see exactly what was underneath.

Once the dishes were away I topped up our wine glasses.

"So, what do you actually do for a living?" I asked the Irishman, watching his face, but there was no awkward flinch at the question.

"My family has several businesses."

"Such as?"

"Import and export mainly as well as business consultancy."

"Uh huh? So all above board stuff?" I asked, watching his reaction.

The muscle in his jaw flickered slightly. He took a sip from the glass.

"Why do you ask?" his voice was low with a hint of a growl.

"I like to know who I work for, assuming I'm not fired yet?"

"What are you really asking me, Charlie?"

His eyes held mine, now watching for my reaction.

"I've heard things. From a number of people."

"Heard what things?" he asked, turning to stand in front of me.

"That you're not a nice person."

"Mmmmm," he grumbled, pushing the glass onto the bench behind me, his arm brushing mine.

He didn't move back again, instead standing close to me so I had to look up at him to meet his eye.

"And what do you think that means?" he asked as my attention moved to those full pouty lips that were just a step away.

"I don't think you're a serial killer."

"Why not?"

"You're too good looking."

He stood looking down at me, his hazel eyes intense, intoxicating. I felt a swell of warmth in my stomach, a tingling sensation creeping across my skin. He brushed a strand of hair off my face that had come loose from my ponytail, tucking it behind my ear, my skin turning to goose bumps under his touch.

Then he stepped back, creating space between us, his eyes softening a little.

"I come from a long line of an old Irish family," he said, more composed, "we haven't always conducted ourselves to the full letter of the law. Not too unlike you, I hear."

I smiled.

"I only roughed a few bullies up, Cian. I expect you are a little further up the criminal hierarchy than me."

"Maybe? But *I've* never been caught."

He smiled back, his lips pulling into a sexy grin as his eyes lit up. The warmth in my belly was turning to something else and I needed to go before I did something stupid.

*****

I got up to driving rain the next morning; a total put off for getting out of bed at the tiny hour of 5 o'clock and had already gone through one full set of clothes by the time I'd fed all thirty horses their breakfasts. It was just going to be one of those days.

81

Soaked to the bone for a second time after my third ride round the gallops of the morning, I was untacking when Cian's car pulled onto the yard. He got out and marched across to the stables.

"Charlie, I need you to come with me," he said abruptly.

"Is this where I salute, click my heels together and say 'yes sir'?" I snapped.

The man was a real Jekyll and Hyde.

"Christ sake Charlie, just get in the car. You, untack that horse for her," he ordered a passing stable boy.

I stared at him and he sighed.

"Please," he continued.

"I need to get out these clothes first," I commented.

Grabbing my arm he pulled me to him, his lips hovering near my ear.

"Charlie, it's Bobby. I need you to come with me now."

My stomach dropped like I'd jumped down a hole, anxiety and fear flooding my entire system. I nodded and followed him to the car, climbing in the passenger side. Then we sped off up the road to the house.

"What's going on, Cian?" I asked as we flew up the drive, water spraying into the air behind us.

"I'm so sorry, Charlie," he started as dread trickled through my veins, "Bobby's died."

I opened my mouth to say something but no words came out. I blinked and stared at Cian blankly.

"Where?" I didn't recognise the voice, the strangled whisper that had come from my lips.

I ran up the stairs, taking two at a time until I stumbled over the steps near to the top and fell onto my face, banging my shin on a wooden step covered in a threadbare carpet. I scrambled up quickly, throwing Bobby's bedroom door open, clanging angrily off the wall behind it.

The old man lay there, his skin grey, his eyes closed; peaceful. Running to his side, I pressed my fingers into his neck, the coolness of his skin taking me by surprise. I couldn't feel a flicker of anything.

"No, Bobby, no," I whimpered, pulling the covers away from him and feeling for his breast bone.

I felt for his sternum, his flesh stiff under my fingers. I counted the fingers below it, replacing them with the heel of my hands and pushed my weight through my arm until the muscles stung and only my sobs called out the rhythm.

"Cian, help me," I cried.

The Irishman moved to my side, covering my hands with his.

"Charlie, stop. He's long gone."

I shook my head, knocking his hands from mine, and continued.

"I can't let him die. He can't die. Don't just stand there! Call an ambulance. Do something!"

I heard the floorboards creak under Cian's weight as he moved to the outside of the door, his voice low, talking to someone, words I couldn't hear.

"Don't leave me Bobby. Come on, old man. All this. We can sort it out. I promise."

I kept pumping his chest and stopping to feel for a pulse, but there was nothing.

"Come on, Bobby. I need you. Don't do this. Please."

I don't know how much time had lapsed but my arms had got heavy and my shoulders ached. The room felt colder, Bobby felt colder. A hand rested on my shoulder.

"Come on now," the low voice rumbled behind me.

Shrugging his hand off, I stopped and straightened myself up, staring at the old man. His eyes were closed, a bluish tinge to thin lips. I crossed his hands over his chest, my own resting on top of them, squeezing his fingers, hoping there'd been some mistake; that he would squeeze back any second. But his hands lay still. I bit my lip, looking round the room. Nothing disturbed. He hadn't thrashed about, just closed his eyes and..... gone to sleep. A half-drunk bottle of whisky sat on the dressing table, tablets spilled across the surface next to it. I looked from the tablets to Bobby and back again.

He'd been so sad; so withdrawn for days. His life was falling apart around him. Everything he'd worked for gone. Anger built inside me. Pressure rising. I turned.

"This is all your fault!" I spat at Cian, my voice erupting in the silence.

He looked at me, shocked.

"You and whatever gambling, loans, shit you've got going on. All of it. Your fault!"

Tears were flooding down my cheeks and I hadn't realised I'd advanced on Cian until my fists started pummelling a chest made of fucking stone. And he stood there and took it until my arms grew weak and my legs threatened to crumple underneath me and his hands wound around my wrists.

Chapter Nine

༄ Cian ༄

I watched her pump the old man's chest. She'd stop, try for a pulse and go again. Several times I tried to stop her, but she shrugged my hand away and carried on, tears silently rolling down her cheeks, dropping onto the stone-cold corpse in front of her. I don't know how long I watched her efforts for, but eventually I walked to her, placing a hand gently onto her shoulder. She stilled.

She watched the old man for a while, as if convincing herself that he really had gone, and then something caught her eye on the bedside table. I'd seen it earlier and I assumed she was about to form the same conclusion that I had. Yet in a split second, she turned and flew at me. Fists flying into me, rebounding off my chest as she pounded her hands against me.

"It's your fault!" she shouted over and over, "it's all your fault!"

Her face was becoming angrier and redder, her fists coming at me faster and with more force.

I took a breath and grabbed hold of her wrists. Yelling, she tried to shake me off and I moved my legs quickly to miss the flailing toes that were thrown in my direction. Tugging at her wrists, I pulled her into me, forcing her tight against my body, holding her still.

Her shouts gave way to sobs and she sank against me. I could feel the shake of her body against mine as I held her close, listening to her break her heart in my arms until she had no more left in her. Her body went limp and her knees buckled and I grabbed her before she hit the ground.

"Come on, Charlie," I spoke quietly, "let's go downstairs."

The paramedics and the police arrived a short time later. I directed them to Bobby's room before going back to Charlie. She was huddled up in the armchair by the fire, cradling the now cold cup of tea I had made for her a while ago. She was lost in the flames, staring blankly as the fire crackled and popped in front of her, her clothes still wet from the weather outside.

"Charlie, put these on. Please." I added when she looked at me, a faint flicker of defiance in her eyes.

But it had extinguished as quickly as it ignited. She turned over the clothes I had given her with her free hand, eyeing the jogging bottoms and jumper tiredly. Then did nothing. I left her staring into the flames while I dealt with the police and the paramedics. Eventually, we were left almost in peace; one lonely policeman sitting in his car outside the house as we awaited the coroner.

It was late afternoon by the time the coroner came. Charlie had sat in the same seat in her wet clothes, occasionally mopping a stray tear from her face. The fire had burnt away to embers and the late winter daylight was disappearing. The rain had continued all day, hammering the house in symbolic fashion.

She looked up as they entered; tired and swollen eyes following them up the stairs. But it wasn't till the body encased in the black bag was brought down the stairs that the true realisation hit her. Charlie got up off the seat on shaky legs, shuffling closer, watching as the body of the old horse trainer was carried out of the house. Tears streamed down her face and she clasped her arms around herself. Then, as they carried him away, she sank to the floor, her head in her hands, sobbing into her fingers.

I dropped to my haunches in front of her, pulling her back up to her feet.

"Come on, sweetheart," I said, pulling her into me, cuddling her into my chest.

For what seemed like ages I held her, letting her sob and cry and scream. Her blonde hair had fallen from the ponytail and hung listlessly around her face, and she shivered against me, a mixture of fatigue, damp and hunger. Eventually, she pulled away from me, rubbing at her arms.

"What do you need?" I asked softly, gazing into her light blue eyes, sparkling from the tears still welling there.

"A shower," she whispered, "I'm so cold."

"Go. Go get a shower," I scooped my clothes off the floor and handed them to her, "I'll sort us something to eat."

She nodded silently, then looked around the lounge, her eyes filling with tears once more.

It was nearly an hour later before I saw her again. She wandered quietly into the kitchen, wet hair hanging down her back, my jumper and joggers swamping her. Even with all of her body covered by the baggy clothes, seeing her dressed in my clothes did something to me.

I'd never seen her so quiet and vulnerable. Her spark had gone, replaced with a pain even I felt. Or maybe it unearthed memories of my own pain and loss. Feelings I'd buried and ignored, instead focusing on vengeance. But at least I had someone to blame for the death of my family and that made the grief tolerable. Sharing this day with Charlie was something else. Her grief affecting me in ways I could never have expected. My chest had burned with a hideous tightening from the moment I'd had to break the news to her.

I'd seen loads of death, caused an awful lot of it, but today it had taken its toll on me. There was nothing I could do to take her pain away. There was nothing I could do to make it better. And that's all I'd wanted to do, to make it easier for her. Christ; fucking England was running a real number on me.

"I need something stronger," Charlie said quietly as I reached for a bottle of wine from the fridge.

Nodding, I pulled the whisky off the bench and poured two glasses. She perched her arse on a bar stool at the breakfast bar and I slid across the huge pizza box. She wrinkled her nose and at first I thought she would refuse to eat, but she opened the lid tentatively.

Soon she'd eaten a load of slices and the colour had returned to her face; her eyes looking a little less red.

"Thanks for today, Cian," she mumbled, staring at a slice of pepperoni on the pizza in her hand.

"I'm sorry it's been a shit day for you."

"It's been a shit few weeks," she sighed.

She looked so vulnerable tonight. No resemblance of the fire-breathing demon I'd come to know over the last few weeks. She took another swig of the whisky.

"You know I thought of Bobby as family?" she said suddenly.

I nodded. I'd heard the old man's stories of her.

"I lost my way a bit as a teenager. I'd never had an easy life. Never felt I truly belonged anywhere. When I was sentenced to community service to shovel horse shit, I was so pissed off."

She smiled at me weakly.

"I spent the first sessions being as slow and as annoying as I could. Making as much mess on the way to the muck heap in the hope they would get rid of me. But Bobby was so patient. Then I found the horses. They do something to me; I can't describe it. I just feel at peace around them."

I heard myself sigh. I didn't think I could recall what peace was. I couldn't remember the last time I didn't feel so angry.

"If it hadn't been for Bobby giving me a chance, I don't think I would have come back from where my life was leading me. He saved me. Somehow. But I couldn't save him. Not when he really needed it."

A tear rolled down her cheek.

"You couldn't have saved him. The situation here, with Bobby's debt. I didn't mean for it to end like this," I said quietly.

Another time she would have flown at me with a venom loaded tongue, but tonight she just stared at me sadly. I felt like I'd broken her spirit.

"The debts were enormous. The land and the horses they would never have been enough to clear it all. When we called it in, we knew there would be a loss."

Something stirred in her.

"Who are we, Cian?"

I sighed. There was no easy way to answer it or avoid the question.

"You weren't too far wrong with your idea about me and my family," I answered eventually.

"So what? You're mafia?"

"Yes, something like that or whatever you want to call it. Mafia, firm, gangsters, all the above."

"Mmmmm," she said and took a sip of her drink.

"What about your family, Charlie? Do you have someone you can call?"

"I have a sister, Natalie. You'd like her; she's obedient."

A flicker of her character had ignited again, and I couldn't help but smile.

"The rest of my family are dead," she continued, "I didn't have many in the first place. I was adopted."

"Oh."

"Yeah, I'm sure its sucks. My adoptive mother died when I was young and my father died a year ago. They were good parents, but I always felt like I didn't fit them. But Bobby? I felt at home with him. Like I was meant to be here."

"He loved you like his own. I could tell," I said.

She nodded, her face turning sad again, then slugged back the last of her drink and I stifled a laugh at the face she pulled.

"I need to go home. Can you drive me down to the yard?"

I pulled the car up onto the yard in the dark. The rain had eventually stopped but the ground was saturated and the water still ran off the stable rooves and into the drains. Charlie was staring straight ahead, her face tense.

"Stay with me tonight, Cian? I don't want to be alone. I've been alone all my life, but I can't cope with it now."

"OK, sweetheart."

Christ, I didn't know what had fucking got into me. I wasn't *that* person. I didn't do comforting people. I took lives and I moved on, not this. But lying in Charlie's bed, both of us fully clothed, with her nestled into my side, was something else. Something I'd never felt before as she lay in my arms, her breath coming in slow, light waves.

Chapter Ten

☙ Charlie ❧

The little red convertible pulled into the car park on the stable yard as I looked over Brian's door. I patted the angry black horse on the neck, hoping he would behave himself for just a couple of days, but I wasn't holding out hope he could contain himself. He was already snapping his teeth at anyone who came too close to him this morning.

"This your ride?" Cian asked, coming to a stop outside of biting range.

I nodded, watching my sister sitting in the car, not daring to get out and get her shoes dirty.

"I've left a timetable for each horse for a couple of days. Jonjo will understand it. Just make sure he doesn't try and grow a pair while I'm gone and attempt to get on Brian. We don't need any more bodies on the place," I added wryly, my sarcasm hurting me more than I wanted to acknowledge.

"Don't worry. We can afford a few days without you," Cian answered softly.

He went to put his hand on my shoulder, but I ducked away from him. I didn't need to add complication to my life. I lost myself to vulnerability last night. It couldn't happen again, no matter how innocent it was. He was dangerous, in all ways. I needed to remind myself of that.

I felt a pang of guilt so turned back to him, "thanks for letting me get away for a few days."

Cian nodded, his coolness returning. That would make life easier for both of us.

I bounded up the stairs to my flat above the stables and grabbed a bag with the basics. Natalie eventually got out of the car, looking at disgust at the ground she had to put her probably ridiculously expensive shoes on. But as I approached, her distaste for the premises faded and she pulled me into a hug and I felt the tears flow again. After a few moments she guided me to the passenger seat, taking my bag from me and stowing it in the boot.

The car revved to life and she pulled away down the road and I watched in the rear-view mirror as the yard and Cian faded away into the distance. It was a relatively short drive to my sister's house. I'd told Cian this morning that I needed a few days to get away from the yard and the horses. And him. He seemed to have understood and for once, I was thankful he'd brought someone like Jonjo on board. I'd never have thought I would be responsible for running the yard without Bobby. Maybe I never would. It was quite possible that Cian had every intention of bringing Jonjo in to take it over, but for now the sadness was too deep that even my anger couldn't resurface.

"You've been decorating," I commented, stepping into the hallway of Natalie's home.

Natalie's house was huge. It was a four bedroomed, mid-terraced Edwardian house in Gateshead. The area was family central, houses filled with screaming kids on either side of her. I always thought her desire for a family had drawn her there, but her love life was just as exciting as my own.

Nat dropped my bag in the hallway and I followed her through to her kitchen. It was beautifully modern and sterile. Every surface was immaculately clean and shiny, every dish had been put away, and even the flowers in the vase looked like they had been picked that day. It was almost a show home.

"Who was the tall, serious guy at the yard?" Natalie asked.

"You wouldn't like him. He has a tattoo," I deflected.

I picked the wine glass that she had slid towards me off the bench, enjoying the gentle crispness of pinot grigio against my tongue. This was so much nicer than whisky.

"He seemed to like you," she said after a long pause.

I hated when she did that: study me. Natalie was an excellent solicitor and a great judge of character.

"He's my new boss," I said after a while, keeping my eyes fixed on the pale gold liquid in my glass.

"Hmmm, that's what we are calling it these days, huh?"

"Nat, please. He's got a stick wedged up his arse. And he's Irish."

"What's wrong with Irish? We've got Irish way back in our family history."

"You have. Not me. No one knows where I've come from. All those secrets died with Dad, remember?"

She rolled her eyes at me. It was a distraction, though; being here with her. A different sadness of a troubled childhood and lack of my own identity, but it was a sadness I could bear, or was used to, and that was good right now.

We talked long into the night, the wine flowing freely, as we reminisced about our childhood and my waywardness. Natalie had been the model child. Me? I was the devil incarnate; or that's sometimes what my father had thought. She'd gone on to University, got a degree, qualified in a respectable profession and then practiced alongside our father. I'd just played with horses, or at least that was what he thought I did.

I slept a lot whilst Nat was out at work, resting in the comfy attic bedroom and enjoyed lounging around the three-storey house during the day. I even watched daytime television which was a real novelty.

I talked her into a night out, which was pretty unusual for Nat, and so we drank and danced and then staggered home at the small hours of the morning. I needed something different; distraction from my thoughts of Bobby. But I couldn't distract myself from my thoughts of Cian. And that had disturbed me. It was time to go home.

Chapter Eleven

ഔ Cian ൕ

I clutched the hand of cards close to me, glancing over at the men seated around the table in the underground gambling den in the centre of Cork. Stacks of chips of various heights sat in front of them, everyone desperately perfecting their best bluffing faces. Yet I noticed the twitch of the grey-haired suit's right eye and the slight furrow of the brow of the man sitting next to him.

The stakes were high. I'd already lost a few grand and my stack of chips was sinking lower and lower. The man immediately opposite from me was glowing and couldn't keep the smile from his eyes. Placing my cards face up on the table, I watched his expression, his lips pulling into a huge grin, and I lost another load of chips to him.

He smiled and flipped his cards over and taking the chips from the middle of the table for what seemed like an unfair amount of times that night. I took a slug of whisky as the grey-haired suit decided he was cutting his losses and retiring from the game. Sensible plan.

That left the three of us. The dealer flipped out the cards again and I slid mine towards me, seeing my opportunity. I pushed another pile of chips into the middle, watching the other two men as I did. The man with the furrowing brow rubbed his face, clearly deciding whether he was in or out, before finally deciding he was folding. I watched the middle-aged man look at his cards, then at his chips. He pushed a small pile forward to match mine.

"I'll raise you another grand," he stated, trying to study me.

I took another sip of whisky while I considered, sneaking another glance at my cards and holding my breath. I eyed my dwindling chips, letting my eyes roam over them before slowly letting my breath out.

I pushed the lot forward.

"I'm all in."

The man across from me couldn't keep the curl of a smirk from his lips still as he pushed his chips into the middle of the table to meet mine. The dealer nodded at him and he turned his cards over, his smile widening. My eyes lingered on the cards for just a moment, then without a flicker of emotion I flipped mine over. The man's face fell and for a moment I thought he was going to cry. He knocked back the last of his drink and sat there staring.

I followed him to the bar a short while later, propping my arse on a bar stool next to him and ordering a whisky.

"Wanna drink?" I asked, but signalled to the barman to get him one anyway.

"Thanks," he mumbled when the tumbler was passed to him.

"Unlucky, that," I continued, watching the man's reflection in the mirror in front of me.

"Fuck," he moaned.

"You've got a nasty habit of losing a lot of money like that, haven't you?"

His head shot up and he looked at me suspiciously.

"How do you know that?"

"I know a lot of things about you, Sean."

He turned sideways to look at me.

"How are you going to get me the money I just won? I know you don't have that sort of cash."

"I, err, I'll get it."

His eyes were engulfed in defeat.

"What if you could pay it a different way?"

The man looked at me timidly.

"Y, you're not my type."

"No, you're not mine either," I knocked back my drink and turned so that I could see him properly.

"There's something else you can do for me, though."

*****

There were a few of us in the office crowded round the computer watching CCTV of various areas of Cork city on the screen in front of us. We watched my father's car pull through the traffic in the centre of town.

"There," Osh said, suddenly pointing to a van a few vehicles behind the big black Mercedes, "It's been in a few frames since the Merc got into the outskirts."

I looked closer, then went back to the footage from the other cameras. Oisín was right. It was there in several other cameras that covered the suburbs of the City. It had to have followed them from the house. The Mercedes pulled into the back lane and the camera lost sight of it. But it also lost the van as well.

"Zoom in on that van," I instructed Riley, "can we get a registration plate?"

"Possibly. I can get a partial. I'll keep playing with it, see what I can get."

I nodded, moving out of the office seat and letting him get to work.

"How'd you get all this anyway?" Osh asked, collapsing onto the leather sofa across from the desk.

"I won at poker."

"Nice one. How did you manage that? You're shit at poker, brother."

"Riley was my eyes."

Riley popped his head above the computer screen and flashed us a smile. Osh shook his head.

"Thought you might have improved your game while you were in New York? Instead, you just took up cheating."

"Got the CCTV didn't it?"

"Got it!" Riley announced excitedly from behind the desk, "and an address."

"Good. Let's go."

We parked the car a little way from the main door to the shabby block of flats, watching people come and go until most had settled down for the night. I was getting bored and agitated.

"What do we know about him?"

"Not much," Riley said from the front of the car, "doesn't seem to have any connections. No record. He's a total unknown."

"Gambles? Drinks? Fucks prostitutes?" Osh asked impatiently from beside me.

"Dunno, Osh. I've got nothing on him. He's a chef in an Italian restaurant in the City centre. Doesn't seem to have a girlfriend or boyfriend. Goes to the gym, but that seems to be about it."

I picked the dirt out of my nails with the tip of my knife, watching the sharp edge glisten in the street light that flooded into the car. He was too plain. Too boring. Too insignificant.

Eventually there was a rumble as the souped-up van rolled into a parking space in front of the block, the low vibrations of the oversized exhaust stopping as the engine was shut off. A tall man got out, typed a code into a keypad at the main door, and disappeared inside.

"Riley, Mad-Dog, stay here. Osh with me."

I pressed the button of one of the lower flats on the telecom keypad, buttoning my suit jacket as I awaited an answer. A lady's voice crackled over the system.

I flashed my wallet quickly across the camera, "Garda, I need access."

The door clicked open. Osh shot me a glance, and I shrugged my shoulders. We took the stairs to the tenth floor. The flats smelt stale. Many scents all mingled into one; cigarette smoke, cannabis, chips, flowers, cheap air fresheners. We walked along the corridor, stopping outside a blue door. I knocked loudly and for a moment we heard nothing, but then eventually the sound of muffled footsteps. The door was opened a crack as the man peered out into the hallway at us.

"Who the fuck are you?" he said gruffly through the one-inch gap.

"People who would like to speak to you."

"Not a fucking chance," he said, closing the door.

I rammed my shoulder into it and it sprung open as the man staggered backwards. Stepping inside, I glanced around at the flat. It was nicely done out; light and airy with white paintwork and abstract art pictures hung on the wall. Not at all what I had expected. Oisín followed me, closing the door behind him, locking us all in the small flat together.

"Sit," I instructed at the stunned-looking man.

He was broad shouldered, not a dissimilar build to me, and tall.

"Tell me who the fuck you are."

His hands had balled into fists and he stood defiantly, his feet planted. I sighed and took a step closer to him so that there was barely a foot between us.

"Just a little over a month ago, someone killed my father and my brother and my little sister. I want to know who that someone was and you're going to tell me."

The man looked even more stunned.

"I have no fucking idea what you are talking about!"

"No? Your van," I cocked my head towards the direction of the window, "it followed my father's car from the outskirts of town right to where he was taken."

"The v, v, van? I only bought it a few weeks ago!" he fell over his words.

"You expect me to believe that?"

"I swear that's the truth."

"Who'd you buy it from?"

"I dunno. I got it from an auction. Hold up. I've got the receipts somewhere," and he turned and walked into the kitchenette, rummaging in a drawer. Osh caught my eye.

"Here," the man said, holding a piece of paper in his outstretched hand, not daring to come any closer.

I snatched it from him, my eyes scanning over it. Just the auction company's name, nothing else apart from a date of purchase three weeks ago. I gritted my teeth and tipped my head at Osh, signalling it was time to leave.

"Dead end," I grumbled when we got back in the car, explaining the exchange to the other two men.

"It's got to be the O'Malleys," Riley commented.

"It probably is, but we need proof."

I wanted revenge. Someone needed to pay for the deaths of my family, but if I was going to declare war on the O'Malleys, I had to be pretty fucking certain it was them.

Chapter Twelve

ℂ Charlie ℮

The yard felt different with Bobby gone. It was quieter, less full of life than it had been. There was no one to watch enthusiastically from the top of the hill while we trained, no one to cook dinner for me as we talked over wine by the fire on the night time. I missed the old man like crazy, like there was an enormous hole where my heart used to be.

A few days' break had only distracted me from reality, made me forget about the pieces of my life that were falling down around me. The pain in my chest was crushing me and making me more of an arsehole than I already was.

To make it worse, I had all the admin and paperwork to do. We'd been a great team. I would ride and train the horses, run the yard and the yard staff. Bobby would pay the bills, take care of all the registrations, and the owners' accounts. Now that had all come to rest with me and I felt as though I was drowning in it.

"Hey, Charlie, how you doing?" Jonjo said softly, sitting beside me on the cold stone mounting block where I was lost in the darkness of my coffee.

I sighed.

"I didn't expect this," I answered, lifting my head and looking around, horse's heads resting over doors as I scanned the yard.

"I know it's shit. Can I do anything to help?"

"Don't suppose you know much about accounting, huh?"

"Actually, I do. A bit anyway. What can I help you with?"

"The owners' accounts, firstly. If you help me, I'll pay you with food?" I felt the smile creep across my face.

"It's a date," Jonjo said, laughing when he turned to look at me, "kidding, I value my testicles too much!"

I laughed back. It was the first time I had laughed or smiled in days and it actually felt good.

We sat in Bobby's office that evening, the log burner in the background, going through all the admin I was struggling with. The house was filled with the smell of Chinese takeaway and smouldering wood and I crunched noisily on a prawn cracker.

"How can you eat so much?" Jonjo complained, shaking his head as I offered him the bowl of crackers.

"I work it off," I shrugged.

"Yeah, so do I, but I'll have to do two extra runs every day for the rest of the week just to burn off what we ate tonight. You're a bad influence, Porter!" he nudged my arm and I spilt beer down my face.

"Aw, man, what a waste," I complained, then reached for another spring roll.

"Jesus, Charlie, you're going to pop," he chuckled, turning back to the accounts.

"What's going on in here?" a voice growled from the doorway and I was sure the temperature had just dropped a notch.

"When did you get back?" I asked, ignoring the dark expression on his face.

"Just now. What are you doing?" Cian's tone was icy.

Jonjo looked at me helplessly whilst I stared back at Cian, quietly challenging him as I folded my arms across my chest.

"OK, Charlie. That's most of it done and I've set it up in a spreadsheet for you, so it'll be easier next time," Jonjo stated, looking between me and Cian, "so I'll see you at the track tomorrow."

Jonjo grabbed his jacket and slid past Cian, who was blocking most of the doorway.

"So what *were* you doing?" he asked again.

"Spring roll?"

"Charlie, I asked you a question."

"So did I?" I bit the end off the spring roll I was waving in front of him.

"Are you drunk?"

"I've had a couple of beers. I'm not drunk. Prawn cracker?"

"Fuck's sake, why do you have to be so difficult all the time?" Cian asked as he moved into the room.

"I'm only offering you some left overs," I taunted, moving towards him with the bowl of prawn crackers so I was just a foot away from him.

"I don't want any fucking leftovers."

"Then what do you want? Waltzing in here with your stony-ass face and the warmth of a fucking snow storm?" I turned away from him, but he grabbed me, knocking the bowl out of my hands, prawn crackers spilling over the floor.

He spun me round and pushed me into the wall, as I stumbled in shock, his hand wrapped in the material of my jumper at my neck, his other beside my head, leaving me no means of escape. I tipped my head up to spit some more insults at him, my face only millimetres from his, our bodies almost touching. I could feel his breath on my face, his plump lips only a brush away from mine. For a moment, I expected him to pull away until I felt him crush his mouth against me, forcing my head back into the wall behind me.

His tongue pushed roughly into my mouth, swirling and tangling with mine. He was angry and this was his way of punishing me, intimidating me. I fought back, forcing my lips into him with the same ferocity, the same anger and intensity. He released the collar of my jumper, pushing his fingers into my hair, grabbing handfuls and pulling, little pricks of pain erupting in my scalp. I kissed him harder, nipping his lips with my teeth, enjoying the gasp he exhaled. My breath quickened, my hands ran up the front of his shirt, feeling the hardness of muscles under the thin white cotton. Then he pulled away, leaving my lips exposed, tingling and hot from the scratching of stubble on my skin.

"What the fuck, Cian?" I breathed, my heart pounding against my chest.

He stepped away from me, wiping his hand across his jaw line.

"I think you should go before I do something stupid," his words stinging.

"You've already done that," I shot back, turning towards the door.

It slammed loudly in the frame, the house rattling and creaking around it.

*****

We travelled South the next day with the horses and had a few in nearly every race. I'd

111

hovered round the stables, making sure each horse was properly settled and the stable hands knew which horses needed to be out and in what order.

I had Brian with us for the 1.30pm race and he was looking wild-eyed and tense in the stable at the end of the block, snapping his teeth at everyone in his usual manner. I'd avoided Cian all morning, using every excuse to stay with horses and let him entertain the owners.

The first couple of races had gone smoothly, and we'd had one winner, which Jonjo had ridden. The big jockey was growing on me. Now that he had taken his head out of his arse and actually started to listen I could really see him for the incredible jockey he was. We'd worked out between us which horses he was best suited to and our 'understanding' had now morphed into a friendship. And I sure as hell needed a friend right now.

"Good call," he nudged me casually as he walked past with his tack after weighing out after his first race.

"Told you I'm good," I winked, before backing into Brian's stable with a box of brushes.

The stallion greeted me at the door, nuzzling my pockets, looking for treats. I set the box down beside him and was just about to brush his neck when I noticed three men in suits wandering the length of the stables, sticking their heads over the doors of my horses. I let myself out of the stable, the hackles already prickling over my back, and strode towards them, getting to them before they got to Brian, for all our sakes.

"Can I help you?" I asked, "this is a restricted area."

The taller and broader of the three men looked at me, tipping his head sideways as his eyes roamed from my feet to my face.

"You are woman rider," he said, his voice heavy with an accent.

"I am a woman and I am a jockey, yes," I answered, returning the gaze.

He chuckled before adding, "dah, I've heard about you."

"Who are you?"

"Alexei Lebedev," the man introduced himself, just as Jonjo came to stand behind me.

I looked at the outstretched hand, then back at the man who was holding it towards me. Jonjo reached over the top of me suddenly, grasping the man's hand and shaking it enthusiastically.

"I'm Jonjo Moore," he said, "and this is Charlotte Porter."

I resisted the urge to stamp on his foot for using my full name.

"*Charlie* Porter," I corrected, shooting Jonjo a warning glance over my shoulder.

"Sorry, what do you want?" I asked again.

"I'm looking for boss, Mr O'Sullivan,"

I gritted my teeth, stopping myself from being an absolute arsehole to the foreign man in the suit and his miserable looking friends.

"You'll find him in the lounge, with the owners," I tilted my head toward the bars and restaurants that overlooked the race track.

Lebedev nodded and walked off in the direction I had indicated. I watched as they left, one of his minders glancing back, giving me a stony stare.

"Christ, Charlie, do you know who that was?" Jonjo hissed in my ear.

I shrugged, "I have a funny feeling I'm about to find out."

"Alexei Lebedev is a Russian billionaire. He's fucking loaded. If he wants to see Cian, it's more than likely he's interested in having horses with us, or at least, he was interested until he met you."

I rolled my eyes, "I need to see to Brian," I answered.

I was soon sat on top of the feisty black stallion. Brian was snorting and jogging but had managed to keep all four feet on the ground and so far he was feeling a lot less tense than normal. There were a number of good horses and jockeys in this next race. I was thinking through my strategy, Jonjo's idea ringing in my ears. I assessed the other horses, watching to see how settled the horses were, which ones were absorbing the atmosphere and which ones were bouncing off it.

Dickie Hargreaves caught my eye, smirking in my direction, the dark red of the chestnut horse's coat looking almost on fire as the sun caught its flanks. The horses made their way to the start line, and I watched where Dickie placed his horse, steering Brian away, trying to put as much space between us, until we were fed into our allotted stalls. Brian settled quickly, dancing slightly from foot to foot, but as soon as the gates sprang open he sat onto his hind legs and bounded forward.

Brian's legs thundered underneath me, his body stretching with each stride, his breathing steady and I eased the pressure off the reins, letting the black horse find his rhythm. He covered the ground in quick, long strides, breaking away from the rest of the horses. We sat two off the lead horse, staying in space, giving the horse time to relax and focus on the hurdles that were approaching, jumping each one cleanly and confidently. Dickie Hargreaves edged towards us, the flash of red catching my eye. I let Brian go on a little faster, keeping him in the space we had created as we passed the roar from the grandstand for the second time.

I counted each jump, Brian clearing each one with a regular faultless stride until the final straight came into view. The pounding of hooves vibrated through me from the horse behind and I checked over my shoulder. The chestnut horse of Dickie was gaining on us. I swapped my hands on the reins, shortening them, signalling to Brian to go faster. He surged on beneath me, passing the second horse and gaining quickly on the lead horse. Soon we flew past them, leaping over the next hurdle, now two from home.

The hammering of the hooves behind me grew louder, closer, and I felt the brush of a jockey's leg against mine, pushing us towards the rails on the last turn. Dickie's horse was almost neck and neck with us and I could feel his knee as he pressed it further into my leg. He glanced at me and grinned and then pulled away just a stride out of the penultimate hurdle. Brian stumbled, veering left, twisting me slightly, my foot slipping from my right stirrup. The black horse reached for the jump, adding a clumsy short stride and landing awkwardly, sending me flying over his head.

I lurched forward, hanging off the left-hand side, the ground suddenly soaring up to meet me. I prepared my body for impact, tucking my arms and chin to my chest instinctively, just like we'd all been taught. But, just as I thought I was about to eat dirt, I stopped, my foot twisting in the stirrup as I hung upside down around Brian's belly. Hooves flew past my head as I tugged on my leg, my foot stuck fast, the last fence approaching. I wiggled my leg again, keeping my head up and off the ground. It was no use. There was no way I could break free. The saddle slipped over to the left as the glint of metal shoes passed right in front of my eyes. The last fence got closer and closer with each stride.

Chapter Thirteen

৪০ Cian ରେ

"Mr O'Sullivan," the Russian billionaire greeted me, having found me in the lounge.

"Mr Lebedev. Nice to finally meet you. I hear you are interested in your horses training with me?"

"Yes. I would assess your jockeys more. You have two main riders, dah?"

"That's correct. Jonjo Moore and Charlie Porter. Charlie's also the trainer."

"Is she? I've had pleasure of meeting her," the tall man mused.

Shit. I'd not wanted Charlie to be let loose on the Russian, not without having some control of what came out of her mouth. Although unless I actually gagged her, I didn't know whether controlling that mouth of hers was ever going to be possible.

The commentator suddenly broke through the introductions.

"And they're off. Charlie Porter and Messiah Complex getting a good start."

"Perfect," the Russian continued, "now we see what girl can do," and he moved us to the windows to watch.

This would not have been the race I would have wanted him to watch. If the black stallion was in a difficult mood it would be a car-crash. Instead, as we watched, the black horse seemed composed. Charlie kept him close to the lead horses but in good space and he was gliding around the track, relaxed and easy.

"Bit early letting horse out?" Lebedev muttered beside me.

"She knows what she's doing."

Charlie eased the horse forwards and soon she had the advantage as she pulled away from the leaders. But there was another horse coming through on her right-hand side.

"Charlie Porter takes the lead with Dickie Hargreaves and Attack the Morning coming alongside," the commentator called out.

The other jockey was riding really close to them, too close, and I squinted at the screen several times, trying to work out whether he was actually touching them. Charlie checked back over her shoulder.

"Oh no. Messiah Complex has hit the rail."

The horse chipped in an extra stride, just before the jump, and landed clumsily, throwing Charlie out of the saddle and over his head. I sucked in a breath, waiting to see her body tumble, but the black horse found his feet and thundered on as she dangled from the side of him.

"Charlie Porter is stuck in her stirrup!"

A taut silence descended on the room, the swish of whispers as everyone's head turned to the screens, tension suspended in the air between punters. My heart jumped. The next fence was approaching fast and she was still hanging from the horse. The cameras focussed in on her. Her hands tugged at her stirrup, trying to wiggle her foot out. There was no way she could get free of the horse and he was still approaching the last fence, locked on, ready to jump.

I watched as she lifted her head, looking forwards towards the hurdle approaching, and for a split second I wondered what was going through her mind. My stomach lurched and nausea thumped me from the inside. Then she moved her hands further up, her face tense and straining. Bit by agonising bit, she pulled herself upwards and then, two strides before the fence, swung her leg over the back of the horse, hitting the saddle just as he took off.

Without Charlie in charge he leaped wide over the hurdle, jumping too early but miraculously coming down cleanly on the other side. Charlie picked up her reins, leant forwards and sent the black horse running onwards. He ate up the rest of the track with furious long strides and I watched, her left foot still twisting out to the side, as she crossed the finish line in second place.

The room erupted in cheers. People I had never met before coming and congratulating me. The commentator was going wild.

"That is incredible jockey," Lebedev patted me on the back, "I'll take your terms. Let me know when and where to sign contracts."

I nodded my attention on the television screen as Jonjo dashed out to Charlie. She leant down and hugged him and he helped ease her foot from where it was still jammed in the stirrup, touching her gently. My stomach flipped and I gritted my teeth, my insides confused with emotions of jealousy and relief. Then the press flocked to her side, microphones thrust up into her face, a TV camera beaming images of her around the racecourse, flushed and animated.

I missed her in the winners' enclosure after organising a further meeting with Lebedev. The steward pointed me toward where she was last seen as the stable hands led the stallion back to his stable. The whole racecourse was buzzing, regaling the moment she got herself back in the saddle, the television screens replaying her fall again and again. But every time I saw the replay, it filled me with anxiety and an ache of dread weighing heavily in my stomach.

I pushed the door open to the changing room.

"Do we not knock now?" she bit as I walked in.

She was standing in only a white thong and white lacy bra, scooping her hair up into a ponytail high onto her head. Her stomach tensed, showing a line of muscle running down each side, her legs lean but toned, with strong well-muscled calves. But it was the tattoo that stretched from under her arm, all the way down her side and over her hip and thigh that caught my eye; a black horse rearing up onto its hind legs, its mane and tailing flowing out behind it.

She walked over, coming to a stop when she was only a few centimetres in front of me, and I noticed the way she had limped.

"What do you want, Cian?" she held my gaze defiantly, a smirk coming to her lips, "or do you just like what you see?"

"You hurt?" I asked, ignoring the insinuation.

"My ankle a little," she said.

"Sit. Let me take a look."

"Since when were you a doctor?"

"Just do as you're told."

She raised an eyebrow and stared at me, rebellion written all over her face. I rolled my eyes, wrapped an arm around her middle and carried her back to the bench seat behind her, depositing her roughly on her arse.

"If you ever touch me again…."

"You'll do what?" I asked, dropping to my knees between her legs and pulling her injured foot towards me.

She winced as I gently pressed my fingers over it, her skin mottled with a bruise developing.

I felt along her ankle, her skin smooth under my fingers as I ran them down her foot.

"Doesn't feel broken; just bruised."

"So what? You have X-ray vision now too?" she said, pulling her foot back, but I didn't move away from between her legs.

"I was a medic in the forces, a long time ago."

She cocked her head, looking at me suddenly with interest. I changed the subject.

"What happened out there, Charlie?"

She sighed, glancing at her foot as she turned it side to side.

"Jonjo and I had a plan. Run Brian close to the front runners, keep him in space and then risk opening him up early on and keep him in the lead. It almost worked. I just needed to hold some back till we got over the last fence then let him go. But I couldn't shake off Dickie. He rode me into the fence. He meant to push us into making a mistake. And we did. Thankfully, my foot got stuck or I would have been clean off the side."

"Thankfully? You could have been killed!"

"I got second, didn't I?"

"At what cost, Charlie? Fuck, I thought you were gonna be a write off."

"Why do you care anyway?" she poked at me.

Why did I care?

"You're a fucking good jockey, Charlie. I don't want to lose you till I've at least made a fortune off you."

"Ah, so as soon as you've taken what you wanted I'll be expendable?"

Her baby blue eyes held mine, a shadow of darkness in them as her lips pressed together. She was even more beautiful when she was pissed off. I kept my eyes fixed on hers, trying not to let them wander all over her almost naked body. Trying not to focus on the rush of blood to my stomach, or the swelling of my cock, or the warm smell of her naked flesh so close to me and her smart little mouth that had felt beyond good on mine the other night. I breathed deeply.

"I don't mean it like that, Charlie."

"Then what do you mean, Cian?"

Jesus, I wanted to kiss her again. I wanted to wrap my hands in her hair, pull her head back and ravage her mouth. My cock twitched angrily in my pants.

I squeezed my eyes shut, trying to regain control and when I'd opened them again she'd stood up, my face now in line with her belly button, the white thong just in reaching distance of my teeth. I could smell the sweet scent of her cunt, and I was sure if I touched her there, licked her there, I would find her soaking wet. I glanced up, catching her watching me intently, nipping her bottom lip with her teeth.

I stood up, watching as her eyes followed my every movement, and then I was towering over her again. A piece of blonde hair had fallen over her face. I brushed it back behind her ear, feeling the smoothness of her face and the prominence of her cheek bones and then let I let my fingers slide down her neck, stopping on her collarbone. Her lips were parted slightly, her breathing just slightly heavier. I ran my fingers across her neck, lightly closing round her throat as she kept her eyes on mine, daring me. She licked her lips, the tip of her pink tongue brushing the pronounced peaks of the cupid's bow, and I couldn't help increase the pressure of my hand on her throat.

"I mean you're valuable to me, Charlie," I answered her question eventually, my voice coming out more husky than I intended, "you're useful both in terms of money and physically."

The door clicked behind us.

"Charlie, the horses are ready to go….. oh shit… Cian. I'm sorry. Erm, I'll er, I'll get the stable lads to start loading them on to the horsebox."

Jonjo left us.

"You'd better let me get dressed so I can continue being useful to you," Charlie said as I dropped my hand from the soft skin of her throat

I left her alone in the changing room, fighting every urge to walk right back in there, push her into the wall and fuck her into submission. Jesus Christ, she was getting to me.

Chapter Fourteen

❧ Charlie ☙

I'd limped around the yard for the next couple of days, dosing myself on painkillers to dull the throb in my ankle. But after a rough ride on the gallops with one of the younger horses, I dreaded getting off. The grey horse jogged back into the yard, its feet clattering noisily on the concrete road.

Jonjo jumped off his horse, passing it to a waiting stable hand, then came round the side of me.

"Need a hand off?" he asked as he took the dancing horse's reins whilst I kicked my feet free from the stirrups.

"I'll get her," Cian said, striding up towards me.

I rolled my eyes.

"I got it, I answered

Swinging my leg over the back of the saddle, I lowered myself to the ground carefully, taking my weight on my good leg but unable to hide the audible wince as I stepped onto my left foot. Cian grabbed my arm as I staggered backwards and I shot him a look.

"Coffee?" he asked, feigning disinterest in the look I'd given him.

I did need a coffee and more painkillers. Sighing, I nodded.

"Yeah."

"Go on," Jonjo urged, "I'll sort him out," he motioned to the impatient grey horse.

I limped away after Cian, failing to keep up with his long strides as I hobbled along behind him catching the smug look on his face as he glanced at me over his shoulder, but decided the pain in my ankle was dulling any thoughts of sarcasm.

I sank into a dusty chair as he switched the kettle on, scooping coffee into two clean mugs on the bench.

"Alexei Lebedev will be bringing his horses at some point today," Cian said as he handed me a mug, steam pooling off it in the chilly March air.

I blew onto it, making the steam swirl before my eyes and the rich, nutty smell making my stomach rumble hungrily. I took a sip of the hot liquid and recoiled at the burn on my tongue, but instantly going back for more, ignoring the burn in order to satisfy my caffeine desires. Then I turned my attention back to the Irishman.

He was out of his suit again today, dressed in blue denim jeans, thick-soled boots and a black jumper, that was pulled tight over the muscles of his chest. The sleeves tightened over the bulge of his biceps and showed off the neat taper of his waist as he leant against the bench.

"I'm guessing that is a 'behave yourself, Charlie' instruction?" I asked, taking another hot slurp.

"More of a request. If I say 'please', would that sweeten it?"

I smiled.

"Pass me a few more of those pills," I beckoned to the cupboard above his head, "and that may make me more favourable."

Cian tossed me a box of tablets and I pulled the capsules out of the foil packets and popped them into my mouth.

"So, drugging you makes you easier to manage then?" Cian asked, a slight smile forming.

"You like your women drugged, huh?"

He pushed away from the bench and bent over the table, hazel eyes bearing down on me.

"I like my women submissive; obedient."

The smile had disappeared and his eyes held another look, his lips pushed together just a few inches from mine. My heart rate picked up a notch, beating against my ribs, pounding through my body. Then he stood up, drained his coffee as the steamed spilled from it and walked out, leaving a formidable tingling forming between my legs. Why the fuck did that affect me like that? I needed more painkillers.

By the afternoon Alexei Lebedev's horses had arrived. We'd settled them into stables, making them comfortable. There were three of them. All bay and tall. They were well muscled and looked amazingly fit, but they were all jumpy, flinching at the slightest sound and one had taken to walking round and round its box.

Lebedev arrived an hour later in some expensive car. It was just as huge as I'd ever seen and clearly driven by a chauffeur. It parked in the yard, and I watched Cian walk across and meet the tall Russian.

Lebedev was mid-fifties with greying hair and cold grey eyes. He had a grey goatee to match but seemed in good shape for his age. He stepped out of the car dressed in a suit with a heavy wool overcoat, wary of where he was putting his feet, despite the well-swept concrete of the stable yard. I watched him grab Cian's outstretched hand, grasping the back of the Irishman's elbow as they exchanged pleasantries.

His minders got out after him. Like bookends, they both sported the same shaved hair, mid-length leather jackets over dark suits and thick-soled boots, looking more like nightclub doormen than bodyguards to some billionaire. The men stared around the yard, following behind the Russian as he and Cian moved towards me.

Stopping in front of me, Cian spoke, "you've already met my rider and trainer, Charlie?"

"Yes," the man held out his hand and I limped forward, shaking it dutifully, catching Cian's eye as I did, "I see you're injured after ride Saturday," he noted

"Just a bit of bruising. It'll go down in a couple of days."

"You were incredible. We don't get women riders where I come from. It's man's sport."

Gritting my teeth, I forced away the sarcastic comment forming on my tongue. I'd heard the same thing for years and it frustrated the fuck out of me.

"It's becoming more common here in the UK," I managed in the end, watching Cian let out a silent sigh.

"I'm pleased," the grey-haired man said, "you do fine job. I'll be honoured to watch you ride my horses."

"Thank you," I muttered.

"Come, I'll show you round the facilities," Cian said, probably desperate to move his new billionaire owner away from me before my halo slipped, "Charlie, can you help Mr Lebedev's friends find the coffee?"

I nodded and then beckoned for the men to follow me to the kitchen. After making them a coffee each I hobbled away back to my jobs, leaving the men talking to each other in Russian, or something, in the kitchen.

I'd taken a wheelbarrow full of nets to the hay barn a short time later and was busy stuffing them full, coughing occasionally as the dust filled my lungs, when I felt a presence. I stood up, glancing at the shadow standing in the doorway. One of Lebedev's men stood watching me, his arms folded across his chest, his shoulder propped against the wooden frame of the barn door.

"Can I help?" I feigned politeness.

"Carry on," he said in his heavy accent, "I'm enjoying view."

Shaking my head, I ignored him and turned back round to finish filling the net. As I reached for another armful of hay I felt him behind me. The smell of stale cigarettes filled the air as he breathed over the top of me.

"Do you want to back the fuck away?" I growled.

"You know, I could give you much better ride than any of these nags here," he said, running his hand up the back of my leg.

I stiffened. His fingers trailed over the back of my arse cheek. Anger uncoiled within me and I snapped up, grabbing the pitchfork out of the wheelbarrow in front of me. Spinning quickly, I pushed the prongs of the metal fork towards his throat, almost touching the soft skin of his neck. He retreated and I kept going until he had backed out of the hay barn with the point of my fork mere millimetres away from his neck.

"Shit!" I heard from across the yard, and keeping my attention focussed on the minder in front of me, watched Cian appear in my peripheral vision.

"Charlie, what the fuck?" Cian shouted.

The minder stared down the pitchfork at me, unmoving, unphased, willing me to do something.

Ignoring Cian, I turned back to the man at the end of the prongs, "what do you think happens to the colts here when they get too big for their boots?"

He smiled at me, a gold tooth sparkling in the daylight.

"Let me help you with the answer," I dropped the prongs from his neck and pushed them towards his groin.

He exhaled slightly as I pushed the metal spikes against him.

"They get castrated."

"Careful, Charlie," Cian's voice was softer.

I took the pressure off a little, pulling the pitchfork back an inch.

"Touch me again and I'll have your balls on the end of each prong."

Cian's face darkened and he turned to Lebedev.

"Tell your boys they can wait in the car for you."

The Russian paled and he nodded, beckoning for his minder to move out of my way.

"I'm sorry about that," Alexei Lebedev offered me, then turning to Cian he said more quietly, "I love this girl. She's one of a kind."

I didn't look back at the men in the yard. Instead, I pushed the pitchfork back into the wheelbarrow and went back to filling the hay net.

*****

The morning of Bobby's funeral had arrived. I'd been up early and exercised a few of the horses, completed numerous yard jobs, and now I was sitting at the end of my bed in just my underwear staring out into the distance. I felt odd. Empty. Lonely. I'd dreaded this day; the finality of it. Now I just couldn't get the motivation to get ready. My hair lay wet, dripping down my back and onto the bed and my makeup was spread out over the top of my dresser, untouched.

I glanced at the letter on the end of the bed. The report from the coroner had arrived the same morning. I should be relieved it hadn't been suicide, that it was cancer that had taken Bobby. But I felt a sickening guilt. He had never told me and I had never guessed. He'd kept it well hidden, but I'd seen the signs, seen him grow paler, weaker, thinner and I'd dismissed them. He'd never told me. And I'd never asked.

Butterflies swirled in my stomach, bouncing off each side and then rebounding. I felt sick. I looked over at the dress hanging on my wardrobe door, black and ominous, the way I felt inside.

Eventually, I managed to dry my hair and put some makeup on and made my way up the drive in my heels, my feet already aching when I got to the front of Bobby's house, waiting in the cold for the hearse to arrive.

The red convertible got there first, pulling round to the side of the house next to Cian's car.

"What are you doing here, Nat?" I asked, surprised to see my sister dressed immaculately as always.

"A certain Irishman told me you could do with some support today," she smiled sadly at me.

I nodded, feeling the rush of tears to my eyes. Blinking hard, I chased them away, focusing on the comfort of her arms as she wrapped them around me.

"Thanks for coming," I heard the rumble of a deep voice behind me.

Cian stood on the doorstep behind us, clad in the same sombre clothes. A thin black tie hung from his neck and his hair was swept messily to one side. The smell of his aftershave lingered in the light breeze. He distracted me for a moment, my eyes scanning over him as he stood waiting with us. There was a pain in his face, a sadness, but I didn't think that was for the old horse

trainer. He stared off into the distance, his jaw
tight.

Chapter Fifteen

ഇ Cian ര

I followed the small funeral procession from the main house and down the drive. As the hearse got into view of the stable yard, I saw the line of people. Stable hands, jockeys and exercise riders lined the road, paying their respects as Bobby's coffin was driven slowly past.

The funeral was well attended. Cars flanked the road at the crematorium and there was a sea of people clothed in black milling around at the entrance. I parked a little way from the entrance and stood to the side, watching the undertakers pull the oak box from the back of the hearse, adorned with all manner of racing related wreaths.

The service was short but effective. The vicar gave the usual non-personal reading from the Bible and then a short piece based on Bobby's life and racing career. I sat a few rows from the front, my attention fixed on the blonde jockey, not on the words or the haunting music. And not on the memories of weeks ago.

Charlie had remained incredibly composed, but I'd noticed the way she clasped her sister's hand tightly, her eyes fixed straight ahead, avoiding focussing on the service and the words. But to me she looked like a horse that would bolt at any second.

I didn't blame her; I hated funerals too.

A few hours later, I was sat at a bar in a busy pub sipping a glass of water, bored with forced conversations and explanations of my connection to Bobby. Charlie pulled herself onto the bar stool beside me.

"Drink?" I asked.

"Please. I'll have a vodka and coke."

"Onto the hard stuff today, huh?"

"Bobby would have preferred wine, or whisky. I just need something stronger right now and I don't like whisky."

I slid the drink across to her when it came and watched as she took a long swig and then pulled a face. Despite the circumstances, she looked stunning. Ash blonde hair fell to the middle of her back as the beautiful light blue of her eyes was framed in thick, dark lashes. The tight black dress hung against her neat curves. She had good shaped tits, small and round and a gentle swell to her hips. But it was her legs that I couldn't keep my eyes off. The black heels exaggerated the bulge of her calves, strong, lean and toned, tapering off to slender ankles.

"Thanks for getting Natalie to come today. I didn't realise how much I needed that," Charlie said, taking a break from gulping down her drink.

"I know how hard funerals are and how much you need a sister to look after you," the sadness I had been pushing down threatened to bubble back up, and I only had water as my weapon.

"Do you have a sister, Cian?"

"I used to," I stared at the ice cube floating round my drink, "she died recently."

Charlie put her hand on my leg, "I'm sorry, Cian. I didn't know."

"I didn't tell you."

"Can you take me home? I've had enough of talking about Bobby for one night."

"Where's your sister?"

"Had to go. Some kid's got himself arrested," she shrugged.

We drove back in silence, the only noise coming from the radio. Just before we pulled onto the drive Ed Sheeran's voice filled the car, the song gentle and light but evocative, reminding me of Fiadh. It had been one of her favourites, something she would listen to with tears in her gentle eyes. I forced the lump from my throat. Charlie stared out of the window, keeping her head turned away from me.

I pulled up on the yard.

"Do you want to come up to the house and we'll order food?" I asked, my own stomach grumbling loudly.

She shook her head, "no thanks. I don't really want to be up there right now. I just need to be alone."

Charlie didn't look at me. She got out of the car and walked around behind it. I watched her go across the stable yard. She didn't go to the door of her flat above the stables, instead she turned the lights on, popping her head over each stable door, checking the horses. I drove off up to the house.

But as I sat there, outside in the darkness, the engine of the car still purring, my mind whirred along with it. It had been an odd day. The house was in darkness, hostile and unwelcoming. I knew Charlie had been upset in the car, that as she sat in the quiet, away from the wake, it had all come crashing down on her. I knew because that was the way I had felt the day I buried my mother and then when I buried the rest of my family and my beautiful little sister.

I turned the car around and drove back down to the stable yard. The lights were still on and I could see a few horses' heads over stable doors, but there was no sign of Charlie. Treading carefully in my good shoes, I walked the same route she had, popping my head over each door until I got to an empty stable at the far end of the yard. In there I found her, sat in the straw, knees drawn up to her chin, her coat and arms pulled around herself. She was staring at the wall, tears falling down her cheeks. I sat beside her, the straw rustling loudly underneath me. Putting my arm round her I pulled her into me and she rested her head against my shoulder. We sat there for some time, saying nothing to one another, just staring at the wall of the stable in front of us.

Eventually, Charlie shivered. I could feel her body shaking against mine as the steam from our breath swirled in front of us.

"Come on. Time to go in," I said, squeezing her gently against me.

"I need to put some more hay in for Brian," she said softly and stood up, walking off to the hay barn in her heels.

I followed, watching her throw armfuls of loose hay into the wheelbarrow. Her calf muscles tensed, straining under the height of the black heels, the loose curls of her hair swaying with each effort.

"Surely, Brian has enough. The stable lads stayed late tonight to feed everyone."

She ignored me and carried on.

"Come on, Charlie," I coaxed, but she just shot me a glare.

I walked over towards her, grabbing her hand gently.

"Get off me, Cian," she warned, "I don't need your sympathy!"

"Really? So you frequently sit in an empty stable crying by yourself?"

"I don't need you, Cian. If you'd never turned up here, none of this would have happened!" she spat, anger lacing her voice.

"You saw the coroner's report. Bobby was dying. It was cancer, nothing to do with me. If I hadn't have come to take what he owed me he would still have died."

I shook my head. I should have left her to it but the change in her tone, her defiance, it did something to me. I pushed the wheelbarrow out of the way, standing in front of her. Flinching, I saw her reaction before she'd even realising she was doing it herself. Her arm flew towards me, her fist clenched. But she was too slow. I grabbed her, stopping the punch before it got anywhere near connecting with my face and pushed her back into the bale of hay.

I should have let her go and walked away, but I didn't. I grabbed a handful of her hair, yanking her head backwards so her throat was exposed, staring up at me with defiant eyes, daring me. I crushed my lips against hers; filling her mouth with my tongue. She breathed against me, lips pushing into mine, her tongue wrestling against me. Pulling away slightly, I bit her bottom lip and she moaned loudly, pushing her perfect body into me.

My cock strained against my trousers and I forced her further back. My lips worked down her slender neck, sucking and biting, each murmur from her making me hungrier for the taste of her. Her fingers dipped to my stomach and I felt the gentle caress of her hands as she skimmed over the waist band of my trousers, untucking my shirt and gliding her fingers up underneath it, sending red-hot pulses shooting over my skin.

My mouth found her collar bone and as I nipped at the skin I heard her gasp and push her hips into me, her fingers roaming under my shirt, her nails grazing my stomach muscles. I pushed my lips harder into her skin, tasting, biting, teasing, gliding over the dip at the base of her neck. My hands moved from her hair, stroking across her waist, feeling over the curve of her hip and the flat of her stomach to the swell of her tits, hidden away from me behind the black fabric of her dress. Reaching behind her, I pulled the zip of her dress down.

"Take this fucking thing off," I growled into her ear and for the first time since I had met her, she complied, and my cock grew harder.

She slipped the dress off her shoulders, sending it and her coat falling to her feet.

"Stand still," I instructed.

Taking a step back, I took a long look at her. The black lacy bra and thong were stark against her creamy skin and the tight definition of her legs. Her swollen mound pushing against the fabric of her knickers was begging for me. Her hair, now messed up, fell over her shoulder and bobbed over round, pert tits, screaming at me to take handfuls while I fucked her senseless. Charlie watched me, her blue eyes intense, pink lips slightly parted. She was incredible. My dick throbbed.

"Lose the bra."

141

She obeyed, hooking the straps off her arms, unclasping it at the back and letting it fall to the floor, her tits suddenly exposed, her nipples hardening instantly in the cold air.

I closed the last of the space between us, dipping my head and taking a nipple in my mouth, Charlie gasping as I gripped it with my teeth. She pushed her chest forward as I pinched her other nipple between my thumb and finger. I sucked harder, and she leaned back against the hay, moaning with each bite and suck as I feasted on her tits.

Then my fingers strayed down her body, sliding over the hint of muscle in her stomach and pushing the thong down her legs. She kicked it off the rest of the way so that she was now standing naked in front of me, wearing only in her heels. Nudging her legs apart, I kneeled, watching her as I moved down her body, her eyes dancing with need and excitement, her breathing rapid with anticipation. I brought my face just above that pretty cunt, inhaling the musky scent, tracing my way down, my lips brushing the small patch of hair just above the entrance of her pussy, her clit and lips already swollen.

I pulled a leg over my shoulder and pushed my face into her, holding it there for just a moment as I enjoyed the feel of the heat coming off her, the smell of her, her went cunt pressed against my face. Her hands went to my hair, trying to push my face closer, but I denied her, making her wait for the punishment I was about to unleash on her sopping wet pussy. Then I slid my tongue across her engorged lips, tasting the dampness between her legs. She groaned, shoving her hips forward into my face and any resolve I'd had, got up and left. I buried my face between her legs, my lips engulfing her like I hadn't eaten in days, driving my tongue into her pussy, lapping and sucking, thrusting in and out of her relentlessly.

Charlie shouted, her hips bucking against my face with each assault of my tongue; each swirl against her swollen nub, her juices spilling into my mouth. My phone vibrated in my pocket. I ignored it.

She pulled at my head, forcing me closer, her hips thrusting, riding my face, moans growing louder as she started to tense, as she used my tongue and my lips to take what she needed. My phone vibrated again.

"Fuck!" she swore as I increased the pressure on her clit.

Then with a shudder and a cry she came, grinding against my face as I licked up every last bit of her orgasm, until her breathing slowed down and she relaxed her grip on my hair. My phone vibrated again in my pocket. Fuck's sake.

I got back to my feet, leaving her panting against the hay bale and took the phone from my trouser pocket checking the display. Three missed calls from Riley. I pressed the call button and rang him back, watching Charlie leaning naked against the bale, her eyes trained on me.

"What?" I asked gruffly when Riley answered.

"Cian, it's Oisín. He's been shot!"

"Fuck!"

I hung up, looking at Charlie. Beautiful, bare, and primed for me. My cock twitched.

"I'm sorry, I've got to go."

"Go where?" she hissed.

"Ireland."

"What? Right now?"

I nodded. Her eyes changing from lust to fury. I bent down to help her pick up her clothes.

"I've got them. I don't need your help."

Her voice had taken on its usual venomous tone as she snatched up her underwear and dress. She pulled her coat around her and walked away, leaving me in the hay barn by myself, the smell of her pussy all over my face.

Chapter Sixteen

ଔ Charlie ଓ

I'd started training the Lebedev horses. They were all skittish, unruly, and confused. The two geldings were bad mannered and every time I'd put a saddle on, they'd tensed their backs and exploded as I tried to get on. It was as if they were channelling their inner Brian.

I was working with one of them in our jump pen, sending it over hurdles without a rider on its back so I could assess it better, when Jonjo wandered over, leaning on the gate to watch.

"How's it going?" he called across the arena.

I turned.

"Yeah, these are difficult. Not what I'd expected. They seem much further behind in their training," I explained.

"What do we know about them?" Jonjo asked.

I shrugged, "not that much. I didn't get much chance to get any info out of Cian before he pissed off back to Ireland."

"Charlie!"

I didn't see the horse coming at me quickly enough. The brown blur caught me off guard, deviating from his course over the jump, coming directly for me, teeth bared and ears flat back. I jumped sideways, keeping my head just out of kicking range as the glint of metal flashed across my eyes. The horse's leg struck me hard in the thigh, sending me staggering backwards, pain followed by numbness.

I yelped, my leg giving way, and I sank to the ground. Jonjo vaulted the gate, running towards me as the angry bay horse doubled back and advanced again. Scrabbling to my feet, pain pulsing through my thigh, I stood, watching the horse come towards me until he was mere feet in front, then I dropped a shoulder and scooted sideways.

Jonjo had already made it to the side of the arena and I ran across, limping badly from the dead feeling at the top of my leg. Just as I reached the fence and squeezed through a gap in the rails, the horse ran past again, kicking out and clattering the perimeter, smashing the wooden rail in two.

Safely, on the outside, I watched the bay racehorse run round angrily, avoiding the hurdles, kicking out furiously every time he came past them.

"Jesus! It's Brian with anger management issues," I laughed as Jonjo looked at me quizzically.

"Charlie, that horse is mad!"

"He'll be OK. But I really need to know more about it. Can you do the next few rides while I do some paperwork?"

Jonjo nodded. I limped up towards the house, leaving the furious horse charging round the arena. Hopefully he would have tired himself out to submission by the time I got back.

The house hadn't been the same since Bobby had died. There was no welcoming cooking smells, no smell of wood burning on the fire when I walked in. The place was cold and had acquired a damp, stale smell, as if sadness poured out of it. A pile of post lay on the floor at the door. There were the usual junk letters, letters from companies that did not know yet that Bobby was no longer here. I'd not done much of the formalities. The solicitor was dealing with wrapping up what was left of the estate. Bobby's possessions and belongings remained where they'd been left by him; some in the packing boxes and some in his bedroom. I'd done nothing with them, either.

I picked up the pile of post and took it through the house to the office, dropping them to the side of the desk and flicking the old computer on, listening as it whirred to life. Casting my eyes around the desk, I found the folder that had come with Lebedev's horses. Opening it, I thumbed through the paperwork, eventually finding the

147

three little books that were the horses' passports and scanning my eyes over their details, picking out the one I was particularly interested in. The bay gelding that had tried to kill me; his name was Killer's Kiss. Ironic.

When the computer had fired itself up, I opened an internet search bar and typed in his name, looking for details of the races he'd run in. The search brought nothing back. Not the tiniest mention of the horse anywhere. I opened up the Horseracing Authority's database and typed in the name. Nothing. Grabbing the other two passports, I typed in the names of the other horses. Not a thing.

I sat back in the office seat. None of these horses were registered to race. I flicked through the passport pages, checking the covers, looking for anomalies. Using all the information the passport contained, the breeder's name, the vet's name, none of the information brought anything up. It was all fake.

What was Cian playing at? Some sort of racing scam? Had his mafia family bought into some sort of ruse that was going to play out on the racetrack? Through me?

Something started in me. From a tiny ember, the anger, fuelled by the feeling of betrayal, ignited. Why had I been so blind to him? To who and what he was? I was about to be fucked over big time.

My mind jumped, latching onto an idea whilst suspicion and a dull, nauseating knot formed in my stomach. How much did Jonjo know? How embedded was he in all of this?

*****

"What are you doing to me, Charlie?" Jonjo complained as he stuffed another slice of pizza in his mouth.

I shrugged and smiled back at him.

"One little pizza won't hurt."

"One? It's two and they're not little."

Jonjo drained the last of his beer and I passed him another. We'd finished off yard jobs, and I'd suggested a takeaway and beer night. Being a taller, heavier jockey, I knew how strict he had to be with eating and drinking and tonight I was exploiting all of it. I plied him with a few more beers, watching for when he was just a bit looser.

"Did you get any info about those lunatic Russian things?" he asked when the last crumb of the pepperoni pizza had been hoovered up.

"They're not registered."

"What?"

I watched him, genuine surprise on his face. Either that or he was as good an actor as he was a jockey.

"Why would we train unregistered horses here?" I asked him.

"We wouldn't. Why would you ask that?"

I eyed him, watching for any falter as I formed my next question, "I'll re-phrase it. What benefit would running unregistered horses have for a mafia family like the O'Sullivans?"

His eyes flickered, and I noticed how he swallowed nervously, his Adam's apple bobbing.

"I don't know what you're getting at, Charlie," he answered, his voice wavering slightly.

"I know what Cian is, Jonjo, he told me."

"He did?"

"How did you get involved with a group of gangsters, Jonjo? What hold do they have over you?"

He sighed, a look of defeat across his face.

"I used to work for them; before I was a jockey. But Cian knew it wasn't what I wanted. I'd always loved horses. Me and Cian used to race our ponies against each other when we were kids."

"Cian can ride?"

Jonjo laughed, "he's Irish, of course he can ride!"

I was getting distracted.

"Cian helped the rest of the family realise that there was more benefit to them if they helped me get into the career I'd always really wanted."

"What sort of benefit?"

"There's a lot of money to be made from throwing the odd race," he sighed, sadness creeping across his face, "there was always going to be a price for them getting me where I am today."

I don't know why I was so shocked? I'd heard rumours of race fixing for years, but hearing of it so close to home? I struggled to contain my anger. Is that what Cian would want of me? Was he getting me hooked with his bad-boy demeanour and skilled tongue like some sort of druggie?

"So running unregistered horses, Charlie," Jonjo broke the strained silence, "it makes no sense. There's no reason to do that."

"So what?"

The tall jockey shrugged, and I continued, "so Cian thinks he can get me involved in this too? Throwing races? Is that what he wants of me?"

My words were running hot with anger.

"I dunno, Charlie. Just be careful how you go. The O'Sullivans are dangerous. Disloyalty is dealt with in the only way they know how…."

Jonjo stopped realising he'd said too much.

"Hey. It's getting late. I'd better get going."

"I'll ring you a taxi," I offered.

"Nah, it's OK. I need to walk off all that shit you just fed me."

I'd tossed and turned all night, trying to sleep but distracted by my thoughts and emotions which ran riot around my head. The faint thrum of a car engine woke me again. I must have been just dropping off and the fucking noise had brought me back to consciousness. I lay in bed for a while listening and just as I thought I'd made the whole thing up in the chaos that had filled my brain, I heard the screech of a bolt sliding in the door in the stable yard below.

Flinging my almost bare legs out of bed, I pulled on my long yard coat over the vest top and shorts I wore as pyjamas and slid my legs into a pair of cold wellington boots that stood by the door to my flat. I pulled the coat around me as the cold air hit me and wandered onto the yard below. Horse's feet shuffled on the straw in their stables and I could hear one or two noisily chewing on hay. Using the torch from my phone, I checked every horse and every bolt as I made my way past each stable.

As I moved further across the yard, I noticed the hay barn door was open. I was sure Jonjo and I had made certain everything was properly closed up for the night. Had he returned? Had he decided to sleep his beers off in the barn?

Making my way to the hay shed, shaking my head as I poked it in through the door, the light from my torch caught a person at the back in the corner.

"For fuck's sake, Jonjo. What are you doing?"

The figure turned, the orange glow from something in his hand illuminating his features, creating a shine to his bald head, the only bit of him not covered in dark clothes.

152

"What the fuck?" I blurted.

The orange glow coming from his hand was a lighter; aflame and way too close to the hay bale. Shit. He looked at me and extinguished it, relief momentarily washing over me.

"Well, look who it is," the accented voice said from behind me.

A chill coursed down my spine, mixing with the bolt of dread that struck my stomach. Hands clasped the top of my shoulders roughly, catching me by surprise and then my arms were tugged behind me, my coat pulling open and exposing the thin fabric of my pyjamas as I clutched hard to my mobile.

"Not brave without your fork, are you?" the man hissed into my ear, flecks of saliva hitting me on the side of my neck.

The man with the lighter advanced from the front, his eyes fixed on me. Shit.

"Get the fuck off me!" I shouted, wriggling to get my arms free.

The advancing man smiled sickeningly, moving forward, his hands grabbing at my coat and pulling it off my shoulders, cold air hitting my almost naked skin. Leaning back into the man behind me, I kicked out my legs, hitting him hard in the chest and sending him staggering backwards.

"*Suka!*" he spat.

Pain exploded in my jaw, flashes of light crossing my eyes and my head lolled to the side.

153

Colours burst in front of me and I heard the tearing of fabric. Something warm trickled down my chin and then rough hands were inside my top, grabbing at my breasts. I forced my eyes open; forced them to focus. The man's bald head dipped to my neck, stale cigarette smoke assaulting my senses. His ear brushed my chin.

I dived forward, grabbing at his ear with my teeth, crushing them together. He screamed, trying to get away, but, focussing on the pain in my jaw, the anger sparking inside of me, I squeezed my teeth together as hard as I could. With an agonising yell, he pulled backwards. Warm liquid gushed down over my chin and splashed my face, the pressure on my arms relaxing slightly.

I tugged an arm free, shoved my hand into my coat pocket, feeling metal cold against my palm. My yard knife! I flicked the blade up between my fingers and spun quickly, throwing my arm behind me, the blade from the multi-tool finding something other than fresh air, and I pushed against it as hard as I could as a shout erupted from behind me.

The hands left me completely, and I pushed my way out of the stable and ran. My fingers fumbled over the display of the phone, the light temporarily blinding me as it came to life. Then with a thud something heavy crashed into me and I fell forward, hitting the concrete floor hard, my phone bouncing away, into the open doorway of an empty stable.

I kicked out, fear gripping at my stomach and crawled forwards towards the stable and my phone and any chance of getting help. My coat snagged on something. I glanced behind, seeing the bald man caked in blood, half his ear flopped over at the side, his hand gripping my coat. I shrugged out of it and on my hands and knees I crawled forwards into the doorway of the stable, reaching for the phone.

But he was on me before I could reach for it, grabbing my leg and yanking me, my knees grazing against the concrete of the stable floor as I was dragged backwards.

"I'll take you like this," he hissed in my ear, his body over the top of mine, one hand fumbling against my arse, and I heard the zip of his trousers. Oh god no!

I scrabbled forward again, my eyes fixing on the object at the back of the stable.

"Stay fucking still," the man behind me instructed, "I promise you'll enjoy a real stallion between your legs."

Summoning all my strength I rolled sideways, pushing him off me just enough to wriggle free and turnover, crawling like a crab backwards and away from him.

"That's right. You'll look at me while I fuck you."

My fingers touched the cold metal prongs. I pulled the pitchfork from where it was propped up at the back of the wall, holding it out in front of me. The man stopped a moment, giving me just enough time to get to my feet as I held the prongs pointed up to his throat. He smiled, a creepy grin forming at his lips, then came at me fast.

Lowering the pitch fork as I backed away, I drove it upwards, pushing it as hard as I could when it struck resistance. There was a horrific squeal, like a pig being slaughtered, and then silence. The bald man put his hands on the fork, surprise and agony across his face.

"That's right," I said, thrusting the fork further into him as I glanced at the other man in the doorway behind him, "you'll look at me while I castrate you!"

I gave the fork another thrust and a twist, feeling flesh tearing. The bald man gave a soundless cry, his eyes bulging, his hands clasping the handle, and then I tugged the prongs free, blood pouring from his groin, soaking through his jeans and onto the straw of the stable floor beneath him. He fell to his knees and tipped sideways, his hands cradling the spot his manhood used to be, staring at me in silent hate.

The other man looked from me to his friend and then bolted and I watched on from the stable floor as his fleeing shape got smaller and smaller before being engulfed into the night.

Eventually, I looked back to the crumpled heap of what was once a man on the stable floor. I crawled past him to grab my scattered coat, pulling my arms into it and wrapping it round me protectively before returning to watch the life fade from his eyes. Then I rang Jonjo.

Chapter Seventeen

හ Cian ලෙ

I got home just before dawn, the orange glow of sunlight casting deceptive warm tones on the house. My car purred as it idled at the gate as I leaned out and punched in my code. The heavy iron gates inched open slowly as I sat tapping the steering wheel impatiently.

The house was quiet; the only people awake were those operating the security systems. Sipping a coffee, I wandered into the lounge, kicking off my shoes and rubbing the tiredness from my eyes. I'd driven nine hours from Durham, pulling over once when it felt my head was going to roll clean off my shoulders with exhaustion. I necked the rest of the coffee, tipped my head back and let sleep take me, at least for a little while.

By the time Osh had got his lazy arse out of bed, I'd already showered and changed and was waiting for him in the office with the rest of my men.

"Nice of you to join us," I grumbled at him when he limped in.

"Christ, can't a brother get some sympathy?"

"Shut up, sit down, and tell me what happened."

"I'll stand, thank you. The hole in my arse cheek doesn't take kindly to being sat on right now," Oisín replied.

"Come on, Osh, just turn the other cheek!" one of the men quipped, slapping him on the shoulder.

"Not fucking funny," he shot back.

I rubbed my hands over my eyes, my patience wearing thin under my tiredness.

"How the fuck did you manage to get yourself shot?" I asked.

"I was picking up profits from one of our dealers. There was a problem with the figures, so we were sorting that out. Then I went to the club. When I came out someone shot me."

I looked towards the accountant, "has our CCTV guy come up with the footage?"

"Sure has."

I watched the CCTV on the computer screen. We saw Osh go into the flat over the pizza shop from the back lane. And then I sat waiting for him to come out. And waited. After fast forwarding the footage, I looked across the room at him.

"What were you doing in there for an hour?" I asked.

Osh shrugged. "The fella was a few bob short. So I fucked his girlfriend and let him off with the rest."

"For fuck's sake! I'd rather we got our fucking money!"

"She was hot as fuck," Osh answered me, unabashed.

He was a fucking liability half the time. I shook my head and looked back at the CCTV screen. I watched Oisín leave the flat, get in his car and drive across the City to one of the strip clubs on the far side. Flicking through a few frames, I watched for anything unusual but seeing nothing, I fast forwarded the recordings watching for Oisín leaving the dingy club. The footage showed Osh going round the back of the club to his car. A figure moved in the shadows, almost unnoticeable.

A flash of light lit the screen and I saw Osh duck instinctively, diving in the car as two further flashes followed. The lights of the car came on before it pulled away haphazardly.

"The bullets. Have we got them?" I asked.

Osh nodded. "I sweet-talked the sexy blonde nurse to get them for me."

He smiled like a schoolboy and I rolled my eyes.

"The only problem, boss, is we have no one in Ireland on our books who can run ballistics for us," the accountant piped up.

"I know someone," I said, pulling my phone out of my pocket.

*****

Two days later, we were sat in an Irish bar in the outskirts of Soho on the West side of London; Riley outside in the car waiting for us. The Pogues and the Dubliners sang out in the background and I sipped on a pint of lager, watching revellers getting rowdy to the rousing music as people jostled against one another.

Osh shifted uncomfortably in his seat and I glanced across at him, not keeping the amusement off my face.

"When I find the sorry fuck that shot me, I'm going to rip him a whole new arsehole," he grumbled into his whisky, his eyes scanning the crowd.

Eventually, a man moved through the bar. Dressed in a black leather motorcycle jacket and jeans, his blonde hair pulled back into a ponytail, he attracted a number of looks from men and women. He sidled up to the table we were sitting at.

"Long time Kee," he said, blue-green eyes sparkling, his face animated by a wide grin.

I stood up and held out my hand.

"Howay," he responded, grabbing me and pulling me into some sort of manly hug, "you suddenly sat on a stick since you've been honing those *entrepreneurial* skills of yours?"

I couldn't help smile at him.

"Nice to see you again, V."

Osh watched us suspiciously.

"Oisín, this is the Viking. V this is my little brother Osh."

Osh seemed wary of holding out any body part towards the biker and V just nodded at him.

"I served with your brother," the Viking explained, noticing the confused look on my brother's face.

"And you can help us how?" Osh replied, looking unconvinced.

"The Viking can get us what we need, Osh. No need to go into detail how."

I explained what I needed to V and handed him two envelopes; one containing the bullets and one containing his fee. He secured them inside his jacket.

"What brings you to London, anyway?" I asked after we had discussed business.

"I've a job on for the Chinese," he said, offering no more detail.

My phone vibrated against my chest where it sat inside my suit jacket. Pulling it out, I checked the display. Jonjo. My finger hesitated over the cancel button, but something stopped me. Jonjo at 2am? I held the handset tight against my ear.

"What?" I asked, not hearing him properly over the heavy Irish beat of the music.

I moved out of the bar, standing in the frosty night air on the street outside.

"We have a problem," Jonjo said again, "Charlie's been attacked. She's OK, but the perp is dead. Could do with you back at the ranch to sort this body."

"On my way," I shut the call off. A stab of anger hit me in the pit of my stomach and I felt the unravelling of fury engulfing me.

Striding back in the bar, I beckoned for Oisín.

"V I could do with you North with me. I'll double your fee for delaying your Chinese job."

The Viking studied me for a second, recognising the darkness in my eyes and nodded in agreement.

*****

When I pulled up on to the yard just before 6am it was quiet, apart from the soft whicker of the horses who were expecting their breakfast. The main door to Charlie's flat was open and there was a light coming from inside. I knocked on the door, the sound harsh in the silence.

"Charlie? Jonjo?" I called tentatively.

Jonjo came to the top of the stairs.

"She's still in the stable," he said, bounding down the wooden steps as they creaked noisily beneath him and led me past the row of thoroughbreds, expecting their breakfasts.

I popped my head in the empty space finding Charlie tucked up against the back wall, her knees drawn up against her chest and her arms wrapped around her legs. Her thick padded stable coat was pulled around her and there was a horse rug draped over her shoulders, yet I could see the slight shake of her body underneath it all.

"How long has she been in here?" I asked Jonjo.

"Since it happened."

"And the body?"

"Round the back. I've put it in one of the storage rooms, but we need to get rid of it before the staff get here."

I nodded.

"Osh, Riley, V. Take Jonjo's car and the stiff up to the house. Jonjo, I need you to clean up any evidence round the yard," I instructed as Oisín limped closer.

Moving through the scattered straw as it rustled under my feet, my eyes swept round the stable. There wasn't too much to clean up. The straw had taken the brunt of the blood and although there was a huge dark patch, it was contained mainly in one spot. The spot that Charlie's focus was fixated on.

"Hey, sweetheart," I said, dropping to my haunches in front of her, blocking her view of the pool of blood.

She lifted her head slightly, looking at me with a faraway expression. There was an angry cut to her lip and a bruise growing around it, dried blood still smeared across the side of her face and chin. The hands clasped around her legs were tinted red, her coat smeared with dark patches.

I tilted her chin up with my thumb and forefinger, inspecting the depth of the cut. It was nasty but would heal by itself, no need for drawing any unnecessary attention of medical staff.

"What are you doing in here still?" I asked softly, searching her eyes for what might be going on in her mind.

For a moment she didn't speak, looking over my shoulder into the space of the stable.

"H, h, h, he was going to rape me," she said eventually, her voice shaking with shock and cold.

I clenched my teeth together, the heat of rage washing over my skin, controlling the explosion that was building in me because she'd seen enough monsters for one night.

"Come on," I said, repositioning myself so I could scoop her into my arms, "you need a shower."

I carried her, pulling her into my chest as I walked to my car, placing her carefully in the passenger seat and taking her up to the main

164

house with me. Lifting her out the other end, she clung to me tightly, her face nestled against my chest. The stairs creaked under the weight of both of us as I took her to the room on the opposite side of the big house that I had claimed as my own.

Leaving her sitting on my bed, I turned the shower on, coming back to find she hadn't moved an inch.

"Come on, sweetheart. You need to get under the water and warm up. I promise you'll feel better."

Eventually she nodded, slowly rising to her feet and peeling off the thick padded coat. She wore only a strappy vest top and shorts underneath. The skin on her arms shadowing where bruises were forming, and I noticed her top was torn down to her naval, almost exposing her to me.

"I'll leave you to it," I said, "there's some clothes in the drawers over there. Just help yourself."

Walking round to the back of the house, I met up with Jonjo's car as it pulled round into the almost empty garage. The Viking pulled down the shutter behind us as I dragged the heavy tarpaulin off the body in the boot.

The greying corpse was hunched up, its eyes wide and mouth gaping open, his right ear was almost torn clean off, flapping loose around the side of his face as a thick red smear of blood had dried on the side of his face and neck. The front of his denim jeans was soaked in the dark claret of his blood, his trousers gaping open at the waist and what was once his crotch merely a mangled piece of meat.

"Jesus, she did a number on him!" Osh said from my right-hand side.

"Charlie said he tried to rape her," I answered stiffly.

"Looks like the twat deserved all he got then," Osh continued, his voice more sombre, "who is this fucker anyway?"

"One of Lebedev's bodyguards," I answered.

"What, that Russian billionaire you just got into bed with?"

"Yes, that one. Although what this fucker was doing here, I don't know."

I pulled down the lapel of his coat, slicing the top underneath open with my knife, revealing an inked canvas of tattoos on his skin. Nothing of any sort of artwork, just numerous one-off tattoos.

"What do you reckon V? Anything on here you recognise?" I asked the biker, who was looking over my shoulder.

"There's a couple that look familiar but I'm not sure where from. One or two of them look like tags," the Viking answered, "what do you know about the Russian, anyway?"

"Not a lot. He's a big name in racing. Well known. It was a good opportunity to run some well backed horses."

The Viking shook his head.

"There's something off here."

"What are you thinking V?"

"I'll tell you when I know. You can take care of this yourselves, yeah? I got an errand to run."

Leaving the body wrapped in Jonjo's car, I moved back inside. I needed a coffee and sleep, probably not in that order. Riley and Osh followed me, the loud rumble of the Viking's motorbike growing to a purr as he took off down the drive.

I crept back up to my room, getting comfortable in the armchair across from my bed where Charlie lay asleep. For now, she looked peaceful, content; no longer the vulnerable young woman in the stable where I had taken her from. I watched the rise and fall of her chest, the small peaks of her tits under the white hoodie of mine she had on. Her wet hair spilled onto the pillows and my eyes gazed at the thick dark lashes, down to the prominent cheekbones and her pink lips as I drifted off into a light sleep in the corner of the room.

Chapter Eighteen

ଔ Charlie ଓ

Light flooded the room, and I felt hot under the thick covers. My jaw ached and my lip stung and my head felt thick, like I had a hangover, pounding relentlessly. I edged out of the bed, carefully pulling on a pair of Cian's jogging bottoms and rolling the waistband a few times to make them somewhere near to fitting me.

I could hear multiple deep voices from the lounge at the far side of Bobby's house and, straining my ears, I tried to make out how many people there were as I padded silently closer.

"The bullets you gave me, Kee," an unfamiliar voice rumbled from inside the room, "they were Russian issue. From a Glock. You been pissing off your Russian friends?"

"No. We've all maintained our patches. The only overspill we've had was from the O'Malleys but that's not unusual. They just push the boundaries and we push back."

"Well, it seems some Russians want you and yours dead, Kee. That stiff in the garage, those tattoos are the sort of things we see on people like the Russian mob, although it's difficult to be sure as some of them have been lasered off."

"What the fuck would the Russians be doing up here?" I recognised Oisín's voice.

"I dunno. We need to get Charlie to take us through it when she wakes up. I need to know what happened," Cian answered.

I pushed the door open.

"Charlie's awake," I said, wandering into the room in my bare feet and dressed head to foot in Cian's clothes.

All eyes turned on me and a knot of dread at having to relive the events of last night to this room of men started to form in my stomach.

"I need a drink first," I instructed, focusing on Cian who was already pouring out the golden-bronze liquor into a glass.

I gulped the hideous liquid down, closing my eyes as it burnt my throat and then, taking a deep breath, I recounted the night to the men in the room. The silence made me uneasy as I looked around after I had finished. Cian's eyes were dark, his jaw tight and his hand wrapped tight round the glass of whisky he had sipped from frequently as I spoke.

"So Lebedev sent two bone-heads to burn my place down and put their hands all over my… jockey," Cian added quickly as Osh shot him a smug look.

"Why though? Is Lebedev working with the Volkovs?" the other man in the room asked.

I recognised him from when I first met the O'Sullivans. He was loitering around in the background, not saying much but with them, that much I remembered.

"We've had no beef with the Volkovs for years."

"Old man Volkov is weak and his oldest son is blood thirsty and power hungry. My guess is he's getting greedy," Cian explained.

"But why target the stables?" I asked.

"It's an excellent way of getting rid of bodies and there's lots of combustible materials. Stable yards go up in flames really easily," the biker answered.

I felt the colour drain from my face and nausea seemed to have replaced the knot.

"My horses. All their innocent lives," I whispered.

"And yours too, babe. My guess is you weren't targeted. Wrong place, wrong time. But there's no doubt they would both have raped you and then left you to die in the fire, if you weren't dead all ready," the biker answered.

"Easy V. She doesn't need to hear that," Cian's voice was softer, his eyes watching mine.

"She wants the truth," the tall blond-haired biker answered.

"I do."

But I felt sick now, my cheeks burning hot and saliva gathering in my throat. Dread, anger, terror; driven around my body by the heart that beat like a wartime drum, heavy and ominous.

I shook my head, "no I really do. What's the chances of them coming back?" I asked, my voice betraying me as it wavered.

"They'll be back. If they've started a turf war with us, they'll not stop till we're all dead. Or we kill them," Osh answered.

I nodded, soberly. How the fuck did I get caught up in all of this? I was just a jockey; a normal, boring girl. This was Durham, not the wild fucking west.

Cian shook his head.

"I want to speak to Lebedev," he growled.

"Lebedev will be well guarded. Mafia or not, these Russian billionaires have a shit-hot security detail. Half of them will be ex-fucking KGB. You'll never be able to waltz in there and speak to him," the biker man spoke.

I watched him for a moment. He was taller than Cian, long blond hair pulled back into a ponytail from the nape of his neck. His head was shaved on either side with an intricate tattoo running front to back on one side, replacing where his hair would have been.

"But he will have limited guards at the jockey club ball next week," I piped up, all eyes turning back to me.

I shrugged, "you're already on the list. Bobby would go every year, so you just need to do whatever shit you do when you *talk* to someone, Cian."

Cian looked around the room at the other men.

"Sounds like a plan," he said, "Osh, we're going to need some more men here."

Oisín nodded in agreement.

"Charlie. I don't want you staying on the yard by yourself. You'll stay here at the house."

"Fuck no!"

The room went silent and Jonjo and Riley passed a look between themselves.

"That's not a request, Charlie, that's an order."

I laughed, the noise sounding loud and shrill in the suddenly chilled atmosphere of the room.

"You don't give me orders, Irishman."

"I do now. Riley, go bring her clothes over here."

The other man walked out, running the minute his boss gave him an instruction. If Cian thought I would do the same, he was going to get a fright. Fear and dread had turned to anger. I clenched my teeth together.

"I've got horses to ride," Jonjo said suddenly.

"Yeah, me too," I agreed, getting up onto weak legs.

"You're taking the day off today, Charlie," Cian answered, his tone commanding.

"I'm fine, Cian. There's work to do."

"I don't care whether you're fine or not. I said you're taking the day off."

"Who the fuck do you think you are?" I said quickly, the heat of rage in my voice.

Cian crossed the room towards me, his demeanour imposing, coming to a stop right in front of me. I kept my eyes on his, my teeth gritted, folding my arms across my chest.

"Right now I own your sorry ass," he growled, "you work for me, remember? And that means you'll take orders from me."

"The fuck I do," I spat, almost tasting the fury on my tongue.

Cian looked away from me and glanced across the room, tilting his head and I heard footsteps of heavy boots on the hard wood floors. Then as their footsteps faded, and we were left alone, he pushed me, my legs hitting the back of the armchair and I tumbled into it. He bent down towards me, resting his weight on the arms of the chair, and I shuffled back into the sagging fabric till I couldn't get any further from him.

Sandalwood, cedar, musk, and the faint scent of something flowery were all I could focus on. I should be frightened by him, but I wasn't. The sheer proximity of him made my core clench.

I stared at him defiantly, watching the darkness swirling in his hazel eyes, his eyebrows knitting together as he frowned, the savage look he was giving me making heat collect in my stomach.

"Don't misinterpret me, Charlie. I'm a killer, not a hero," he growled, danger lacing the satin smoothness of his voice, "when I tell you to do something you'll do it."

"Or what, Cian? You'll kill me?" I whispered.

He pushed his lips together, his eyes searching mine. Then he stooped his head lower, the plumpness of those lips brushing mine, a tiny stab of pain from my split lip and my breath that came out like a contented sigh. My pussy pulsed as I remembered the last time he had his lips on me.

"Be a good girl for once. Go make yourself a room up. You're moving in here with me."

He stared at me for a few more seconds, and my stomach somersaulted. I pushed my thighs together, trying to ignore the feeling between my legs. Then he stood up and walked out, leaving me dazed, hot and annoyingly needy.

Chapter Nineteen

๑ Cian ๛

I stormed out of the room, leaving the annoying, petulant undisciplined blonde jockey sat by herself. Why she couldn't just make life easy and do as I told her? I should just leave her out on her own, in her flat on the stable yard and let the Russians do what the hell they liked to her. Yet the moment that thought slipped from my mind, anger and rage raced after it. Fuck's sake.

She'd looked even more stunning in my clothes, too. If it hadn't been for the memory of how vulnerable and fragile she had looked this morning in that stable, I would have ripped them off her and fucked her right then. She was driving me crazy, and she knew it.

The scent of her pussy still lingered on my face after the other night. And no matter how many times I washed my face, it was as if it had embedded itself into my skin. Every time I thought about her, about my face at her entrance, my cock came to life.

Flustered, I stalked to the kitchen, hitting the switch of the kettle, fearing tiredness was getting to me. My men eyed me warily and I couldn't help let out a frustrated sigh, scrubbing the stubble on my face with my hand. I needed action and decisiveness right now.

"Riley," my friend had just walked back in with a bulging black bin bag presumably of Charlie's belongings, "I want that body returned to the Russians. Send them a message. Make it known if they want a war with us, all their men will end up like this one."

"But we didn't kill him," Riley countered.

"He as good as died at our hands. Jonjo, help him."

The tall jockey nodded, his face stoic, and I knew he hated being pulled back in like this. But he was as good as any of my men, on a horse or off.

"V, I need intel on the Russians. Discreet intel. I want to know everything they do. If they are having a shit, I want to know. If they are out fucking, I want to know. I even want to know what they are thinking. That's the level of detail I need."

The Viking chuckled, "Okay, Kee. I think I know just the guy."

"What are you going to do about your little firecracker in there?" the Viking asked, amusement all over his face.

I rolled my eyes, plonking myself onto one of the breakfast bar seats, and sipped on my coffee.

"I'll have someone watch her for now."

The blond biker-man laughed again, deep and knowing, then clapped me on the back with his big hand.

"Whatever, bud. You just keep *watching* her. I'm off to organise your intel."

When the room was quiet, Osh limped over, poured a coffee and joined me at the other side of the breakfast bar.

"Charlie is becoming a liability, brother," he said quietly and I could feel his eyes on my face.

Frowning into my coffee, his words whizzing round my head, I knew he was right. She wasn't any concern of ours. She was collateral. Yet no matter how much I knew it, I couldn't leave her unprotected. She was becoming a weakness, and in this life weaknesses were a death sentence, for somebody.

"You think it was the Russians who killed our family?" I asked Oisín.

"Looks like it," he answered, and I could see the same look of rage and pain on his face that I'd felt inside me for weeks.

I rubbed at my temples.

"We've still not avenged them, Cian," Osh said suddenly, "all this time, and we are no closer to finding their killers. We should have been ripping body parts off anyone we suspected."

"Yeah, and create an all-out war?"

"If that is what it takes. You didn't act. Now we look like a bunch of pussies. We'll have every fucking firm in the whole of the UK trying to take us out soon."

Oisín was right. I'd been too cautious to start something that would take a huge amount of manpower to put out, never mind keep under the radar of authorities. But that was compromising us.

The O'Sullivans had been one of the biggest crime families in the UK for years. My father had been ruthless, he had been feared, and my older brother, Torin, even more so. He was cruel and unnecessary. I was calculating and the strategist, but where was that getting me?

"I need you back in Ireland," I said eventually, "if the Russians are attacking us from all angles, we need to protect our home turf. If anyone takes us on, we will retaliate. If the O'Malleys push their boundaries, I want a message sent."

"Got it, brother."

Osh's face lightened at the thought of violence and revenge, something I'd been trying to contain in him for weeks. But if it was a war these fuckers wanted, it was a war they'd fucking get.

Chapter Twenty

❦ Charlie ❧

I slunk out of my new room the next morning, floorboards creaking traitorously under my steps as I eased the door open. Cian's room was right next door, and I was under instruction not to be alone, but the idea of being followed around by one of his men all day only fuelled my annoyance all the more.

I'd heard voices from downstairs long into the night, so I was guessing no one would be up before dawn today, particularly, as I suspected, they'd just gone to bed. Despite the four big bedrooms Bobby's house offered, I wasn't quite sure where everyone was going to stay. Even Jonjo had hunkered down here too, but at least his company I could cope with.

Bypassing the kitchen, not chancing switching the kettle on, I crept out into the pale orange glow of dawn. There was a distinct spring feeling in the morning air now; the sound of birds singing, the lush scent of grass growing and as I got closer to the stable yard, the smell of fresh hay and horses.

A rustle in a bush behind me made me jump, my heart racing for a moment, my eyes fixing on the little brown bird scratching in the dried leaves on the ground. Normally the expectant faces of the thoroughbreds, the variety of coloured noses sticking out over their doors awaiting breakfast, brought a smile to my face. Today, instead, my eyes were drawn to the empty stable, my chest constricting as my thoughts tapered off. The smell of cigarette smoke prickled at my nose and panic rose in me as I looked around urgently.

A dark figure stood in the doorway of my flat, the end of a cigarette burning red with each pull on it. My chest squeezed tighter, resolve and rationality leaving me and I ran across the yard to the kitchen area, slamming the door closed behind me and propping myself up against it, knowing my barely eight stone of body weight wasn't going to stop anyone getting in there with me. My breaths became frantic as the footsteps grew louder and I clamped my hand over my mouth to prevent the screams in my throat from escaping into the thin air.

"It's OK," I heard the Irish voice on the other side call out, "I'm Tommy. I'm with you today. I'm one of Cian's men. Sorry to frighten you," he said again when I didn't answer.

Forcing my heart to slow down and doing my best to push away the panic from keeping sense hostage, I rose to my feet and opened the door. I looked the man up and down. He was young, even younger than me, I guessed, and dressed in a dark suit and formal shoes.

"You're my shadow today, huh?" I asked, my voice coming out calmer than I felt inside.

He nodded, smiling warmly.

"You're going to need to get out of those clothes," I said, turning from him and putting the kettle on for a much needed coffee.

He looked at me quizzically when I turned around again.

"The suit. You got something else? Jeans? Boots?"

"Yeah, I got jeans."

"Good. Go put something on. You can't shovel shit in those clothes."

Tommy looked at me in surprise.

"You're going to look well out-of-place following me around dressed like that," I continued when he didn't move, "at least look like a newly appointed stable lad then it'll not be quite as obvious the yard is amidst a fucking mafia takeover."

"Oh. Aye. I see."

Yet he still stood there.

"Well? Off you pop. I'm sure I can get a cup of coffee without supervision."

When he turned and left for my flat I let out a long breath, some of the earlier tension leaving my body, my hands still shaking as I scooped coffee into a cup. I really needed to get a grip.

The day continued like that. I didn't see Cian or the other men, only Tommy, who diligently followed me around, more like a lost puppy than a protector, but no one seemed suspicious or asked questions. Admittedly, he was fairly useful and picked up the yard jobs quickly, wrinkling his nose up every time he inhaled a lung full of horse piss, which made me smirk each time.

While I rode, he waited on the hill at the top of the gallops, where Bobby used to watch me and I gave him the job of timing each horse. And each time we finished he looked elated, like Bobby used to.

"Wow, that was fast, Charlie," he said after I'd ridden a particularly well-behaved Brian.

"Can you ride, Tommy?" I asked on the way back to the stables.

"Nah. Never sat on a horse in my life. And that's the way it's staying. Motorbikes, yes, horses, no."

By evening Jonjo, another rider, and I had trained every horse, paying particular attention to those running at the weekend. As the night closed in, I stood in the bay filly's stable, brushing her beautiful coat before she was rugged for the night. Turning her head, she blew into my ear and I rubbed her soft nose in response. I ran my hand over her body, feeling the hardness of muscle under the soft velvet of her coat. She'd been Bobby's favourite. A strong character but honest and brave and aside from Brian, she was the fastest horse on the yard.

A bang overhead made me jump, and I automatically looked about, my stomach jerking with panic, the deep rumble of men's voices from above making me hold my breath momentarily. Another muffled bang from above made me flinch, but this time my brain had kicked into gear, not controlled by the irrationality of fear. What were they doing to my flat?

I left the stable, securing the bolt behind me, watching Tommy stand up from his perch on the mounting block and follow me. I bounded up the steps, the voices and laughter getting louder as I got up there. Pushing the door open, my eyes roamed the space. My lounge stunk of cigarette smoke, cups and dishes lay strewn on the coffee table beside a man's feet that were folded at the ankle, his head lolling back on the settee and a cigarette between the fingers of his outstretched hand. The end table where there should have been an expensive lamp was knocked sideways and an angry black mark had formed on my brilliant white walls.

"Get your fucking feet off my table," I said, walking over and kicking his feet sideways.

I plucked the cigarette out of his fingers and took it to the sink where I extinguished it with a hiss. The man stood up. He was tall with dark hair and nasty scar from his eyebrow to the corner of his lip, making him look like he was sneering.

"Get this fucking place tidied up," I continued, "or you can sleep in a stable."

"Who the fuck are you?" he spat, eyes dark with anger, sidling up to me, his hands balled into fists either side of him.

"Easy, Mad-Dog," Tommy warned from the doorway, "she's the boss' girl."

The man released his fists but didn't move away from me as I shot Tommy an irritated sideways glance.

"You can fuck off coming in here with your attitude," he said, his voice low and intimidating, "unless the boss gave the order, *I* ain't following it. Now piss off back to playing with your ponies."

My temper rising, I moved into the man's space, my brain firing me warning signals.

"Get. The. Fuck. Out. Of. My. House," I snarled, my voice low, my heart pumping hard against my chest, fuelled by rage.

The man looked down at me; and laughed. I moved to step around him, but he caught my arm and stopped me. Hot rage flooded to my cheeks and without a second thought I drove the toe of my riding boots into his shin.

"Fuck!" he shouted and released the grip on my arm as I pushed past him and through to my bedroom.

The bed had been slept in and the duvet was chucked back, half on the bed, half on the floor. The sheets were crumpled and pillows strewn all over the place. I grabbed a hold-all and stuffed as much as I could in there, flinging it over my shoulder and bursting out of the room, bashing the heavy bag off 'Scar Face' on the way past. Tommy followed me a couple of steps behind, as

I stormed up the drive to the house, the bag quickly becoming heavy on my shoulder.

The house was quiet when I got in. Not a soul around, which was probably just as well given the mood I was in.

"I'm going in the shower," I said to Tommy, who sensibly stepped aside and let me pass.

It was a couple of hours before I heard voices downstairs. Outside, daylight had yielded to darkness. My rage had simmered down a little, but the moment I heard voices it sparked back up again, like a fire not quite burnt out. Storming down the stairs and into the kitchen where a collection of men stood, including 'Scar Face', I didn't hold back.

"Cian, I want my flat back," I burst out, fixing my eyes on the scarred man watching me with a smirk on his face.

Cian sighed, wiping his hand across his face.

"Not happening."

"Like fuck it's not."

"I'm not debating this now," he said, leaving the room, "I need a shower."

I followed behind him, not letting him get away from me until I was standing outside the bathroom door; Cian somewhere on the other side.

"Your men, they're wrecking my flat," I called to the sound of water running against tile in the bathroom.

Silence. The only sound the rhythmical patter of the water. I pushed the door open. Unbuttoning his shirt, he looked straight at me, raising an eyebrow, but didn't stop, shrugging off the white cotton fabric and letting it fall to the floor.

"Can we talk about it later?"

"No we can't."

I crossed my arms across my chest. My eyes were drawn to the white vest he'd had on under his shirt, how it clung to the bulge of his chest, exposing the round cap of his shoulders and the veins that jutted out of muscled biceps. My eyes meandered over the tattoos on his upper body; patterns and pictures extending over his shoulders and exaggerating the sinewy muscle of thick arms.

"I'm busy," he answered, his eyes piercing mine.

Cian crossed his arms over, pulling on the bottom of his vest and lifting it over his head, his stomach muscles rippling underneath. Lines of text were tattooed across his chest, covered slightly with the sprinkling of light brown hair. I tried to focus.

"My flat smells of cigarette smoke. There were feet on my furniture…" I started angrily, stopping short as I watched his fingers unbutton his trousers and push them to the floor, wispy hair trailing down the over the tight 'v' of his lower abs.

"Uh, huh," he answered, his fingers dipping under the waistband of the snug boxer shorts that clung to his legs bulging in the middle over his cock.

Then he slid off his boxers, and I watched as they moved over the thick muscles of his legs, his dick hanging in between, foreskin pulling back slightly over a bulging head.

"My face is up here, Charlie," he said, his full lips pulling into a lop-sided grin.

Heat licked at my cheeks, my eyes dropping back to his groin. Cian turned his back on me, stepping into the shower, my eyes lingering over the muscle definition of his back, down to the plump curve of his arse cheeks. He turned, dipping his head under the stream of water and pushing his hair back over his head, his arms flexing, his stomach tight, his cock right there enlarging in front of my eyes.

"Something you like?" he asked, his voice dark as he watched me watching him.

"Stop changing the subject," I bit, moving closer to the shower door, "My flat..."

His arm reached out, suddenly grabbing me and yanking me forwards. I wobbled for a moment, caught off guard, before being pulled into the shower with him. Water soaked my white t-shirt instantly, running over my hair and down my jogging bottoms.

"Cian," I squeaked, but he'd already spun me away from the door, his hand wrapped tight in my wet hair.

My head was pulled back, my chest pushed out into him and I stared up into his eyes, his face dark, and his jaw clenched as he studied me. His other hand cupped my breast over the now see-through fabric of my t-shirt.

"Hmmm, no bra," he murmured, his lips brushing the side of my face, stubble scratching a path on my skin.

I gasped as he tweaked my nipple roughly, his hold in my hair tightening, and then he captured my mouth with his and I ignored the sting of pain in my lip as he slid his tongue between my lips, water cascading over the pair of us. His tongue thrust in and out of my mouth, his lips pushed hard against mine, heat rising in me. Then he pushed me backwards, my back hitting the tiles behind me and I felt his erection against my stomach, sending my insides somersaulting, a pulsing heat radiating between my thighs.

Breaking off the kiss, his hands skimmed down my sides, tingles erupting under his touch, and then he was sliding my wet bottoms off, pulling my thong down with them. I gasped again as his fingers wound up the inside of my thigh and I parted my legs as rough finger-ends brushed over my folds and clit, heat and need igniting in me instantly.

Towering above me, water running off his head and onto my face, my head pulled back so my eyes could only see his, a finger thrust inside me. I cried out, feeling my pussy clench around him, moaning as he pulled it back and forth. And then I felt the push of a second finger filling me, rough thrusts stoking the fire in my stomach, a harsh pulsing pace in and out of me, as his thumb rubbed circles over my clit, heat bursting through me. Then, just as my body started to shudder, he pulled his hand away, and I let out a squeak of frustration.

"So what were you saying about your flat?" he whispered in my ear, his husky voice adding to the flames licking at my insides.

"No, it can wait," I breathed.

"No, Charlie, it was important to you. We'll talk about it now."

"Later, please," my voice was nearly a whimper; I couldn't cope with the heat that was still building between my legs.

I grabbed his hand and pushed it back towards me.

"You wanted to talk about it so desperately."

"Fuck, Cian, please?"

The fucker was making me beg.

"Please what, Charlie? What do you want?" releasing his hand from my hair, he wrapped it round the side of my throat, his thumb brushing against my lips, his other stroking lightly over my already tingling pussy lips.

"Fuck me Cian," I said looking straight in his eyes.

He pushed his lips together and then his hands fell to my hips. He lifted me up, pulling both my legs around his waist, forcing my back against the tile of the shower. I felt the tip of his cock at my entrance. He paused, staring at me, and I moaned and wriggled in anticipation, feeling the bulge just there, just waiting to push its way inside me. Then he plunged into me in one hard thrust, impaling me, filling me full of him, and I let out a cry, my pussy stretching around him.

Cian didn't wait for me to adjust, didn't build up the tempo, didn't slide slowly in and out. He hammered his cock into me, ramming my back into the tile, thrusting harshly, fast and furious. Heat flooded through my body, my own cries ripped from my throat at the ferocity of each stroke, of each urgent thrust from him. He was an animal, hard and fast, punishing my pussy over and over, crushing his pubic bone against my clit. The tingles and pulses from inside of me came like spasms, my cries echoing around the bathroom. Cian grunted with each thrust, deep and throaty, pounding me, stretching me, hurting me with delicious pulsing pain.

God, I couldn't take anymore. I clung to him, my nails digging into the skin of his back, my eyes closing as I came, shaking against him, my thighs clinging hard to his waist. Cian growled into my ear, burying himself in me as far as he could, jamming me between the wall and his cock, and then he stilled, leaning his forehead against the wall, holding himself into me as the last surges faded away.

190

"What were you saying about your flat?" he breathed into my ear.

Chapter Twenty One

ﻬ Cian ﻬ

I breathed deeply, my cock still inside her, her tight pussy still caressing it as I pushed my forehead into the tiles of the shower behind us. Charlie's muscular legs were clamped around my body and my back stung, water running off the scratches she'd left on my skin. I eased out of her, tightness stroking my cock, pressure building in me once more.

Putting her down, I stepped back under the shower stream, washing myself, my eyes trained on the blonde jockey in front of me. Her t-shirt, soaking wet, clung to her body, see through. Her tits were round and perfect underneath, the dark pink of her nipples visible under the wet material, just the right size, and had felt so good between my teeth. There was a glistening sheen between her legs, the muscles of her inner thighs firm and all I could think about was burying myself in her again.

I left her in the shower. There were things I needed to do, and I really didn't need a distraction. But as I wandered off to my room, she was all that was in my head.

Charlie followed soon after, wrapped in a towel, her hair hanging down her back as she clutched her wet clothes against her. I tried to ignore her and the hardening feeling of my dick, raking through my drawer for something comfortable to wear.

"My flat, Cian. I want it back," she said softly from behind me.

I sighed, turning to find her moving towards the door.

"I want you here at the house," I answered. I wanted her here for more than one reason and I tried to push that out of my mind, "I'll talk to the boys down there and make sure they treat your place properly. You can move back in as soon as I say it's safe for you to do so."

"I'll decide what is safe for me and what is not."

Charlie's face darkened, the defiance in her returning and it induced that same response in me. The need to dominate her, to control her, to make her submit, and it made me hard again. She'd seen it too, her eyes dropping to my crotch, her pink lips parting so slightly that if my senses hadn't been so fucking heightened I would have missed it.

I crossed the room in easy strides, grabbed her round the waist before she'd even realised what was happening.

"What the fuck, Cian," she raged, struggling in my arms, making my cock grow harder for her as I carried her to the bed and flung her down on her back.

I ripped the towel from her, exposing her body to me properly this time, and crawled over the top of her. The petulant look she had given me moments earlier morphed into something else: desire, excitement. Her pupils dilated. I barely had to nudge her legs open, she was already wrapping her incredible thighs around me, wet and ready for me to take her again. My cock twitched, resting against her wet cunt, and she arched her back to edge herself closer. I pushed against her, feeling the warmth of her pussy, her juices letting my tip glide in easily and she gasped from under me. But I didn't give her anymore and after a second, she glared at me.

"If you want my cock, you'd better start behaving," I growled, dropping my head and biting the lobe of her ear.

She moaned and rocked her hips towards me. I slid further in before stopping again, annoyance crossing her face.

"You want me to beg for your dick again, Cian?" she asked, her voice hoarse, sending a shiver over my skin.

I took a breath. I could be the most patient predator in the world, but right now, half way into Charlie's tight cunt, I was losing my resolve.

"Be a good girl and do what I tell you and you can have as much of my dick as you want," I continued.

194

"Not gonna happen, Cian."

Her pussy tensed around me. How could she still fight me? I knew what she wanted; what she needed yet would she fucking give in?

I pulled away from her suddenly, watching the look of disappointment creep over her face that she tried to hide by biting that gorgeous bottom lip. I dipped my head back down, taking her bottom lip between my teeth, nipping down on it hard until she squealed with equal parts pleasure and pain. Then, releasing her, I flipped her over onto her stomach. Her arms flailed in surprise and I grabbed them both, pulling them behind her, pinning them tight into my left hand. Then I pulled her arse up where I could see it better and slapped her hard across the right cheek.

Charlie's head shot back as she yelled out.

"Cian! What the fuck?"

I slapped her right cheek again, the sound of my hand hitting her soft flesh and the delicious cry, a mix of pain and arousal, the way she wriggled to get free making me want to sink into her right now. I rubbed her arse cheek, a slight pink tone coming to the creamy smooth skin. Charlie cried out, the tone low and sensual.

"You like being punished, sweetheart?" I purred into her ear, letting my cock slide against the folds of her pussy, wet and slick.

She moaned as I forced her head into the duvet. I dipped my hand between her legs, my fingers sticky from her own wetness, and I brought them to my mouth, tasting what I was doing to her. Then I slapped her backside again, and she yelled out, a cry so primal I was sure she was going to come from just a spanking alone.

And so was I. The feeling of dominating her, hitting her gorgeous round arse, punishing her; it was enough for me to shoot my load right now. Taking my cock in my hand, I positioned it at her entrance and she moaned, moving her hips back into me.

"If you want this, you'll have to be a good girl and do as you're told. Can you do that?"

"Yes."

"Don't move," I growled, tightening my grip on her wrists.

Charlie stopped wriggling and held still. I stroked the head of my dick through her wet slit, rubbing it over her clit as I listened to her breathing coming faster, waiting for me to fuck her. And then I pushed into her, sliding myself all the way in slowly. Once I was inside her to the hilt, I stopped a moment, admiring the view. Impaled from behind, she was finally cooperating face down on the bed, her arse red from my hands. Her pussy clenched around me, sending bolts of electric up my shaft to my balls. I slapped her again and she jumped, her pussy clamping down on my shaft. I grunted.

Slowly pulling back, I listened to her rapid breaths and then I thrust roughly back in, the tip of my shaft hitting her hard and she yelled loudly. I repeated, dragging out and hammering back in, holding still for a second, pushing myself in as far as I could get, making that gorgeous, tight cunt take every inch of me. Then I started working my hips faster, grabbing hers with my spare hand, pulling her back into me with each thrust while she screamed from underneath me.

God, she was so insanely tight. Her pussy clenched around my cock with the slightest of movement, holding onto me like a vice and soon I was grunting like an animal, pulling at her arms held in my hand, yanking her back into me with each urgent thrust of my hips, hitting her arse as hard as I rammed my cock into her.

Her body shook under me as I fucked her as hard as I could, punishing, controlling. Whimpering, she cried out, shouting my name as she came, sending me spiralling out of control and over the edge, pumping into her madly until I shot load after load inside of her.

Releasing her arms, I leaned into her, forcing her flat to the bed, keeping my shaft pushed into her tight space till every ebb of my orgasm faded away. And even then, as we lay still together, the feel of her wet hot pussy still holding onto my dick after I'd ravished the fuck out of her, still flooded my groin with the most incredible feeling I'd ever had.

I came downstairs to the smell of fresh pizza some time later and, following the scent to the lounge, my stomach grumbled loudly. I helped myself to a decent slice and grabbed a beer off the table before plonking myself into an armchair in front of the fire.

The Viking had already arrived and was leaning against the fireplace, supping a beer, as nearly all my men had filled the large room.

"Pleased you bothered to join us, Kee," he rumbled, a knowing smile on his face that I ignored.

"What you got for me, V?"

"My intel man is in place, so we've now got eyes on the Newcastle Russian branch. But we need to coordinate with Osh about what's happening South."

I nodded, shoving the last lot of pizza in my mouth and digging out another slice. I was starving.

"Anything in the surveillance?" I asked, hopefully.

"Nope, not yet. All the normal things you would expect."

"What about our message?" I asked Riley.

"Delivered."

I hated having to wait. I'd much rather go running in, break a few bones, take a few fingers and get things sorted, but I needed to bide my time and start a war I knew we could win. And to do that, I needed to know my enemy better. Lebedev was key to that. He would talk. It was well known he was hiding out in the UK to stay away from the motherland's reach. A bit of pressure in the right places and I'd have him singing.

"V, what can you get on, Lebedev?" I asked, swigging back the last of my beer and reaching for another.

"I know he loves the women. The harder to get, the better."

I gritted my teeth, knowing where this was headed.

"You need to use your girl for that," the Viking continued.

"Not gonna happen."

"Why not?" a voice from the doorway added to the conversation.

All the men in the room turned their heads, each one of them lingering on Charlie far longer than I liked. She leaned against the door frame, her arms folded across a strappy vest top, her legs crossed at the ankles, bare to the top of her thighs, the linen shorts she wore exposing the creamy skin of her toned legs.

"Because I'm not dangling you in front of him like bait," I grumbled.

"Again, why not? I'd be good as bait."

"Yeah, jailbait," I heard someone whisper from behind me.

"Because I don't want you in any danger. This isn't your world."

"Seems to be too late for that now you lot are here," Charlie said, "besides, I know racing and horses and you don't."

"I do," I protested.

199

"No, you know black and white ponies. These beasts are different. This industry is different. Let me do the talking about horses. You do what you do best; be the threat in the background."

Before I'd had a chance to respond Charlie turned and walked off in the direction of the kitchen. I stood, running a hand through my hair.

"Thought you'd got that one broken in tonight, boss," Mad-Dog piped up from behind me as the younger ones in the room erupted into sniggers.

Rage flashed before my eyes, hot and wild.

"Whoa, boss, steady on," Riley said, putting his hand tentatively on my outstretched forearm.

I followed my arm, the eyes of Mad-Dog bulging out, a shocked expression on his face, his fingers groping against my hand where I had wrapped it round his throat. Shocked, I relaxed my grip, letting him slide down the wall I'd pinned him against, his feet finding the floor again.

"Get the fuck out of here," I growled to the younger men.

The room had descended into an uneasy silence. The younger men and Jonjo scurried out as the Viking watched me from his spot at the mantelpiece, a grin just pulling at his mouth.

"Haven't you got shit to do V?" I asked, my voice harsher than I meant to be.

The biker-man laughed, grabbed his black leather jacket, and left the room.

"Cian, what the fuck's got into you?" Riley asked, his face full of concern, "you're losing your head over a woman, mate. That's not like you."

I walked to the drinks cabinet in the corner of the room and poured myself a whisky, ignoring Riley as I sat back in front of the fire, staring at the red and orange of the flames as it licked at the grate. Riley was right, that wasn't like me. Durham was doing something to me, diluting me. I needed to sort all this shit out and get back to my life in Ireland.

Chapter Twenty Two

∞ Charlie ∞

Activity in the stable yard was ramping back up by morning. Tommy was sat on the mounting block, wrapped up in a thick black coat, a scarf and woolly hat; the steam from his coffee and his cigarette creating white trails in the freezing air before him.

My fingers were numb, stinging as I fastened saddles and bridles, then turning to burning hot after a few rounds on the gallops, blood pushed round my system from exertion and adrenaline. The stable hands were hard at work, scurrying between stables, keeping warm with activity and to get the outdoor work completed as quickly as possible.

The cold was getting to the horses too. Many were fresh and on their toes, bouncing and jogging to the gallops and back. Tomorrow's runners needed gentle exercise and for once I was pleased that I wasn't taking Brian over the hurdles this morning, knowing he would be particularly enthusiastic.

"Where are you taking those?" Jonjo asked as I leaped into the saddle on the black stallion's back.

"Down to the river," I answered.

"Charlie," Jonjo warned in a low voice from the horse he was on, "Cian doesn't want you out of sight of one of the men."

"Tommy can't ride and these horses need to be walked out," I answered, uncaring.

Jonjo was training on the gallops all morning, so I was riding out with one of our exercise riders who was now looking between us quizzically.

"It's a direct order, Charlie. Not even you should go against it."

"If Cian thinks…."

"If Cian thinks what?" the voice behind us grumbled.

I turned to look in the direction of the deep Irish tone. The tight black hat he wore made him look even more threatening as he stood staring at me with his arms folded and his lips pursed. My stomach fluttered.

"These horses need riding out," I replied stiffly.

He raised an eyebrow at me; the movement lighting his face, a small tug at the corner of his mouth.

"So if you've a problem, you'd better get your arse in the saddle," I continued.

The air seemed to still and Tommy looked nervously between us. I watched Cian shrug, then walk towards the grey horse that was accompanying Brian. Standing at the side of the horse, he beckoned for the rider to dismount before sticking his foot into the stirrup and swinging his leg over the back of the horse and gathering up the reins.

"All right Irishman, let's see if you can actually ride?"

Brian jumped forward, snorting and jogging as we made our way down the drive towards the gates, the horses' shoes ringing off the concrete. After a few minutes Brian had relaxed, allowing the grey horse to come alongside him.

A half mile down the road, I pointed to an opening in the woods that had flanked us; a single track winding away in the trees. I led the way as Brian picked his feet over branches that had dropped off in the wind and the odd rock. The wooded path eventually ended and the trees cleared, revealing a lush hilly field. I steered the horses so that we skirted the edge, the rolling land dropping gently away.

"Can you trot?" I asked, eyeing the muscled man on top of the grey horse.

Cian nodded, a smirk growing on his face. I ignored him, pressing my legs against the horse and pushing him into a ground-covering pace. Cian kept up well, the grey horse under him relaxed. He was a big man but carried himself lightly in the saddle, his hands gentle on the reins, his legs wrapped strongly around the horse's body; in control of the half tonne animal in a careful yet commanding way. My stomach fluttered again.

The land had started to rise under the horses' feet and I suggested we picked the speed up again. The Irishman nodded in agreement and I pushed the black horse onwards at the foot of the hill. The trot morphing into canter, the rhythmical beat of the horses' hooves pounding on the grass under us, as wind whipped at wisps of my hair that had escaped from my hat.

"Is this all you got to throw at me, Charlie?" Cian shouted from behind me.

I looked back, glancing at his face quickly, seeing a sparkle in his eyes and a grin pulling at the side of his mouth. He pushed his heels into the grey horse, tightening his reins. The horse's ears flicked backwards and then with a surge it pushed forwards, the steady beat of canter transforming, the grey horse stretching forwards, its feet striking the ground as it increased in speed.

Brian scrunched his back up as the horse passed alongside him, doing his best impression of a triangle as he threatened, momentarily, to throw in some good old-fashioned rodeo moves. I tightened my reins, leant forwards and allowed the black horse to glide forwards, catching up with the grey horse with easy strides.

Wind pushed against me, pulling tears from the corners of my eyes, cold air hitting my face, freezing the skin on my cheeks and making my lips tingle. The field and the aligning hedgerows became a blur, turning to streaks of green as we thundered on, the drumming beat of the horses' hooves like a percussion-only orchestra. All too quickly the hill ended, and I sat back into the saddle, coaxing Brian to drop to a canter as we reached the soft peak.

"Where did you learn to ride?" I asked Cian as the horses slowed to a walk.

"Why? Didn't think I could?"

I grinned at him in answer.

"My mother taught me," he answered after a brief pause, "she loved horses, their gentleness and grace, and their unpredictability."

"That's a pretty accurate description of them."

"I think they reminded them of herself. My mother married into this life and hated it. The horses were her release. She was a showjumper. That was her passion."

"So, how did she get tangled up in all of this?" I waved a hand in the air, and Brian jumped slightly at the sudden movement.

"It's just this world. Money attracts money, but not nice people. The rich and the corrupt travel in all the same circles."

"Uh, huh. But that didn't answer my question," I prodded.

Cian paused, a look of sadness crossing his face.

"My father watched her at a competition one day. Decided she was his. So he chased her, pestered her until she gave in and went out on a date with him and eventually they got married. But as the years went on, she grew tired of this life; tired of the constant scheming and staying ahead of the law. The incessant fighting for power and using each other's loved ones as pawns in some sick game of chess. I understood that more as I grew up. I wouldn't have chosen this life and for a while I thought I'd escaped it to some degree; first in the army and then when I went to live in New York. Guess you can never outrun fate after all."

"So when Jonjo wanted something else, you didn't mind helping him?"

"He told you about that?"

I nodded.

"Guess you're not such an arsehole after all, huh?"

Cian grinned at me, the plumpness of his lips thinning slightly as they pulled into a wide smile. He was the most handsome man I'd ever set eyes on, but when he smiled, it felt like he'd put my stomach in a blender; that I was merely a schoolgirl, and he was my first crush.

"I'm pleased you hold me in such high regard," his voice came alive with a chuckle, "what about you, Charlie? Where did you learn to ride?"

"Until I met Bobby, the only times I got to sit on a horse was a pony at a fête. I remember

207

one day spending a month's worth of pocket money just to keep joining the back of the queue to ride the pony at the school fair. I think I was there all day."

"So your parents weren't into horses then?"

I shook my head, "Nat's parents weren't in to horses. I have no idea who my biological parents are. My father, Nat's father, he destroyed all the records for some reason. I don't even know if the day I celebrate my birthday is even mine."

"Did you get on with your adoptive parents?"

"Yeah, they were great. My mother died when I was quite young and my father was a top end solicitor. He died a year ago. Me and Nat spent a lot of time without him around so we're pretty close. It was never a secret I was adopted but as I got older, the kids at the school started to take the piss out of me for it. Eventually, I retaliated, developing my right hook. Guess I gave one too many and it landed me in the Youth Court."

I could feel Cian's eyes on me, watching me intently, the horses' feet clanging noisily underneath us as we turned back onto the road from the wooded path.

"It was Bobby who taught me to ride," I continued, the mention of his name sending tears prickling at the back of my eyes, "he caught me stealing a ride on his horses and instead of sending me packing he made me learn to do it properly."

The cold had set back into the ends of my fingers by the time we got back to the Yard. Swinging my leg over the back of the horse, I dismounted, bracing for the shot of fire that would hit my ankles as my frozen feet connected with the concrete below. I glanced across at Cian, who'd left the stable hands to lead the grey horse away and moved towards me stiffly.

"Hey, cowboy," I called over my shoulder as I took Brian's saddle and bridle back to the tack room, "fancy a coffee?"

"Sure do, ma'am," he answered playfully, following me with a slight hobble.

"Hmmmm, I quite like the sound of 'ma'am'. Think you should call me that more often." I teased.

Placing the saddle on the rack, I turned straight into Cian. His eyes were darker, the cheekiness gone. He pushed the door to the tack room closed behind us, the only light filtering in from the small barred window off to the side. Reaching behind me, I felt him wrap his hand in my pony tail before pulling my head back roughly.

"The only fancy name shit round here, sweetheart, will be when you call me, Sir," he growled at me, his expression intense.

I wasn't one for taking orders, for submitting to anyone, but when Cian talked to me like that, grabbed my hair like that, I couldn't stop the pulsing from beginning between my legs. And the bastard fucking knew it.

"So not happening," I fought back, pushing memories of last night from my mind.

He yanked my head back harder, brushing his lips against mine, leaving a trail of hot tingles where he touched me. Ice-cold fingers moved under my jumper, against the skin of my stomach, making me jump; the same cool fingers biting into my flesh as he pulled my hips towards him. I felt his hardness through his jeans as he dipped slightly, pushing his erection against me, sending a red hot throb directly to my pussy. Pressing my eyes closed to keep my reactions to him under control, I bit my bottom lip hard.

"You know I can make you beg for me like you did last night," he whispered, his face millimetres from mine, breath hot on my cheek.

His hand sank into the front of my breaches and I moaned against the tightness as his fingers teased over my entrance, pushing my knickers aside.

"You want more, sweetheart?" his finger circled my clit.

"Yes."

"Yes, Sir."

"Fuck off," I answered, breathlessly, cold fingers slipping inside me.

"You really gonna spoil all this because of your stubbornness?"

Cian's fingers moved in and out of me and I pushed myself against his hand, parting my legs further.

"Say the words."

"Never."

He pushed another into me, stretching me open. Heat and wetness pooled between my legs as he thrusted and twisted them, his hand jammed against the material of my breaches. His other hand wrenched my head back, so I had no choice but to look him in the eye as he fucked me with his fingers. I pushed into him as the heel of his hand rubbed against my clit. He watched me for a moment, and then, as if dissatisfied with the effect of the onslaught in my pussy, he took my mouth as well, forcing my lips apart for the assault of his tongue. His kisses worked hard and fast, stealing my breath and sending my head spinning.

The scrape of wood on the floor behind me made me jump.

"Oh. I'm er, I'm sorry," the youthful voice from behind Cian squeaked, and I broke away, peaking over Cian's shoulder at the red faced stable boy who stood in the doorway.

The door scraped on the floor again, footsteps fading quickly.

"Shit," I cursed.

"You'd better start practicing those words, sweetheart," Cian said to the top of my head, tugging his hand free from my breaches.

"Don't be a dick," I hissed at him as he stepped away from me.

He opened the door, letting daylight flood the room before winking at me and then walking away across the yard.

Chapter Twenty Three

ഌ Cian ര

Newcastle Racecourse was buzzing with a huge atmosphere. There was a sea of spectators, bright colours clashing as spirits were high and drinks flowed. I watched out over the racecourse. Charlie had been having an amazing day and so far had won every race. The O'Sullivan name in racing seemed to be blazoned in lights like a beacon, and I'd found myself making small talk to a number of other owners.

"Your female jockey is quite the thing," a man approached me, holding out his hand, and I shook it obligingly.

"She's very good," I answered him.

He was a young man, sporting an expensive suit with a distinctly corporate vibe; handsome, rich and arrogant.

"Matthew Keegan," he introduced himself.

Stinking rich, in fact. I recognised the name. His family owned several big financial businesses, but most notably a bank. Not the usual high street thing, but a bank for rich people: footballers, entrepreneurs, regular millionaires. And maybe even Russian billionaires. And he was the stereotypical rich, playboy, a reputation he had duly earned.

"Cian O'Sullivan," I returned the introduction.

"I'd really like to meet that jockey of yours. Is she available after her races?"

"I'm sure she will be."

"You'll introduce me then, won't you?"

I nodded coolly, watching him turn away from me and re-join the group of men at the windows overlooking the racecourse.

The commentator introduced the next race and I scanned the parade ring for Charlie. It didn't take long to find her; the black horse she rode was putting on his regular performance of leaps and bucks. The lounge was full of electric energy and I caught snippets of conversation from either side of me as I watched her scratch the stallion's neck, Jonjo keeping tight hold of them both. Off to the side, I caught a glimpse of Tommy watching intently.

A big chestnut thoroughbred kept close behind the stallion, too close and occasionally it would dance sideways, dangerously close to Brian's back legs. The black horse would tense up and Charlie would glance at Jonjo, who would say something back to her and she would relax again.

"Who's riding that big chestnut?" I asked Riley, who was watching from beside me.

"Dickie Hargreaves," he mumbled, thumbing through the race card.

I frowned, something niggling in my stomach. The horses and their jockeys made their way onto the racecourse and Charlie immediately popped the black horse into a strong canter. Hargreaves caught up with her quickly, keeping pace. The television screens focussed in on them and I noticed a conversation passing between the two of them.

"And there's Charlie Porter on the black stallion, Messiah Complex," the commentator called through the tannoy system, *"the pair took a tumble at their last race but miraculously recovered to take second place."*

The younger men in suits stood with Matthew Keegan, all muttering as they watched my jockey on the screen, joking between themselves, slugging back shots. I curbed my annoyance.

"Dickie Hargreaves rides Russian Doll. Tipped as the favourite, he'll have to ride that mare hard as Porter will be looking for a win here today."

The horses slowed to a walk, Brian looking calmer as handlers started feeding the thoroughbreds into the stalls. I watched Charlie carefully, anxiety gathering in my stomach. She kept the horse at the back of the field, making sure she was the last one pushed into the metal cage. The horse's feet paddled the ground as he started

215

to get wound up, but within seconds, the gates sprung open, setting them free again.

Charlie rode him wide at first, keeping him in the middle of the horses but almost on the outside of the track. The chestnut horse of Hargreaves edged out towards them, coming away from the main runners. She had clocked them creeping closer and flicked her reins, sending the horse on faster, pulling away in front, giving Brian plenty of space. Hargreaves edged closer. My heart moved to my mouth.

Then, with only a few hurdles left, Charlie surged forwards, the chestnut hanging hot on their heels as she brought Brian over towards the rail, taking advantage of her lead. Hargreaves moved to her right-hand side, closing off the space she'd created. She sailed over the final fence, checking back over her shoulder as she landed; the red-coloured thoroughbred squeezing ever closer until they were neck and neck.

The television screen zoomed into them. Hargreaves was saying something to her, his head flicking from eyeing the finish line to turning into Charlie. Something was being exchanged. Charlie scowled. The horse Hargreaves was riding bumped into the stallion and Charlie's head shot towards him, the camera zooming in on her just at the right moment. Then I watched as she shortened her reins and touched the stallion's sides. Her head shot sideways and she smiled. The black horse bounded forwards, power surging from its hind legs as it propelled itself towards the finish line, stretching and soaring like someone had just injected it with nitrous oxide.

"*And Messiah Complex takes the win for Charlie Porter*," the commentator shouted over the tannoy.

The lounge erupted with cheers and I felt myself smiling, a flood of relief replacing the knot of anxiety that had been sitting in my stomach for the entire race. The bankers in suits beside me talked excitedly, and I watched as they flagged over a waiter who quickly arrived with champagne and glasses. I guessed Charlie had won them a fuck load of money.

The television focussed on the blonde jockey as she rode the jogging black horse into the winner's enclosure. She patted his neck as he danced underneath her, Jonjo loyally at her side. A microphone was pushed towards her, Charlie's voice singing through the television speakers full of excitement and elation, telling the reporter how proud she was of Brian, who had been written off by all the other trainers, yet had chosen her. The reporter went to pat the horse's neck, and I watched as the stallion bared his teeth, taking a swipe at the man's hand for touching him uninvited. They were one and the same, that jockey and her horse, I mused, watching the reporter jump backwards out of Brian's biting range.

By the end of the day, the punters were queuing up to meet her. I'd lost count of the number of people who had asked for an introduction or who wanted to talk to me later about their horses and what Charlie could ride for them. She was almost famous and the reporters and commentators had spoken little of anything else all day, speculating that she could make history at two of England's biggest races in the next few months.

I wandered off towards the changing rooms, pushing the door open tentatively. Charlie had her back to me when I walked in, a blue long-sleeved blouse skimming the top of her buttocks, exposing the bulb of her arse and her strong slender legs. I stood behind her, revelling in the smell of her freshly washed hair and the light floral perfume that was evaporating from her skin; feminine, sexy.

"I'm sure it wouldn't kill you to knock occasionally," she said, not even glancing over her shoulder at me.

I didn't answer her. Instead, I ran a finger up the back of her bare leg, feeling her silky smooth skin, tracing up over the curve of her arse, then over her hip bone, increasing the pressure as I pushed my fingers down her stomach towards her groin. She let out a gasp, breathless, aroused, losing control. I cupped my hand over her the front of her thong, letting my fingers splay out between her legs, feeling the heat of her from underneath the thin fabric. Snaking my other hand around in front of her, I grabbed hold of her throat, pulling her head back towards me as she let out another moan, my lips trailing down the side of her neck.

Slipping my hand under the fabric of her thong, I could feel her hot sticky wetness lubricating the satin of her pussy, waiting for me. I pushed a finger inside of her and she tensed around me immediately, making my cock harden even more as it strained against my trousers.

"What do you say, sweetheart?" I whispered into her ear.

"Fuck me, Cian," she breathed.

"Those aren't the right words."

"No chance."

I slid my hand away and I heard the exhalation of air from her pretty mouth. Fumbling with my zip, I pulled my cock out, hard and ready, rubbing it against her arse, gliding it down between her plump arse cheeks, sliding it against the material of the thong covering her from me. Charlie pushed herself backwards, rubbing against my shaft.

"Please, Cian," she murmured.

I pulled her thong to one side and moved the head against her, enjoying the needy whimper that left her lips.

"The words, Charlie," I whispered into her ear before biting the end of her lobe and sending her gasping.

She shook her head. I pushed the head of my cock against her swollen pussy lips, the promise of ecstasy only a few words away.

"You know what you have to say."

"Bastard," she hissed.

Reaching round the front of her again, I pulled the fabric further away from her, my fingers circling her clit and she cried out. I pushed in a little further, gently tugging and rubbing at her clit as she rolled her head backwards. Then I took my hand and my cock away and turned her to face me.

"You know what I need, Charlie."

Her eyes were intense, her lips parted, her breathing erratic.

"You want me to fuck you, sweetheart?" I asked, watching her eyes drop to my cock, her tongue dragging across her bottom lip.

"Yes."

"Yes, what?"

She looked at me, want and need burning deep in her eyes, her pupils dilated and her breath ragged.

"Fuck me, *Boss*," she breathed.

So fucking stubborn, but so fucking hot. I spun her back round to face the wall, heat throbbing in my veins.

"Hands against the wall," I ordered.

Charlie propped her palms against the wall and I pulled her arse towards me, kicking her legs apart. For a moment I stood admiring her, waiting for me, hands and legs spread out, her racing whip sitting on the bench beside her. My cock stiffened painfully. I picked the whip up and trailed it down her back. She tensed and glanced over her shoulder.

"Eyes on the wall, sweetheart."

I slid the whip over her arse, watching as her pert cheeks tensed. I ran it over the curve of her flesh, dragging it down her thigh. Then thwack. The sound of the whip hitting the skin on her leg and her strangled cry was delicious. I slapped her again, her cry vibrating through my body, red marks forming on her skin. And then again, moving up to her arse cheek. And again, increasing the size of the red welt on her backside. The cries from her mouth deepened, arousal hiding the pain of the whip on her skin. I stroked over the redness, heat rising from her skin, and she moaned under my touch.

Dipping my hand to her wet slit, my fingers were soaked at the lightest touch, her pussy lips swollen. I plunged a finger inside of her, bringing the whip down on her arse again at the same time.

"Cian!" she cried out, her pussy gripping me.

I whacked the whip off her again, rubbing her clit at the same time, and she screamed out, pushing herself onto my fingers. I hit her again, her head snapping back as she screamed my name. My cock pulsed and my balls tensed. Fuck, I loved this.

"Cian! Please," she whimpered.

"Say it," I growled at her, delivering another slap of the whip to her arse.

"Boss, fuck me," her voice was strangled with need.

Fuck. I pulled away from her, taking my cock in my hand, and slid it against her. Even in

221

her tight pussy it slid in easily. She was soaked. I listened to her breathing, the erratic rasps and little whimpers. Then, wrapping one hand into her hair and pulling her head back, I moved against her. I meant to savour her, build it slowly, but she just felt so good that soon I was pounding into her roughly, enjoying the cries I ripped from her lips.

I pulled harder on her hair and she cried out again as I pumped my hips into her, fucking her as hard as I could, dominating and punishing, until I felt her legs quiver and her cries turn to strangled gasps. Such. Beautiful. Sounds. Releasing her hair I pushed her further into the wall, her head turned sideways against the brick, thrusting my cock into her hard and fast until my own cry joined hers, my balls tensing as I filled her full of hot cum in a few more thrusts. I stayed there as my erection softened, listening to Charlie's breathing as her orgasm faded away, my hands on either side of her as I pinned her against the cold wall of the racecourse changing rooms.

Gently withdrawing from her, I turned her round. Her cheeks were flushed red and her eyes still held that dazed look. I pushed a lock of blonde hair from her face as her blue eyes sparkled back at me. I tipped her face up to mine, a quiet, subtle tension hanging between us. Everything about her was perfect; the delicate features of her face, the baby blue eyes, high cheek bones, perfect lips. She smiled at me, the dimples in her cheeks appearing; something I really didn't see enough of.

I dipped my head, taking her lips with mine, kissing her gently at first until she groaned into my mouth and then I pulled her head into mine, my tongue thrusting into her.

"Better get dressed," I muttered against her lips a few seconds later, reluctant to see her beautiful body covered up, "there's people out there who want to meet you."

Charlie joined me again a short time later, making her way through the lounge dressed in the baby blue blouse that matched her eyes and the crisp black trousers. The race goers dwarfed her as she pushed gently through the crowds towards me and Riley. I smiled warmly at her as she approached and got a show of her dimples in return.

"Can I get you a drink?" I asked, my hand settling just on the top of her arse.

She moved away from me instinctively, stifling a wince, and I could feel the heat of her red arse cheeks through her trousers.

"An iced water, please?"

When I came back with her drink, the corporate boys had already moved in on her, Matthew Keegan grasping her hand lightly as he towered over the top of her. The man was taller than me, leaner and dressed in a petrol blue three-piece suit. My eyes scanned over him as I approached, noticing the bold navy over-check on the fabric, the gold tie pin that secured the gaudy burnt orange tie, the matching handkerchief and polished tan shoes, the skin of his ankles exposed by the lack of socks.

Keegan held a champagne glass out to Charlie and I watched as she shook her head at him, yet he still pushed the long-stemmed flute of liquid towards her, smiling like a regular Prince Charming. It took every effort to hide my annoyance as I joined them with Charlie's water.

"I see you've met my jockey," I said, straining to keep the possessiveness from my voice as I watched each of the men with their eyes roving all over her.

"Yes. I've thanked her. She won me a lot of money today," he said dismissively to me before turning back to Charlie, "I would love to thank you more personally. I don't suppose you would like to have dinner with me?"

My stomach clenched and my jaw tightened.

"You're right," she answered him, "I wouldn't like to have dinner with you."

I almost laughed out loud at the look of shock on Keegan's face. Hazarding a guess, I would say the arrogant prick hadn't been dismissed like that in a long time. I could tell he wanted her, and I smirked inwardly, knowing that a few minutes ago it was me who had punished her tight cunt; my name on her perfect lips as I'd fucked her against the wall, and my cum that now leaked out of her.

"It was nice to meet you. Now I've got horses to see to," she said before walking off.

"I know *I'd* like to give her a good seeing to," I heard a voice from beside Keegan.

I reeled, grabbing a fistful of expensive suit jacket, pushing my nose against the shocked punter.

"Whoa, man!" the corporate dickhead held his hands up at me in surrender as a hushed silence fell upon the lounge.

"Disrespect my... jockey again and I'll happily fashion you some cufflinks out of your own balls," I growled at him.

A hand touched my shoulder and I released my grip from the man, my eyes burning into him as I set him back on his feet. I flattened the collar of his suit back down, my hand clasping his tie and wiggling it back into position, tightening it sharply as his eyes widened, staring at me fearfully. Then I patted his chest and turned away.

"Cian, what was that?" Riley hissed at me as I left the lounge.

I shrugged. I knew what it was: rage, possession, jealousy.

"It was nothing."

"Didn't look like nothing to me. You need to get your head in the game," Riley cautioned as a friend this time and not one of my men, "Charlie will be your ruin. You need to let her go before it becomes more than it should."

I was beginning to think it was too late for that. Every time I looked at her, I wanted more of her; more than just her body. I wanted her loyalty, her exclusivity, all of her.

Chapter Twenty Four

∝ Charlie ∞

"You look amazing," Cian said in a low voice from his seat beside me in the back of the black 4x4.

I smiled weakly, feeling slightly self-conscious in the thin satin material of the dress I wore. A jeans and top kind of girl, this dress felt uncomfortable, and I pulled the ruby red material over my leg, covering the vast amount of skin it exposed.

"Don't know why I couldn't have just worn a suit like the rest of you," I grumbled.

Cian rolled his eyes in mock annoyance.

"I need Lebedev to spill it all to you, sweetheart. And for that, he needs temptation."

Cian smelled incredible. He wore an aftershave I hadn't noticed on him before; the woody, musky scent mixing with the fresh smell of soap and clean clothes, sending a tingle running through me. He'd actually styled his hair today, and it was gently pushed over the side of his head and his face was freshly shaved. It took some amount of self-discipline to refrain from running my fingers over that smooth jaw line and across his lips.

"Do we have a plan?" I asked.

"We find Lebedev, you make him talk and we all listen," Cian grunted, taking out his phone and checking the display, "then we get out of there."

"Not much of a plan, huh?"

The Irishman took a box out of his pocket, gently eased the lid off, and held it out to me. Inside sat three small objects; a tiny circular disc that looked a like a watch battery, something that looked like an SD card and a black rectangular object.

"We're going to fix his watch for him while we're there, too?" I asked, raising an eyebrow at him.

"You're going to swap out the memory card of his phone for this one and then drop the bug and the tracker in his pocket. That way, we can listen and track him."

"And I'm going to do that how?"

"Distract him. That's what I bought you that dress for."

"For fuck's sake," I swore, partly under my breath, "next time leave me to deal with the horses and you lot go off to do your mafia shit without me."

Jonjo snorted back a laugh from the front passenger seat and Mad-Dog eyed me disdainfully from the rear-view mirror. I stared back at him, holding his glare until he had to look away to watch the road in front of him.

I watched out of the window as the Durham countryside slipped by. The Jockey Club Ball was held at the hotel beside Newcastle racecourse and as we pulled up outside, I felt like I'd never left the place all day. The three of us got out, leaving Mad-Dog behind the wheel, and I was thankful for not having him glare at me all night. It only made me want to punch him in the mouth. I pulled the dress around me, trying to cover up my left leg exposed by the huge thigh high split. My nipples hardened against the cold, pushing against the thin glossy fabric, the intricate pattern of lace, rhinestones and tiny beads that wound from the very top of my thigh and over my chest, obscuring my reaction to the night air.

Cian rested a hand on the small of my back, his palm warm against my skin where the dress dropped away. He couldn't have picked a more revealing dress for me to wear, the red stark against his black dinner suit and bow tie, making him look like the grim reaper in his party clothes. He guided me forwards as I teetered on high heels beside him.

The hotel was buzzing, a mix of conversation and atmosphere and there were several people I recognised, many of which looked at me with hideous gawping faces when they eventually recognised me. I was so far out of my comfort zone, I wanted to beat Cian with the next injury-inducing object I could find. Instead, the cool gentle bubbles of the champagne I plucked from a passing tray calmed my thoughts, my potential to maim diluted by the sweet tasting alcohol.

I scanned the room, trying to make out my target against the sea of black suits. Jonjo had wandered off in another direction and I watched him head towards a group of people, whose faces I recognised from underneath riding hats and colourful racing silks. I would have joined them, but every so often Cian would nudge me gently as he introduced me to some rich politician or other businessman and I was forced to smile and practice being pleasant to people.

I pulled another glass from a tray, my mind drifting into defensive day-dreaming as I blocked out the pull of the hungry eyes that raked over my over-exposed body. Bored, I threw back the last of my champagne and signalled to Cian that I was going to the bar. I pushed in beside Jonjo, elbowing him playfully to move out of my way.

"You scrub up well, Porter," he grinned as I fired him a look.

"Don't. Just don't," I complained, waving at the barman who duly rushed over to take my order, "God, this is awful"

"You've never been to one of these events before?"

I shook my head. "Not my sort of thing. Give me a night club and a shiny disco ball any day. All these how-do-you-dos and shaking of sweaty hands. You lot can keep it."

Jonjo laughed heartily, and I leaned against the bar, a vodka and coke in my hand and watched Cian as he talked and laughed and engaged the wealthy, over-fed businessmen.

"He seems in his element," I commented, unable to keep the surprise from my voice.

"There's more to being a mafia boss than killing people, you know?" Jonjo chuckled.

A tall, grey-haired man caught my eye, moving confidently through the crowd and smiling warmly as he greeted people, shaking their hands enthusiastically. I raked in my purse, then sighing, slid my glass from the bar and teetered over towards him, holding my dress up slightly so I didn't trip on the hem. Just as I got almost alongside him, I stumbled, lurching forwards into him.

Resting my hand against his chest, I steadied myself, tucking the battery sized listening device into his jacket pocket.

"I'm so sorry," I gasped, mopping the drink up that I'd spilt on him and immediately wishing I'd not tried to make such a sacrifice of it.

"Ah, Miss Porter," he cooed, his accent sharp under the softness of his words.

Lebedev's eyes roamed over me, coming to rest at the top of my leg, the red material dropping away either side.

"You really are delightful."

I scowled, and the man put his palms in the air in surrender.

"I know, I know," he continued, "unwanted attention. Why don't I replace drink you just threw at me?"

"Thank you," I replied stiffly, "I'd hate to waste it on you," I said, unable to soften the hatred bubbling underneath the surface.

Lebedev chuckled, unphased, and waved me back towards the bar. With another glass in my hand, I turned to face him. Lebedev raised his glass of clear liquid towards me.

"To success," the Russian said, his accent rumbling over the words.

"Hmmm," I answered, taking a sip of my drink, "there'll be little of that since you sent me ringers to train."

The grey-haired man's eyes widened, the initial shock on his face hardening to stone.

"Yes, I noticed," I continued, "where'd you get them from? Not one of them is legit."

"I have no idea what you're talking about."

"Oh, you do. That big bay would have killed me."

I rolled my dress up, showing the huge spreading bruise on my right thigh, the purple tinge morphing into greens and yellows as it aged.

"Luckily I'm quick. What's the game play here, Lebedev? Get me out of the racing scene? Bet against me? What exactly?"

His jaw tightened and a muscle in the side of his cheek jumped.

"If you'll excuse me. I've got people to see."

Lebedev pulled his mobile out of his breast pocket and checked the display as he turned to leave me at the bar.

"I haven't finished," I growled, reaching for his hand to turn him back to me.

Losing his grip on the phone, it tumbled from his hand, hitting the hard floor, the back falling off as it bounced under my dress. My heart jumped. I turned away from him reaching into my purse and thumbing the little box open. Stooping down I grabbed the phone at my feet, sliding out the SD card and replacing it with the one from the box. Then I turned it in my palm and handed it back to him.

"If you ever try to sabotage me again..."

"You'll do what exactly?" he answered, his face glowing red with anger, "you're woman. You're novelty and men just want to think about putting their cocks in you."

"Is that why you sent your men after me?"

Lebedev had his hand on his phone now, the tension in his knuckles making them glow almost white.

"Are you OK here, Miss Porter?" a male voice behind distracted me.

My grip on the phone softened and Lebedev slid it from my grasp, staring at me intensely before turning and moving away through the crowd.

I turned towards the voice that had eased the tension between me and the Russian and looked up into the familiar face of the man Cian had introduced me to earlier today. His dark hair was swept back over his head and dark eyes looked down at me, a radiating smile across his face.

"Fine thanks," I eventually answered.

"I'm pleased to have run into you here," he continued, his voice deep and velvety.

I hadn't remembered that. And I hadn't noticed earlier just how handsome he really was.

"Are you?"

I took a sip from the glass Lebedev had bought me, regretting my inability to keep my anger in check and, inevitably, my failure to get any information out of the Russian. The man next to me had asked me a question again, but I wasn't paying attention. I looked up at him blankly.

"I'm sorry," I confessed, "I didn't catch that."

"Are you happy with O'Sullivan?"

I looked at the banker quizzically.

"In his employment, I mean," he said again, eyeing me with interest.

I nodded.

"I have a lot of connections in the business. If you fancied a change of team, I can find you a better contract."

"You mean act as my agent?"

"Yes, something like that."

"And what would your fee be?" I searched his dark eyes.

"Well, that we could discuss another time. Over dinner, perhaps?"

"You seem to like food, don't you? Or is it something else you're really after?"

I watched his expression change, the tug of a smile at the side of his lips, the arrogance I had noticed in him earlier at the race track return.

"Excuse me. I have to go powder my nose, or go to the little girl's room or something like that," I answered, turning my back on him and walking away, hoping that I didn't add to the drama of the last few moments by catching my ridiculous heels in this ridiculous dress and landing on my face.

Cian stood a little way off watching me and I moved towards him pointedly. Despite the suave and arrogance of Keegan with his dark hair, dark eyes and sophisticatedly handsome features, there was nothing quite like the Irishman. The scar on his eyebrow, the point to his chin, the softness of his features that hid the shrewd gangster underneath. His eyes never left me as I approached, his lips pushed together, exaggerating the pout as he chewed on a cocktail stick, leaning against the wall and swilling a glass of gold-liquid nonchalantly.

Chapter Twenty Five

ജ Cian ര

I'd watched nearly every man in that room look at her tonight as she moved past them. Charlie was stunning in her breaches and sweaty racing silks with her hair stuck to her head, and everyone could see it. But tonight, dressed in the ruby red silk dress I had bought her, she was a goddess. Her hair fell in soft curls around her shoulders and down her back, and her minimalist make-up enhanced her natural beauty.

She'd smiled graciously, the dimples in either cheek making her look gentle and womanly, yet I could see the insecurity as she pulled at the slit in the skirt, hiding the bare skin of her leg.

Her altercation with Lebedev had not been what I had planned, but she'd managed to slip the bugs on him and I had confirmation we had at least got ears on him now. But the attention she received from the rich banker, Keegan, had built a knot of anger in my chest. Seeing them together, how she had tilted her head back to look up at him; it had sent my mind wild with jealousy. It had tested my resolve to the limit, and it had taken everything I had to stand and watch them instead of walking across and putting my fist straight in the middle of his face.

Yet now she walked towards me, the creaminess of her toned leg peeking out of the red of her dress, the silk clutching her skin, pulling in at the nip of her waist and bulging over those beautifully pert tits. I sipped my whisky, trying to get hold of the errant thoughts rushing through my brain and into my groin.

I slipped my hand around her waist, my fingers brushing the bare skin of her back and pulled her closer towards me, casting a quick glance over her shoulder and meeting the faraway stare of Keegan who continued to watch her, watch us. And I liked that. I liked this: possessing her.

Charlie looked up and smiled at me, the dimples coming to life as I studied her face, the ballroom of people and Keegan blurring away in the distance. She smelled delicious; jasmine mixed with a gentle floral scent, giving her usual badass demeanour a gentle vulnerability.

"I'm pleased I made you wear that dress," I spoke into her ear.

"Why is that? Didn't do me any favours with Lebedev."

"No, but it's doing lots for me."

"Hmmm. It really doesn't leave much to the imagination."

"I know," I whispered into her ear.

"Then you ought to know I'm not wearing anything underneath it."

"I know that too. I enjoyed the sight of you as you got out into the cold."

Charlie smiled, and, cocking her head to one side, she pulled my hand from around her back and pushed it towards the slit in the material and I let her trail my fingers up the smoothness of her leg and underneath. There was no familiar feeling of fabric between her legs but the warm, silky feeling of her pussy, naked and accessible.

Heat hit my stomach immediately, wetness pooling on my finger ends. My gaze dipped to her chest, the swell of her breasts, bare under the fabric as my fingers danced between her folds and my cock strained against my trousers.

I dropped my hand, feeling for her slim fingers before pulling her down a corridor away from the revellers in the room behind us. Away from prying eyes, I spun her around, grabbing her head between my hands and launching an assault on her mouth, forcing my tongue roughly between her lips. Charlie's hands peeled my shirt from my trousers, her fingertips stroking my skin, teasing as they swiped back and forwards across my stomach, tickling the tiny trail of hair down to my groin.

I pushed her back against the fire exit door, leaning into her as the bar behind her clunked and depressed and the door sprang open and we stepped into the darkness of the hotel car park. As the fire doors closed behind us, leaving us in the cold air, I cupped my hands under her arse and lifted her onto the bonnet of the car behind us.

Charlie gasped at the cold metal and I pushed her legs open, settling in between them as I buried my face in her chest, my tongue trailing over the top of her tits. She moaned, leaning backwards and my fingers found her wetness, sliding easily in, straight into that relentless rhythm I knew she needed.

She inhaled suddenly.

"Cian," she gasped.

I sucked on the side of her neck as I rammed another finger into her, enjoying the way her pussy clenched around me the minute any part of me was in her.

"Cian!" she said more urgently this time.

The familiar cold feeling of metal pressed against the back of my head.

"*Dobry vecher*, Mr O'Sullivan," the low voice behind me said, "come with us please."

Covering Charlie up, I slid her off the bonnet of the car, squeezing her hand as I turned away from her, staring down the barrel of the gun to the man at the other end.

"Come with us please," the man repeated and I glanced around, counting three men standing behind him, no doubt well-armed.

I pushed my hands up slightly and one of the men stepped forward, opening my suit jacket and patting me down and then nodding at the man with the gun. Then I was spun and pushed against

238

the car onto my stomach as my hands were pulled roughly behind my back and pinned in place with plastic ties.

Charlie watched me with eyes wide, her teeth worrying her bottom lip, her gaze darting from me to the men and me again. I was tugged upright before being pulled away.

"Bring the girl too," I heard the deep voice of the armed Russian behind me say.

"Don't fucking touch me," the bite of Charlie's voice rang through the air.

"Leave her. She's just an escort, a hooker."

"I'll give you a fucking right hook, you prick," she called after me, the men behind me breaking out in low chuckles as I rolled my eyes. Fucking liability.

After what seemed like hours sitting on the hard floor in the back of a van, bouncing around as the vehicle was flung round corners and over bumps, we came to a stop, trepidation niggling in my stomach. The door creaked open and rough hands bundled us out. I scoured our surroundings for some clue to where we were. The van had been backed into a loading bay, the place barren except for a few parked cars treating it like an underground carpark.

We were nudged from the back of the van and along a corridor flanked by a load of armed Russians, pushing and pulling us, and I heard Charlie behind me stumble in the heels she wore.

"For fuck's sake, you dick head. Have you ever been kidnapped wearing these things?" she

239

complained, "leave off the pushing. I don't need any encouragement."

The man let out a low laugh and as I glanced over my shoulder, I noticed he'd taken his hands off her. All the men that had taken us had raked their eyes over Charlie, hungry eyes and exchanged glances. She looked nothing short of incredible. And I was really regretting making her wear that dress. She was over exposed in here and vulnerable for it. I was trying to stay detached from her, rational, but each time someone laid a hand on her or looked at her, I wanted to rip their eyes out.

Pushed through a room on our left, I scanned it quickly. It was some sort of storage area. Boxes were stacked on metal shelves on either side in a haphazard, uncared for fashion, and a table and chairs sat in the middle of the room. We were deposited around the other side and pushed into the seats; the man lingering next to Charlie as he looked down at her cleavage.

"It's a good job I'm tied up or I'd poke your fucking eyes out right now," Charlie spat, looking at him defiantly.

I groaned inwardly and considered whether I should ask them to gag her. We had a better chance of us both getting out unscathed if I did. The broad Russian grinned, winked at her, and then left the room.

"Where the fuck are we, Cian?" she asked as the door closed.

"In a whole load of shit, sweetheart, and you're not making it any easier with your smart-ass mouth."

I sighed and tested how tight the cable ties on my wrists were, careful not to make them any tighter.

"I need you to listen to me right now, Charlie," I turned to her, my voice low, "no matter what happens next, I need you to not say a word. Do you understand? Not one word. Let me do the talking. Listen, but don't speak."

"Why? Because women should be seen and not heard in your world?"

"Because I want to get the both of us out of here alive and in one piece, and you'll likely get one of us killed, or worse."

Charlie pushed her lips together, the sulk in her eyes clear.

"Call me a hooker again and I'll kick you in the balls," she said, eventually breaking the few minutes of petulant silence she sat in.

"Noted."

We sat in silence again, waiting. Eventually, the door pushed open and a tall man walked in. His dark hair was shaved so short his head was coated in dark stubble and a five-o'clock shadow covered his jaw.

"Cian," he greeted me.

"Lukyan."

He looked across at Charlie and she held his gaze before his eyes trailed down her body and the exposed leg she had crossed over the other. Charlie never took her eyes off him, watching him intently.

"And this is?" he tipped his head in her direction.

"She's irrelevant."

Charlie flashed me a warning glare, and I knew her well enough now to know the threat wasn't empty.

The legs of a chair scraped across the floor, the sudden sound making Charlie jump slightly and Lukyan's attention settled back on her.

"I got your message," he continued in his heavy Russian accent, "that wasn't very friendly. But what I really want to know is why you sent me a random dead body. Do you know how much attention that could have drawn to my door, Irishman?"

"Thought you might like your boy back?"

The Russian smiled. But it wasn't one of warmth or jest.

"That was not one of mine," he said, his tone now colder.

"That's convenient," Charlie's voice piped up from beside me.

I took a deep, slow breath and willed her to shut the fuck up.

"Is your woman talking to me?"

Lukyan looked back towards her, studying her. I opened my mouth, but Charlie got there first.

"His woman? What is it with all you gangsters, huh? You think you own everything that has a heartbeat?"

I saw the anger cross his eyes as he sprang to his feet. Leaning back in the chair, I pushed my weight backwards and kicked at the table, sending it slamming into his thigh. He exhaled and bent over and then changed direction, smashing his fist into my mouth and I felt the pop of skin and a warm trickle run from my lip. Charlie startled beside me, staring at me in shock.

"Yes, that's my fucking woman," I growled at him, "so keep your fucking hands off her."

He raised his eyebrows, "fair enough," he said, shrugging, then sat back down opposite us.

I kept my eyes trained on him, not wanting to show the anger I had for Charlie right now, and I pushed the throb in my lip from my mind.

"Someone targeted one of my businesses," I continued, "these were soldiers acting on orders, not on their own. They mess with my property, I find them, I kill them. Simple as that and then I deal with whoever sent them."

"And you think I sent them?"

"They had soviet tags, so yeah, I think you sent them. And we know Lebedev is involved with them, so it all points back to you."

"Lebedev," Lukyan spat on the floor next to him, "Lebedev is Russian by breeding only. That *shestiorka* is not one of us."

"Don't fuck around with me, Lukyan. If you sent them, then it's an act of war. We all but wiped you out last time."

Lukyan tensed, anger at the memories flashed across his face and then subsided, replaced with a sneer.

"I could kill you now, the head of the biggest crime firm in the UK. Then it only leaves one of you left to crush, doesn't it?"

I clenched my teeth, keeping my reaction under control.

"We didn't kill your family, Cian, even though you'd love to pin the blame on us," he continued, "if that was what we were going to do, *I* wouldn't have left any of you alive."

I searched his eyes, looking for anything which would give away that he was responsible for the death of my father and Torin and Fiadh. I wanted it to be the Volkovs. I wanted to drive the Russians away one last time, but I couldn't be sure.

Lukyan stood up, pushing the chair out noisily behind him.

"But I will send you home with our message, Irishman," he grinned wickedly at me, then glanced across to Charlie, who had managed to stay quiet for the last few minutes. Then he walked out, leaving us alone, surrounded by shelves of boxes.

Chapter Twenty Six

☙ Charlie ❧

We sat in silence briefly and I let my shoulders relax a little, flicking out the blade of the pocket knife I'd swiped from the tall Russian's trouser pocket. Carefully, I angled it towards the ties and gently tilted my wrists until I could feel the bite of the blade against the plastic.

"Any idea where we are?" I asked Cian.

He shook his head.

"So what, are we just going to wait around for them to come back?" I said, looking around the room for escape points, "I don't like the sound of this *message*."

Cian seemed to be bracing himself, focusing on something, maybe on the threat that loomed over him.

"I have no idea what they have in mind," he answered eventually, "but knowing the Russians, it usually involves sending you home missing a piece."

"Even better reason to get out of here then," I said, getting to my feet and moving to the door.

I carefully twisted the handle left and right and the door sprang open. Cian sat staring at me, disbelief pasted across his face.

"How the fuck have you got out of those?" he hissed.

I smiled, dangling the knife in front of me by the handle.

"I didn't just go to youth court for punching someone," I said shrugging, "I was a pretty good pick-pocket too."

"And why have you not cut these ties before now?" he spat, beckoning to his hands with his head.

I sidled over to him.

"Didn't think I was *'relevant'* enough for you. So I thought I'd wait to see how you were going to get us out of here. Seeing as it looks like your plan involves losing a digit or a limb or something equally horrible, I figured we'd better turn to plan B: escape."

Cian rolled his eyes and I stepped around behind him, pushing the blade between his wrists and pulling until the plastic popped falling into two pieces. He stood up, rubbing at the skin where the ties had cut into his flesh. Reaching down, I undid the straps of my heeled sandals, kicking them off my feet.

"What are you doing now?" he hissed at me.

I rolled my eyes at him, "I can hardly make the great escape in these things, can I?"

He shook his head and grasped my hand, pulling me behind him as we crept forward towards the door. Turning the handle carefully, easing it open just a crack, Cian peered out into the dimly lit corridor beyond.

We skulked out quietly, both of us listening intently for the subtle sounds of anyone approaching. My heart beat harder and faster in my chest and I pushed my hand over the top of it in case it was as loud as it felt in my ears. Silently, we moved forward, my feet cold as my bare skin dragged across the floor tiles, occasionally catching on the roughness where some parts had worn away from years of use.

Eventually, after the corridor bent round to the left, and we crept precariously past closed doors, fearing someone would come rushing out at us, we reached the end where a single metal door barred the way. Slowly, Cian pushed the bar down, listening for any loud noise it might make. But the door opened with only the tiniest clink as the bolts inside slid back.

A rush of cold air hit us, making the hairs on my arms stand up and my nipples contract to peaks in an instant. I shivered.

"Get low," Cian whispered, and I ducked down, following close behind him as we ran across the underground garage in crouch-like poses towards the cars that were parked on the other side.

Cautiously, Cian tried the door of the big 4x4; the panel didn't budge. He tried again at the car next to it, but that was locked up tight as well.

"Who'd have thought the bastards were so security conscious," he muttered to himself.

I moved around to the last car. It was older and covered in scratches and dents. Moving to the driver's side, I wiggled the handle and got the same response as Cian. I flipped out the blade of the flick-knife and slid it between the window and the panel. Giving it a wiggle until I felt the mechanism below, I rocked the knife back and forth, feeling for the pop of the lock springing open.

"Get in," I whispered to Cian, pulling the driver side door open.

Cian climbed in and pulled the lock up on the passenger side, allowing me to slide in beside him. I watched him pull the visor down, swipe a hand across it and then check the glove box for keys. Frustrated, he hit the steering wheel in front of him.

Resisting the urge to roll my eyes again, I reached across, nudging his leg out of the way and felt for a dip in the material in the foot well, pulling it away and grabbing a handful of the wires underneath. When my fingers found the thin, rubber-encased strands, I ripped them towards me, slicing off the casing with the knife and pushing the exposed wires together. The car coughed and spluttered into life.

"Yeah, I've pinched a car or two. Didn't get caught for that though," I smiled at him as he gawped at me in disbelief.

Just at that moment, the door sprang open and men poured into the garage. With a roar of the engine, Cian forced the car forward, driving at the shutter in front of us. The vehicle caught the sensor as it whizzed past and the garage door started to rise. Not waiting for it to go up the full height, Cian drove straight at it and I ducked instinctively as metal clattered and screeched off the top of the car.

Then we were out into the night, Cian forcing the old car faster and faster along a deserted road. Darkness flanked us as we whizzed past redundant street lights, where there had been once an attempt to light the pot-hole plagued road. The car hit a deep rut, sending us lurching sideways, and Cian pulled the steering wheel hard in the other direction. I glanced in the mirrors, seeing small spots of headlights behind us. Cian had seen them too. Muscles in his jaw bulged, his teeth clamped tight together and his hands working hard, swapping gears and steering around holes. I fumbled for the seatbelt, securing it round me with a reassuring click as it locked in place.

"Any idea where we are?" I asked Cian.

"Not yet. Seems to be an old industrial park. Concentrate on any sign or indication of a way out onto a normal road," he ordered and for once I didn't resist him, but tried to focus on making out the black shapes that loomed up on us quickly.

"Fuck!" Cian cursed loudly, "we've already been this way."

He revved the car's engine, pulling across the junction the opposite way now, the spots of light in the wing mirrors growing bigger. I scoured the blackness, looking for something, anything, and then I saw it. Tiny flecks of light travelling fast in the distance.

"There," I pointed through the windscreen, "there's a road up there. Can you see the lights in the distance?"

Cian nodded, "just need a way out of this maze first."

The car sped down the road, the headlights illuminating the rough surface, a mix of concrete and tarmac that had been patch-repaired for years, now sat crumbling. The wheels skidded on some debris and I clutched the handle of the door tightly, watching the concentration on Cian's face as he controlled the car from sliding into a disintegrating brick wall to the left of us. We missed it by a fraction, but as he straightened up, a huge hole appeared in front of us. The car bounced over, metal grunting under us. The headlights behind were getting closer and then in front, in the distance, another set of lights shone.

"Shit!" Cian hit the steering wheel as the car spluttered to a stop.

I looked around wildly, cars approaching us from either end. Cian threw his door open, leaving the engine vibrating and ran around to me.

"Quick. Out," he commanded, yanking the passenger side door open and pulling at my arm.

I swung my legs out and Cian tugged me across the road and we scrambled over the partially dilapidated wall and into the darkness. We ran on through trees and bushes and I closed my eyes each time my feet found something hard and sharp, the fear in my chest numbing the pain in my feet.

My face stung where I'd run into a sharp branch, catching me just under my eye as we pushed through bushes and trees that had thickened out. It was darker still amongst the trees, the only light from the silvery glow of the moon casting deep shadows around us. Pain throbbed in my feet, and despite our exertions I was cold. I stifled a cry when my foot caught on something sharp.

"Cian, I need a second, please," I was close to begging as searing pain coursed through my foot with each step, making me limp.

He slowed down and turned to look at me, his eyebrows knitting together as I hobbled behind him. Tugging gently on my arm, he pulled me into a pool of light that had breached the unruly canopy of naked tree branches. Guiding me, I sat on the decaying trunk of a fallen tree as Cian dropped to his knees.

"My feet hurt," I tried not to whine, but as I took the weight off them, the pain escalated.

Cian pulled one closer, gently feeling across the sole as I winced and pulled away at the combined sensation of pain and the tickle of his fingers on my foot.

"I can't see anything in your foot, but they're pretty bashed up."

The cold had me in a tight grasp as my breathing slowed and body shivered so hard I felt like I was having convulsions. Cian took off his suit jacket and wrapped it round me.

"Can you keep going?" he asked, concern in his voice, "we can't be far away from that main road now."

I nodded, hearing the dull roar of traffic in the distance. Putting his arm round my waist, he helped me to my feet, taking my weight as we moved forward, more slowly now, my feet stinging painfully with each step.

Eventually, the trees and bushes ended and I felt the coolness of smooth tarmac under my feet. We padded along the unlit road in the dark, Cian frequently checking our surroundings as we edged closer to the main road.

"What's the plan when we get there?" I asked.

"Flag someone down, convince them we're not lunatics and get them to give us a ride to the nearest shop or petrol station or something," Cian shrugged unconvincingly.

The glow from car headlights cast our own shadows in front of us and dread awakened in me as Cian looked around.

"Quick, over there," he pulled me towards what I could make out in the dark as wall. I winced at each painful urgent step, tiredness consuming me, the headlights getting brighter and brighter until we were washed in the bright glow.

"Shit!" Cian cursed from beside me.

We stilled and turned, facing into the flood of light. A car door creaked, and a man got out. The dull thud of a heavy booted foot hit the tarmac as the engine purred in front of us.

Chapter Twenty Seven

ജ Cian ര

"Boss, get in," I heard the familiar voice as the sweet feeling of relief swept over me.

I scooped Charlie up into my arms, taking her off her shredded feet and carried her to the car. She wrapped her arms around my neck and lay her head on my shoulder, shivering against me. Riley opened the door, and I slid her in gently.

"Crank that heating up, boys," I instructed, climbing in the other side and feeling the cold for the first time myself.

The blowers came to life, and the car cruised away down the unlit road.

"How the fuck did you find us?" I asked after a few minutes when we'd made our way safely to a bigger busier road, the big car travelling along smoothly.

"That tracker," Riley replied, continuing after I stared quizzically at him.

"What tracker?"

Charlie chuckled beside me and rummaged in her cleavage before pulling out the tiny little rectangular black box.

"I never got this one on Lebedev."

She was incredible for all sorts of reasons. I should be mad she failed to follow my orders, multiple times tonight, but had it not been for her inability to do as she was told, we wouldn't have made it out of there in one piece.

"It was Jonjo who'd noticed one of those fucking Russians sneaking about at the Ball," Riley commented from the front passenger seat, "Took us a little time to get a hack on the security cameras to find you, but we managed to get a grainy image of a couple of people being thrown into the back of a van."

"Where are we anyway?" I asked, not recognising any of the landscape.

"Just outside Doncaster," Riley answered.

"Since when was Doncaster Russian ground?"

Riley shrugged, "no idea boss but seems they're inching in on other people's patches."

I dragged my gaze from out of the window as we hit the motorway; the car speeding up with ease, and looked across at Charlie. She smiled at me faintly with tiredness in her eyes as the shivers still rocked her body. Pulling her towards me, I wrapped an arm around her. She snuggled against my chest, the gentle smell of coconut in her hair teasing my senses.

"What do you want to do now, boss?" Mad-Dog asked from the driver's seat.

I touched the cut on my lip, the throb from the break in the skin having dulled a little.

"Drop an anonymous tip to the Filth about that warehouse. The Russians are definitely running something from there. I want that supply chain cut off."

"Volkov just kidnapped the pair of you and gave you a good whack and all you want to do is shop him to the Police?" Riley complained in an exasperated tone.

"Shut the fuck up, Riley," I bit back, "this wasn't a question for a committee."

The two men stared straight ahead, Riley duly chastised as an uncomfortable silence descended on the car.

I spent the drive up north to Durham with my eyes loosely focussed on the gentle rise and fall of Charlie's chest, the rhythm soothing as she snuggled safely under my arm. I teased the hair carefully from her face, watching the lights from passing cars cast shadows over her as she lay against me, sleeping peacefully. For a moment I wondered what it would be like to have her in my arms every night, cuddled against me, content.

We eventually turned into the dark driveway, the dull golden light under the canopy of the stables the only thing welcoming us home. Charlie stirred against me, blinking quickly as she gazed at me with slight surprise. Tipping her chin up towards me, I searched her eyes, the light blue just shades of grey from the darkness of the car.

"We're home, sweetheart," the words fell softly from me.

Charlie edged out of the car behind me, pulling her dress across her legs, but as she took her first step onto the tarmac of the drive, she hissed loudly. Scooping her back into my arms, I carried her from the car and all the way through to the back of the house, greeted with the warmth of the fire burning in the hearth. She sank into the old armchair that I set her down on and I dropped to my knees at her feet, lifting each one up and carefully assessing the damage.

The soles of her feet were angry and red; cuts and grazes criss-crossing all over like a road map of outer London. Stones, grit and splinters of tree were wedged in some of the cuts and I pulled a couple of the easy ones out as Charlie's fingers gripped the arm rest sides.

"We need to get the rest of these out", I mumbled, my fingers moving gently over her feet as my eyes traced up her toned legs to the slit in her dress, knowing what was beyond.

She watched me intently, her head cocked to one side, wincing every so often as my fingers moved over a sore part.

The door to the lounge creaked open and Riley and Mad-Dog walked in. The drinks cabinet creaked to my side, followed by the familiar chink of a bottle against the lip of a glass. Riley handed the liquor to Charlie.

"Looks like this will help," he said to her, and I watched as she gave him a thankful smile before lifting the glass to her sculpted pink lips.

Handing one to me, he continued, "are the Russian's responsible for Fiadh? And Torin and the old boss then?" he quickly added.

"I don't know," I sighed, "my gut says no or else why kidnap us? Why not just kill us? They had enough opportunity. It's what I would have done."

"Is it?" Riley's tone was loaded as he looked at me pointedly. I fired a warning look back.

Charlie's gaze flittered between us, interest fixed on her face. I threw back the rest of my whisky.

"Drink up sweetheart, we need to get these feet cleaned up," I looked across at Riley as I stood, "we'll finish this conversation later."

Charlie stood carefully, her eyes drawing closed as she put her weight on her injured feet.

"I got you, sweetheart," I said softly as I picked her up carefully in my arms and carried her up the stairs.

After I'd bathed her feet in the bathroom, I set her down on my bed and took another look. The skin looked cleaner, the dirt and grit washed away, so the wounds now took on a pink hue. They were still in a bad way.

"I'll get some dressings for these."

"Kitchen. Far right cupboard," Charlie instructed.

The house was still alive, despite the early hour, and I could hear the drone of low, male voices from one room not far away. Digging in the cupboard above my head, I eventually found a first aid kit, plucking out some salve and dressings. Shutting the door, I suddenly came face to face with Riley.

"Fucks sake!" I cursed, refraining from punching him square in the nose in shock.

"Sorry, Cian. Drink?"

I shook my head, waving the bandages in my hand in gesture. Riley frowned, his brows knitting together, unease across his face.

"What?" I asked impatiently.

"Look, mate. What is going on between you and Charlie?"

"What do you think?" I answered abruptly, tension creeping across my jaw.

"You're losing your edge, Cian. The Russians…. you're letting them musclc in on us."

"We still don't know they had anything to do with the hits on my family, Riley. We start throwing muscle around the place, the shit's gonna hit the fan and it won't all miss us."

"But if we don't. If you don't, all the other firms are going to think you're weak, Cian. You need to be the boss we all need you to be, and she's a distraction. Get yourself one of the girls

259

from the club if that's what you need, but stay away from her. *She*'s making you a pussy."

My jaw tightened, and I wondered whether if I had punched Riley in the face when I first thought about it I would have avoided this conversation; avoided this feeling of confusion and uncertainty. Yet I knew he was right. Charlie was dampening my responses, distracting me with thoughts of what I might actually want from life, from her.

"Fine," I responded, petulantly, "burn the fucking warehouse down then. If they want a fucking turf war, then we'll have one."

"I'll give the order," Riley looked satisfied, and I felt a twinge of dread, something that had been eating away in my stomach since I was forced to return from New York.

Contradicted, deflated, I retreated to my room. And there she lay, peacefully asleep in my bed. Ash blonde hair spilled over my pillow, lazy curls softening her features as her perfectly sculpted lips pressed gently together. Charlie hadn't taken the dress off and it still clung to her slender body, the slit exposing the milky skin of her leg as the red silk dropped away from both sides.

I walked closer, cautious not to make a sound as I watched her sleep. Her chest moved in slow rhythm, her tits swelling beneath the tight, embroidered bodice and it took every inch of control not to run my fingers across the peaks of her nipples, prominent under the dress because of the chill in n the room.

Her eyelashes almost touched the top of her cheek bones, thick and long, and I wanted to touch her, to trace my finger along the smooth skin on her face and the hint of the dimples in her cheeks as she slept contentedly.

I left the cream and dressings on the bedside table and stripped out of my suit. Climbing in beside her, I pulled the covers over her, casting out the cold and covering my view. I turned towards her, my arm wrapping round her stomach as I moved her closer to me, inhaling the scent of her hair and the perfume still on her skin. The curly tendrils of blonde tickled my nose, the smooth silk of her dress lightly caressing my bare torso, and an alien feeling crept across me, a different sort of warmth igniting in my chest and cascading outwards like a web. I closed my eyes, dread fighting contentment, fear grappling with happiness. The stark emptiness I'd felt for so long I had lost count, yielding to these sharper feelings that were unknown to me until recently. And for a while I lay there, enjoying the tender warmth of her body in my arms; Charlie filling that void inside me and for once, in those moments before sleep took me, I felt whole.

Chapter Twenty Eight

❧ Charlie ☙

Fingers traced up my inner thigh, stroking, trailing, sending my skin into reactive convulsions, my body awakening as a familiar tingle grew between my legs. An involuntary exhale left my lips escaping across the pillow and the fingers caressing me stilled. The bed dipped as Cian rose above me, pulling me into the centre and nudging my legs apart, the red silk dress from last night's ball falling open and exposing me to him. His gaze intensified.

I looked up at him through sleepy eyes, his dick hard in his hand, the tip bulging and the veins swelling over the top of its thickness. I would have squeezed my legs together to dull the throb that had now formed if they weren't spread open by him. His eyes were dark, dangerous, and I lay watching him looking at me, devouring my body with his gaze alone, his fist pumping the hard shaft in his hand.

Then, suddenly, he grabbed the skirt of my dress and pulled, fabric screaming as he ripped it in two.

"Cian! The dress. That was expensive!"

"It was my dress. Mine to rip off you," his voice was low and deep as he stared at my nipples that had tightened to little pebbles, cold air assaulting my skin.

Leaning over the top of me, he pulled my hips towards him, the threat of being speared on his cock making my pussy pulse before he even touched me. He dipped his head to mine, taking my lips roughly, forcing his tongue inside my mouth as I yielded to him, to his control over my body.

My hands slid over his chest, feeling over the hard muscle of his pecs, the ripples of his stomach, my fingers lingering on the rough scars that interrupted the smoothness of his skin. Following the line of wiry hair to his groin, I reached out, my fingertips brushing the smooth head of his cock. Cian moaned into my mouth as I swirled my thumb gently over the tip, my hand sinking over the ridge that separated the head from the shaft, feeling the veins that bulged under my hand.

I rubbed the tip against my slit, Cian pushing against me slightly, then pulling back again, teasing me, making a flood of wetness pool between my legs. He pulled his lips from mine, grabbing my throat and positioning me so he could stare right down at me. Then with a sudden thrust, he pushed inside me in one swift movement, filling my pussy roughly as I gasped and closed my eyes at the sensation.

"Look at me, Charlie," he commanded, following his words with a sudden deep thrust, hitting my cervix with his cock.

"Cian!" I breathed out.

My hands wound round the back of him, my fingers kneading the flesh of his arse, my nails scratching into his skin as he pumped into me slowly, hard, forcefully. Pushing his hand between us, his thumb found my clit, swirling with each heavy thrust, his eyes trained on mine, building the orgasm within me as I rocked my hips to reach him.

Then as suddenly as he entered me, he pulled out, flipped me over so I was face down into the bed, pushing my legs open wide and pulling me back towards him. With one hand, he captured both my wrists, holding them behind my back as he positioned the bulging head of his cock at my entrance.

My pussy clenched, waiting for him, waiting for him to fill me, to pound into me, fuck me, but he stopped, and I felt the tickle of breath against my ear.

"You want me, sweetheart?"

"Yes!"

"Then what do you say?"

"Fuck me, Cian!"

Teeth nipped the back of my neck, making me inhale a sharp breath, heat erupting again in my pussy. His fingers dipped between my legs, sliding across my folds before nipping and rubbing my clit. I tried to throw my head back as I moaned, but I could barely move beneath him, pinned under his weight, waiting to be fucked by him, trying desperately not to beg him.

"That's not how you ask me to fuck you, sweetheart," Cian whispered in my ear. His fingers swirled my clit, the head of his shaft rubbing against me, dipping in ever so slightly.

"Cian, stop being an arsehole and fuck me," I growled into the pillow beneath my face.

He moved his hips, pushing all the way into me, and I screamed. Then he pulled out, slowly, unbearably.

"You know what I want, Charlie. I know what you want. Say it."

His cock entered me again, sending a shuddering sensation through me as it hit off my cervix before he took it away again. The swipe of his fingers through the wetness he was creating only making the throb in my pussy intensify. I whimpered.

"Say it," he growled.

"Please, *Boss,* fuck me,"

I compromised because I needed to feel him inside me. I needed him to put out the fire that raged within me. I needed him to fuck me; hard.

His shaft slammed into me, a scream erupting from me again and again and again with each hard thrust as Cian ground his hips against my arse. Pulling my right leg outwards he pushed his weight into me, pushing me into the bed as he fucked me relentlessly.

I screamed with each thrust, my pussy clamping on him, dragging him back into me with each withdraw, until his grunts grew louder, and he pumped harder and faster. Releasing my wrists, he grabbed my hair, pulling my head back and half rolling me onto my side. His other hand slid beneath me, his fingers assaulting my clit as his cock took my pussy and then lights exploded behind my eye lids before everything went black. From the darkness I heard Cian groan loudly and then collapse down on top of me.

We lay there together for a time, the feel of his heart pounding against my back, encased in his arms, as rain hit the windows. Silently, I listened to Cian's breathing, feel the warmth of him beside me and I closed my eyes, enjoying the moment too much.

Cian turned me to face him, studying my face with his hazel eyes as he pulled my body into him. We lay there wordlessly for a while; just a jockey wrapped in the arms of a mafia boss. My heart fluttered, feelings of warmth chasing away the unease that hung around on the outskirts of my mind.

I sighed.

"What's wrong, sweetheart?" Cian asked gently.

"I like it here, right now, with you. But the horses need feeding and exercising."

"I'll tell Jonjo to sort them today. Take a day off."

"I can't. We're only a couple of weeks away from the Festival of Racing. I need to be out training them, training me."

"It's one day, Charlie. Jonjo can handle them. Brian can have some downtime and I'll train you."

I looked up to see him smile at me, cheeky and delicious, his scarred eyebrow pulling in to a high arch. And then he dipped his head, not waiting for an answer, and kissed me long and passionate, his full lips massaging mine, his tongue caressing the inside of my mouth.

"Ok, you've convinced me," I breathed into his lips when he stopped.

Pushing him over onto his back, I straddled him, feeling his cock grow under me.

"Good. It was an order anyway."

I swatted his chest, and he grinned back at me. Then, bending down, I ran my fingers through his thick hair. He pulled me towards him, sucking a nipple into his mouth, grasping it between his teeth until I gasped, a mixture of pain and pleasure, and I rocked my hips against his erection that was now teasing at my entrance. When he finally let go, after he'd squeezed and nibbled at me until I was wet and hot, I leant back away from him, watching his expression as I lowered myself slowly onto his cock.

I took every inch of him, my clit rubbing against the base of his shaft, igniting the fire deep inside me again. Cian folded his arms behind his head, muscle bulging, his eyes moving from my face to my breasts and to where I rode his dick, taking what I wanted from him, selfishly building my own orgasm as I rocked and tilted my hips.

A shudder started to build through my body and I threw my head back, savouring the feeling as it intensified. His hands grabbed my hips, fingers digging into my delicate flesh, as I moved faster.

"Good girl, ride me harder," he commanded, his voice thick, squeezing my hips tighter, letting out a grunt, as I slid back onto him.

My stomach tightened, and I quickened my pace, closing my eyes as the sensation took over me.

"Look at me, Charlie. Tell me when you're going to come. I want to watch you."

"Soon," I whispered, struggling to keep my eyes on him.

My pussy clenched with the next stroke of my hips, a shiver running down my spine, my clit on fire.

"I'm coming, Cian," I gasped.

Pressing his thumb to my clit he rubbed it at the same time as I pushed against him, a cry coming from my lips as ecstasy consumed me and I fixed my eyes on the man beneath me as it raced through my body, exploding within me with delicious, delirium inducing bursts.

"Fuck!" I shouted, the apex hitting me and sending me spiralling out of control, Cian still circling and rubbing at my clit until I fell forward on top of him.

"You're not finished yet, sweetheart," he whispered into my ear, as I lay on top of him, soaking up the last ebbs of my orgasm.

Urging me upright again, he dragged my hips back and forth and I took the rhythm back, this time watching him.

"Legs wider," he demanded, nudging my legs further apart, "I want to see all of you on my cock."

Pushing myself upwards, I took my knees out from under me, leaning back slightly as I let my legs fall open, moving up and down his shaft, hearing him groan with each movement. His fingers curled around my ankles, restraining them while I used the full length of his cock, sliding off him and slamming back down, a new feeling building in my stomach with every movement.

"Fuck," Cian groaned loudly, pushing his hips in to me as I pushed down on him, "faster, harder," he commanded.

Yielding to his instructions, I quickened my pace, watching his face tighten each time I sank onto his shaft, till he was gripping my ankles almost painfully and pushing his hips to meet me. And with each movement of us together, felt like electric was flowing through my veins, the pounding heat in my pussy intensifying.

"Fuck, Cian, I'm coming again," I shouted, bouncing on his cock, and then it came, the orgasm blinding, pulsing through me as I screamed his name.

Cian grunted loudly not even a second later. Pushing his cock so far into me I felt his balls rammed against me, sticky warmth exploding within me.

I collapsed on top of him for a second time and he pulled me into him, my face buried into his chest, inhaling his scent, a mix of spicy aftershave, sweat, sex and us.

We lay for a while, Cian's arms wrapped around me, our bare flesh touching, lost in the peace of our own breaths and the rain that hammered the windows. I closed my eyes, enjoying the feeling of him around me, in me, warm in his bed, in his arms. His fingertips trailed over my back, sending delicious shivers up and down my spine. I closed my eyes, savouring the feeling.

"What was it like for you," I asked suddenly, "you know, growing up in all of this?"

"What? You mean as part of the mafia?"

"Uh-huh."

Cian sighed and fell silent and for a moment I wondered whether he was just going to ignore me.

"I hated it," he said after a time, "nothing ever felt normal, even though I knew nothing else. I knew what we were from an early age.

Fuck, I'd even pulled a trigger and killed someone before I was even thirteen."

"Jeez," I whispered, not expecting that.

"It's a different life, Charlie," he continued with sadness in his voice, "not one I would ever have chosen. Not like my mother had. She'd regretted it later. It tore her apart eventually. She tried to put it past her, the fear of never truly being able to keep us safe, not knowing whether we would be gunned down from one day to the next. Yet she kept going till we were all raised, old enough to look after ourselves, then she left us."

"How did she die, Cian?" I don't know why I asked. I already thought I knew the answer.

"She hung herself in the stables," he sighed again, "I found her. She'd done it in the place we shared, the place we both went when things were tough, when the only peace we could find was with the horses. After that, I got rid of all the horses. I didn't want to go down there, seeing that image of her every time I went. And I was so angry at her. Angry at her for leaving us and angry that she'd ruined the only place, the only things I really enjoycd."

I shifted against him, propping myself up on my elbow, watching his faraway expression, the pain in his eyes.

"She'd never got over Riley's mother dying. The O'Malleys came after her, but got Riley's mother instead. She never forgave herself for it; it plagued her for the rest of her life. They killed her really, killed her by proxy."

Cian pushed away the hair that had dropped over my face.

"I was never like my oldest brother," he continued, changing the subject slightly after a long pause, "he was born ruthless. The mirror image of my father: hard, tough, merciless. It should have been Torin who took over as head of the family. But they killed him: Torin, my father and my little sister."

"Who's they?"

"We don't know for sure. The Russians, the O'Malleys; maybe someone else entirely. But I will find them and I will destroy them."

"Why not just call the Police?" I asked.

"Apart from the fact we don't want them digging around in our business, it's all about power. The slightest sign of weakness, and we might as well surrender and hand over everything to any of the other firms. I have to avenge my family's deaths. It's my duty."

"So why not just slice off the top people in all those other gangs you talked about? You know, send that message you keep banging on about?"

Cian turned onto his side and smiled at me.

"You sure you're not secretly a gangster?" he asked.

"Course not. It just seems sensible if you're after power and revenge."

"Maybe you'd make a good mafia wife after all?"

"Cian, I'm not wife material full stop, never mind playing any sort of dutiful gangster bitch."

Cian flipped me over onto my back, covering his lips with mine, his hand winding up my neck and cupping my head, pulling me into him harder as he deepened his kiss. His erection pushed into my leg, ready to go again and my pussy throbbed a mixture of anticipation and the ache from the punishment Cian had been giving it. My stomach growled loudly.

Breaking away from Cian's kiss, I gently pushed him off me, waggling a lone finger in his direction.

"No more sex before I'm fed. I'm starving. Want a sandwich?"

"Sounds good," he answered, a hunger in his eyes as he watched me slide out from the covers and pull on one of his T-shirts, the hem coming down to the middle of my thigh.

I made my way downstairs to the kitchen, the house quiet and peaceful, the old stairwell creaking under my weight. Pulling out a loaf of bread and a couple of plates, I hastily made two sandwiches, hurrying to get out of where Cian's men might pop up at any point when I had nothing but a t-shirt on. But just as I was squashing the top slice of bread onto the sandwiches I had flung together, I heard the drone of male voices just outside the kitchen door.

"What's Cian's plan, Riley? He's messing about with that girl and not focussing on what needs to be done. We're sitting ducks here,

273

waiting for the next strike," the first voice complained.

"I know, Mad-Dog. She's a weakness. He knows that. I'll talk to him again."

Two men pushed through the kitchen door and I hastily stacked the plates on top of each other and grasped the pint glass of juice. They drew quiet when they spotted me and I wished at that point I had a spare hand to pull the t-shirt down further.

"'Scuse me," I muttered, sliding past them as I made my way to the door.

Both men looked at me; Riley pursing his lips at the evidence of where his boss had been all morning. But Mad-Dog's gaze almost burned into me, making me recoil as the eyes that swept over me, resting on where the white t-shirt ended just short of the middle of my thigh. I hurried away, hoping my arse cheeks remained covered, bounding back up the stairs noisily.

Chapter Twenty Nine

ಹಿ Cian ಲ

Rain still smattered the windows and had done so most of the night, but it was the noise of the shower in the bathroom next door that woke me up. That and my raging hard-on. I glanced at the red numbers on the display of the alarm clock, almost offended at the time on the display. I was not used to being woken up so early in the morning. I could have just rolled over, but I pushed back the covers and padded quietly into the bathroom.

Charlie had her back to me, water and frothy soap suds washing over her skin, falling down over the intricate horse tattoo and over the curves of her hips and that perfectly shaped arse that was round and taut. I gently slid the shower door open and stepped inside with her, the heat of the steam swirling about me. Feeling the dip of the shower tray, she peeked over her shoulder, startling as she saw me behind her.

Snaking my arm around her waist, I kicked her legs apart and ran my hand down the slippery surface of her stomach, over the top of her mound, feeling for her pussy.

"Hands on the wall," I growled the instruction into her ear, my fingers sliding over the smoothness of her skin at her entrance.

"Yes, sir," she answered playfully, her words sending me into a frenzy.

Pushing her forwards, I rammed my cock straight into her, one hand grabbing the back of her neck, the other pushing against the tiles on the wall to steady myself as I pounded into her from behind. Charlie squealed as I thrusted, fucking her furiously, her pussy clenching round me, grabbing onto me with each movement. And then, just as I knew I couldn't hold back any longer, I let go of her neck, my fingers finding her clit. She threw her head back and screamed my name into the water that fell against her face. Leaning forward, I placed my mouth on the top of her shoulder, the kiss turning into a bite as my cock throbbed inside the tightness of her pussy, my balls pulsing as I filled her with thick, hot cum.

Pulling myself out, I slapped her arse, my hand making a loud noise between the sheen of water and her flesh. She yelped, beautifully, still braced against the wall. I spun her round and took her mouth, forcing her back into the shower wall and groaning at the taste of her tongue. She was intoxicating, and I was obsessed, hooked on her.

Charlie eventually left to the feed the horses after I'd fucked her another twice, punishing her pussy in every way possible, my body and my mind desperate to claim every inch of her.

The next few days started and finished in much the same way. Charlie hadn't moved back into her room and instead every moment I wasn't with my men and Charlie wasn't dealing with the horses we spent in my bed. I explored every part of her, every chance I could steal, and I'd got used to falling asleep with my arms wrapped around her and waking next to her in the morning. My obsession was growing, and so was the formidable swelling of my heart.

The rain was hammering the windows again that morning, sending ominous hints to my brain. Charlie's alarm clock had not yet gone off, but I lay there awake, worrying. Worrying about what I was doing, how I'd let myself fall for someone, wondering how she'd crawled in through the cracks in my walls and settled in my heart and worrying whether she felt the same or whether I just offered her some comfort and company. I inhaled deeply, enjoying the smell of coconut from her hair, my arm wrapped snugly around her stomach and her tight arse nestled into me as she lay on her side, sleeping serenely.

I slid out of bed, scrubbing the stubble on my face with my hand and rubbing at my eyes that felt dry and disorientated at the ridiculous time of the morning. I pulled the curtains back an inch or two and stared out into the dark, tiny specks of lights twinkling away somewhere out there in the Durham countryside, before dropping the heavy material back into place as soft hands snaked around me. Gentle fingertips smoothed over my chest and I felt her warmth at my back as she ran her hands down the front of my stomach.

"What are you doing, Cian?" she murmured softly against me and I closed my eyes, savouring the feel of her nakedness against me.

Soft lips were placed carefully on my back, gently caressing my skin, her tongue skimming lightly across with each kiss, gently teasing, carefully tasting. Pulling in a long breath, pushing aside the growing feeling of doom and trepidation that was tangling with the warmth in my heart, I leaned my head back, concentrating on Charlie's touch.

"Come back to bed," she whispered, her voice still laced with the vulnerability of sleep, and my cock stirred at the thought.

I turned, gazing down at her as she raised her head and her baby blue eyes met mine, her mouth curling up at the sides, her dimples coming alive with the smile. My heart and my dick swelled, and I realised I was helplessly falling deep.

Walking her backwards until the bed hit the back of her legs, I pushed her down. Dropping to my knees in front of her, I pushed her legs open, resting my face at the entrance to her pussy, inhaling her, breathing in the sweet earthy smell of her cunt, her velvety lips swollen and slick, ready for me. Then I buried my face in her, devouring her pussy, my tongue lashing her clit. Charlie's fingers twisted in my hair, bucking her hips against my face as I listened to the beautiful gasps and the sound of my name on her lips as I licked and lapped, and sucked and nibbled. Strong thighs clamped round my head as Charlie rode her orgasm out on my face and soon we were once again entangled, thrashing around together on the bed.

When I woke again that morning, a murky grey light was peeking through a gap in the curtains. The rain was lighter now than it had been at 4.30am, but it still struck the window full of threat. I rolled onto my back staring at the ceiling, the smell of Charlie all over the sheets, over me and immediately the bed felt huge and hostile without her in it. Fuck. She was killing me.

Black coffee held my wayward thoughts at bay, at least for an hour and, leaning against the kitchen countertop, I watched the horses training on the gallops in the distance. I could get used to this; fucking Charlie like a wild animal every chance I got, then watching her ride those magnificent beasts from the comfort of a warm kitchen. No drugs operations to oversee, no people that needed reminding of their status and mine.

"Ready to go, boss?" Riley asked from the doorway, his eyes following the path of mine out of the window.

"She's got a great chance at the festival next weekend," I said, ignoring his question, my eyes never moving from the faraway horses and their riders.

"So you're going to ask her to throw the race?"

The question hit me hard in the chest and I didn't know why it rocked me so much. It was what we did after all: own jockeys, fix races, make a fuck-ton of money in the process. But the thought of it made me feel sick. I shook my head.

"You know she's got a great following. The money we could make from her. It would be our biggest one yet."

"No!" I snapped and Riley looked at me, surprise all over his face, "no. I can't."

"Boss... Cian. This is what we do. Just because you two are fucking each other's brains out, you can't forget what makes us the money."

The coffee cup smashed into pieces as I hurled it across the kitchen into the ceramic Belfast sink on the other side of the room. It was the cup or Riley's face.

"I fucking told you, no, Riley. You'd do right to remember who's the skipper here," my tone was threatening as I sidled up to him, my face inches from his, ready to smash his nose with my forehead if he uttered another word to piss me off.

"Now, let's get on with some proper work. Yes?"

Riley nodded at me, not taking his eyes from mine, watching my every move suspiciously but dutifully following me out of the kitchen when I stalked away from him.

*****

A couple of hours later, we parked the black SUV a mile from the warehouse, scrabbling over rough footing and through thick trees

280

masquerading as woodland. A twig snapped noisily underfoot, and I stilled for a moment, my eyes scanning around me, on edge even though we were a few hundred meters away from the warehouse and anyone noticing.

Through the myriad of bare branches criss-crossing our line of sight, two huddled figures waited for us. I patted Mad-Dog on the shoulder as we got to them and he glanced up at us, his eyes red and bloodshot.

"Rough night?" I asked, trying to keep the amusement from my voice.

"Fucking freezing, boss. Think my dick has dropped off."

Tommy snorted, trying to rein in laughter beside him.

"Go on then, you two, fuck off."

We took over their watch and for once I welcomed being the one calling the shots. The rain was still light, but the temperature had risen from nearly freezing overnight. Pulling my jacket around me, I crammed on a black woolly hat over my head and ears and hunkered down in the bushes.

Riley and I sat next to each other till the daylight faded, the rain having stopped hours ago, not once speaking to each other than to acknowledge movement into and out of the warehouse, noting the times that people came and went, their number and what they were driving. Lukyan didn't show, and it seemed it wasn't one of his more frequented venues, but it was certainly well stocked. I'd estimated a good half a million of product was being stored in there. It was a pretty big operation. Ballsy. Arrogant. And I knew it would kick him right in the balls when it burned down to the ground.

"Right, I've seen enough," I grunted at Riley, "let's go."

I took advantage of the silence between us and that Riley was driving on the way back up north to Durham, dozing in the heat from the car, now finally dried out from sitting in a bush all day. I woke up again just outside of Durham, the golden glow of the Cathedral illuminated in the distance against the night sky as we got closer.

Then eventually we pulled onto the long driveway that led down through the stable yard and up to the house at the top of the hill. The yard was virtually deserted as the car rolled past and I glimpsed a small figure in the glow of the hay barn.

"Let me out here," I instructed Riley.

He nodded, his eyes fixed straight ahead on the road, but I saw the jump of muscle in his jaw as he brought the car to a stop.

"See you back at the house."

I stalked away to the hay barn and the woman in it. The yard was quiet. There was the occasional snort from a horse, the odd ring of light aluminium shoes on the concrete and the rustle of hay being pulled from hay nets. The night was still and the rain had held off for several hours. It was peaceful; tranquil. The smell of damp earth and fresh hay lingered in the air and with it, the faint smell of coconut, apricot and vanilla.

I pushed the hay barn door open with a rumble and Charlie whipped round to face me, shocked and defensive until she realised who it was and then I was welcomed by her beautiful smile and dimples. I pulled her into me, pushing my lips into hers, our flesh cold between us. Charlie's long blonde hair was secured in a plait, I noticed as my hand slid around her back and grasping the end of it I yanked it back, pulling on it roughly to expose the delicate skin of her neck. She moaned as I kissed her neck.

My fingers snaked under the thick jumper, pushing her bra from her tits so I could squeeze the soft buds as she whimpered. Every noise she made under my hands sent me crazy with need, and my dick was already straining against my trousers.

"Get these off," I demanded, popping the button open and yanking the jeans open as far as the zip would allow.

Without hesitation, she kicked off her boots, pushing her jeans down her legs. I pulled one leg from them, the feel of the silky smoothness of her skin on my finger ends as I touched her, my hand moving up the inside of her leg as she moaned loudly and pushed her hands into my hair. I trailed a finger along her pussy, wet and warm, and she pushed her hips towards me.

"Fuck me, Boss," she taunted.

Those words, on her lips, every time; they weakened me. I pushed two fingers into her, gliding quickly into her wetness as she cried out at the sudden intrusion. I swirled them inside of her, listening to her gasp and writhe against my hand. Then, fumbling with the button on my trousers, I popped it open, pushing them down and letting my dick spring free. Pulling my hand from her, I held my fingers to her face.

"Taste yourself," I demanded, pushing my fingers into her mouth, her pink lips sucking at me, her tongue swirling my fingertips, whilst I guided my cock into her with the other hand.

I pushed her back into the hay bale behind her, my fingers still in her mouth, my cock impaling her as I hooked her leg around my waist, thrusting into her tight fucking pussy with deep fast pumps. I took my hand from her mouth, cupping the arse cheek of the leg that was round my waist. Charlie cried out as my fingers bit into the flesh of her buttock and I quickened my pace to a frenzy, my balls hot and tingling, ready to shoot my load into her any second. I grabbed her head, forcing her mouth to mine, our tongues tangling as we came together, hard and fast. As the last ebb of orgasm dropped away, I kissed her more gently, my eyes searching hers for something more than just desire and lust.

"Good show," a voice from behind me in the doorway interrupted us.

Charlie squeaked, and I glanced over my shoulder to see the Viking leaning against the

284

lintel of the barn, his leather jacket clad arms crossed across his chest.

"Fuck's sake, V. I'm busy!"

"I can see that, bud. Hi, Charlie," he called around me.

"Hi V," Charlie giggled into my neck.

"Jesus. Give me two minutes. I'll see you at the house!"

"What? Round two?"

I shot him a warning look, and he held his hands up in mock surrender and then walked away. A few moments later I heard the loud rumble of the exhaust from his bike, growing quieter as he rode the fucking thing up the drive.

I pulled out of Charlie, tucking myself back in and watching as she climbed back into her jeans, a slight sheen on the inside of her legs. I liked the evidence of my claim on her. I liked it way too much.

Chapter Thirty

❧ Charlie ☙

I followed Cian into the lounge. The fire was roaring in the hearth, warmth quickly filling the room, for which I was thankful. The bite of cold on my finger ends was excruciating. Although March was nearly out, the weather had taken a turn for the worse recently, reminding us that winter was yet to yield to spring. I cupped my hands round the coffee cup, blowing on the hot black liquid inside before taking tentative sips.

Cian stalked around the room, clutching the neck of a beer bottle between his fingers, and I sensed an atmosphere between him and Riley as they eyed each other continuously. The Viking was sitting across from me in front of the fire, shooting a big wide grin in my direction, and I smiled back at him, feeling the heat of embarrassment licking my cheeks.

"Pleased you two could join us," he said mischievously, giving me a wink.

"What have you got for me, V?" Cian interrupted, his tone irritated.

"Lebedev. We lost one of the bugs that Charlie planted; the one in his jacket. But we expected that."

"Did you pick anything up from that?"

The Viking shook his head.

"Not much. Not on its own, anyway. He picked up an expensive escort after the Jockey Club Ball; not unusual for Lebedev," the blond biker commented, more at me when I screwed my face up, "he didn't talk to anyone significant that night and not to the Volkovs or any of their men that night or afterwards. But the bug Charlie got into his phone picked up some interesting conversations."

The Viking took a long drink before continuing.

"Seems our Russian billionaire has been supplying the Northern Pipeline."

"Northern Pipeline? What's that?" I asked, noting that everyone else in the room seemed to understand what he was talking about.

"Human trafficking," Cian answered, "people are trafficked through cities here in the North and then out over Europe, or in that way, depending on who has ordered what. It's big business."

"We're not just talking about slavers here either, Cian. Lebedev is really up there with this shit," The Viking gesticulated, holding his palm above his head.

"So what? He's coordinating the whole thing?"

"He's not right at the top. I can't figure out who is. There were a lot of code names mentioned; none that I could decipher, though. But he is using his hotel business to move stock. He'll recruit down and outs, girls with shit families, girls that no one cares about and then suddenly they quit and go missing. Only a few of them ever get reported to the Police and mostly the cases are closed. All the girls have long record sheets."

I glanced around the room. Cian's jaw was taut, his grip had tightened around his glass and Riley shifted uncomfortably from one foot to another.

"So, what?" I asked, "this not normal mafia behaviour?"

The blond man grinned at me and Riley passed a look to Cian.

"Cian, this one's yours," the Viking deflected.

The Irishman rubbed his hand across his jaw and looked to be struggling with whether or not to answer my question.

"Some do. Not us. We are a lot of things, do a lot of things, but enslaving women to be systematically raped and abused is the absolute fucking pits."

I hid my relief and nodded silently at him.

"The Russians don't traffic either, though," Cian pointed out to no one in particular.

"Not at the minute. But old man Volkov weakens by the day and Lukyan is a greedy bastard. I wouldn't put it past him to see a few easy quid to be made from getting involved in this," Riley commented, looking uneasy.

"That's not the only thing, Kee," the biker continued, "my guy hacked some of the cameras. Lebedev's systems were pretty well protected, but eventually he found a vulnerability, just for a few minutes, before he was detected and shut down."

The biker looked towards me and I felt the eyes of everyone in the room follow his gaze.

I swallowed, glancing about, "for fuck's sake, spit it out," I complained, a knot of dread forming in my stomach.

"My guy found some info laid out on a table in what looked like an office. Photographs of you, Charlie. And he also saw your rap sheet, which was pretty extensive. Seems Lebedev has a real interest in you."

"By interest, what do you mean?" Cian asked, his voice laced with anger as it rumbled across the room.

"There was a pile of info of girls on the desk from what we could see. Charlie was in that pile. Lebedev's interest in her was more than just because she's associated with you. She fits the shopping list. Young, an extensive record, plenty of episodes of being missing from home when she was younger. Someone, who, if she goes missing, it wouldn't be unusual. He'd get good money for someone like Charlie."

The knot tightened as bile rose in my throat. I swallowed, trying to push the sudden nausea away. I looked across to Cian. His face was passive but his lips were pressed together, his jaw tight and a darkness had settled in his eyes.

After what seemed like a long silence, Cian nodded, as if he'd just made a decision. Moving towards me, he squeezed my shoulder as I looked blankly at the biker, my head whirring at the conversation, the revelation flooring me. Fear crept up inside of me, making me unable to speak, think or move.

"That doesn't make sense," I said eventually, "not to toot my own trumpet but I'm hardly going to disappear quietly now? I'm all over the news, not just some little ol' orphan anymore."

Cian shrugged.

"I dunno. But I'm not taking a chance. V, you and I will pay Lebedev a little visit. You kept the footage as evidence, didn't you?"

"Kee, Kee, Kee. Don't ask stupid fucking questions."

"The rest of you stay here. I want eyes on Charlie at all times."

"Boss," the collective of voices answered.

"Good. Now you can all fuck off for a minute," Cian instructed and everyone, including

290

the Viking, trooped out, the door closing softly behind them.

Cian came around and kneeled in front of me, tipping my chin up so my eyes met his, covering the hand that scratched manically at the other, tearing the skin with my nails, blood oozing from the scratches I hadn't realised I'd made.

"Charlie. I'll sort this. By the time I've finished with him, he'll know you're off bounds."

"And what about all the other girls on his list?" I asked, my voice wavering, weakness showing.

"I can't promise I can sort that. The Pipeline is much bigger than us. It would take much more than one pissed off firm to take the whole thing down."

He touched his lips to my forehead, his hand wrapping around the back of my head and holding me to him.

"Please stay in the house."

I nodded, the fear he had momentarily chased away back to haunt me. I felt sick.

Chapter Thirty One

ജ Cian ര

The anger I felt as I drove to Lebedev's place was consuming. My knuckles had turned white where I'd gripped the steering wheel. How had I been so short-sighted not to have seen through him when we first met? I was normally good at reading people. Instead, I'd let his reputation, his business assets, and the promise of a small fortune blind me.

"Do you have a plan, Kee?" V asked from beside me, breaking the silence we'd sat in for the last twenty minutes.

"I want any trace of her in his house wiped out. I want to know who he was planning on selling her to and then I'm gonna make sure he never looks at Charlie ever again."

"Sound enough plan. There's a fuck load of security on Lebedev. I'm guessing I'm the diversion?"

"Sure are. Just don't kill anyone. Well, not too many, anyway."

The Viking chuckled.

"Not much room for many more tattoos these days, Kee. I'm choosing my inspiration more wisely."

Eventually, we moved through well-lit streets sporting million pound houses. Long driveways to huge sprawling properties lined the road on either side, the orange glow of streetlights casting soft shadows beyond the walls. We swept past Lebedev's ludicrous suburban mansion a number of times, looking for guards or patrols of any kind, but the property was dark, quiet. Too quiet.

"Something's off," V said quietly beside me, peering down the driveway for the second time, "this place is usually lit up like a Christmas tree."

There were a few small squares of light at the end of the driveway, dotted across the face of the huge property. The driveway lights were unlit, creating an ominous vault of darkness consuming the little road to the house. It obscured our view, restricting the opportunity to see the dark shapes of men patrolling or gauging the level of occupancy by the number of cars there were. Although the lack of illuminated windows hinted that there were few people home, I wasn't banking on it.

"Think we're going to have to get closer," I said.

We parked the car a few streets away, finding a small local shopping area to deposit it without arousing much suspicion, and walked back towards Lebedev's mansion. Finding a shadowy corner, we scaled the high perimeter wall and dropped down with a soft thud into the bushes the other side.

We crept around the outside of the property, skirting in and out of the safety of the shadows to avoid camera contact as much as possible until we were hiding in a patch of bushes just a few metres from the main entrance. There had been no movement into or out of the house at all. No guards patrolling. Nothing. Unease was starting to gnaw away at me.

"Go around the back," I instructed the Viking, "give me two blasts on my mobile if there's anything suspicious."

I stood up, dusted mud and dirt from my suit, and went to step forward. A tug on my trousers stalled me.

"What are you doing?" V hissed from his crouched position in the dark.

"Might as well give Lebedev a knock," I answered, shrugging my shoulders boldly, stepping out of the copse of bushes.

I left the Viking and strode across the lawn, the thick, well cared for grass soft and spongy under my feet. Pulling the arms of my jacket back into position, I straightened my appearance and stepped up to the huge oak front door. I knocked loudly, the sound against the wood in the quiet of the night, stark and hostile.

I waited for a few minutes, but there was no answer. The bushes rustled to my left and I knew

V had started to move into position towards the rear of the house. I knocked again, but this time the door clicked open slightly from the frame. I pushed tentatively on in, a gentle stream of light growing brighter as the door swung fully open into the vast hallway.

A soft glow emanated from the lights on the stairs, although the bottom hallway was dark. Creeping in the shadows, I moved past the many rooms on the ground floor, my hand resting on the handle of my gun tucked at the back of my trousers, as I peeped around the doorway of each room, finding nothing but emptiness. A scratch caught my attention, followed by the muffled pad of feet. Pulling myself into a dark corner, I pushed my back against the wall, watching all sides of the property that now flanked me. Exhaling, I relaxed as the dark, creeping figure came into view.

"The place is deserted, Kee," the Viking whispered as he joined me.

"Sure is. We need to find this shit and get out of here. Something's not right."

"Agreed."

We climbed the decadent staircase; the light shining from the landing upstairs catching on heavily gilded picture frames, and sparkling as it bounced off an over-the-top crystal chandelier hanging over the double stairwell. The house was dripping with opulence; every ornament and painting dowsed in gold and worth a fucking fortune. Even the heavy drapes covering the windows were gaudy, bold, and expensive.

We took turns tentatively pushing open doors, ready to be met with the barrel of a gun, but the house remained eerily quiet, the rooms pristine and undisturbed. Eventually at the far side, light spilled out of a room onto the thick carpet of the corridor we had been carefully creeping along for the last few minutes. I pulled my gun out, clasping it snugly in my hand, cautiously removing the safety.

I nodded at V and then, holding my breath in anticipation, bounded into the room. The dark oak desk sat in front of an enormous bay window, gold and black curtains secured tidily at either side. Papers were strewn across the leather top, blood soaked from the body that was slumped over the top of them.

"Fuck," I cursed, flicking the safety back on and tucking the gun back in my trousers.

Moving closer to the body, I leant towards it and pulled the head back, about to check for a pulse.

"He's totally gone," V spoke from in front of me as Lebedev's head rolled backwards under the grip of my hand.

"You reckon? Feels like his head's about to fucking fall off," I grunted.

It didn't take much of a search of the desk to find the details he had on Charlie and I pulled them from under his corpse, blood almost covering the papers entirely.

"We need to get rid of these and anything else that mentions her," I waved the soggy sheets towards V, the metallic scent wafting in front of my nose. The Viking nodded, taking out a pair of leather gloves and pulling open drawers, checking everything inside as I raked around the desk Lebedev was lying on with the barrel of my gun.

"I don't like this, Kee," he grumbled, pushing a drawer back into place.

A mobile vibrated, and I looked up, the Viking pushing the small phone to his ear, grunting and then sliding the phone into his pocket.

"This is a trap," he said suddenly, "that was my man. It's bothered him how easy it was to get through Lebedev's firewalls. He reckons they took the network security down. We were let in to their CCTV, Cian. They've lured us here tonight!"

The rumble of a car engine below us distracted me. I edged to the window, peeking around the curtains and out onto the driveway below.

"Shit! Police are here," I called across the room just before the sound of the front door opening below us.

"Fuck."

"We need to get out of here."

Blue lights lit up the walls of the study, increasing in brightness till it seemed the entire room was bathed in an azure glow. Pulling my gun out of my jeans, I thrust it and the bloodied papers at the Viking.

"Take these and get out of here. Get Riley to get me a decent solicitor," I instructed.

Then I strode out the study door into the arms of the awaiting police officers.

Chapter Thirty Two

❧ Charlie ❧

It had been a couple of hours after Cian had left and I'd had a couple of glasses of wine to settle my nerves. The Lebedev revelation made me feel physically sick. I'd heard about people trafficking for years, but to find out that someone I knew was knee deep in it, even if I'd only met him a few times, had been enough to rattle me. And then to find out that he had some sordid interest in me, that I was a target, that I could have been, still could be a victim of all this; that had been enough for the unease to seep into every inch of me.

I pulled on Cian's jogging bottoms and a white t-shirt of his, my own clothes not as comfortable, and a silly part of me enjoyed the comfort and safety I felt having his clothes envelope me. I half-dried my hair with a towel, leaving it damp and hanging down my back, and wandered downstairs.

"Are they back yet?" I asked softly as I entered the kitchen, the conversation between

Tommy, Mad-Dog and Riley, ceasing immediately when they saw me.

Tommy smiled encouragingly, "not yet. I'm sure Cian's fine, Charlie."

Mad-Dog scowled at me, his features dark as his eyes lingered on the clothes I wore, and Riley watched me with interest. I pulled a mug out of the cupboard, dropped in a teaspoon of instant coffee and clicked the kettle on, keeping my back to the men, my concentration fuzzy as I listened to the water in the kettle heat.

A rumble outside of the house caught my attention and, flinging a glance over my shoulder, I noticed the three men behind me eye up the door expectantly. It opened, the black leather jacket of the biker filling the doorway, his blond hair spilling on to his shoulders. I looked past him, watching for Cian.

"Where's the boss?" Riley asked, a tone in his voice.

The biker ran a hand through his hair.

"We've got a situation," he started.

"What do you mean, a situation?" I interrupted, dread expanding in my stomach, "where's Cian?"

"Lebedev's dead," the biker man continued, addressing Riley, leaving my question unanswered.

"Hey, where's Cian?" I cut across him, grabbing his arm and pulling him to face me.

He looked irritated, stressed.

"Police got him," he answered gruffly.

"What?"

"What she said," Riley's voice sounded from the other side of the kitchen, "what's going on V?"

Moving into the lounge, we followed the Viking, as I brought up the rear, not failing to notice that they kept trying to cut me out of the conversation. I flopped into the armchair next to the fire, watching the biker squat an arse cheek on the arm of the sofa.

"The house was deserted when we got there," he explained, accepting the whisky tumbler that Riley passed to him and recounting the news that Lebedev was dead.

"Why didn't you help get Cian out of there?" I asked, anger having erupted in me half a story ago.

"It doesn't do any of us any good if we both got lifted. I took Cian's weapons and all the information about you. The only one that's currently implicated is Cian. Now we just need to find someone to get him out of there."

"Know anyone local?" Riley asked.

The Viking shook his head, "my guy's out of the country. He'd be the only one I'd trust."

"I know a good solicitor," I piped up, reading the concern on the men in the room, "my sister."

"And what do you think she'll do when she realises what we are, Charlie?" Riley asked abruptly, "it's bad enough that Cian's let you in on business details. What makes you think your sister is gonna be able to sort this shit out?"

Riley pulled his phone out of his pocket, "I'd better ring Oisín. We're gonna need someone sending up from Ireland. Might take a couple of days, but at least it'll be in the family still."

"Look, Riley. Nat is a defence solicitor. A fucking good one at that. There's very little that can surprise her, and even if did, she'll do it for me, because I asked."

Riley and the Viking looked at each other, the biker man shrugging at the other. I didn't wait for any further agreement. Taking out my phone, I pulled her contacts from my list, then pressed the phone to my ear. The phone rang a few times, too long, but eventually the line clicked and I heard her voice.

"What's up, Lottie?" she asked, her voice sounding tired.

"I need a favour."

"You always need a favour. What have you done now?"

"It's not me. It's Cian…."

I explained the situation as Nat listened quietly to me, and once or twice, I heard a resigning sigh on the other end of the phone.

"Ok, Lottie," she said eventually, "I'll get him out."

"Thank you."

*****

I don't know how many hours I'd been asleep in the armchair for. Someone had covered me with the throw from the other sofa, but the fire that had been roaring in the hearth had reduced to embers. A soft touch on my cheek woke me up, and I opened my eyes to find Cian bending over the top of me.

"Hey, sweetheart," he said softly.

I couldn't keep the relieved smile from my face. Reaching up and pulling him towards me, I kissed him like I hadn't seen him in months. A feigned cough from behind us made us stop, Cian pulling away and straightening up.

"When you two have finished eating each other," V's voice vibrated in the background, "I see Charlie's sister got you a pass out?"

"Aye. She's a regular ball buster, had nearly the whole fucking station cowering from her," Cian turned back to me, "good call, Charlie."

I smiled and looked across at Riley, "she's shit hot. One of the best in the North of England, now our father is gone."

"So, are you totally off the hook?" Riley asked.

Cian nodded, "Lebedev's throat was cut. By someone left-handed, apparently. Natalie had their forensics confirm it there and then. Police had to actually bring a guy in to check it. She's serious. She pulled a few strings, got access to the body. They'll still be sniffing around though, so we're gonna have to keep our heads down."

Cian walked across to the liquor cabinet and poured himself a whisky. His face strained. Something was eating at him.

"There was something off the minute we got there," he said eventually, "there were absolutely no guards, but Lebedev didn't look like he'd been dead long. The blood, it was still pretty wet, not yet congealed."

"What are you thinking, Cian?" Riley asked.

"A set-up. We reckon V's man was allowed access to the cameras just at that point. They knew I was coming."

"Could it not just be coincidence? Bad luck?"

"No, Riley. I'm telling you I was set up. We walked into a trap. Who called the Police? They got there just after us. Someone is watching us."

I watched the reactions of the men in the room. Mad-Dog and Riley exchanged glances and Tommy swallowed, as if there was something stuck in his throat. What if we, they, were being watched from within? I glanced around again. How loyal were Cian's men? My eyes focussed on Mad-Dog. His jaw was tense, his hand clutched around the neck of a beer bottle, and then, as if sensing my eyes on him, he looked my way, meeting my gaze, his face dark.

"So what now, Kee?" the Viking asked, his huge muscled arms folded across his chest.

"Test my theory, V, find out from your man whether he found a vulnerability or whether someone let us in to those cameras. Then I want to know who. And as for you two," Cian turned towards Mad-Dog and Tommy, "go burn the fucking Russians down. If they set me up, I'll take the whole of the fucking Volkovs out."

"Boss," Mad-Dog acknowledged, turning to Tommy and cocking his head, the pair of them following the order just given.

"And you," Cian said gruffly, suddenly turning to me, "bed now."

"Boss," I repeated, watching the glint of wickedness cross his eyes.

"Cian, a word," Riley interrupted.

Cian tipped his head, signalling for me to leave them and for once, outside of the bedroom, I complied, leaving them alone in the lounge. I stopped outside the door for a few moments, listening, but all I could hear was the rumble of low voices. I gave up and headed upstairs to Cian's room.

He joined me less than ten minutes later, stalking across the room as he shrugged out of his jacket and unbuttoned the neck of his shirt. The shirt was smeared with faded red, stark against the crisp whiteness. Swinging my legs out of bed as he moved closer, I grabbed the waistband of his trousers and pulled him towards me, positioning him between my bare legs as my fingers danced over the remaining buttons on the blood streaked shirt, popping them free. Tracing my fingertips over the waistband, brushing the smooth skin underneath his shirt, I dipped forward, pushing his shirt aside and placing my lips on his exposed torso, just above the button on his trousers.

Cian groaned as my lips and tongue worked across his skin. He fumbled in his pocket, taking out his phone and pushing it onto the bedside table next to us. I pulled him closer, slipping the button of his trousers free and sliding the zip down, the top of his erection escaping out of the waistband of his boxers. I pushed my face into the hard flesh of the 'v'. Beside me, the phone vibrated on the bedside table, the display lighting the dullness of the room.

Cian looked across and frowned, and I watched his eyebrows knit together in frustration.

"Just a sec," he grumbled, grabbing the phone and moving his thumb across the display.

I sat patiently. His eyebrows furrowed even more and eventually the sound from the handset amplified further. A man begged, a woman screamed, joining in the voices of multiple men, and Cian's eyes widened in horror. Darkness washed over his face, his hazel eyes blazing with a hatred and anguish I'd never seen on him before and, for the first time, he actually frightened me. Then, with a roar, he threw the phone across the room and marched towards the door. He shouted again, an angry, animalistic snarl that made me jump, tensing with fear. Cian's fists pounded the door, wood cracking and splintering. Then he yanked the door open and thundered down the stairs.

"Cian!" someone shouted from downstairs.

I sat for a few moments, my body shaking, watching the door, waiting for him to charge back in. But the house had descended into an eerie stillness, as if its entire occupants were holding their breath.

The phone lay on the floor, miraculously unscathed, and I got to my feet, my legs shaking as I crossed the room. The display was still on, the lock screen not yet barring my access, and I could see a video on the screen. I hit the play button and watched.

It was dark at first and then the screen adjusted, providing enough light that I could see relatively dark shapes of two people on chairs. They looked up at the screen and then shadows moved across it, momentarily blurring the view. The heads of the people on the chairs followed the movement and then the camera changed angles, the focus becoming sharper.

A woman was struggling between two men, their faces concealed in the shadows. Her face was bloody, with dark shiny cuts on her eyebrow and lip and thick red blood bulging in her nostril. Her arms were pinned behind her back, her clothes were tattered and hung off her, her chest bare and she wore nothing on her bottom half but a pair of knickers. My stomach dropped.

A deep, accented voice drawled in the background.

307

"We'll spare her, what's left of her, but you shoot him and then yourself," the voice said.

"Get your filthy fucking hands off her!" a thick Irish brogue shouted back.

"Or what, Irishman?"

"We'll sort out patches. I'm sure there's some arrangement we can come to. Something we can do."

"There is," the accented voice agreed, "you kill your father."

A gun slid across the floor and the Irishman looked back at the camera as men moved behind him, before his hands sprung free.

"Kill your father, or we rip her apart. Make the choice O'Sullivan. Who will it be?"

The man beside him shouted through the gag. Indiscernible muffles.

"O'Sullivan needs some help with his decision," the voice behind the recording continued.

The camera tilted back towards the woman. A man pushed her towards a table and kicked her legs apart. She screamed, thrashing and throwing herself around, but his weight pinned her in place. The camera moved back to the men on the chairs, but I could hear her sobs mixed with the sickening grunts of the man.

"Stop it! Leave her!" the strained Irish voice said to the side of the camera, "please!"

"Shoot him, and this all stops."

The man shook his head, "I can't....m, m my father," he stammered.

"Do it."

The camera turned back to the helpless woman and I watched in horror as the man stepped away and another took his place. The screen flashed as a shot rang through the air. The other man in the chair slumped. The woman screamed. Another shot was fired and followed by a dull thud. Bile rose in my throat.

"*Suka*!" the voice from the corner grunted over the sobs of the woman.

The video stopped, and I stared at the screen, my heart racing and my hand shaking. Then I dropped the phone and ran to the bathroom.

Chapter Thirty Three

ℬ Cian ℛ

I sat in the cold. Daylight was breaking from the east, a tiny amber glow rising over the horizon, a ribbon of gold spreading in the night sky. I'd sat on top of the hill overlooking the gallops for hours. My thoughts swirling though my brain as I leaned against a tree, my toes and fingers numb with the cold, the thin shirt no match for the sharp night air.

In the darkness, I could see her face. Distorted, pained, humiliated, tortured. We'd always known what had happened to some extent, but the brutality of it, the video, the look on her face. I didn't know what I felt: anger, despair, sick to my stomach. Everything. Every emotion had hit me like a sledgehammer. And then there was guilt and disgust. Guilt because I should have been at home to protect her, to keep her safe, to keep Oisín in check. Then it would have been him, not her. And disgust at my brother. He should have fought harder. He should have ripped those men in that room apart just for laying eyes on her. Instead, he'd begged for his own life, begged not to be made to kill his father.

I would have killed them both to protect her. I would have ripped all of their eyes out just for looking at her and I would have done it whether I was bound to a chair or not. Torin had sat there doing nothing. They had offered him a gun, his hands were free and instead he was too chicken-shit to save her. He deserved to die. But his death had been quick. A shot between the eyes, like our father. Fiadh had been tortured. Her body was a mess, her insides torn apart from what they did to her, what they continued to do to her after the camera had stopped rolling.

I leaned to the side and vomited on the ground. Not for the first time that night.

And then anger. Burning white hot from the inside that it hurt. I would find them and I would rip the skin off their very backs. By the time I'd finished with them, they would regret breathing. Riley was right. I'd been soft. I'd tried to be measured, rational. No longer. I'd start with the O'Malleys. I'd make an example of every syndicate in the UK until I found the ones responsible. The need for revenge was ravishing my body, my mind. I wasn't sure whether I was shaking from the cold or the anger pulsing through my veins.

A gentle hand touched my shoulder and for a long minute I thought it was just the cold, a whisper of the wind at my back.

"Cian," her voice was soft.

I stared straight ahead, hearing but not really processing. The gold on the horizon had melded into bronze, the sky becoming a blaze of orange and red, pinks and purples, colour flooding to the land.

"Cian," she said again as she crouched down beside me, "I saw it. I watched the video."

I nodded silently, my eyes fixed on the myriad of colours in the distance. She moved round in front of me, kneeling on the ground so her face was in line with mine, my eyes forced to look at her.

"I'm so sorry, you had to see that," she whispered.

Something wet dripped down my face and she wiped at it with her thumb. And then, almost involuntarily, I wrapped my arms around her and pulled her towards me, burying my face in her chest, inhaling the sweet remnants of her perfume.

Eventually, I was numb from the cold and I felt Charlie shivering against me, the arms wrapped around me loosening with every shake from her body. She'd knelt there, in the dank soil, holding me, waiting for me as I buried tears into her chest. I pushed away from her and she looked at me, her blue eyes searching mine.

"You ready to go do whatever it is you need to do?" she asked softly, and I answered with a wane smile.

I wiped my face with the heel of my hands and then got up onto numb legs I could barely

312

feel. I pulled Charlie gently to her feet, kissing the top of her head, and we walked hand in hand through the early morning and back to the house.

*****

"I'm sorry, Cian, but I'm gonna need to see that video," the Viking said quietly as my men gathered in the lounge.

I nodded wordlessly and passed my phone to him. He and Riley gathered round the screen, watching. I let out a breath when it finished, struggling with hearing it again, the images forming in front of my eyes every time I blinked. Riley's face was ashen, abstract anger etched across it, the same anger that I felt consuming me.

"Jesus!" the Viking hissed.

"Wait," Charlie suddenly spoke, and all eyes turned to look at her, "play that last bit again, V."

"Suka!"

She stared into the flames of the fire.

"Again," she instructed.

The Viking played the last part again. I nipped the bridge of my nose and stared at my feet.

"Once more."

"What the fuck are you playing at?" Riley roared, "are you trying to torture him? What's this shit about?"

313

Charlie turned to me, dropping to her knees, searching my eyes.

"I'm sorry, Cian, please trust me."

I nodded, looking at Riley with an unspoken order. He turned away, pulling his hands over his head, distressed.

"Suka!"

The video played again.

"There," Charlie said abruptly, "it's the same voice, I'm sure of it!"

"What do you mean?" Viking's voice rumbled, looking at me.

I shrugged.

"The voice in the video. The man who tried to rape me, the one I killed… it's him."

My eyes snapped to her, searching her face. The unease, the fear, the humiliation and the rage. It was all there in her eyes, mirroring my own emotions.

"He said that same word to me that night. I'll never forget it, Cian," she spoke to me, lowering her voice, unsettled memories coming back to her.

"Fucking Polish!" I shouted, slinging my glass into the fire as it split into pieces and fell into the grate, the flames dancing higher from the alcohol.

The Viking moved towards Charlie, smiling encouragingly at her, a reassuring hand resting on the back of her shoulder.

"Nice work," I heard him say.

Turning to Riley, I spoke, "the Polish won't have orchestrated this by themselves. They knew too much about us. Do what you need to do to find out who gave the order, but leave them alive for me."

Riley understood me, understood my order. This meant war. War with anyone who got in my way, with anyone who was the slightest bit involved. Hatred and loathing, it fuelled me now, eating away in my chest.

Sometime later, my men traipsed out. Jonjo went with Charlie to see to the horses and everyone else to get some sleep; everyone but Riley. He caught my arm as I moved to go past him, his face concerned.

"Boss," he started carefully, "you know this means war and bodies?"

"Course I fucking do."

"Then is this the place for Charlie?"

I looked at him quizzically.

"She's in danger just by being involved with you. The attack on the yard. They were targeting your business, and it caught her in the crossfire. Being taken by the Russians. They were after you, not her; she just got carried along for the ride. Lebedev…."

"What are you saying to me, Riley?" my voice came out more like a growl.

"If you love her, let her go. You don't want to see her in a video?"

Everything went dark, anger erupting, and with a roar I wrapped my fingers round Riley's neck and drove him backwards into the wall, his feet scraping for purchase on the floor beneath him.

"Cian," his voice garbled under my hand, his fingers scraping at the flesh, "she's not yours, Cian. She can never be yours."

Relaxing my grip, Riley fell at my feet clutching his neck. For a moment I stood over the top of him, then I turned, walking out of the room and left him crumpled on the floor.

Chapter Thirty Four

෬ Charlie ෧

The house had descended into a strange atmosphere, a brittle quietness making the ominous mood more amplified. Cian and I had passed like ships in the night the last few days. He slept till late morning whilst I was up at the crack of dawn, training and tending to the horses, then by the time I came in on an evening he had gone out. The men talked in hushed voices, conversations stopping when they saw me, eyes casting me suspicious looks.

I woke up alone and ate alone, and the longer it went on, the more pissed off I was getting. Cian seemed to do all he could to avoid me. There was just a hint he had been around; the faint smell of his aftershave lingering on a chair in the kitchen where he'd sat, the smell of fresh soap in the shower, suspended on the steam in the bathroom.

I'd made a conscious effort the next day to catch him. Once the horses had been ridden out, I left the stable hands to muck out and stalked back up to the house. Tommy and Mad-Dog were in the kitchen drinking coffee and inhaling cereals. I didn't even spare them a look as I kicked my boots off at the door. Purposefully, I moved through the house, scanning each room for the illusive Irishman. I found Riley sat in the armchair in the lounge, a coffee in hand, reading something on his phone.

"Where's Cian?" I asked abruptly.

He looked at me, the startled look quickly fading to annoyance as he turned his phone upside down on the arm of the chair.

"He's not come down yet."

"Don't worry," I said, my voice dripping with sarcasm, "I can't see what mafia shit you were doing."

Taking the stairs two at a time, irritation biting at my heels, I bounded along the corridor, not concealing the angry stomp in my footsteps. I didn't knock on Cian's door, instead, I flung it open.

Cian raised an eyebrow at me as I barged in. His hair was still wet from the shower and he was standing in only his boxer shorts as he twisted the thick brown tufts under his fingers, the muscles in his arms bulging with each snippet of movement.

"What's wrong, Charlie?" he asked.

"You tell me? What's the cold shoulder for?"

"What are you talking about?"

"You know what I'm talking about. Stop treating me like an idiot."

He sighed, annoyance melting into sadness.

"I'm sorry. I'm just distracted."

"Not by the right things, Cian. I know this must be shit for you. I can't understand how you are feeling. But I'm not the enemy."

"No, sweetheart, you're not."

He smiled ruefully at me, his eyes still distant. I walked up to him and he watched me advance, his stature guarded, cool almost, but as I watched his expression as my fingers ran over the ripple of the muscles of his stomach, he rested his eyes shut as if cherishing my touch. When they opened again, the sadness was still there, swarming in the hazel orbs, confliction torturing him. I traced my fingertips over the tattoos on his chest, following the letters of the words on his skin.

"What does this say?" I asked, my voice almost a whisper, as I stared at the four lines of writing on his left pec.

The words were indiscernible, a language I didn't recognise, scratched into his skin in italics.

Neart san aontacht

Onóir i dioltas

Riamh toradh

Gan trócaire

319

"It's Irish. It's the rules we live by, our family motto. Strength in unity, honour in revenge, never yield, no mercy."

"And that's what you're going to do now, isn't it?"

He nodded. I could feel the fear creeping around the edges, trying to take hold. Dread at the thought as to what was to come next, what he would do, and what would happen to him. When had I fallen so badly for this man? The man I had hated. The man who I longed for when my bed was empty of him.

Stretching on the tip of my toes, I reached up and kissed him gently, feeling the fullness of his soft lips, of his hard body against me and the strength in his arms as he wrapped them round me, kissing me back. My hands moved through his thick hair as I pulled him into me, the roughness of the thrusts of his tongue igniting need in me and he walked me backwards towards the bed until my knees hit the side and I fell backwards. He was on top of me in seconds, pulling my jumpers off and yanking my riding breeches down my legs, not waiting to pull them fully off before I felt the head of his erection pushing against me. And with a long, full thrust he'd entered me, our bodies connecting physically as well as emotionally.

*****

I'd put Tommy to work that afternoon, as he'd been left to babysit me. Not that I was complaining. The only other babysitter was Mad-Dog and the looks he gave me, full of disdain and disapproval, did nothing to make me feel safe. Tommy was a sweetheart, dressed in Mafia clothing. And he enthusiastically did what I asked. Currently, that was shovelling the last of the horse shit out of stables and bedding the boxes down with fresh straw, ready for the horses to come back into.

"You really don't need a gym with this lot?" Tommy mockingly complained in his Irish accent as I handed him a cup of coffee, steam forming in clouds in front of our faces.

"Are you struggling? I thought you were a big, tough gangster? Speaking of which," I took a sip of the hot black liquid as Tommy eyed me reproachfully, "how does Cian seem to you?"

"He's fine. He's just being Cian."

"And what is just being Cian?"

Tommy took a long sip of his drink.

"I'd better get on. You'll be wanting to bring these horses in soon."

"Tommy, please. Give me something, some way of understanding what is going on in his head," I asked, pulling on his arm as he turned back to the pile of muck.

"I'm just a foot-soldier, Charlie. I follow his orders. I don't know him all that well," he said with a sigh, "but I can tell you he's been distracted since he met you. His reactions are less impulsive, more measured, more merciful; until the other night. I don't think I've ever seen him

321

more angry. It seems to have woken him up. Now he'll be the boss we need him to be."

That knot of dread that had been forming in my stomach tightened. I nodded wordlessly to Tommy. I'd asked for his honesty after all and then I baulked when he reminded me of who Cian really was.

I went back to my yard jobs, switching on the radio as I washed the coffee cups in the yard's kitchen, watching the sky acquire the orange glow of late afternoon as the sun started to sink into the horizon. Tommy popped his head in the door, his finished cup in hand, and I took it from him as the song on the radio finished and a news reader took over.

"Fire fighters battle a huge fire in a Doncaster industrial estate," the woman's voice read out excitedly.

My attention piqued, and I paused, concentrating on the newsreader.

"The fire was discovered at an old warehouse this afternoon," she continued, "fire fighters have been on the scene tackling the blaze for a number of hours after reports of explosions from inside the building."

I looked over at Tommy and he nodded, then walked away, leaving me with my attention focussed on the radio.

*****

Cian had gone back to being distant. There seemed to have been a lot of activity in the house, almost a war room setting in the lounge, and I was actively excluded from it. I'd retreated to my room and hadn't tried to approach Cian again. I would leave him to do whatever it was he needed to do. I understood, in part at least.

I was fortunate to have my own distractions whilst I waited for Cian to wage his war, but my bed felt conspicuously empty, and somewhere in my chest there was an ache. And the day before the biggest race of my career nerves and anticipation were setting in. I'd woken up with an apprehension creeping over me, making me restless and fidgety. I ran an extra few miles that morning to clear my mind and regain focus, but that had only made me feel sick, an annoying nausea that I'd not been able to shake off all day.

By the evening, we were on the road, horses and equipment packed onto the massive horse box, and headed south to settle the horses into their stables for the night. The racecourse was bustling when we arrived; stable hands and staff rushing about, unloading horses, tacking others up. Brian came off the horsebox like a fire-breathing dragon, snorting like a mad thing and bouncing around at the end of his lead rope. It had taken every ounce of strength I had to hang on to him.

The following morning, the atmosphere had taken on an electric buzz as the Festival of Racing got underway. Punters poured into the racecourse dressed in their best and the crowd was a sea of bright and beautiful colours and crazy hats. The horses were groomed within an inch of their lives, their coats gleaming and manes neatly plaited, showing off the ripple of muscles in slender necks. Brian was tense with the atmosphere and shifted from hoof to hoof, almost knocking me off the stool I was stood upon as I rolled the plaits in his mane into tight balls to sit just on the crest of his neck.

"Looking good, Charlotte," a voice jeered over the stable door, "the only thing you'll win today is best turned out."

Dickie blocked the light, the loose box turning darker from the shadows he cast over it. I sewed in the last plait and patted the black horse, climbing off the stool.

"Let's just see what happens out there today," I muttered, trying not to be wound up by him as I left the stable.

"You really think you're the dog's bollocks, don't you? This race is mine and I'll do anything to keep it that way."

"Is that a threat?" I snarled.

"It's a promise. This is my race. Get in my way and I'll…"

"What Dickie? What will you do?" I cajoled, watching his face contort.

An arm grabbed mine, fingers sinking into the flesh of my bicep.

"Just be a good little girl for once and stay out of my way if you want to finish the race in one piece."

"Get that hand off me," I warned, my temper flaring.

"Or what? You'll go running to your new sugar daddy?"

"Or I'll break your nose."

Dickie laughed and then stopped abruptly as my fist connected with the bridge of his nose and he let out a roar of pain, doubling over as blood poured between the fingers cradled over his face.

"You'll fucking pay for this!" he shouted, straightening up slightly.

"Really? You look better already Dickie," I said, shrugging my shoulders and walking away to the tall man in a suit watching from a little way off.

"What was that all about?" Cian asked as I approached him, his arms crossed in front of his chest.

"Just a few friendly, pre-race tips."

Cian's expression was dark, a storm swirling behind those hazel eyes.

"Who is he?" Cian asked, his voice thick, a low grumble which reverberated through me.

"Dickhead Hargreaves. He's an ex, Cian. An ex for a reason," I continued when the tall Irishman pushed his lips together.

I moved away from him. I still needed to get changed, and I could feel a bunch of nerves jostling for attention in the pit of my stomach.

Cian's hand wrapped around my upper arm, his fingers curling round the muscle lightly but with the threat of restraint. His eyes were a confusion of irritation, desire and fury, looking at me as if he didn't know whether to be angry with me or devour me. I made his decision for him.

"You did just see what happened to the last man who grabbed me, didn't you?"

His lips twitched at the corners, his eyes clearing from the storm they held for a split second, before the darkness returned. I shrugged him off, walking away.

Nerves had hit me square in the stomach once I'd put my breeches and racing colours on and I'd had to make a bolt for the toilets to evict the meagre breakfast I'd had that morning. Wiping my mouth on the back of my hand, I stared into the mirror, doubt threatening a hostile takeover of my usually focussed state. And then my mind flittered back to Bobby. How he would have loved to have been here to watch this. How he would have patted me on the back and told me to go get that win, even if he wasn't so sure himself. I smiled sadly at myself in the mirror, noticing for the first time the paleness of my face and the tiredness of my eyes. Squeezing my eyes shut, I willed my head into a better place, took a deep breath and left the changing rooms.

The atmosphere had ramped up into nothing short of electric outside as I walked across to the parade ring. Brian was easy to find in the huge field of racehorses. Jonjo hung on one side, a nervous stable hand on the other, as the black horse tossed his head around angrily, dancing from one foot to the next and letting out a row of explosive bucks. Pushing my earlier tension to one side, hiding it from the volatile beast of a horse that depended on my calmness, I approached the side of him and nodded at Jonjo, who legged me up without breaking pace with the horse.

Brian felt like a coiled spring and was soaking up the atmosphere like a dry sponge in the bath, but other than a few small leaps, he managed to keep his feet mostly on the ground. I watched the other riders mounting their horses, noting where Dickie was so I could keep an eye on him. In the crowd, I saw Cian. He was talking to another man in an expensive-looking suit, who was smiling widely, his face animated. I recognised the wealthy young banker immediately. Yet Cian barely looked at him, his gaze finding mine from across the space between us. A mask of tension and apprehension.

All too soon we were making our way to the track, the horses jogging and jostling each other as they got too close. I looked left and right, scanning the throng of riders, trying to keep space between me and Dickie. I knew he would come after me the minute we started. Then we were under orders and the mass of horses made their way to the tape, dancing and bouncing, not one remaining composed in the atmosphere. Then we were off.

I guided Brian, moving him quickly from the middle and close to the front, trying to keep him in space, watching my flanks for anyone closing in on us. The fences were coming thick and fast; huge leafy obstacles rearing up before us, almost as wide as they were tall. Brian sailed over them, never faltering, eating up the ground between each fence, his legs hammering the track as he ran ever faster.

Blood and hoof beats pumped in my ears, wind whipped the tears from my eyes. We passed the fourth horse, moving round him quickly, gaining on the third. I didn't check the black stallion. Instead, I willed him to stay calm, remain focussed. Glancing around, I could see Dickie two horses back and gaining. I needed to keep him away from us, keep us out in front. I tightened my reins and Brian flicked his ears back, stretching his neck out as he thundered towards the next fence. He flew over it, landing nimbly, safely on the other side.

We were neck and neck with the second placed horse with two fences before the finish. Dickie was coming up hard on my right flank. If he got alongside us, he would push us into the rail. The hooves of Dickie's ride were directly behind us now and I pushed Brian on, kicking a little with my heels as we passed the first placed horse and took the lead. I took another look behind me, seeing Dickie tight on my tail, forcing the young chestnut he was on to catch up to us. As we took off over the last fence, I held my breath, almost closing my eyes in trepidation of landing, in case we hit the ground slightly wrong and it sent us stumbling. But despite the huge steeplechase fence and the giant leap from Brian, we landed safely.

I pushed off the rail, tightening my reins again, sending the black horse flying onwards, leaning forwards, sinking myself down towards his back, making us as aerodynamic as possible. The thunder of hooves behind me faded slightly, and we surged ahead, crossing the finish line to win the second most coveted race in the United Kingdom.

Chapter Thirty Five

ঙ Cian ৪

The racecourse was crammed. Women dressed in their best dresses, high heels exaggerating long legs, hair and make-up that had been carefully planned and executed, complete with hats of feathers and organza. Men were equally immaculate, many coordinating the colours of the ties with the women they were with and all too many sporting a top hat. I felt out of place, despite the navy suit I wore.

I gazed round, sipping on my whisky, waiting for the man I was here to meet. I eventually saw him enter the lounge, over dressed in a three-piece suit of light grey with a bold black over check and the silver chain of a pocket watch visible against his waistcoat like some Victorian nobleman. He saw me and nodded, moving in my direction purposefully.

"Cian," he opened, "I'm really pleased you agreed to meet me."

I nodded, feigning a smile at the young billionaire banker.

"So you're ready to sell?" he asked excitedly.

"Yes, for the right arrangement. I'm going back to Ireland and have no need for businesses here."

He beamed.

"So what sort of money are we looking at?"

I outlined my price and Keegan looked at me for a second, taking me in.

"And that is the land, the business, assets, and the staff? Yes?"

"Yes. Their contracts will transfer to you, but must be on the same, if not more preferable, terms."

He smiled widely, a look of triumph on his face.

"And the jockey?"

"It's Charlie's choice whether she stays with you, but the stance is the same. If she does, her current contract must be honoured, or bettered."

"Deal," he said, holding out his hand.

"I'll get the paperwork drafted up and emailed to you. Give your details to my man here," I gestured to Riley.

The bustle from the crowd was growing with the atmosphere as winners were toasted and losses commiserated with alcohol and more bets. I drank alongside Matthew Keegan for a while as he eagerly discussed the horses racing today. And then it was time for the race. The commentators were stoking the crowd up and I watched the screens, observing the odds ever decreasing until Charlie was the favourite.

I made my way down to the parade ring as the runners started to be led out. Charlie's black stallion was making a spectacle of itself as usual, the worried looking stable hand trying desperately to save their toes as its hooves went everywhere but where they should. Jonjo soon joined the horse, swapping sides with the anxious lad as Charlie approached. Then, with a caber like toss, he threw her up into the saddle.

Matthew cooed beside me, babbling excitedly as he watched her take up the reins and quickly move the horse out onto the track. The field of horses gathered together like a swarm of bees, walking away and then doubling back, breaking into a trot as they approached the starting line. Then with a pop, the line sprung upwards, and the horses were off, hooves thundering as they jostled for position.

I watched Charlie steer the stallion through the throng, quickly getting him into the space and stride he liked, and I noticed the chestnut that was making a beeline for them. Yet, she kept the horse away from Hargreaves, pushing it out in front and devouring the huge steeplechase fences at each approach.

The racecourse commentator was shrieking loudly, the thrill of the race consuming him as Charlie passed the third horse, then the second. Then she sailed past the first, Hargreaves hot on her heels, checking over her shoulder a couple of times before she gave the horse the last push and he stretched his entire frame, leaping towards the finish line.

The crowd erupted, a surreal roar going through the racecourse as punters jumped and jostled. Keegan slapped me on the back.

"She's one incredible jockey," he said, delighted.

My eyes locked on the screen in front of me, Charlie filling the entire monitor. Her face flushed, a broad smile revealing the dimples in her cheeks and her light blue eyes full of elation. She was an incredible sight, on a horse or not. And I had all but sold her to the younger man standing next to me. My chest tightened, my hands gripping the tumbler of whisky in my palm as her beautiful smile and those fucking dimples stared down at me from the screen. The last time I would see them. I knocked back the rest of my drink and gathered my men, leaving Charlie to bring home the horses.

*****

The first cars were packed up by the time I had returned home and the men were moving boxes into the rest, placing them in the boot snuggly. The house was quiet, pensive almost, as we moved our belongings out one last time. I glanced around the rooms, closing doors on the emptiness as I'd checked each one. A sadness was settling in my chest, unease weighing heavily in the pit of my stomach.

Eventually, I heard the door click and saw the slight frame of Charlie as she tugged her boots off as I waited in the kitchen. She glanced around the room, her eyes scanning her surroundings and her brows furrowed.

"Where is everyone?" she asked.

"They've left already."

Charlie cocked her head to the side, looking at me with eyes full of questions.

"Left for where?" she asked suspiciously.

"We're going back to Ireland."

"Oh. When will you be coming back?"

"We won't. I won't."

I watched her reaction; the hint of realisation.

"Ever?"

"No, Charlie," I said softly, struggling to part with the words.

She looked at me unblinking, processing the information, and I watched as her eyes became glassy, tears welling but not allowed to fall. The heavy feeling in my stomach was spreading throughout my body, my breath hitching in my chest, despair and regret taking hold.

"So, what's happening with this place, Cian?"

Her voice wavered slightly.

"I'm selling it. To Matthew Keegan."

"That arrogant fucking banker?"

I nodded.

"Fuck you, Cian!" she spat, and she turned to walk away from me.

I hadn't expected that.

"Charlie, wait," I grabbed her arm, and she set her eyes on me, burning with pain and anger and betrayal.

She shrugged under my grip, looking at me furiously.

"Get the fuck off me, Cian."

Normally I would have held on to her, bent her to my will, taken her to my bed. But I couldn't do that. I had to let her go. So I released her and watched as she stormed out of the kitchen and back down to the yard.

I sat there for a few minutes, watching as her dark shape was swallowed into the night, the house stilling into silence around me so that all I could hear was the slow beat of my heart, feelings and emotions hitting me all at once. Sadness, emptiness, regret, guilt, jealousy. I squeezed my eyes shut, rubbing my temples. Then, getting up, I picked up my bags, turned off the lights and threw the last of my belongings into the car and drove away into the night, leaving the yard and Charlie behind me.

Chapter Thirty Six

ೞ Charlie ೦

I heard the deep, guttural roar of the big 4x4 car as it drove down the drive. Bright red tail lights faded gradually until it reached the bottom of the drive, disappearing onto the road beyond the gates. I sat on the mounting block reliving that last angry exchange with Cian, confused and rejected, and angry.

Eventually, after my arse had gone numb from sitting on the cold stone of the steps, I made my way back up to the house. The building was in darkness, its quietness hostile. I flicked on the lights, bathing the rooms in a brightness that didn't quite chase away the shadows; the loneliness threatening to smother me. I wandered, opening each door, gazing at emptiness, the only possessions the faded furniture. Bedding was neatly folded and left clean on the beds, preparations for departure clearly having started much earlier than I had even realised. How long had Cian known he was leaving?

My eyes burned from the tears gathering there, tears that I desperately forbid from falling.

Until I walked into the last room. It was the biggest room of the house, occupying the gable end, with views of the gallops and the stable yard. And now it looked barren. The mattress lay bare; the bedding washed and neatly stacked at the bottom of the bed, curtains open, vulnerable to the dark outside. I'd not stepped a foot in here for weeks, not since I'd found Bobby lying there. The first tear fell, dripping down my face, then another and another, and sobbing, I closed the door.

I didn't even bother to light the fire as I sat in the gloom, an ornate lamp in the corner of the room casting a dull orange shadow. The house settled around me, the groans and creaks of the structure amplified in the silence. I'd got used to the hustle and bustle and the stomp of men's boots, of the grunts and laughter, the smell of aftershave and liquor. Now, though, the place felt as far from home as I had ever experienced. I felt unwanted; rejected by the man I'd shared my body with and cast out by the house I'd spent the best part of my adulthood visiting.

The cold clung to me and I wasn't sure whether the sudden shiver was because of the emotions that leaked out of me, the chill in the night air or both. I turned off the lamp, wandering up to the room I had moved into. Grabbing a handful of belongings, I stuffed them in a bag and made my way to my flat on the yard. The only place I was wanted; my only place of solace.

My flat had shared the same fate. Tidied and cleaned, no sign of the young mafia foot soldiers that had taken up residence, save for faintest of smell of men, the only clue that it had been inhabited by anyone other than me. Shivering in the cold air, I flicked the heating on, made my bed and jumped under the covers. Yet every time I close my eyes he was all I could see, him and him alone. I let the sobs rip through my body, my pillow becoming wet with tears until there was nothing left to cry.

Over the next few days, I became an automaton; wandering the yard, unable to focus on what I was doing and avoiding human contact. I'd managed to go a couple of days before the questions from the staff were raised.

"What's happening, Charlie?"

"Where have the Irish gone?"

"Where is Jonjo?"

Cian and his men were conspicuous by their very absence. They'd become the excitement and noise of the place over the last few weeks that it was now insanely quiet without them. I avoided conversation with the staff for fear they would see my great display of weakness. I kept busy, training the horses, training myself, harder and harder till it reduced me to vomiting. The National was fast approaching and my mind needed to be on that race, but it was focus that I was struggling with, unless that focus was on Cian and what he had done to me.

The horses were running the best they ever had, their coats gleaming, their muscles rippling. Brian was anxious, sensing my mood and had spent a lot of time in the air rather than keeping his feet safely on the ground, although it had provided a few minutes of distraction as I fought to keep him under control.

As the day of the National arrived, my stomach was in turmoil. I'd felt sick since arriving at the racecourse the night before, my insides wringing themselves into a knot. The horsebox felt like a cage and I'd woken several times in the night, hot and stressed. By the early hours of the morning, I'd spent over an hour with my head in the toilet, nerves and stress getting the better of me. But as day broke, and the first shreds of sunshine crept into the horsebox, I'd eventually managed some form of disturbed sleep.

As I sat in my changing room, alone, I could just hear the distant roar of the huge crowds outside. I felt sick. My stomach had been somersaulting all morning, and I'd barely tolerated a coffee. I needed to chase these nerves away before I got on Brian. He would react to anything other than my calmness.

A soft knock on the door broke me from the depths of my thoughts. I recognised him immediately; tall and lean, over dressed in another garish suit, thick dark hair, almost black, thick black eyebrows and eyes just as dark.

"Nice to see you again, Charlie," he greeted me, holding out his hand.

I stared at it, not moving to put my hand in his.

"Hmmm."

"I can't wait to work with you and your horses."

"Not sure I can say the same."

His smile remained, not put off by my rudeness.

"We'll talk about your pay rise after this race. I'm sure you have plenty of prep left to do?"

"Yeah. I'd better get on."

Matthew Keegan glanced around the room pointedly and I gave a feigned smile, both of us knowing there was nothing I needed to do as I stood in my breeches and racing silks.

"Good luck out there. I'm sure you won't need it."

"Thanks," I said, watching the billionaire banker retreating from my changing room.

My stomach tensed again, and the nerves came flooding back, setting a swarm of butterflies off inside me. I rushed to the toilet and brought the rest of my coffee up.

The horses gathering on the starting line bumped and jostled each other, each jockey going through their own pre-race rituals. Some chatted to fellow riders, others surveyed the course ahead, and some fought with horses that bounced underneath them with excitement. Surprisingly, Brian was calm, and I trained my eyes on the obstacles on the course ahead, working over my game plan.

Not only was the National the biggest race of my career, it was the biggest field of horses I

340

had ever raced in. There were nearly forty horses forward, all of them running as a herd for the first part of the race. The course itself was long; four miles of galloping and jumping and was often more of a game of luck than skill, praying that another horse wouldn't mis-jump and bring you down. There was no way I was going to be able to keep Brian in space over the first two miles. Instead, I just had to count on the hours of training I'd put in and hope he'd listen to me.

Then, with the rhythmical thump of hooves and the jostle of bodies, we turned back towards the starting line, coming towards it at a steady trot. The tape sprung up in the air as we approached and we pushed forwards, the horses surging onwards onto the track towards the first fence.

Brian settled quickly into a good rhythm and a steady pace and I could glance about, watching the surrounding horses, ready to change course at the slightest sign we were going to get in trouble. I couldn't see Dickie and his ride amongst the horses, but I knew he was there. It seemed we'd both had the good sense to stay out of each other's' way, or he just didn't fancy another black eye.

Brian cleared the jumps over the first mile and I watched a few horses and their riders fall. This wasn't the race for mistakes and there was little space to come back from one. As the field thinned out, we edged into the first half of the horses. Even with Brian's talent and stamina, it was far too early to even attempt to push forwards. We just needed to stay in a good position.

As we came halfway through the second mile, the black horse suddenly put his ears back and slowed very slightly. I checked around me, looking for any cause of his sudden discomfort. He dipped his head a little and something in his back felt a little off. But a fraction of a second later, I felt the power return to his hindquarters and his ears prick forward again. We cleared the next jump, flying through the air and landing without a falter in his stride and then again with the next jump.

But as we took off over the third jump, a big leafy thing which felt almost as wide as it did tall, he just dropped a front leg, not quite picking it up as quickly as the other one. It hit the jump, and I heard the rustle of the leaves and brush beneath us. But as we landed, Brian's front legs suddenly buckled under him and we lurched forward towards the ground. I pulled on the reins and tried to lean back, giving the horse the help he needed to make it back up to his feet. But instead of bounding straight back up, he scrabbled around, skidding and bobbing. Something crashed on top of us, sending us to the ground hard. Pain erupted within me.

Chapter Thirty Seven

ஐ Cian ൽ

The rustle of the newspaper's pages as I turned each one tentatively was enough to make my head feel like it was being held in a vice again. I'd already sunk two black coffees and almost a pint of orange juice as I chased the thump of a hangover headache away, the slightest noise bringing it back.

"Morning. You look like shit!" Osh said too loudly as he joined me at the oversized dining table, a plate of breakfast clattering onto the oak.

"Shut the fuck up," I grumbled, rubbing my temples in an attempt to ease the pressure building in my head.

Oisín chuckled, shovelling a fork full of bacon into his mouth.

"You will keep raiding the liquor cabinet, brother."

It had become a habit since I got back, or at least when I realised it was the only thing that encouraged sleep to come and drown out the thoughts of Charlie. Whisky dampened the incredible guilt that ate away at me, the aching loneliness and the consuming emptiness. But it didn't take away the anger.

I opened the next page of the noisy paper and laid it out on the table as I nibbled on some toast; the cardboard-tasting-square leeching my mouth of any moisture. Pushing it to the side, I poured another cup of coffee, sipping at the bitter hot liquid as I read the article with familiarity.

'Body pulled from the River Lee.'

"That should send the Gardaí sniffing round the O'Malleys," Oisín commented, his neck looking like it might snap as he strained to read the article at an angle as he scooped up the last of the scrambled eggs from his plate.

"I don't want the Police getting too close to the O'Malleys or we won't get close to them either. Tell Paddy to be more careful where he disposes bodies in future. Fucking amateurs, the lot of you."

Osh opened his mouth to complain, but the look I shot him made his retort retreat inside his head.

"About the Gardaí," he continued, and I took a deep breath, reading the look in his eyes, "they've taken one of our factories out."

"Fuck!" The word came out more strangled as I didn't dare shout, my head already resuming its incessant thumping, "how bad?"

"The whole operation from there is gone. At least for now. They have seized everything of any use."

"Do I need to guess where the tip-off came from?"

"Can only be the Polish or the O'Malleys. No one else is pissed off with us enough to fight back, and the Russians are behaving themselves at the moment."

I drove home the night I'd left the racing yard, my heart ripped to shreds once more and anger gluing those pieces back together. The minute I'd stepped foot in the O'Sullivan mansion in the small hours of the next morning, I dragged all my officers out of bed and my father's study was instantly transformed into a war room. That night we took the first of several strikes against both the Polish and the O'Malleys.

"I want everyone in the office in thirty minutes," I ordered.

Nodding at me, Osh got to his feet, pouring himself a cup of coffee before seeing that the men were woken. I sank yet another cup myself, the rush of caffeine in my body making my heart feel like it was going to beat its way out of my chest. Passing the liquor cabinet before I left the heavy wood panelled room, I gave it a glance. Osh was right that it had become my friend and sleeping partner these last few nights. I'd even woken up this morning with only the dregs left in a bottle on my bedside table.

Tearing my eyes from the cabinet, I walked the long corridor to the kitchen on the far side of the house, digging around in a messy drawer for some pain killers before making it back to my office to slump into the worn leather chair. By the time my men filed in, my headache was almost tamed.

"Riley," I turned to my best friend who was sitting closest to me on the saggy, russet brown leather sofa, "have we contacted the families of the men lifted from the factory raid last night?"

He shook his head, and I stopped myself from rolling my eyes for fear they might actually fall out of my face.

"For fuck's sake. Get someone to speak to whoever depends on them. Make sure they know we'll pay for a lawyer and support them till their men are out."

I turned to Osh.

"Sort a solicitor out. I want them at the Police station as soon as that shift changes. None of those men will talk. Make sure the lawyer understands that."

"We're losing a load of product from our street level business," the accountant looked up from behind his laptop, "and we're pissing money with it."

"Word on the street is that the Polish are pushing back. They're either buying out our street operations or running people clean off their patch," Riley stated, watching me carefully for my reaction.

He was right to be wary; fury was building at every mention of the Polish bastards.

"We've gone through the CCTV surveillance from your contact, Boss. Looks like Ronnie O'Shea's sold out to the Polish too," Mad-Dog spoke up from the back of the room.

The office descended into an uncomfortable silence, the atmosphere thick with unease. Running the palm of my hand against my jaw, three-day-old stubble prickled my skin.

"Osh, looks like we've got a game of poker tonight."

*****

I looked over dressed in my black suit and thin black tie when we arrived in deepest, darkest Cork. The bar sported a huge neon signing that hung precariously lop-sided over the doorway. Faded curtains were drawn across the window, a crack spreading across the glass from the bottom right corner, and smashed bottles in the gutter.

The door creaked as we entered, catching on a lump on the floor, sending nearly every head in the packed pub turning in our direction. Both Osh and I stood out like a scene from The Matrix and had we been anyone other than the O'Sullivans, then we would have retreated immediately. I glanced around, watching people divert their eyes and tug on their fellow drinkers beside them.

Sidling up to the bar, I didn't even need to push past the small crowd gathered there. A thin man scurried away, clutching a half-drunk pint, leaving a gap for me. The barman was round, a dirty tea-towel slung over his shoulder that he wiped his hands on as he approached, watching me carefully, eyes flicking over every part of me visible above the bar-top, scanning for any weapons I might have hidden on me.

"Two of your best whiskies and a game of poker," I raised my voice against the beat of the music.

The middle-aged barman nodded in understanding and tilted his head, directing us to the edge of the bar. The floor fell away down a series of six or seven steps that led to a corridor, the ground damp underfoot from fluid that had leaked out of doors on either side with tatty signs depicting the customer toilets. I stepped carefully through the puddles, the smell not filling me full of confidence that it was anything other than watered down piss.

A door barred our way and the barman took a set of keys from his back pocket, taking one last, long glance at us, before unlocking and pushing the door inwards and stepping out of our way, allowing us to walk through.

"Don't you think we should have brought more men?" Osh asked, his voice low yet still stark against the silence in the long corridor.

I shook my head, "nothing we can't handle ourselves."

We didn't need escorting into the right room. A slice of orange light peaked out from a crack where the door at the very far end of the corridor stood ajar; the smell of cigarette smoke drifting out.

A huge round table and several people occupied the windowless room. The air was thick; smoke mingling with the acidity of alcohol and varying scents of aftershave competing against each other. The atmosphere suddenly stilled, faces turning towards us, men shifting uncomfortably in wooden chairs, the padded seats bursting and threads dangling underneath.

"Cian. Oisín," a man at the far end of the table stood up, flustered, "err… we didn't expect you."

"Thought we'd call in for a game," I said coolly, eyeing the scene, working out who would have twitchy fingers first, "you don't mind if we join in?"

I pulled a battered chair from a collection in the corner of the room placing it next to a man sitting off to the right. Metal squealed against the floor as Osh brought a chair on the other side of him and the chubby man with the shaved head looked at each of us warily.

I slapped him casually on the back, making him jump and spilling his drink across the bare table, "long time, Ronnie."

All eyes remained on us, no one speaking, only watching, waiting for something to unfold. The man who greeted us cocked his head in the dealer's direction, who slid some cards towards us. I peeled them off the table, leaning against the uncomfortable metal backrest of the chair as I studied them. The room stayed silent.

"It's nice to see our business partners tonight," I broke the silence, signalling to Ronnie

349

to pour me a glass of liquor from the bottle placed next to him.

He turned an empty glass over and I noticed the slight shake of his hand and a tiny splash of liquid escape. Taking the tumbler from him, I held the glass in the air.

"I'd like to raise a toast to your loyalty and continued partnership. As you all know, if you look after the O'Sullivans we look after you. To continued partnerships."

The room of men raised their glasses and a muttering of 'partnerships' added to the smoke filled air. I swigged the liquor back, the cheap Irish whisky burning at my throat and making my eyes water, then I slammed the tumbler back onto the table, the bang echoing around the room. Grabbing the back of Ronnie's head, I smashed his face into the table, the thud and resulting crunch this time even louder. The room descended back into an eerie half-silence, the only noise the shocked gasps of Ronnie as blood ran between the crack in his fingers.

"Apart from Ronnie here, who neither has loyalty nor a partnership. Isn't that right, O'Shea?"

"I, I, I don't know what you mean," he spluttered, spitting flecks of blood across the table.

"Someone bring me a bottle of vodka," I instructed.

The dealer left the table, scurrying away to rake through some boxes and come back with a bottle of clear liquor, a gaudy red and white label slapped on the front, not quite straight. I indicated for him to pass the bottle round and everyone poured a glass and I watched as a few of the men stole nervous glances at each other.

Pouring myself a glass, I raised it in the air once more and the rest of the room followed. Osh nudged Ronnie, who dutifully clasped a bloodied hand around his glass and lifted it in the air.

"To Ronnie. Who has moved on to bigger and better things," I said, bringing my glass to my mouth and swallowing the disgusting drink as it burnt skins cells off my tongue and the back of my throat.

Ronnie hesitated, eventually putting his glass to his lips, when I slapped him on the back in encouragement.

"Again," I motioned to the dealer and the bottle was passed around once more.

"To Ronnie," I continued, raising my glass in the air, watching everyone, including Ronnie, follow my lead, "who has made new friends with our Polish enemies."

I necked back the drink, watching as looks tore through the poker players.

"Drink up," Osh growled from the other side of O'Shea.

"So, Ronnie. Would you like to tell us about this lucrative deal you made? Does it pay better than me?"

"I, err, I, I don't know what you're talking about, Boss," he stuttered, colour draining from his face.

"You do. Try again. How much more?"

"I told you. I haven't a clue….."

Ronnie's head hit the table hard again, an agonised wail coming from his mouth and I looked over to Osh, who shrugged his shoulders in response.

"How much?" I lowered my voice to almost a growl.

"They said they would up my cut by 20%", he whimpered, blood now falling from a large cut across his eyebrow.

"Another toast," I called across the room, signalling for another bottle of the disgusting cheap vodka to be passed around.

I was the last to fill my tumbler, the clear liquid sloshing haphazardly into the glass. Filling Ronnie's glass for him, I tipped my head, gesturing for glasses to be raised once more.

"To loyalty," I called, watching the room repeating the word back to me.

As everyone slugged back their vodka, I grasped the bottle's neck. The sound of smashing glass broke the uneasy atmosphere as I brought the bottle down onto the table, reducing it by half and shoving the jagged end into the side of Ronnie's neck, twisting sharply. His hands clutched at the wound as I dragged the remnants of the bottle away, blood rushing out of the hole, across the table and onto the floor. For a few seconds his fingers scrambled at his neck, trying to hold the flesh together, trying to stem the flow of blood.

I stepped away from him and surveyed the room. My eyes caught the terrified eyes of a man on the far side, who still had his raised glass in his hand.

"McGivern, you take O'Shea's patch," I nodded in his direction, "the rest of you, no deals with the fucking Polish."

I didn't need to spell out what would happen if they did. Fastening my suit jacket, I covered the dark red stain on my shirt, pushing back from the table as the chair legs screeched angrily across the floor and leaving the men to their poker as Osh followed on behind me.

*****

The thumping ache returned the next day as I groaned from under the covers, daylight flooding the room and amplifying the pain in my head. My mouth felt as dry as a desert and once I'd finally dragged myself from the pits of my bed and survived the trek to the kitchen on weak legs, I stood and drank a lake's worth of water, diluting the alcohol playing havoc with my system.

Osh and I had met some of my men at one of the City's strip clubs; part business, but mostly pleasure for those who had been interested enough. We'd secured another one of the O'Malleys' businesses, offering a mixture of extra income and the threat of violence, and the O'Sullivan Empire was expanding.

Taking the entire coffee pot with me, I locked myself in the office, switching the television on, while flicking the sound down. I was supposed to be forgetting about her, leaving behind all the memories of the blonde who had no fear of me, who resisted me at every turn, until I had her naked. I shook my head, trying to rid the images of her from my mind but only rattling my dehydrated brain around my skull and reigniting the pain.

Massaging my temples, I watched the figures on the screen, the horses milling about the paddock, a black horse bouncing around as the handler worriedly patted its neck, anxiously awaiting the jockey. I should have switched channels or even turned the television off entirely, but I didn't. I sat watching. Watching her jump into the saddle and take up the reins, watching her calm the horse as she made her way towards the start, a huge field of horses and jockeys jostling around her and watching as the tape shot up in the air and the horses lurched forward.

I didn't take my eyes off the screen. Each jump was clean, each time she moved the through the field, following the strategy she knew would work, the horse powering on beneath her. The cameras continually focussed on her, never allowing me to look away. The fences were huge, yet she rode towards each one without fear, watching for her stride, positioning the horse to keep him clear of anything that might get in his way. Each landing she eased him closer to the front of the group and I watched her glance around, keeping an eye on the other riders.

Dickhead Hargreaves wasn't far away and my eyes kept flicking back towards him, a lump of tension in my throat each time he crept closer, but he wasn't putting the pressure on her yet. Charlie was already well into the race, with just under two miles to go. The television commentator was getting more and more excited and all I could hear from the TV was the sound of her name as, with each long stride, they surged onwards.

Suddenly, the horse faltered, its ears flicking backwards and forwards and backwards again, and Charlie looked around and down to the ground. But then he seemed to recover, stretching his neck out and lengthening his stride, and I'd wondered whether I'd actually seen anything at all.

They soared over the next few jumps. A huge leafy, wide fence stood in their way. The front runners leapt over in varying styles and then came Brian. The horse took off, its weight pushed back onto its hind legs but unusually it trailed a front leg, leaving it dangling and touching the top of the hurdle. Yet as the pair landed, the black horse's front legs seemed to fold under it. Charlie leaned back in the saddle, her legs pushed forward, waiting for the plucky stallion to correct his mistake. He skidded, pulled up and then collapsed forwards. Charlie wobbled on top of him like a rag doll. And just as the pair of them hit the ground, the horses behind them came crashing over the fence.

I held my breath, my heart drumming in my chest. The commentator shouted, hooves and horses became bundled into a blur of thrashing legs; colourful racing silks buried under writhing bodies and tangled limbs.

Three of the four horses got to their feet, their jockeys following and running off to side of the track as the rest of the field launched over the top of the fence, the black horse lay there, his legs moving but unable to get any purchase. I couldn't see Charlie.

The camera cut back to the race. The commentator was babbling. I'd moved to the television screen, standing in front of it, although I'd not even realised I had got up from my desk. I heard her name and the mention of screens, and I stood there willing the camera to go back to the fence. My stomach ached from the tension, I balled my hands into fists, and it felt as if my heart had stopped beating altogether.

It seemed to take an age for the race to finish. I don't know who won. I didn't care; I wasn't listening. Only watching. Watching for a glimpse of that fence, a glimpse that Charlie was OK, a glimpse she was alive.

The camera reverted to the fence, replaying the fall. I scrutinised the screen, watching where she fell, and this time I could a snip of the burgundy of her racing silks under the tangle of horses. The next shot on the screen made my stomach drop. White screens, people hurrying between them and the ambulances, and a smaller veterinary car shrouded the fence.

"We have no news from the racetrack," the commentator's voice filled my office, *"I'm afraid it looks very serious. Thoughts are with Charlie Porter and O'Sullivan racing. We'll bring you an update when we know more."*

Chapter Thirty Eight

ೞ Charlie ೲ

The incessant beeping noise was enough to drive me insane. It cut through my dreams and brought me out of a peaceful sleep to the unwelcome throb of pain. Everywhere. I would have groaned but my throat was so dry not a sound could pass. My hand curled around the thin sheets, screwing them into a ball in my fist as pain pounded in my head, my eyes adjusting to the glare from the lights. A pang of nausea made my mouth water.

Warm skin touched my hand, someone covering it with theirs, and for the first time, I felt the presence of another.

"How are you feeling, honey?" the soft voice fussed from beside me with a squeeze of my hand.

Carefully, painfully, I turned my head; each tiny movement sending swathes of agony to beat my eyes, pressure pushing from inside my forehead.

"Nat?" I croaked.

"I'm here."

"I feel like shit."

"Trust me, you look like it, too."

"Thanks," I grumbled, "I need water."

My sister helped prop me up and then passed a clear plastic cup towards me, guiding it to my lips for me to take a sip. Each small gulp was painful; from the sting of my lip, the dryness of my throat, to the searing agony in my side.

"What happened?" I asked eventually.

"Do you not remember?" Natalie asked, concerned.

I did remember. Some of it, at least. I closed my eyes, remembering the mistake, a mistake that we should have recovered from, but instead his legs went from under him as we landed. There were so many horses behind us, we didn't stand a chance. I felt the rush of air as the ones that missed us flew over the top of us and then the thud, air being sucked from me as the ones that didn't, hit me, hit us.

I remember trying to get up, of my head spinning, my eyes unable to focus, and the feeling of something heavy writhing about on top of me. There were so many legs. Tangled, kicking in panic, metal flying at my face, cutting my arms. I heard the thud of hooves, the rush of the wind and it seemed to take forever for all the horses to have jumped that fence, jumped us, before the ground stopped shaking and the thundering of hooves coming towards us stilled.

And I remember trying to scramble to my feet, of the poker hot pain in my chest, but I couldn't get up, I couldn't get my eyes to focus on anything other than the black horse lying on the ground in front of me.

He just lay there, his breathing erratic, his eyes half rolled back in his skull and his nostrils flaring with pain and fear. Eventually, with lead-like limbs, my body screaming with each tiny movement, I crawled to his head, to calm him, comfort him. He didn't move when the screens went up around us; a flush of white and the bustle of racecourse staff.

The vet was there before the ambulance and I saw the look of sadness in his eyes and the small shake of his head, the pain of the impending loss hitting me in the chest, the lump in my throat nearly choking me.

I'd fought off the paramedics who tried to peel me off the black horse, who tried to force me to lie back down, who wore masks of worry as they looked at me and then at each other. I was there until the gun was brought, my hand scratching at the base of his neck, as I whispered to him, telling him he was a good boy, that the pain from his shattered legs would be gone soon. And he looked back at me, the panic in his eyes subsiding for one moment, watching me, listening to me. His ears pricked at my voice, his breathing calmed.

And I watched as the gun was pressed to his head, wincing at the sound of the bolt being fired, his eyes rolling back and his body finally relaxing, life snatched from him.

I remember the strange wailing noise I could hear, the hot liquid rushing down my cheeks, the paramedics easing me onto a stretcher, the worry and pity in the eyes of the racecourse officials as they crowded round me, sheltering me from the cameras as I was taken to the ambulance. But I didn't remember anymore.

And now all I could feel was this; the throb of agony all over my body, the hideous feeling of bile burning as it rose to my throat, nausea caused by the pain and the half-numb, half-raw feeling of loss and emptiness. My eyes burned hot, and I squeezed them shut, taking a deep breath.

"What's the damage here then, Nat?" I asked once I composed myself, glancing down over my body covered in the thin hospital gown, wires protruding from every angle.

"You've done a number," she said lightly, squeezing my hand again, "broken collar bone, broken ribs, lots of bruising, but the doctors were mainly worried about your head."

"Wouldn't be a first," the joke was empty.

"They put you in an induced coma for a couple of days as they were worried about the swelling and a possible bleed on your brain. There'll scan you again in a couple more days."

"Fuck no! That means I'll have to stay in here. I've got horses to look after."

"They're taken care of. Cian…" she paused, clearly uncomfortable at saying his name to me.

I rolled my eyes, regretting it instantly when a flood of heat and pain hit my head, the room spinning at a speed of knots as I clutched the sheets for fear I was going to fall off the bed.

"The O'Sullivans have briefed the staff," Nat continued as I stared at the door in the far side of the room, emotions running rampant inside my head and a familiar prickle starting in the corner of my eyes, "the horses, their training, the yard, it's all taken care of. You just need to rest."

I would have rolled my eyes again, but I remembered the pain that brought, so instead I sighed, loudly. That hurt too. Red hot, searing pain across my left-hand side. I clamped my eyes shut, immediately making a mental note that any eye movement was going to lead to agony of varying degrees.

"Shall I get you more painkillers?" Nat asked, reacting to the hiss that left my lips.

"Uh huh," was all I could muster.

As quickly as Natalie left the room, a nurse popped her head in the door.

"There's a man here to see you. Shall I bring him in?"

Involuntary excitement hit me, the little bob of my stomach, my pulse quickening. I nodded too quickly, instantly regretting it, but anticipation distracted me from the sudden pulsing behind my eyes.

But the tall dark-haired man was not who I was expecting as he walked in the room, a ridiculous sized bunch of flowers clutched in his hand. My excitement was short-lived, replaced by the heaviness of disappointment and the treacherous prickle of tears at my eyes. I swallowed, forcing back the emotions threatening to consume me.

"Charlie," he purred, his voice low and rich, as he approached my bedside in his expensive three-piece suit, the gold chain of his watch hanging across his waistcoat, "how are you?"

"Feeling as good as I look," I answered, unable to hide the disappointment that laced my words.

"That was a hell of a fall. You're very lucky that it wasn't more serious."

"It was for some of us," I answered bitterly.

"I know. I'm sorry about the horse."

"Are you? Or just about the amount of money that was lost?"

Matthew Keegan pushed his lips together, a flash of darkness crossing his face, dissipating as quickly as it came.

"The horse is a loss, of course, but not as much as you would have been," he said with a forced lightness.

"Well, I'm out of action for a while now anyway," I glanced down at myself, at my left arm in a sling, a huge angry hoof-shaped bruise on my right fore-arm.

"Don't worry," the tall man continued, "the sale of the business is progressing well. I'll have the best physiotherapists work with you. I'll pay for the best health care you could possibly need. I'll get you back on that racetrack as soon as I can."

He smiled at me encouragingly, waiting for my outpouring of gratitude. It didn't come and I could see the flash of annoyance cross his face, his jaw tightening just a little, the tiny narrowing of his dark eyes. A rustle from the doorway distracted both of us.

"Who is your visitor?" Natalie asked suspiciously, eyeing the billionaire banker interestedly.

"Matthew, this is my sister, Natalie," I introduced them, thankful to move his attention away from me, "Nat, this is Matthew Keegan. He's buying the racing yard from the O'Sullivans."

Keegan moved towards her, holding his hand out in greeting and shaking her neat palm with a certain sort of masculine grace.

"Nice to meet you, Mr Keegan," she greeted him in her best lawyer voice and I couldn't hide my smile as she matched him with her air of authority, "we appreciate your concerns and gifts. But my sister needs rest now," she quickly added in response to the face I was pulling at her.

"Of course," Keegan agreed before turning back to me, "perhaps we can talk about my plans for the business when you're feeling a little better?"

He smiled brightly at me, his face full of encouragement and expectation. Handing the bunch of flowers to Nat, he flashed me another smile, perfect white teeth contrasting against the slight tan of his skin and the darkness of his hair and eyes, and with a respectful nod of his head towards Natalie, he left.

I managed a faint smile, a fresh fear of nodding, or moving any body part no matter how small consuming me.

"And that was?" Nat asked with interest, her eyes following the tall dark shape as he moved out of view.

"He'll be the new owner of the racing yard when the deal goes through," I answered softly, trying to keep the emotion from my voice.

But emotion or not, Natalie could see right through me.

"What's wrong with him?"

"Nothing. He's just not… he's just not got any industry experience."

"He's an investment banker. He'll have done his homework and his successes speak for themselves."

"I thought you didn't know him?" I raised an eyebrow, a flood of pain hitting my forehead.

"I know of him. I was more interested in what he was to you?" Nat smiled mischievously, but I couldn't align with the amusement of her words.

"He's just a rich bloke. Where are those pain killers?"

My head felt like it had been run over by a tractor, repeatedly. Heat burned in my side and my whole body alternated between a dull throb to a sharper ache. I was tired. I was empty. And what I really needed was relief from all of this; the pain, the anguish, the emotion, disappointment and despair.

Chapter Thirty Nine

ᴆᴑ Cian ᴐᴙ

Guilt gnawed at me like a starving rat whilst terror chipped away at me from the other side, and, although it faded with each day, remorse filled the gap that it left. I'd watched the racing footage over and over, nausea, dread, fear eating at me with each minute that ticked by whilst I waited for an update from Riley.

He'd acted on my instructions to contact all the local hospitals, to find out by any means necessary how Charlie was. I'd not done it myself. I couldn't risk my resolve breaking. I couldn't risk acting on the constant thoughts that haunted my nights. She was safer this way; safer away from this life of treachery, violence, and death. And yet still she'd nearly been killed in that fall.

When I'd eventually located her, she was in a serious condition. She had multiple breaks, but it was the head injury and the swelling on the brain the doctors had been concerned about. Through Riley's contact at the hospital I was provided with daily updates until at last, they'd brought her out of the induced coma and she was awake and responding.

I'd wanted to be there, to hold her hand, to be the first one she had seen when she opened her eyes, but that would have meant bringing her back in; back into danger. I had to let her go. For good. No more dreaming of her, no more thinking of her when my hand finds my cock for relief, no more wondering if things had been different, if I'd been part of a different family. It was torture. It was worse than torture. That I had been trained to endure, trained never to yield to, but this, this was something else.

Cradling my head in my hands, I focussed my eyes back onto the boring lines of text on the papers in front of me. Lawyers had drawn up the contracts for the sale of the racing business and transfer of the staff and I'd been sitting trying to get my head round the boring legal waffle, making sure that the staff, that Charlie, would be properly looked after.

My office door opened following a soft knock that I'd barely heard, my mind anywhere but where it should be.

"Hey bro," Osh announced his presence, Riley stepping in behind him, and the rest of my men pouring in behind them, finding seats where there were any, others leaning against the furniture in the room.

Passing the paperwork towards the plump middle-aged man in the room, I rubbed at my temples, today's headache not quite faded away yet.

"Looks fine to me. Have a read, see if there is anything in there we need. I want the staff properly protected as the transfer goes through."

The older man raised a greying eyebrow, and I shot him a look that told him not to voice the thoughts that just formed in his head.

It was a full office this morning, more than just my more high-ranking officers. Operations were moving on. We were steadily pushing back against the Polish, discovering their strongholds across Ireland and the UK, burning factories, tipping off police where we had solid contacts and fewer chances of repercussions from the law ourselves. But the O'Malleys were also moving in on the spaces we were creating and I'd yet to really deal with them.

They were barely a step behind us, picking up the patches we had been clearing before we'd really had a chance to ourselves. They were carrion, scavenging off the benefits of our kills, swooping in like vultures. And it was pissing me off. They knew too much.

My eyes swept the room, studying faces. There had to be a leak in the organisation; someone high enough that they knew what our strategies were, where we would strike next, and when we were coming. It had happened a few times. The Polish had picked up my father and Torin just too easily, I'd been sold out to the Russians at the Jockey Club Ball, Northumbria Police nearly had me for the murder of Lebedev, and now back home the O'Malleys were just too close.

I watched Tommy and Mad-Dog. They were merely foot soldiers despite how close I'd got to them over the last few months; would they betray the family? Anyone would for the right price. Tommy was born and bred in the firm. His father had been a loyal member, as did his grandfather, and he'd always been proud to be one of us. Mad-Dog, on the other hand, had been found on the streets. He was vicious, but had the loyalty of a starving dog toward the person feeding them. Oisín had found him, and he'd taken some training at first. He was quick-tempered and ruthless; as much a liability as Osh himself.

The older men had been loyal to my father for many years and whether they approved of my decisions or not, they didn't let it show. But somewhere in this room, in this organisation, was a traitor; leaking our plans just enough that our enemies were half a step ahead.

We'd not quite cracked the Polish backs. We'd not found their stronghold nor got a handle on all their businesses, but we had been chipping away at them for a while. Brick by brick, we were taking apart their empire.

"We've got a lead on one of the Polish heads," Riley started, "seems he has a healthy appetite for O'Malley pussy."

"Siren's?" I asked excitedly.

Riley nodded, "seems he's there most nights."

"Looks like we're having a night out in Kilkenny, boys."

370

*****

"Talk me through the night they were taken," I asked Osh quietly as the car hurtled down the motorway, my eyes flicking between the road lit by the car's headlights to my mirrors and back again. I noticed the slump in weight against the passenger seat as I waited for him to respond.

"Dad and Torin were supposed to be meeting McNally. He wanted support for the upcoming elections and he was paying big. McNally wanted intelligence against who he was running against. We knew he was likely to win and it would mean we'd have him in our pockets. It was a good move to expand operations with the protection from the politicians."

"Who knew about the meeting?"

"All of us. We'd discussed it as we usually did."

That implicated everyone in my leak theory.

"Anyone else who wasn't in the meeting?"

"Just Torin's wife and Fiadh. What are you thinking, brother?"

"I think we have a traitor. I just don't know who."

I glanced in my rear-view mirror, watching the headlights of the car behind.

"How did they get Fiadh, Osh?"

371

He went silent beside me, and I waited patiently for his answer.

"She borrowed my car. I was supposed to be at the meeting. I was driving myself there, it was always the plan, but then Fiadh asked for a lift into town. I said I would take her. And I would have. But McCormack was short with the rent and the protection money again and his lass came over to, err, pay it off. I didn't know she'd taken the car. She'd got fed up with waiting for me."

"So you were too busy fucking someone to take our sister to where she needed to be or even go to the fucking meeting you were supposed to be at?"

The car went silent again. The only noise was the purr from the engine.

"They would have got me too," he mumbled.

"Yeah, but they wouldn't have taken Fiadh."

I wanted to reach across and punch him; open the door and shove him out into the road without slowing the car or just smash his head through the fucking window. She was our baby sister. He should have protected her, even if that meant with his life. We sat in silence for the rest of the journey, not even glancing at each other.

The strip club was located down a back street; red neon signage leaving no room for doubt to what it was. The figures of women in provocative stances were painted in red against the black walls. There was no queue to get in and

372

having parked the cars some streets back, the five of us bounded up the stairs, bantering with each other in feigned excitement as we fit in with the rest of the punters.

Slipping a doorman a few crisp notes, he emptied out a booth at the back of the club, giving us a vantage point of nearly every corner of the venue. The club wasn't packed. Its décor was dated and stereotypical and a number of the tables housed single men, fantasising over the women who danced on the stage whilst sipping the cheapest drinks on the menu.

In the furthest corner of the club, a group of men were positioned in a booth. They were loud and brash, knocking shots back and cajoling at the women that danced on the podiums nearby. The shorter man in the middle seemed particularly interested, beckoning over each dancer when they finished on the small stage only a few metres in front of him, his hands marauding over their bodies. The dancers were familiar with him, flashing him smiles and looks, and I watched him tuck a few notes into the black thong of one before she climbed into his lap, his comrades watching on with interest.

I sat watching him for an hour; observing the numerous rounds of drinks he ordered, the way he whispered in the brunette barmaid's ear every time she approached the table before she hurried away again as quickly as she could prize his fingers from her. His eyes followed her everywhere she went. The woman was pretty. Thick brown hair hanging down past her shoulders, tits pushed together, almost escaping out of the white shirt that tried in vain to remain in control of them and the tight short skirt that showed off long toned legs. She shrugged off every bit of interest from the punters, serving their drinks and moving on quickly. She wasn't one of the dancers, I could tell that from her demeanour.

As our drinks ran dry, I left our booth, sidling up to the bar and perching an arse cheek on one of the bar stools. I watched the barmaid serve some others, smiling politely but making little small talk despite the customers trying their best. She needed this job, either as an extra income or to fit around studies or something. Her financial situation was her weak point. When the other men cleared off with their drinks, she approached me, forcing a smile. I ordered another round of drinks and watched her as she worked, glancing up at me occasionally, keeping tabs on where I was and what I was doing.

"Have you worked here long?" I asked, looking for a reaction and finding little. She was used to that question.

"Couple of years," she answered with disinterest.

"Do you like your job?"

"It's a job."

"That's not what I asked."

She stopped and looked at me with more interest this time. I offered a friendly smile and watched her sigh.

"It pays some bills."

"Again, not what I asked."

"Why do you want to know?" she studied me, her eyes narrowing.

"You just don't seem to have much enthusiasm. Not like the other girls. You don't engage with the punters. You don't talk to the doormen or the other girls. You need this job to pay off a debt, make ends meet, don't you?"

She pushed her lips together, her brow furrowing into a scowl. But her brown eyes told me the truth. There was a soberness there, a tiredness.

"What if you could earn two years' worth of this salary and walk away tonight? Would you do it?"

"I'm not a whore!" her tone was filled with disgust.

"I know you're not. But if you could pretend to be *available* for a few minutes, I'll help you get out of here."

She cocked her head to the side; I'd interested her.

"The man in the middle of the booth right at the back…."

"He's the new owner," her eyes narrowed on him, something just short of hatred crossing her face.

"Is he? Interesting," so the O'Malleys sold to the Polish. The dots were joining up, "I need a word with him, in private, away from his crowd."

"I'm not aiding and abetting a murder. Do you know who they are? They'll come after me."

"I won't kill him, but I can't promise he won't look much uglier by the time I've finished with him. Tell you what; I'll add a couple more grand towards your relocation expenses."

She looked back at the man sat in the middle of the pack, groping the almost naked girl on his lap. Then she turned to me and nodded.

A short time later, I watched the brunette walk across with another round of drinks for the table. She leant over in front of the man in the middle, sliding the drinks across towards him. Whatever she said to him made him smile, a grin that took up most of his face, and he shot a look sideways, smirking. Then he got to his feet, wrapping an arm around the girl's waist, pulling her into the side of him and sliding his hand down to her arse. They walked past me, the girl not making eye contact, and disappeared through a door that led towards the toilets.

I watched the other men at the table, their attention taken up with the next girl that walked onto the podium not far away from them, their eyes fixated on her huge tits that bounced and threatened to spill out from her bra as she danced seductively against the pole in the middle. They jeered and threw notes onto the small stage and she tucked them into the front of her lacy thong, letting her fingers linger there.

Nodding at Riley and Osh, we left Tommy and Mad-dog as sentries and followed the barmaid down the corridor. She hadn't gone far and I could see the shape of the two of them at the end of the long corridor. The Pole had his hands all over her, and she was doing her best at keeping him from getting too intimate. I strode down the corridor, crowding in on the couple, and the man stopped, shooting me an annoyed glance.

"Busy here, mate," his voice rumbled through a thick accent.

"Not anymore."

I flicked my head and the bar maid pulled away from his grasp, hurrying past us. Tilting my head, I watched her from the corner of my eye, Osh stopping her and handing a wad of notes. She turned her head back towards me, looking at me one last time before darting back down the corridor and hopefully never ever coming back to this shit hole.

"Who the fuck are you?"

"You don't know?"

The man looked at me blankly at first, then looked at Riley and Osh before a hint of realisation crossed his face.

"Get the fuck out of my club, you Irish cunts," he growled.

I smiled and then smashed by fist into his face, sending him staggering backwards and through the door behind him. Exactly where I wanted him. We followed on inside the room, Riley leaning against the door.

I punched him some more; in the side of his face, in his stomach, in his ribs till I felt a dull crunch, anger and hatred spilling from me with each connection of my fist to his body.

Once he was a bloodied mess, I took a step back, admiring the work of my fists, a slight ache forming across my knuckles.

"Where do I find your boss?"

"Like I'd fucking tell you."

I nodded at Osh and Riley, who was already advancing on him. Grabbing an arm each, they pulled him to the table in the middle of the store room and opened the fingers out on his right hand.

"You've got five chances to tell me," I said, sliding my knife out of the back of my trousers.

"*Pierdol sie!*"

The man screamed as I hacked his little finger off.

"Four."

He shook his head. I brought the knife down again, skin popping and bone crunching under the blade.

He screamed again as he lost his index finger. Blood spilled out onto the table, thick and gooey, and the man panted between struggles and shrieks. But he didn't give the Polish stronghold location out.

"OK, OK," the man gasped as I hacked the third digit off, only his thumb and middle finger left intact on his right hand.

Tipping my head at Osh and Riley, they loosened their grip on him and he straightened up, cradling his butchered hand.

"I won't tell you where the boss is, but I will tell you this," he hissed, hatred burning in his dark eyes, "that nice little blonde jockey of yours. She won't last the night. Our boys are on their way. They'll fuck every pretty hole she has and then cut her throat. Just like we did to your sister."

The darkness hit me like a hammer, my eyes losing focus, my vision blurring. I brought the knife down on the last of his fingers, his agonised scream fuelling my rage and then my fists flew at him, pummelling his face till it was merely a bloody pulp and his body slumped to the floor.

"Come on," Osh urged. We need to get out of here.

"Charlie," I mumbled, terror and fear ripping at my throat, my voice coming out dry and shaky, "I won't get to her in time!"

Chapter Forty

❦ Charlie ❧

"How are you feeling?" Natalie asked, her heels clacking on the wooden floor as she moved through the house.

"OK," I lied from my slumped position in her armchair.

Nausea had plagued me all day, and I was so tired it had taken my last ounce of energy to get up from my seat in front of the television and hunt for the painkillers. It had been a long day and today I'd grown bored with daytime TV.

Nat kicked her shoes off beside the sofa before padding through to the kitchen and rifling through the fridge. I heard the chink of a glass on her granite kitchen bench followed by the glug of liquid.

"Tough day?" I asked, glancing sideways towards where she stood, raising the wine glass to her lips and taking a long mouthful.

"Hell of a day. Want one?" she asked.

I shook my head, my brain feeling as if was ricocheting side to side with the movement and my mouth flooding with saliva as nausea rushed back to remind me of its presence.

"I think I'm gonna head to bed soon. It's hard work watching TV all day."

"It's early still, sis. I'll make us some tea."

"I'm not hungry."

"Have you eaten today?"

"Had some toast."

I heard Natalie sigh before muffled footsteps moved towards me.

"I'm worried about you Lottie," she said softly as she sat across from me, sinking into the heavily cushioned sofa, grasping her wine glass, "I know you've been through a lot but this… this isn't you."

She waved a hand, drawing an imaginary bubble around me. Tears prickled at the back of my eyes and despite biting my bottom lip whilst I concentrated on something else, anything else, I couldn't stop them spilling down my cheek.

"It's just been a shit few weeks," I mumbled as my phone vibrated beside me, the display not showing the name of the person I longed for.

I slid the button across, rejecting the call.

"Who was that?" Nat asked, her head tilted to one side as she watched me.

"Matthew Keegan."

"Shouldn't you have answered that?"

"Why? He's not my boss yet."

"He seems a nice sort."

I shot her a look.

"What?" Natalie continued, "he's tall, handsome, doing well for himself and, well, not a criminal.... as far as we know."

"Nat," I complained, sighing, "I'm not interested in him. In that way or any other."

"Did you love him? Cian?" she added when I feigned confusion.

Chewing my lip, I considered all the answers I probably should give. Instead, I nodded silently, letting another tear fall more freely this time.

"You know what they say? It's better to have loved and lost...."

"No. No, it's not," I snapped, "I'd rather not have loved him then I wouldn't feel like this. Wouldn't feel so... whatever this is."

Nat sat quietly, looking at me with pity in her eyes. I didn't need her pity. I just needed not to feel. I wanted to be numb to this emptiness, to the loneliness, to this feeling of loss. It was eating me from the inside out. It was all I could think about from the minute I woke up to long after I went to sleep. It haunted my dreams and it hung out in my nightmares. Everyone I'd loved, they'd all gone. I'd lost them all. Bobby, Cian, Brian, Dad. All. Gone. I didn't want to feel like this ever again; I couldn't feel like this ever again.

"I'm going to go back to the yard tomorrow, Nat," I didn't dare look at her, "I need to get back to some normality. Sitting in front of a TV all day isn't me."

"Lottie," she answered softly, "you're not fully healed. You should be resting."

"Being around the horses will help me. I've got the staff there to do all the work. But I need to be back where I belong. "

This time I did glance at her. She nodded in understanding.

"Good night, Nat," I said, pushing myself to my feet, carefully sucking in a breath to mask the pain just from the slight exertion.

Despite the ache, the stiffness and bone crunching pain, nothing hurt as much as the emotional torture. I could bear the physical agony any day as long as I buried this turmoil.

*****

It wasn't as easy as I thought it would be. The minute I stepped a nervous foot onto the yard, I was immediately caught up in the bustle. But even in my most loved environment I felt peculiar, a dull sense of not belonging clinging to me, that it was no longer home. Propping myself against the mounting block, I watched the stable hands working hard, listened to the ring of metal shoes on the concrete as the riders took their mounts off for exercise.

By mid-afternoon, I was finding my rhythm again, although extremely slowly. With the use of only one arm, hay nets were taking an age to fill and I eventually gave up. Instead, I found comfort in grooming the horses, seeing the shine on their coats after the soft, goat hair bristles flicked the dust and dirt from them, watching their muscles ripple under each swipe of the brush. Friendly, soft muzzles nuzzled at my hands and I stood for a long while, enjoying the quiet company.

The stillness and calmness of the yard didn't stay that way for long as the loud rumble of an exhaust broke through my solace. I peeked over the stable door, listening to the richness of the roar from the car, the obscene loudness against the low black sports car signifying money and lots of it. As he stretched a long suited leg out of the door, I had to wonder how he'd folded himself in two to get into the vehicle in the first place.

The stable hands paused, sharing quick glances at each other as they watched the tall man approach, another getting out from the car behind, clutching a black briefcase. Matthew Keegan smiled at me, warm and charming.

"Charlie, nice to see you up and about. Your sister told me you'd come back."

I rolled my eyes, instantly sending me dizzy and staggering backwards. Keegan caught me, gently clasping my elbow as I floundered around one-handed.

"I've brought the contracts. The business transferred to me a few days ago."

I nodded solemnly. It was the final nail in that coffin. The last evidence of the Irishman, of us, swept away. I swallowed, forcing my volatile emotions to stay in check, but I couldn't stop the burn in my eyes and at the back of my throat.

"Can I speak to you separately?" Keegan asked, looking at me pointedly.

I tipped my head, gesturing to my flat above the stables before walking stiffly off, leading the way. Each step I climbed tired me, my legs feeling like they belonged to someone else as I clung to the banister with my good arm to brace myself.

"Here, let me help," Keegan asked, moving towards me with an outstretched arm.

"I'm OK. I got this," I shrugged at him, a warning to stay away as fire bit through my left-hand side and I swallowed the painful hiss that made its way to my lips.

My flat was how I'd left it; tidy and organised. The light floral scent from the plug-in air-freshener greeted us as I opened the door. I beckoned towards the couch and the dark-haired man sunk into the low settee, his long legs stretched out in front of him. Turning away, I clicked the kettle on, fumbling with the coffee jar lid with my only working arm.

"Coffee?"

"Thank you. White one sugar."

"Figures," I muttered, struggling with the milk top and spilling sugar over the bench tops.

"Look," Keegan started from the sofa as I brought the cup towards him, "you're an amazing jockey and I know you've had a shit few weeks, but I want you to stay here and continue to ride for me."

I eyed him, blowing on the hot liquid in my cup as I leaned against the bench top.

"I've doubled your wages; it's all in here for you to look over."

"Leave it on the table," I replied more coolly than I had really intended, "I'll have a look."

"There's something else."

I cocked my head to the side, a feeling of nervousness washing over me.

"The autopsy that was carried out on your black horse…. it found evidence of a substance in its system."

"What sort of substance?" my voice cracked.

"A type of ketamine. The BHA is going to launch an investigation into how it got there."

Even from his seat on my sofa, I could see his eyes searching my face for a reaction. My thoughts jumped around my head, jostling for attention. Brian's sudden loss of power in the race, the slight falter I felt and then the slowness in picking his legs up over that fence. It all made sense.

"Shit," I breathed, hobbling to the sofa and slumping down onto the opposite end.

I felt sick. Really sick.

"How did it get there, Charlie?" he asked softly, eyes full of pity.

Heat rose from the burn in my chest to my face like someone had set me on fire.

"It wasn't fucking me. I don't need to drug my horses to win a fucking race," the words came out through gritted teeth, "but there are plenty people in this industry who did not want to see a female jockey win those races. Maybe the BHA should be sniffing around them."

Keegan nodded, pity turning to understanding.

"The BHA has suspended your licence while they investigate. This doesn't change my offer."

"It'll be a few weeks before I can even get back on a horse, Mr Keegan, let alone race."

"Will you accept my offer, Charlie? I'll look after you, through all of this and more."

My eyes moved to the contract on the table, the typed pages blurring into a mangle of black shapes. Could I stay here? After everything? My memories of death and heartbreak, of violence and threat. I would be safer without Cian. Life might be normal again. Even in those thoughts, the thrill of danger ignited something in me, a yearning, a need, a sorrow. Pinching the bridge of my nose, I closed my eyes.

"Charlie? Are you OK?" Keegan's voice broke my thoughts.

"Err, yeah. Just tired."

It wasn't a lie. Tiredness had hit me again as I had moved into the warmth and the smell of coffee just seemed so strong. It made my head whirl and my stomach tighten.

"You should be resting still. Read over the contract. Let me know that you'll stay with me. I promise you won't regret it."

I nodded as he rose to his feet and I watched as he left my flat. A bag of painkillers sat next to the kettle. Pushing up onto weak legs, I moved towards them, fumbling through the foil packet, pushing the chalky tablets into my mouth and gulping down my hot coffee, a formidable sting starting on my tongue. But I was too tired to pay it much attention and I shuffled off to my bedroom, collapsing onto the bed on my good side. For a few moments the room swirled and my eyes struggling to focus. Closing them helped, and soon I was dropping into a dark chasm of unconsciousness.

A noise in the silence woke me. The room was almost pitch black, an orange glow from outside cascading rich shades of gold and bronze across my bedroom. I'd never moved from where I'd dropped and I didn't know what time it was. The red display on the radio was fuzzy, the numbers jumping around in front of my eyes. I pushed upright, studying the red digits: 3.30am. I'd somehow slept all afternoon and evening. Outside, a rumble of a car caught my attention. My heart beat harder.

388

I got to my feet and staggered across to the window. The orange glow was coming from outside, cutting through a thick haze of…. smoke. My chest tightened, my heart feeling like it had stopped altogether. Fire!

I pushed my feet into a pair of boots at the door, stumbling down the stairs in a mix of haste and stiffness, running onto the yard. Not seeing the dark car parked a little way away.

Horses snickered nervously, the rustle of straw from looseboxes as some walked round and round in panic. I slid back bolts, throwing doors wide and shooing frightened animals out, free into the dark. Looking down at the far end of the yard, the little kitchen was burning a bright russet orange, the red lick of flames rising into the air and black smoke billowing out. Two horses remained, and the fire was moving towards the hay barn. When that went up, there would be little time left.

I ran towards the stable, pulling the bolt free and flinging the door open wide. The bay horse was standing at the back of the stable, eyes wide with fear, nostrils flaring. Running into the box, I got behind it flapping my arm like a mad, one-winged bird, agonising pain screeching through my body. It took a step forward, then a step back. I made a whooping noise, moving my arm again and eventually, after two more faltered steps, it bolted out the stable.

Approaching the last stable, I could feel the heat of the fire. The bay filly whinnied, terror in the high pitch of her voice. The bolt was stiff and

I couldn't wiggle it free. I pushed my weight against the door, sticking my toe under the gap at the bottom. The bolt sprung out, sending me staggering backwards, jolting my ribs painfully. The filly cowered at the back of her stable and no amount of pushing and pulling made her move towards the door.

Reaching for a head collar, I tugged my arm free from my sling and slipped the strap up over her ears, red hot, searing pain shooting through my shoulder and down my side. I hissed, desperately trying not to cry out and scare the horse further. I pulled, I pushed, I turned the horse in a circle, but nothing would make her move closer to the door. A roar from outside made my stomach drop as the hay barn beside us went up, the red-orange glow of the fire creeping closer. Heat and death edging towards us. I couldn't lose this horse too. The last one Bobby and I had bred together. I couldn't lose another one. Tears ran down my cheeks, my breath coming in anxious gasps.

"Come on," I coaxed, my voice weak against the crackle of the flames.

My eyes caught movement just inside the stable; a black, leather-clad shape moved towards me, blonde hair tied back into a ponytail. Shrugging the fabric sling over my head, I thrust it towards the biker, gritting my teeth against the pain.

"Cover her eyes with this," I instructed.

The Viking wrestled with the terrified horse's head, roughly securing the white cloth over her eyes and then getting behind her, he pushed as I pulled the horse, hoof by hoof out of the stable into the fresh night air before letting her go to join the others somewhere loose on the property.

"Ring the fire brigade," I shouted, above the roar of the flames that now consumed the buildings on the far side of the yard, heat licking towards us.

But the Viking just stood there, looking in the opposite direction of the fire. I studied his face. His lips were pursed, his eyes narrowed. His arm reached behind his back, tugging at something tucked away behind his jacket. The glint of metal caught the red of flames as he drew it from behind him; a knife, over six inches long and with an ugly serrated edge. My stomach dropped to my toes, dread and fear gripping me.

Shrouded in smoke, like deathly spectres, three men stood at the yard entrance, a big black car behind them. With his other arm, the Viking pushed me behind him.

"We've come for the girl," a thick voice called from in front of us.

"Not happening," the biker's guttural tone was fearless, "run and hide. I'll find you. Don't show yourself to anyone but me."

I darted away as the blond man stepped forward, swinging the huge knife in an arc through the air in front of him. Feet pounded on the ground and the air erupted with the grunts of men. I tried not to look behind me. My arms pumped, pain replaced by terror as I ran towards

391

the burning stables. But the pull of looking back was too much. The Viking wheeled around, his arms gliding gracefully through the air, blocking and connecting as the three men circled him. He was graceful and lethal at the same time.

A howl broke through the deadly roar of the fire behind him, one man staggering backwards, cradling his side, as the others advanced, but he pulled himself together, advancing again. They moved back towards the burning building, bit by bit, and the biker glanced around, realising they were manoeuvring him towards the inferno behind him. The Viking was nimble, but the three men were fierce and he was outnumbered, the fire at his back another enemy.

My eyes caught the tools lined up against the end of the stables, the prongs of the pitchfork speaking to me. Closing my eyes, I took a breath. These men were killers. I couldn't fight them, but if they killed the biker my fate was worse than death. I'd seen that on the video. The memory of the footage sent bile rising in my throat. My hand curled around the cold metal tool.

I crept forward, inching my way towards the fight, keeping concealed in the smoky shadows for as long as possible, watching each attacker, looking for a weakness I could exploit. The injured one didn't move as quickly and as I got a little closer, I could see a dark patch leaking down onto his jeans. I just needed to even the fight. That's all I had to do. Coming in from the side, I ran at him, the prongs of the fork angled upwards, and with all my strength I pushed hard. There was a pop of flesh, a crunch of bone, and a hideous scream that rang over the sound of the blaze. The men beside him turned. The Viking didn't falter. His arm came quickly through the air, sinking into the neck of the man to his left. The man clutched his throat, shock and horror on the face that was twisted towards me before he crumpled to the ground.

The fork was wrenched from my hands and pulled free from the side of the man I had forced it into, and he came at me. His mouth twisted in a snarl so callous I felt sick. His face a contorted mix of rage and hatred and pain. I swallowed, staggering backwards. A hand clasped my throat, hard fingers tightening around my neck, my feet left the floor before I landed heavily on my back, air rushing from my lungs, pain tearing through my chest.

He was on top of me in seconds, both hands on my throat this time. I couldn't breathe. My lungs couldn't refill what I just lost. His fingertips bit into my flesh. I tried to kick at him, but his bodyweight pinned my legs and agony pierced my side. I couldn't move. He was so much heavier and stronger. My vision blurred, blackness gathering at the back of my head. He smiled, showing gaps in his teeth.

The tip of the knife exploded through his throat, blood raining down on me. His smile stayed in place for a sick second, then his face contorted, and he fell on top of me, iron scented wetness soaking into my chest.

Chapter Forty One

ಋ Cian ಲ

I pulled through the double iron gates and onto the single track, private road that led to the racing yard. The concrete was shiny; the tyres making a whooshing noise through a puddle as rain gently fell onto the windscreen of the big, four-wheel drive. Even in the damp morning conditions, there was a haze in the air; the residue of burnt buildings and the staling smell of smoke.

Rounding the corner and pulling up onto the yard, the entirety of the situation came into view. The kitchen and the hay barn were completely razed to the ground, a few charred posts sticking up against the dull, grey sky. The bottom half of the stables was almost all gone, and the rest were varying shades of grey to black.

A hole tore through Charlie's flat and I could see right into her bedroom from the cavity left in the fire's wake. Her flat was just about destroyed and it took little guessing that any belongings that had survived would be ruined by smoke and the dowsing the fire brigade had given it.

Murky puddles covered the yard, hay and straw floating on top where it had been washed out of the stables. There was no presence of life, or even death.

The door was open a jar when I got up to the house and I pushed on it tentatively, looking around for her. In a corner of the kitchen, she sat on the floor, her knees drawn to her chest and a leather jacket pulled around her shoulders. Her eyes met mine, and I felt like someone had punched me in the chest. Even with my almost constant thoughts about her, seeing her again in the flesh, those light blue eyes sparkling with tears, the vulnerability of her delicate facial features which betrayed the feisty character that hid underneath; just a memory could never have replaced her full beauty.

"What the fuck are *you* doing here?" her voice was strained, but the bitterness was evident, nonetheless.

"Charlie…." I started, walking towards her, ignoring the bulky frame of the biker watching us intently.

"No. Just don't," she warned as I dropped to my haunches in front of her.

Black soot was smeared across her face, tinged with spots of red. I followed the splashes of blood, seeing dark patches soaked into her chest. Peeling the jacket from around her shoulders, she winced, trying her best not to draw attention to her injuries as I inspected her nervously. Her left arm was tucked in against her side and her skin was pale. But there were no cuts or wounds.

"Yeah, I'm OK as well, Kee," the voice behind me caught my attention.

The Viking was holding a scrunched up piece of fabric against his right arm, saturated in red and still trickling. Pushing myself to my feet, I pulled his hand away and inspected the damage. His bicep was slashed open, torn flesh and swelling making the cut an angry mess.

"That's gonna need stitches."

"Tell me about it," he replied, "can you stitch it?"

"With what?"

"Anything, just get the frigging thing closed up," V grumbled, "fuck, that tattoo cost a fortune!"

"There's a drawer full of all sorts over there," Charlie said, her voice faint.

"We need to get out of here," I said as I nipped the skin together and pulled the thin black thread through.

"Yeah, well, we've a load of stiffs in the garage to get rid of first."

"How many?"

"Three."

"All Polish?"

"Sounded like it," the Viking hissed through gritted teeth as I pushed the blunting needle through a tough bit of skin and then tied the last stitch off.

"Done," I said, inspecting my work, "can't say it's not gonna scar."

"Nothing a new bit of ink won't fix."

After we had stashed the bodies in the boot of my car, I came back to the kitchen. Charlie was on her feet, hanging over the sink, a glass of water clutched in a shaky hand.

"Hey sweetheart," I said softly, putting a hand on her back, "we need to get going."

She shrugged me off angrily and turned to glare at me.

"What did you come back for?" she snapped, her baby blue eyes fixing on mine.

"For you. I was trying to protect you."

"Protect me from who? From you?"

"Originally, yes. Being with me put you in danger."

"Then why come back here?" she shot back, her biteable pink lips pushed together.

"The Polish. They were sending people to kill you. I wouldn't have got here in time."

"You didn't."

"I know. I sent 'V'. I knew he could get here before me."

She folded her arms across her chest, then winced.

"OK. Fine," she said eventually, "you can go now."

"We are going."

"No. *You* are going. I'm staying here."

"You can't stay here."

"I'll go to my sister's."

"You can't go there."

"Why not?" Charlie tilted her head to the side, watching me.

I sighed. Why was she so fucking stubborn?

"Until this war is over, you're coming with me."

"The fuck I am."

I pinched the bridge of my nose. This was giving me a real fucking headache.

"Look," I said flatly, "I'm going to get the car. You're getting in voluntarily."

"No, I'm not."

"You are. Or I'll tie you up and put you in."

*****

She kicked my head rest again, my head snapping forward as my neck crunched.

"For fuck's sake, Charlie. If you don't stop it, I'm putting you in the boot with those dead fuckers."

398

"I swear to god, the minute you untie me I'm going to punch you," Charlie complained from behind me.

"Yeah, well, I've got nine hours to work out what to do with you then."

I pulled the car over, the rumble of another car behind me. We unloaded my boot, dragging the heavy corpses deep into the woods, and driving the other car in behind them. A screech of tyres to set up the scene before the car crashed through the trees and I kicked out the windshield.

"Thanks mate," I said, clasping the Viking's arm after I'd driven him back for his bike, "I appreciate it."

Glancing at Charlie, tied up in the back of the car, he chuckled before pulling on the black helmet.

"Good luck with her," he said, amused. Then he revved the engine, the motorbike roaring to life, before he spun it off and drove away from us.

Nine hours with Charlie tied up in the back of my car, complaining every waking minute was nothing short of torture, and as night set in, I broke numerous speed limits to make the journey a bit more bearable. At some point, she relented and fell asleep and I carried on in silence, driving through the night.

The crunch of gravel woke her, and I braced myself for a further torrent of abuse as I drove the car up the drive to the front of the house. But she was quiet. Peeking at her in the rear-view mirror, she looked pale and tired. When I stopped at the front doors, I walked round and carefully scooped her out the car and carried her through the house.

"Are we taking prisoners now, Boss?" one of my men asked, smiling mischievously as I walked in.

Charlie leaned in against me, too tired to fight me anymore as I strode up the stairs and towards my room. Placing her gently on my bed, I took out my knife, cutting the thick rope and freeing her.

"Whose room is this?" she asked, her voice croaky as she looked around.

"Mine."

"So where are you staying?" she fixed her glare on me, defiance shining in her blue eyes.

"Here."

Charlie shook her head.

"No way. You're not waltzing back into my life and picking up where you left off, Cian. You were the one that walked away. Not me."

My heart felt heavy. I deserved her anger. I should hold her, tell her how much I'd missed her, how stupid I'd been. Instead, I nudged her legs apart and stood between them. Running a finger along her jaw line, I watched the reaction in her eyes, the dilation of her pupils at my touch and the teeth that bit at her lip as she tried to deny it. My cock hardened.

"When this war with the Polish is over, you can go home. But until then, you stay here," I said roughly.

She kept her eyes on mine, looking up at me, the challenge clear. My stomach clenched, heat swelling in my groin. Her lips looked even more perfect when she was angry.

I turned, leaving her alone in the room.

Chapter Forty Two

∝ Charlie ℘

It was nausea, and the heavy arm draped over my stomach that woke me the next morning. I was tired, my head was slowly spinning and my mouth felt as dry as a desert in a drought. Closing my eyes, I concentrated on the whizzing sensation, trying to keep the images in my brain from picking up speed.

Cian grunted from beside me; his breaths were shallow and rhythmical, warming my skin and sending shivers down my spine at the same time. If it hadn't been for the need to throw up, I would have happily stayed there, but I wriggled out from underneath him and ran to the bathroom.

"I can't decide whether to hold your hair or fuck you," the low, gravelly voice came from behind me.

I shot him a glance over my shoulder as I gasped, the sudden vomiting leaving me breathless under the heavy pain in my ribs.

"Fuck off," I breathed, as his eyes raked over me, on all fours, hugging a toilet bowl in only my bra and thong.

"Come on, sweetheart," he said, this time more gently, pulling me to my feet and handing me a glass of water, "are you OK?"

"Fine. Just the pain," I lied.

I'd been feeling rough for weeks now and a horrible feeling niggled at the back of my head, one that I had been denying any purchase for the last few days, not least because of the implant wedged in my arm. Bile rose in my throat again and I steadied myself against the sink.

"Why did you come back, Cian? Why not just let The Viking deal with it?"

His expression darkened, and he raked his hand through his hair.

"We got some intelligence that the Polish Mafia were coming after you."

"Yeah. You've told me that. Why did you come?" I pushed.

Cian sighed, conflict playing on his face.

"I, I couldn't bear the thought of someone hurting you, Charlie. I need you here where we can protect you."

I searched his eyes, looking for something.

"Someone did hurt me, Cian," I braved eventually as he raised an eyebrow, "you did. Why did you leave like that? No warning. You didn't have the decency to even talk to me before you sold up and left me with fucking Keegan."

"I know. I'm sorry. Charlie, I thought I was doing the right thing. This war between the families… I didn't want you a part of it. Selling the business was the best way to show that we'd packed up and left and that you weren't a part of this, of me."

"Yeah, well, that worked," my voice was gathering anger, "someone targeted me on the racecourse too. Where were you then?"

"What do you mean?"

"Brian was drugged. Someone, somehow, slipped him something. They meant to bring us down that day."

Cian's brow furrowed, surprise across his face.

"I thought the horse just made a mistake. I watched the race."

"Where were you then? Afterwards. I never heard a word from you."

"I sent flowers."

"You sent flowers from the 'business', Cian, not you," I retorted.

He moved towards me, reaching for me, and I moved backwards; fury and hurt flaring as my cheeks flushed with heat.

"Leave me alone, Cian," I said, my voice an angry whisper.

His hazel eyes studied my face for a few moments, an internal struggle playing out behind them. Then, deciding that I meant it, he nodded slightly and left me alone in the bathroom. Tiredness crept over me, and after I heard the door from the bedroom shut, I retreated to bed, alone.

But instead of sleep claiming me, my thoughts ran rampant round and round my head. I wanted to feel something. I wanted to be wanted. But another part of me couldn't let that guard down again. I wanted to hate him for leaving me behind and then rocking up like a fucking hero. But, when I saw his face in Bobby's house, a sense of relief, of want and need, came over me. Those eyes, his lips, the annoyed raise of his scarred eyebrow, the way his brows knitted together when he was angry, worried, or even just thinking. Every day I had sought his face from my memories and nothing did it justice, like seeing him in the flesh. Lying wrapped up in his arms made me feel all kinds of shit: happiness, desire, safety. But the hardest one was the feeling liked I belonged there, that I belonged with him.

This was a nightmare. Was he just going to turn me loose again when this was all over? Was he only acting out of some sort of guilt because he'd somehow dragged me into all of this and then we would be back to trying to forget each other? I didn't think I could take that again.

At some point my thoughts had stilled, and I'd fallen back to sleep, but when I woke again, hunger had replaced nausea. My stomach growled loudly, and I suddenly felt like a starving animal. I wandered around Cian's huge room with its floor-to-almost-ceiling windows covered with heavy curtains and matching pelmets. Once regal wall paper, faded in places, hung limply where it had peeled away in one corner. The carpet was well worn and covered by rugs, all of them a different colour and style.

I shivered suddenly. Spotting the large oak drawers opposite the bed, I rifled through Cian's clothes till I found a jumper. It hung down to my mid-thigh and fell over one shoulder but it was warm and in the absence of any other clothes, my own dumped beside the bed, tattered and grubby with smoke and soot. This would do.

Floorboards creaked under my feet as I made my way across the landing, the carpet worn where many had walked it over the years. There was a musty smell in the air, almost damp, but not quite. It lingered, along with wisps of men's aftershave and wood polish.

The upstairs landing had row upon row of pictures. Some were landscape paintings of indiscernible woods and fields, but some seemed more personal, more meaningful. A woman show jumping, the horse boldly clearing a huge fence of red and white poles and then another of the same woman clearing a massive expanse of water.

As I got to the end of the landing, just before the stairs, one of the pictures stood out. This time the woman was sitting on top of a horse, brown hair flowing loose about her, her hazel eyes bright with happiness and a toddler tucked in front of her. I stood for a while watching the photograph, sadness emanating from it, and I moved away suddenly, feeling the familiarity of despair winding its ugly talons around my throat.

I wandered the downstairs, numerous rooms running off the corridor, all similarly decked out in dated décor and bulky, dark wooden furniture. Eventually, all the way along the far end, I found a kitchen. It was huge; almost like something you would expect to see in a hotel or restaurant and was the most modern room in the house. The floor was tiled grey as glossy white and black kitchen units rose from it. There was a massive range cooker, bigger than I'd even thought they could be and an obscene sized fridge on one side.

I had struggled to find what I wanted in the gigantic kitchen and what I had dug out made little a meal. My appetite was off, so in the end I'd settled for a few slices of toast. I had been drawn to the fancy coffee machine in the corner that was automatically peculating away, but a few sips of the earthy, strong liquid and my stomach was turning again.

Moving through the house to the other end, I heard the rumble of voices, the sound growing louder as I got closer. Eventually, I stopped in front of a closed door, steadying my breathing as I listened through the thick wood.

"We have to move soon. We've scoped out their security and we know how many men they've got," an unfamiliar voice said.

"I want them wiping out, every last one of them," Cian's voice was harsh, laced with anger.

"We can't hit both at once. We don't have enough men," Osh cautioned.

"So we split the men. Attack both at the same time," I heard Riley adding to the conversation.

"We need the numbers. If we take out the Poles first, it will send a message to the O'Malleys. We can deal with them next, one way or another," Osh argued.

"Don't forget what they did to your family," Riley's voice was harder than I'd ever heard it before, "what they did to your sister."

I squeezed my eyes shut at the memory, my stomach dropping. Silence descended on the room, and I imagined the look on Cian's face.

"I'll remember that even when I am dead," I heard him growl as I pushed my ear to the door harder so I could hear better.

The door moved suddenly under my weight and I wobbled, fire bursting in my left-hand side as I tried to steady myself. I swayed harder, right through the door and into the room.

"Hi," I squeaked at the man that caught me and steadied me back onto my feet.

I looked around the room at the amused faces. There must have been over twenty men crammed in there. Some were seated on a worn-looking leather sofa, others with their backsides propped on various pieces of furniture. Their ages varied, many with tattoos and scars on the exposed bits of skin that I could see. And all of them had their eyes on me, watching me intently.

Straightening up, I pulled Cian's jumper down my legs, suddenly feeling very exposed. Cian's eyes held mine, his jaw muscles tight and a look in his hazel eyes that I couldn't decipher. He chewed on a cocktail stick, his plump lips moving against each other and his perpetually raised eyebrow lifted even further in mock surprise.

"Nice of your woman to drop in on us," Osh laughed, his face light.

"I'm no one's fucking woman," I spat.

Osh smiled brightly.

"Everyone meet, Charlie," Cian addressed the room, his tone lighter, and the room erupted in deep chuckles.

Chapter Forty Three

ജ Cian ര

Charlie stood in front of a room full of my officers wearing barely anything. My grey jumper hung off one shoulder, the top of a slender but slightly muscled arm bared to my men. The hem stopped at the middle of her thigh, showing naked toned legs as the 'V' neck fell far too low down her chest. Her blonde hair was a mess of loose waves from how she had slept. She was amazing in every way.

Crossing her arms across her chest in annoyance, the jumper pulled down tighter over her cleavage and I didn't need to look around the room to know that everyone's eyes were on her, enjoying her far too much.

"What do you want, Charlie?" I asked, much too coolly, and her eyes narrowed on me.

"Well, some underwear would be a good start," she answered pointedly, her eyes trained on me.

The temperature in the room felt like it had gone up a few degrees, and this time I looked about, noticing stifled smiles and hungry stares.

"I'll sort you some stuff out. Just give me half an hour to finish this," I tipped my head, indicating the meeting.

"Fine."

Charlie leaned back against the door, watching me.

"I'll come get you when we're done here."

"It's alright. I'll stay. You carry on."

"This is men's business, lass," the grey-haired man we referred to as the accountant commented, "we don't discuss this sort of thing in front of women."

I blinked slowly, nipping the bridge of my nose. The accountant might as well have poked her with a stick. I glanced at her, watching the clouds gather in her eyes.

"Really? Doesn't seem your Mafia mates think that though when they came after me. I'll stay, thanks. I want to know how this is going to end. Then I know whether I have a life to get on with or not."

Her tone was bitter, but I understood. The grey-haired man looked at me expectantly. I shrugged.

"She can stay."

The older men in the room passed a look between themselves, one that was meant for me to see, but my anger was ignited, anyway.

"Cian, your father…."

"My father is dead. Torin is dead and Fiadh is gone with them. All at the hands of the Polish, the same people that came after her. She's mine, she will stay."

Charlie shot me a look, but she said nothing more. I watched Tommy drop his gaze to his feet as he tried to hide the broad smile that had lit up his face, and Jonjo smiled warmly, like the friend he had become to her. When I lifted my gaze to Charlie, she raised her eyebrow at me; a challenge.

"We'll take out the Polish first, then we're going after the O'Malleys," I instructed, looking around the room to nods of differing levels of excitement, "now fuck off, all of you."

The men filed out, the older ones eyeing Charlie with quiet contempt as they passed her but she didn't notice, or didn't care, her blue eyes quietly focussed on me until the room had emptied and the door had clicked shut leaving us alone.

My eyes wandered up her bare legs, focussing over fresh bruises that mottled her skin, yet didn't change the beautiful curve of her calf muscles, the arc of her inner thigh and the tight bulge of lean muscle on the outside before her legs disappeared inside my jumper. Her tits bulged more fully than I remembered under the thin woollen material as it clung to her nipples and my jeans became progressively tighter.

Charlie stared at me from across the room, anger smouldering.

"So if I'm yours," she slowed on the words, rage starting on the tip of her tongue, "why did you just up and fuck off? Don't think for a fucking second you can just waltz back into my life, kidnap me and then expect me to just be OK with it."

"Charlie, I told you, I was trying to protect you. I thought once I'd stepped away, they would leave you alone. That by taking my world away from yours, you would be safe. And I never kidnapped you."

"Really? What would you call tying someone up, putting them in your car and driving nine hours to a different fucking island, then?"

"I was keeping you safe."

"Again, with the strange ideas of keeping someone safe. Maybe you need to ask me what would make *me* feel safe?"

Standing, I sighed, moving to the lean on the front of my desk, "what would make you feel safe?"

"I want you to kill every single fucking member of the Polish mafia so they can't come after me and my horses ever again."

I nodded, "already on it. Until then, though, you stay here, where we can protect you. Once

413

I've dealt with the fuckers, then you're free to go, if that's what you want."

I watched her reaction, hoping for some flicker of emotion on her face, but she was as still as steel, her eyes not giving anything away.

"What do *you* want, Cian?" she asked suddenly, her blue eyes holding mine.

"I want revenge. I want them all dead. I want them to suffer for what they did to Torin and my father. And Fiadh. And you."

Pushing to my feet, I crossed the room in a few long strides, my eyes fixed on Charlie, only stopping till her head was tilted and she was looking up at me. I ran my fingertips up her leg, confirming her claim she was naked under my jumper.

"And most of all," I continued, whispering into her ear, "I want you."

My fingers trailed across the flesh at the top of her thigh, dipping in between her legs, the warmth from her pussy against my hand. She shifted, parting her legs slightly in an almost unconscious movement.

"I want all of you, Charlie, inside and out. You can walk away after this is finished and I'll let you go if that's what you want. But know it's not what I want."

Her face was stoic, unyielding, not letting me have any idea what she was thinking, but her pupils were dilating and her body was responding to my lightest touch. I stroked between her legs, feeling the damp sheen collect on my fingers, watching her reaction, shadows dancing in her eyes as her emotions fought for dominance. But the only dominance in this room would be mine. Moving my hand from between her legs, I grasped the hem of the jumper, pulling it swiftly over her head, uncovering the gentle curves of her beautiful body. She winced, half in pain, half in arousal.

Charlie kept her eyes on me defiantly, watching me as my gaze raked over her body like a starving man at a buffet. I'd missed this, missed her. Grabbing her head with my hands, I pushed my lips against hers, enjoying their softness for a second before I pushed them apart for my tongue. For a moment I thought she was going to deny me, a pit of despair threatening to open in my stomach, but then I felt her stiffened body relax and then she was kissing me back, hands grabbing the material of my t-shirt, heat suddenly erupting between us.

I was hard the minute she walked into the room, but now it was killing me. I should savour her, her taste, her smell, the feel of her lips on mine, of our tongues battling for dominance, the small bulge of her tits and the hardened peaks of her nipples, but the cock straining against my jeans was nearly painful. I needed to be inside her now.

Charlie's fingers tugged at my t-shirt and I didn't need to be told a second time as I pulled it over my head and then kicked out of my trousers. Her hand rubbed my erection through by boxers as it pushed against the material and I couldn't stifle the groan at her touch. Pushing my boxers

415

to the floor, my cock sprung free and her hand closed round it, her thumb swirling over the tip before sliding down the shaft and back up. She was killing me.

I pulled her leg up to my hip and positioned the head at her entrance, feeling heat and moisture and the slightest tension as I pressed myself against her, watching her close her eyes, listening to the brief intake of breath. Then I pushed into her, drawing a cry from her lips, her pussy stretching around me, filling her with every inch of me. I stayed still a second, relishing the feel of being inside her again, connected to her physically and emotionally. Fuck, she was beautiful. And she was mine. Despite what I had said, there was no way I could let her go.

I pulled her other leg around me, lifting her off the floor, pushing her arse into the sideboard we'd been leaning against and at first I moved in and out of her slowly, her tight cunt grasping me, stroking me, pulling me back each time I withdrew. I tried to be gentle, knowing her ribs were fragile, the bruises only just fading.

"Cian, fuck me hard," she breathed, "I need you. I need this."

Supporting her weight, I stepped sideways, pushing her back into the door, her legs wrapping tightly round me. I plunged in and out of her; the door banging in its frame as I buried myself into her with each thrust of animalistic need. Charlie cried out, her legs tensing around me, a shudder going through her, the sensation sending me wild. Her pussy tightened around my cock, her nails

416

scratching at my shoulders, and I punished her relentlessly until I exploded inside of her.

For a moment we stayed like that, Charlie impaled on my cock against the door, both of us breathing hard. I inhaled the scent of her skin, light shining on the slight sheen of sweat on her tits and the smell of us, of fresh sex, and nothing else mattered.

Chapter Forty Four

☙ Charlie ❧

It was dark outside when we eventually stopped. The contents of Cian's desk now lay scattered over the floor, the only light from a dull side lamp in the corner of the room. I shivered, moving myself from where I lay against his chest, my eyes heavy with the threat of sleep.

"I'll get one of my men to get you some clothes tomorrow first thing," Cian said from the leather settee, his voice low and gruff as he watched me pull his grey jumper back over my body.

"I'd rather choose something for myself. God knows what they'll come back with. If it's a dress, I'd have to fucking strangle someone with it."

"I don't want you anywhere but here. It's not safe."

"How would the Polish even know I'm here?" I countered.

"Apart from the fact they're missing three of their men, they know far too much about what our next move will be."

I looked at him quizzically.

Sighing, Cian continued, "I have a leak somewhere. I'm sure of it. I just don't know who."

"Shit! Really?"

"I think so. So, whatever I say to you, don't repeat. To anyone."

Warmth flooded my chest at the feeling of being trusted with information no one else knew. It felt good. But guilt quickly followed, my stomach twisting with anxiety.

"I need some women's things as well, Cian. It's not the sort of thing I can have anyone else buy for me," I stared at him, watching the understanding cross his face.

He nodded.

"OK. There's some clothes in Fiadh's room still. She was taller than you, but they should still fit. As for the others, I'll send Riley with you to get what you need. But it's straight in and straight back out, understand?"

I nodded, watching him as he stood and pulled on his jeans, my eyes trailing down from his hazel eyes to those plump lips, over the writing on his muscled pecs and the undulating curves of the muscles of his stomach. I would never tire of looking at him. I never wanted to look at anyone else. He was equal doses of sin and

419

pleasure, an addiction; one I never wanted to overcome. And more worryingly, I couldn't deny I was head over heels for him, plummeting down a path of no return.

*****

I woke for the second morning wrapped in his arms, his erection pressing against my back and ignoring the faint feeling of nausea, I turned in his grasp. My fingers stroked over the words tattooed on his chest; strength in unity, honour in revenge. My stomach tightened as I recalled the translation of the italic script on the hardness of his muscle. Tonight they planned to hit the Polish and a fresh sensation of bile rose in my throat at the thought of what that would entail; what one of the possible outcomes would be.

Pushing those thoughts aside I slid my hand further down his chest, feeling each bump and swell of muscle, and the light hair on the lower half of his stomach against the tightness of his skin as my hands followed the well-defined 'v' down to where his cock waited for me. He groaned under my touch as my hand slid down his shaft, veins pushing against the satin skin as it strained against my grip. My palm rounded the tip, smooth and bulging, a pearl of pre-cum on the top that I smoothed over the head with a swirl of my thumb.

Cian dipped his head, finding my lips with his, forcing his tongue past mine, kissing me hard, despite his half sleepy state. My nipples hardened, pressing into his chest, and my pussy throbbed, sending tingles of hot pulses through my body. Pushing him onto his back, I straddled him, feeling the bulge of his head at my entrance, pulses moving to near convulsions as excitement shot through my body. I drew myself up the shaft, rubbing it against me, closing my eyes in an attempt at retaining some control, over me, over sex, before Cian could dominate me once more.

"Open your eyes, Charlie," his tone was low and guttural, a shiver racking through my body from the promise of sin dripping off his tongue. I opened my eyes and looked down at him, his gaze fixed on me.

"I want to see you, all of you, when you slide onto my cock."

His voice, half gravelly, half like the purr of a lion, sent my pussy tightening in anticipation. I moved myself into a better position, keeping my eyes on his as I lowered myself onto the head of his erection, the bulging tip forcing me open, filling me, stretching me, warm tingles erupting inside of me. I hovered for a moment. His eyes drifted to his crotch, watching me take his cock, slowly, enjoying every stretch and pressure and movement till he was completely inside of me. I stopped for a moment, distracting myself with the sight of his full lips pushed together as he fought for control, the slight furrow of his brow.

Then I rocked my hips, listening as he took a sharp intake of air. Pushing into him, I dragged my clit against the hardness of his lower abs, fire erupting in the bottom of my stomach, flames licking at my core with each roll of my hips.

Cian's hands moved to my waist, gripping hard and pulling me closer to him each time I moved, our combined efforts building pressure faster and faster. Taking a hand off my hip, he pushed it between my legs, swirling his fingers over my clit, my pussy tensing on his shaft.

"Let me see all of you," he demanded.

I leaned back, opening my legs wide so he could watch me ride him, his fingers rubbing me as I slid up and down his length.

"You're fucking gorgeous," he growled, his fingers picking up speed.

"Fuck. Cian!" I cried out as he swirled, rubbed and tugged at my clit, my insides tensing, my pussy clamping against his cock, riding his swollen shaft harder and faster, my legs burning under the intensity.

Then in an explosion, my body burst into tremors and I threw my head back, his fingers never missing a beat as my orgasm peaked. He pulled his hand away, grabbing my hip, fingers digging into my flesh, guiding me up and down his full length until his own grunts filled the room and his cum filled me. Exhausted, he pulled me towards him, wrapping his arms around me, capturing my lips with his and we lay there, kissing each other until our hearts resumed their gentle beat.

*****

The little shop was cosy, short aisles neatly stocked with essentials. I lingered down each one,

422

Riley following me round like a shadow, a step or two behind. Walking faster hadn't helped, hanging back and reading every label annoyingly slowly hadn't shaken him off either. He was following Cian's instructions to the letter, ensuring he was within reaching distance of me at all times. But I didn't want him to see what I was buying.

Eventually finding the aisle of all things feminine hygiene, I traipsed the row of products, slowing to a stop at the towels and shooting a glance over my shoulder.

Turning to Riley, I handed him two boxes, and he eyed them distastefully.

"What do you reckon?" I asked him waving another plastic packet in his face, "applicator or non-applicator?"

"What's the fucking difference? They both go up your fanny," he grunted.

"Well, one you push in with a finger and one you push in with a bit of plastic," I shrugged.

"Plastic? Sounds fucking painful."

"Or what about these?" I chucked another box at him, watching the others drop from his grip as he tried to catch the airborne one, "these have a skirt too."

"Fuck's sake. Just fucking pick one."

"Well, give me some space then so I can decide what I want instead of breathing down my neck."

"Yeah, well Cian said…."

"I don't give a fuck what Cian said. You can keep an eye on me from over there. There's only one way in and one way out, so not frigging hard to watch for bad guys approaching."

Riley pushed his lips together, annoyance sweeping across his face, but he stepped away from me anyway, retreating up the aisle.

"I'll be over there at the magazines," he signalled.

Waiting till he safely wandered off around the corner, I moved further down the row of products, quickly grabbing a couple of oblong packets, pulling a pack of towels over the top of them and rushing off to the till.

I watched the cashier swipe them through the check-out, glancing at me sideways as I packed them quickly into opaque carrier bags, carefully placing my other items on top and stashing the receipt into my pocket. Nodding at Riley across at the last till, I indicated I was ready to go, and he returned to my side, escorting me from the shop.

Sat on the bed, my heart was steadily pounding in my chest, picking up pace with each second that ticked by until the shrillness of the alarm by the bed made me jump. I half crept into the bathroom to the little stick on top of the sink and looked down at it. Two pink lines. Two. Fuck.

Chapter Forty Five

৯ৃ Cian ৫৩

There was a buzz of excitement and anticipation in the house all day, and I'd spent most of the time watching the clock. I'd gone over and over the intelligence we had on the Polish, the security they had on the main house and was sat studying the blueprints of the extensive property they owned in a leafy Essex suburb.

The sudden vibration of my mobile phone made me jump, and I cursed myself for being so tightly coiled.

"What?" I answered the call more gruffly than I had originally intended.

"Nice to speak to you too, Kee," the Geordie accent of the caller greeted me.

"Sorry," I relented, "My head is somewhere else."

"Yeah? Which one are we talking about, Kee? You've actually managed to get your cock out of that jockey of yours?" The Viking mocked.

"At least I'm sticking to the same one, mate. How many have you been through in the last twenty-four hours?"

The Viking chuckled down the phone.

"That digging you asked me to do, Cian, brought up some interesting stuff."

I glanced around the office, looking at Osh, Riley and Jonjo, then tipped my head towards the door. Wordlessly, they obeyed my order, getting to their feet and leaving me alone with my mobile.

"Go on," I instructed once the door was closed securely behind them.

"I got my man to check out all yours. Took a little while, like, so his bill is pretty hefty."

"Doesn't matter. What did you find?"

"Most of them checked out. You've a few with some gambling problems though, you might want to get that sorted. I'll email you the names over. But the most interesting one is Mad-Dog."

My stomach twisted, the heavy feeling of disappointment and dread creeping over me.

"How did you find him?" The Viking continued, "he's not from any long line of dutiful foot soldiers like nearly all of your others."

"Osh found him on the streets. He was just a street dealer, but violent as fuck. He was just supposed to clean up the real low-level shit for us, but Osh really liked him. He ran a few decent errands, taking out some of the drug-dealing low-lifes that kept trying to double cross us, and Osh

426

thought he'd bring him in a little closer. Why? What have you got?"

"He used to work for the Polish."

"What? He can't have. We checked him out."

"He covered his tracks pretty well, or at least someone did. My boy, Joey, struggled to find anything much on him at first, but that set off red-flags. A street dealer with no record? Not likely. So he dug a bit deeper and found Dominik Banka."

"So Mad-Dog is Polish?"

"Aye, and I reckon he's your grass."

"Fuck."

"Sorry, mate. I know you guys liked him, but looks like he's your man."

"Thanks, V," I ended the call, leaning my head into my hands and massaging my temples. Dismayed, I mulled over the only action left to me.

A soft knock on the door pulled me back from my warring thoughts and I was grateful for the distraction, however momentarily that would be.

"Hey, Boss," she purred as she poked her head through the door.

My eyes searched her frame eagerly, settling on the long-sleeved white-top she wore over some fashionably, faded light-blue skinny jeans. Her hair was pulled onto the top of her head in a messy bun, blonde strands dropping about her face. She frowned at me.

"You look like shit," she said softly, a hint of concern in her tone despite her words.

"Thanks. I'm pleased you noticed," I grumbled.

"Really, what's wrong?"

"I think I've found the leak."

"Fuck. Who?"

"Mad-Dog."

She dipped her head in a half-hearted nod, walking over to the side of my desk. Closing my fingers around her slim wrist, I pulled her into my lap and she looped an arm around the back of my head.

"You don't seem surprised," I noted, inhaling a lungful of her scent; soap and the faint smell of coconut and almond. The only thing missing was the fresh smell of hay.

"I've never liked him. There was just something about him that didn't feel right. What are you gonna do?" she asked, running her fingers under my t-shirt, leaving soft tingles over my chest before her hand lingered over the words tattooed across my pec.

"What I have to," I answered softly, as I nuzzled my nose against her neck, listening as her breath changed slightly.

My hand slid up the inside of her thigh, stopping a moment just a few centimetres from where I really wanted to be, and I listened to her moan at the slightest touch. Leaving go of her leg, I pushed her top up, pulling it off over her head, the nipples of her naked tits already hardening. I sucked one into my mouth, Charlie pushing her chest forward into my face as I rolled and squeezed the other between my fingers. This was the very distraction I needed.

"Cian," she breathed, "I really need to talk to you."

I sucked harder, cupping her tit as I devoured the hardened bud, nipping it between my teeth, Charlie squealing and wriggling away from me. I slid my hand down her stomach, flicking open the button of her jeans and pushing my hand inside, feeling for the wetness between her legs.

"Talk to me later, sweetheart," I whispered, blowing over the peak I'd just held between my teeth, my fingers pushing through the slick of her folds.

I eased two fingers in, her pussy gripping me tight. My thumb found the bud of her clit and I brushed the rough pad against her, enjoying the way she rocked her hips towards me as she rode my fingers.

Over Charlie's shoulder, I noticed a movement.

"Boss," Riley said, entering the room, his eyes catching sight of Charlie, "Cian, we need to go."

"Got to go, sweetheart," I mumbled, looking down at her, a darkness and dread creeping into my chest, "we'll finish this later," I promised.

"You fucking better," Charlie answered, her voice strained and fear in her eyes.

Pulling my fingers from the tightness of her pussy, I kissed her on the forehead, my lips lingering over her skin, remembering the taste of her as if it was my last meal. Time to go to war.

*****

The plane landed a few hours later at London Heathrow and I was up on my feet pulling hand luggage from the overhead lockers before it had stopped taxying along the tarmac, the glare of an air stewardess on my back. As soon as the seatbelt sign had turned off, I noticed my men jump up, the scatter of heads standing over those still seated.

We filtered out of our seats, joining the throng of people who blocked the aisle as they unloaded their luggage and wrestled bumptious kids onto their hips whilst towing another along behind them. I watched Osh up ahead, his arm wrapped around the waist of a dark-haired flight attendant. He dipped his face towards her ear and her lips pulled into a smile, her eyes dropping to the floor, reacting to whatever filth was coming out of his mouth. I'd watched them earlier scurry away behind the curtains and Osh returning with a satisfied smirk. I rolled my eyes.

We picked up hire cars from the airport, travelling loosely in convoy to an undisclosed meeting point. I drove the lead car, having kept details vague from the men that followed me. Only Osh and Riley had pushed for information but I'd kept them both in the dark.

"I hope you've got a plan for weapons, bro, otherwise we're going in totally unarmed," Osh muttered from the passenger seat, "I'm all for some good old bare knuckle but I'd like to not take a hole in the head before that point."

"I've got it covered," I answered flatly, "we're picking a whole load of shit up at the rendezvous."

The disused industrial estate with its crumbling buildings and ransacked infrastructure was an ideal meeting point. Two big SUVs were already parked at the far side of the deserted carpark, mostly concealed in the shadows where the sole, dull street light could not quite reach. Osh glanced at me, sitting suddenly upright in his seat in tension as we approached.

"Relax, Osh," I muttered, turning the engine off and stepping out of the car as the rest of the convoy came to a stop behind me.

Striding across the dark space and pitted ground, I moved towards the SUVs; a passenger stepping out of the nearest and moving towards me. The big man grabbed me in a solid embrace, clapping me hard enough on the back to make me cough.

"Great to see you, Tully," I greeted him, pulling away.

"You too, cus. We've been missing you in the Big City. Not that the punters say the same. I'm sure the bastards are driving around waving at us now they know their fingers are safe!"

He laughed loudly as Oisín approached, eyeing the big bearded man reproachfully, Riley flanking him from the second car.

"Osh. Tully Murphy. Don't think you've ever met."

Realisation swept across his face, a mix of relief and surprise sparring for control of his features. Riley shifted nervously from foot to foot.

"You called in the Murphys?" Osh exclaimed.

"Some of us," Tully replied, his deep voice seeming to boom across the confused silence of the car park, "some of us have to keep New York ticking over. We lost a good enforcer when this one went home," he slapped me hard on the back again.

Osh crossed his hands against his chest, the padded black jacket making him look much chunkier than he was.

"And did the Murphys come with some weapons?" Osh droned on, looking less than impressed with the back-up I brought.

"Sure did, little cus," Tully responded, moving back towards the black cars and we followed, peering into the boot.

432

Riley had come up behind us and reached over our shoulders when the bags of well-hidden weapons were eventually exposed. He pulled a handgun from the bag, turning it over in his hands and staring down the sights.

"Glocks?" Osh asked, looking at Tully quizzically.

"Yes. Looks like my usual contact has been put out of business by your feds. Had to find a different supplier at short notice."

"Russians?"

"Aye, had to do a deal with those Russian bastards."

A short time later, we had positioned ourselves outside the grounds, surrounding the property with groups of well-armed men. I crouched down, using the wall as cover. Riley and Mad-Dog were with me, along with another couple of men. We would breach the property from all sides. I watched the green display on my watch as I stooped in the dark, waiting for the security change-over we knew would come in the next ten minutes thanks to the Viking's intelligence.

I looked around the men with me, the same feeling of dread settling in my stomach as my eyes lingered on Mad-Dog; disappointment, regret and betrayal, challenging each other for dominance as I contemplated my next course of action. I'd purposefully taken Mad-Dog with me, so I could keep him close where I could see him and when I had the opportunity, I would execute him.

433

My watch display flashed, casting an ugly green glow around me. I nudged Riley, and we stood, scaling the wall with its cast-iron fence on top and dropping soundlessly to the earth below. We stalked forward with military finesse, jumping from the shadows and silently dispatching the foot soldiers nearest us.

The house was obscenely big, swamped in lights which cast as much darkness around the grounds as it lit patches up. We hopped from shadow to shadow, coordinating our approach from all sides of the building, our dark clothes blending into the blackness. At the big front doors, I paused, checking around me before I packed them with a small amount of explosives. The bang was loud enough to wake the neighbours and wood tore as it was destroyed in the small blast, but as the next properties were a good few hundred metres away, I wasn't worried the police would join us anytime soon.

Inside, men were running towards the breach, and with double taps, the first of those rushing to respond dropped in seconds. Stepping over a body at my feet, I moved inside, keeping tight to the walls as our guns pointed in all directions, ready to fire at the slightest movement. The occupants had learned from our first onslaught, opting for defensive positions rather than running at us and I heard the groan of floorboards over head as the smoke and debris of the blasted front doors settled into an eerie, cavernous silence.

Watching the others move through the house from the opposite end, I took the stairs, searching for any movement and half expecting a rain of bullets as we climbed. As we slid along the corridor upstairs, the silence thickened and all I could hear were the heavy breaths of the men behind me, full of tension. A sudden movement to my right caught my attention but not in enough time as weight barrelled into me, knocking me sideways, fists connected with my face before a pop rang through the air. The monstrous sized man paused, his face distorted before blood trickled down a hole in his chest and he landed heavily on top of me. Rolling him off, I looked up, following the outstretched hand.

"Boss? You good?" Mad-Dog's voice was low, his gun lowered to his side.

Grabbing his arm, I pulled myself from the floor, watching his expression as he gazed back, confusion a picture on his face. After a few more seconds, I clapped him on the shoulder before stooping down for my weapon that had been knocked across the landing and wiping blood from the cut on my lip. Downstairs voices, grunts and gunshots rang out, the house erupting into a battleground.

Activity exploded behind us and we split up, Riley and Mad-Dog continuing across the second floor as the others engaged, fists and legs flying with the men that had attacked from behind. A dull ominous thump behind me made my stomach drop, and I half-turned, watching one of my men slump to the floor, his neck bent at an awkward angle, wide lifeless eyes staring at me. I pushed forward, mentally wiping the image from my mind, concentrating on what was in front of me, any little movement attracting the aim of my gun. The men from behind us ploughed through those that had turned to fight them. With no cover, they would gun us down in minutes.

I struck the double doors with my foot, the heavy boot and brute strength breaking the lock and splintering the wood as I forced it in over, strips of the door ripping free and landing on the floor as we bundled inside.

"Nice of you to drop in, O'Sullivan," an accented voice greeted me, their face concealed in the shadow at the far side of the room.

I lifted my gun and pointed it exactly at where his forehead would be. Glancing left and right, Riley and Mad-Dog were behind me, their guns drawn and pointing in different directions. Riley kicked the doors closed behind us, yanking a heavy, brass adorned chair against them, though I doubted it would hold the onslaught of men for long.

Tomasz Kaszynski rose from his chair, his half scarred face caught in the lamplight as he strode towards the gun I pointed at him. Looking over my shoulder, he nodded towards Mad-Dog.

"So the *zdrajca* has returned," he addressed him.

I glanced at Mad-Dog over my shoulder, who shifted nervously, his eyes moving from Kaszynski to me and back again.

"I'm no traitor. Just got a better deal somewhere else," he countered, his gun still pointing securely at the other man in the room.

436

A bald man to my left moved into the light, the orange glow bouncing off his head. Staring at me, he gave me a wide, knowing smile, which felt like someone had kicked me in the guts, his familiar face sending my brain into overdrive, remembering the video, remembering my sister's screams.

Pain erupted in my face suddenly and I staggered backwards, losing the grip on the Glock, which was ripped from my hands, blood running down my face. Behind me, Riley moved, changing the direction of his gun, the bang behind my head deafening. Mad-Dog slumped to the floor, eyes wide, and a hole between them.

Three guns pointed at me. Two were Polish, but it was the barrel of the third gun I stared down. The one held by my best friend.

Chapter Forty Six

ෆ Charlie ෨

I watched the cars leave in the dull light of late afternoon. The O'Sullivan homestead was well lit, lamps on the walls at the front and the back, illuminating the old property in a warm glow. But it wasn't comforting tonight. Fear, dread, foreboding. A cocktail of emotions racked my body as I watched Cian and his men load up into the cars.

I knew what they were going to do. I knew it was necessary, and I knew Cian was as dangerous as the Polish he was going to wage a war on tonight. But wars had casualties, even the best soldiers could fall. My stomach somersaulted at the thought.

My nausea had spilled over into sickness today and I had barely kept a slice of toast down. I'd tried to tell Cian earlier, but baulked. I didn't know what he would do. Even when he'd made it clear he wanted me, that this wasn't just something casual, I'd hid away from the truth. What if he decided he wanted something different when he found out? What if it had distracted him tonight? In the end, I'd held my tongue, letting fate decide if he would learn the truth.

Exhausts roared as the cars peeled off, speeding down the drive, the sound of the small stones being thrown from behind wheels captured my attention. Feeling the slight stab of hunger, I pulled Cian's hooded top over me and padded across the thinning carpet down the stairs.

The house was eerily silent. There was no drone from the television, no clunk of pool balls connecting, no male voices swearing and cajoling each other. I glanced in each room as I walked past, lingering slightly longer outside of closed doors for confirmation there were no voices inside as I moved towards Cian's gigantic kitchen.

As I entered the kitchen, I paused. A figure bent over a laptop at the far end of the island, the glow from the screen lighting up his brow from where his head was dipped towards the screen. He looked up.

"Shit, Tommy!" I exhaled, my heart bouncing against my rib cage, "you auditioning for a horror movie?"

He smiled and looked up.

"Jumpy much, Charlie?" he shot back.

"Yeah, I guess. Just, all this," I spun my hand in the air.

"I know. I get you. It's killing me not knowing what's happening."

"Why haven't you gone with them?" I asked, turning away from him as I flicked the kettle on and rummaged in the cupboards.

"Cian wanted me to stay to guard you."

Tommy reached forward, grasping his cup and taking a gulp of whatever was in there.

"There's lasagne in the fridge. It's the best you'll ever taste," he motioned to the American fridge on the other side of the kitchen.

"Do I need guarding?" I asked as I cut a small portion of the pasta dish out and slid it onto a plate.

"Cian didn't want to take any chances."

"I'm sorry you've been left behind to babysit."

"I don't mind."

The microwave dinged, and I opened the door, recoiling at the heavy smell of garlic which threatened to overturn my stomach.

"I don't mind the company either," I told him as I sat across on the other side of the island.

Tommy smiled, and I watched him as I picked at the pasta on my plate. His eyes shifted from me to the screen and back again every few seconds until he leaned back in his chair and sighed.

"This is gonna be one long fucking night," he muttered, holding the cup to his lips.

"What you watching?" I asked, cutting the smallest morsel of lasagne and still struggling to eat it.

"Cameras. There's about thirty of them dotted around this place. It's a right bastard to keep track of them all. We normally have a few of us watch them."

"I didn't even realise there were any."

"Yeah, they're pretty discreet."

"Where are they?"

"Pretty much everywhere. They cover the whole of the outside so I can see anyone approaching and there's more inside."

"In every room?" I paused, the fork loaded with lasagne just in front of my lips.

"Some of the rooms. But if not, there's a camera outside. I can see anyone moving around the house, too."

"What about Cian's office?"

Tommy smiled a wonky, knowing smile, "don't worry. There's none in there. Or any of the bedrooms."

"Why so many, though?"

"There's been shit loads of conflicts and wars. It's just the way of a firm, Charlie. The more prepared we can be for people taking pot-shots, the better. But the cameras really went up after the war with the O'Malleys. That one went on for years and we really weren't sure how it would end."

I watched him with interest as his eyes flicked back to the computer screen.

"How did it end?"

"It was really when Cian came out of the forces."

I raised an eyebrow.

"Yeah. It makes him ruthless, an elite soldier and a mafia boss, and that's what the family needed. And that's why he was made to sign up, although I doubt the old boss thought he'd get into the SAS. With his strategic knowledge of warfare, he got the upper hand. My Da always said he was a born leader. It was Torin who would have been head of the family when the old boss died. Cian never wanted this, my Da would've said. But I'm pleased. Torin was cruel and unpredictable. My Da said his temper was his downfall. Got in the way of good decision making."

I sat for a while with Tommy, chatting as he watched the cameras, until tiredness crept on me without warning.

"I'm going to head up, Tommy," I said, pushing onto my feet from the bar stool I'd been perched on for the last couple of hours, "let me know if you hear anything?"

Tommy nodded, "night, Charlie," he said before his eyes dropped back to the screen.

*****

442

The house still bore an eerie silence when I woke up, alone. Rolling over, I stared at the clock until the red digits came into focus. It was 9.00am. I'd slept soundly for hours. I kicked my legs out of bed, smoothing Cian's white t-shirt down my thighs, and approached the window. The material seemed heavy in my hand as I cautiously pulled it back and peered out across the fields.

A lazy mist clung to the grass. The air was still. No branches or leaves moved on the trees. It was as if nature itself was poised, waiting. Dread crept back into my stomach, kick starting a fight between nausea and hunger, my stomach rumbling, the only noise in the quiet morning.

The stairs creaked loudly under my bare feet, startling in the thick silence. I felt like I should hold my breath and creep so as not to be heard despite the fact that there was only me and Tommy here.

When I got to the ground floor, I pushed open the curtains from the two narrow windows either side of the door, staring out at the fog that was rolling in across the fields. There was no sign of a car, no sign that Cian was back yet. My throat seemed to swell at the thought and I hoped Tommy had heard from them, that the war was won and everyone was home safe.

I wandered the long corridor to the kitchen, wishing I'd put something over the t-shirt I'd worn to bed. The house was cold this morning and a shiver ran up my spine. I almost turned and went back to grab one of Cian's jumpers, but the grumble of a hungry stomach changed my mind.

The kitchen door was ajar, a sliver of light escaping, almost luminescent as it stabbed through the crack between the door and the frame. The door glided open from the small push of my palm and I was met with a flood of kitchen lights. The Laptop stood open on the island but I couldn't see Tommy. I moved closer, aiming for the coffee machine that was awake and percolating, filling the kitchen with a nutty, smoky aroma mixed with something else. It was a strange scent, one I hadn't smelled in coffee before. It was almost metallic.

A shape at the island caught in the corner of my eye. It was dark, slumped over the keyboard. I turned and stared, not seeing at first. Not comprehending the true horror of what I was looking at.

"Tommy?" I whispered, "Tommy! No, no, no!"

My heart jolted in my chest. So much blood. I rushed across the kitchen to him, gently touching his neck. There was a slight warmth in the sickly greyness of his skin as I felt for a pulse. His neck was a mess, a gaping hole in the middle exposing things I didn't want to see. Blood spilled all over the keyboard as his eyes stared emptily.

My stomach tightened and the back of my throat burned, tears gathering in my eyes. He was still warm. Still warm. For a moment I didn't know why my brain was focussing on that detail. Shit.

Fear gripped at my throat and I searched the kitchen looking for someone, every one of senses alert. Holding my breath, I listened, straining to hear something out of place, to smell or feel something. I needed to get out of here, quickly and quietly.

I searched for some sort of weapon, my eyes coming to rest on a block of knives on the other side. Moving towards the end of the kitchen, the sudden scratching of wood on the stone flags on the floor sent my heart racing faster than ever. A dark figure stood in the doorway, stepping closer, the light picking up their features. I let out a breath. Riley.

My eyes roamed his face, from the specs of blood to the dark red splodges soaked into the white cotton of his shirt. Had he found Tommy? His sleeves were rolled up, and I followed the bare skin down to his right hand, the glint of the neat blade partially obscured by the red goo that covered it.

I opened my mouth to speak, but I was devoid of words. He moved towards me. I backed away, the block of knives now out of reach. My eyes flicked to Tommy, anger pooling in my chest.

"Why?" it fell from my lips, a course whisper.

"Needed him out of the way," Riley shrugged, the emptiness of his voice sending a shiver through me.

I slid myself backwards, my brain desperately running through escape scenarios. Keep him talking. Keep him distracted.

"Out of the way for what?"

"To finish this. Finish the O'Sullivans for good."

"Wh, what do you mean?" a lump was forming in my throat.

"They're all dead," his voice was icy and the sudden knot forming in my throat threatened to kill me itself, "Cian, Osh. The Polish got them all."

"No," it was a whimper.

It couldn't be true. My stomach dropped.

"No. You're lying," I pushed back, my voice strained.

"No, *sweetheart,*" I noticed the way he used the word, "I left Cian staring down the barrel of Kaszynski's gun. The Polish took care of the others. So it's just you and me, *sweetheart.*"

There it was again.

"Why? He was your best friend!"

"His family took everything from me. Everything."

Riley's voice was dark, his lips twisting angrily as he spat the words.

"My mother was killed because she was where *his* mother should be. The O'Malleys wanted *his* mother, not mine. It was me that suffered, not him."

446

"Cian's mother died too. From the guilt of what happened to yours," I remembered.

Riley's brows knitted together angrily.

"Then the O'Malleys got my father. Do you know why?"

I shook my head.

"Because Lorcan and Torin wouldn't avenge her death. They told us they wanted to end the war, not keep it going. They treated my mother's death like they would one of their fucking street dealers. So my Da went to avenge her by himself. He killed the fucker who pulled that trigger, but he didn't get out of there alive. I've lost everything because of them. And they would have continued to take anything or anyone. They would have taken them all."

Riley picked at his fingernails and I watched the bloodied knife moving in front of me.

"And then when Cian's mother died, when the coward took her own life, *he* got to go play in America to get over her. *He* could run away and forget it all whilst I stayed here and played the good little soldier to the family, memories around every corner."

Hatred burned in his eyes as he stared at me.

"So what? You just trotted off to the Polish and handed yourself over as their bitch? Helped them kill Cian's father and brother? Helped them rape and torture Fiadh because you're a pissed off minion?"

447

Riley's face contorted. He crossed the space in front of me, the knife pointing at my face.

"Don't you fucking say her name!"

"Why, Riley?" my voice came out more shaky than I intended, as I eased backwards, leaning on the kitchen bench.

"I loved Fiadh. She was never supposed to be a part of this. I told them she was off limits. She was mine. It was Oisín they were supposed to take. He was supposed to be at the same meeting, but he was too busy with his latest whore. Fiadh borrowed his car."

For a moment Riley's eyes glistened, his attention faltered. Now. I reached for the coffee pot, grabbing the handle and throwing the liquid into Riley's face. He howled, steam pouring off his skin. Metal clanged on the tiled floor as the knife fell from his grip, but he was already reaching for it, clutching his face as it turned bright red.

I ran. Bounding out of the kitchen and along the corridor, my heart pounded in my chest, beating out a frantic rhythm. Casting a hurried glance over my shoulder, I caught Riley's dark shape behind me. Faster. Blood rushed in my ears, the only other sound the desperate pounding of footsteps hammering against the floorboards as I ran. The front doors were within reach. I dashed forwards, grabbing for the handles, yanking them down. Nothing. I pushed them down again, pulling with all my might; rattling the doors. They were locked. Desperately, I looked around. Key, key, key. My thoughts pulsed through my head.

Riley's pace was quickening. He would reach me in seconds. There was no key. No means of escape. Panicked, I turned, moving towards the stairs. I bolted up the first few steps, pumping my arms. Fingers wrapped around my ankles and pulled me backwards, and I clattered hard onto my side, my legs pulled from under me. Pain bit, sending a flash of bright white across my eyes. My legs and arms flailed as Riley pulled me towards him, and despite the searing hot pain in my ribs, I kicked, and punched, and scratched with every ounce of energy I had. I heard a hiss as my nails connected with Riley's face and then came the click. Dull and menacing, and I stopped.

Riley's gun was pointed at my face as he sat on top of me, his face contorted in anger and as red as a lobster.

"Where do I start filling you full of holes, *sweetheart?* Your pretty face?" he dropped the gun towards my stomach, "or here? To make sure the O'Sullivan line never continues."

He knew.

"Do you know Fiadh was pregnant with my child when she was taken?"

I shook my head, a single tear falling down my face as I watched the anguish and anger in Riley's eyes.

"All because Oisín couldn't keep it in his fucking pants. We should have had a life together. But she was taken from me too," he snarled and I watched any last bit of control unravelling as he moved the gun back to my head and then back to my stomach.

The gun went off, pain exploding within me.

450

Chapter Forty Seven

ഇ Cian ഈ

I didn't recognise the face of my best friend. Hatred and anger welled in his eyes as he stared back at me, the gun in his hand unwavering as he pointed it in my face.

"Surprise!" Kaszynski chuckled from behind me.

I ignored him, keeping my eyes trained on Riley and the gun he held at me.

"What the fuck is this, Riley?" I asked.

"He's with us, you thick Irish cunt," Kaszynski commented from behind me.

"I wasn't talking to you."

Pain shot through the back of my head and I fell to my knees in front of Riley, closing my eyes and bracing myself against the darkness threatening to consume me. I needed to stay awake. Blood spilled onto my fingers as I touched the back of my head where the butt of a gun had connected with it.

"Stay there, Irish dog. O'Sullivans belong on their knees like the cock suckers they are," Kaszynski's voice came from above me, but I didn't give him even the respect of acknowledging the jibe.

"Why, Riley?"

"All of you. You ruined my life. Every part of it. You, all of you."

"So you sold us out to these pigs?"

The gun slammed into the back of my head again, sending me flying forward onto my hands.

"We bought him, O'Sullivan," the voice from behind me piped up again, "one gambling debt cleared for the lives of the O'Sullivan family."

"And Fiadh?" I asked, pushing myself back onto my knees and searching Riley's eyes.

His gun faltered; just a little, but enough for me to notice.

"They weren't supposed to take Fiadh. If Osh had been the son he was supposed to be, and doing what he was ordered... it was him they were supposed to take. I would never have hurt her. Ever. With the rest of you gone, it would have just been us."

"But you did, Riley. They raped her. He raped her," I looked across the room towards the other man with the gun, who flashed a sickening smile.

"I'm going back for your blonde bitch next, O'Sullivan. Would have had her the first time if the bitch wasn't so fucking wild. Didn't fucking beg like that Irish slut," the ugly, bald man smirked.

Riley's face contorted, his eyes narrowing to slits, and his grip tightened on the gun. Then he turned. The shot ringing loud, and the bald man slumped to the floor.

"What the fuck?" Kaszynski growled.

"You should never have taken her," Riley answered, his gun now pointing at the Polish Boss, "I told you she was off limits."

"You sold me the pup. You didn't deliver. But my men didn't mind. They said the Irish whore was tight as fu……"

Kaszynski hit the floor like a sack of shit, blood pouring out from the hole between his eyes.

"You going to finish what you started, Riley?" I challenged, pushing to my feet.

"The O'Malleys were never a part of this, were they? You just tried to push me to wipe them out, too? Revenge for your parents?"

Riley smiled.

"It would have worked. But your smart-mouth jockey got in the way. She made you weak."

"And Lebedev?" I asked.

"Yeah, that was me. It was fun watching that forces friend of yours trying to get into Lebedev's security and he sucked it all up when the Polish took down the firewalls. It hadn't taken much to get hold of Charlie's record and it made for fun fucking reading. She really was a wild child. You did exactly what I thought you'd do when it looked like Lebedev was coming after her."

"Shame Charlie's sister got me off those charges, huh? I bet that really pissed you off! Is that why you drugged the horse?"

Riley frowned in confusion.

"The horse was drugged?"

I nodded.

"Shit. Was a good idea, mate, but that wasn't me."

I wanted to break his fucking face, but I needed to remain in control or I'd soon have a hole in my head as well.

"I always knew about you and Fiadh. I knew she was pregnant," I watched his reaction, the slight shock of realisation cross his face, "she told me. I told her I would sort it out with my father. I was pleased, for both of you. I never wanted her to be used as a bargaining chip, marrying her off to create alliances and that sort of shit. You killed her, Riley. The one person who was supposed to love her and protect her; you killed Fiadh and your child."

Riley's face twisted, the hand holding the gun wavered. I launched forwards, forcing my shoulder into his chest and shoving him backwards. His back collided with the dresser behind him with a dull thump and a whoosh of air as the force cleared out his lungs. The gun went

454

off behind me. Not missing a moment, I grabbed Riley's gun hand, forcing it over his head and slamming it into the wall. A knee drove into the bottom of my ribs, relaxing my grip on him. I stumbled backwards, eyeing the gun I hadn't managed to dislodge.

Shouts outside in the hall caught our attention. A chorus of deep Irish voices, the rhythmical pop of gunshots and the thump of bodies. I glanced towards the door and in that moment Riley moved past me, running towards the window. He threw the windows open and leapt over the balcony. I followed, wobbly from the blows to my head and ribs, and looked out into the dark. For a moment, I watched a figure moving across the grounds until darkness swallowed it.

Charlie!

*****

My brain whirled, chasing thoughts around my head that I didn't dare dwell on. I'd found the black car in the garage back at Kaszynski's place and, registered to the now dead Polish Boss, was perfect for the speed limits I had broken all night.

The wait for the ferry had been agonising, but eventually I'd crossed the Irish Sea and abandoned the car when, having warned me for several miles, it stuttered to a stop, out of fuel. The house was quiet as the taxi pulled up to the gates, nothing looking out of place. A mist had crept in across the fields, gathering at waist height and creating an uneasy atmosphere. I paid the fare at the gates, watching the house, alert for any sign of movement.

The lamps that lit the grounds still burned, less bright against the dullness of the morning. There we no cars at the entrance, no sign anyone had come and gone. I pulled my mobile out of my pocket, punching in Tommy's number for what seemed like the hundredth time, and despite the lack of answer to my previous calls, held it anxiously to my ear. The phone rang and rang.

I stalked closer, my nerve endings alive as I watched for any movement in or outside of the house. Riley couldn't have been too far in front of me. I moved to the front door, peering through the windows. Could I see dark shapes moving inside? My stomach clenched. Grasping the handle, I turned the key in the lock, the door bounding open.

"All because Oisín couldn't keep it in his fucking pants," I heard the snarl of his voice.

A gun fired. I bolted forwards towards the dark shapes on the stairs, my gun in my hand. Then I squeezed, the noise of a second gun filling the space around us. Riley slumped forward on top of Charlie and I grabbed for him, rolling him off her. His eyes stared at me, unblinking, the front of his forehead puckered from the exit wound of the bullet.

"Cian," Charlie whispered, her voice faint.

Blood oozed through the fingers grasping her side, her arm cradled across her stomach. Peeling her fingers away, I pulled the white t-shirt up over the wound, exposing her bare tattooed flesh and the angry red hole that pumped out blood to the side of her belly. I shrugged out of my jacket, my fingers already flying over the buttons of the shirt I wore underneath, yanking it over my arms and pulling it off me. Scrunching it up into a ball, I pushed it over the wound, holding it with one hand as my fingers slipped over the display of my phone.

"You're going to be OK, sweetheart," I said softly, pushing more pressure against the bullet wound to the side of her stomach.

"Cian," her voice was strained, tears rolling down her face, "Cian, I'm pregnant."

My hands faltered on the wound, my heart skipping a beat, emotions balling and crashing together. Shock, dread, anger, fear. Riley had tried to take my woman from me. And my child. Just like his had been taken from him. He had known.

"Charlie, you're going to be fine. Both of you."

I pressed my lips to her forehead.

*****

There was an atmosphere in my office; an overbearing sense of emptiness despite the number of bodies crammed into the small space. I'd pulled that trigger in anger and I would have done it all over again without hesitation. But that didn't mean I'd not spent the last few nights

457

thinking over my every move, every decision I had made since I'd come home from New York.

The Murphys had left as quickly as they came and we left the English authorities cleaning up the mess and body count. With the evidence we'd stashed about the place, there was little chance they would come after us. Here, though, was another story. The Gardaí had combed the place in the last week and two dead bodies hadn't helped.

"So the O'Malleys weren't involved, huh?" Jonjo grunted.

"Not this time," I answered.

"What about the strip club? They sold it to the Polish?" Oisín asked, looking across the room.

The Viking folded his arms across his chest, "the Polish were making alliances with anyone. My guess is they would have convinced the O'Malleys to share what was left of your turf once they had got rid of you all."

"Those fuckers jump into bed with anyone for the right price. Know a few women like that," Osh chuckled.

"And how was that slimy Russian involved in any of this?" Jonjo asked, still dressed in his breeches, straight off the racetrack.

"Looks like he was a pawn in their game," I answered, "useable and disposable."

"That and his connections with the Northern Pipeline," V added, "rumour has it the

Poles are right in there. Makes sense, seeing as they can get people in and out over Europe. Guess Lebedev was easily expendable."

"And the Polish probably got bored with babysitting him, keeping him away from Mother Russia's reach," Osh shrugged.

"Did you get anymore intel on the bastards who drugged Charlie's horse?" I asked the Viking, the memory igniting an anger that simmered inside of me.

"Not yet. But my man is close. On the day of the race, someone bet a pretty vast sum of money that Charlie and the stallion wouldn't finish the race. I'm not a gambler…."

Half the men in the room sniggered, and the Viking smirked.

"But I'd bet that same person might have slipped the horse that drug," he continued.

"I want them found," I ordered, "I want a name and where to find them. I'll do the rest. I don't want Charlie finding out…"

"You don't want Charlie finding out what?" the voice from the doorway joined the conversation.

"You're supposed to be resting," I sighed, looking up from my desk at her.

"I don't need rest."

"You do need rest. Doctors and my orders."

"Yeah, well, I don't follow orders."

Not unless it was in my bed.

459

I looked around the room of men before tipping my head and dismissing them with a silent command.

Chapter Forty Eight

ങ Charlie ഇ

Cian had left the next morning, leaving me rattling round the huge house. It was full of his men again, laughing and cursing, smoking and playing pool. The atmosphere was strained and certain members were conspicuous by their absence, but even in all of this, I felt some sense of relief. A sense that the war was over. For now, at least.

I wandered into the kitchen, scouring cupboards for something to eat, something that I could stomach between the bouts of morning sickness. Settling for a cup of coffee that I sipped like it might poison me, I propped myself on the kitchen stool at the table in the middle of the floor. It had been scrubbed meticulously clean, not even a pinprick of blood left on the grout of the tiles. My heart felt heavy every time I came in, jolting on my chest as if it had just been restarted.

The newspaper I'd disturbed rustled loudly next to me, making me jump and spill coffee, soaking in and smudging the print. I swiped the

461

excess off, reading the black typed text in front of me.

"Fuck!" I whispered into the loneliness of the kitchen, my eyes fixing on the bold headline on the front page.

'Horror crash ends five-time champion jockey's career.'

I read the article, horror mixed with a strange sense of satisfaction, as it told of Dickie's car crash, leaving him a double amputee and in the back of my mind something sparked. *I don't want Charlie finding out.*

*****

I had expected Cian back that night, or at least those were the whispers from the men as they got progressively louder from the alcohol and the raucous betting on the pool game across the hall. The sounds of their voices carried around the house, and even from behind the thick oak door of Cian's office, I could still hear the banter.

The door eventually creaked open, Cian not seeing me at first as I sat in the shadows of the lamp.

"What? How did you get in here? It was locked," he asked, eventually spotting me at his desk. Then he rolled his eyes, "OK, OK. Did you ever get arrested for breaking and entering?"

I grinned, shaking my head, feeling my smile stretch at the corners of my mouth.

"No. They never got me for that one."

"You know I've bought you your own clothes, don't you?" he asked, moving across the room towards me

"Yeah, but these are more comfortable," I answered smoothing the white t-shirt down to where I'd tied it in a knot above the dressing on the side of my stomach, the top of Cian's jogging bottoms rolled up at the waist.

Stooping over the top of me, Cian's fingers stroked the exposed skin, sending what seemed like millions of tiny electric pulses coursing through me.

"Where have you been, Cian?"

A hand snaked into the front of my grey joggers, cupping my pussy, fingers dancing lightly over my slit.

"You've no knickers on?" his voice was low and husky.

"Stop changing the subject," I warned, trying to swat his hands away.

He ignored me, pushing the thick, grey material over my hips, sliding the joggers and his hands down my legs as heat swarmed in my stomach. His fingers slid between my legs, gliding through the slickness of the folds at my entrance. A moan escaped my throat as the heat turned to molten fiery lust licking at my insides with every slow, teasing movement of his fingers.

"Cian. Where have you been?"

He nuzzled my neck, pulling me to my feet in front of him.

"Cian," I warned.

"I had to go up North. Durham."

"Don't suppose you came across a car accident on your travels?"

His lips hesitated on my neck, and then I felt them part into a grin. He peeled himself from me and grabbed my face in his hand.

"Hargreaves killed your horse," he said, his voice husky, "he could have killed you. And in my world, Charlie, that doesn't go unpunished. No one touches you. And anyone who does will lose more than just their fingers."

Then his lips found my neck again, dancing over the skin, sucking and nibbling, raining a load of hungry kisses over the bulb of my shoulder until he dropped to his knees, his teeth nipping over the bare skin of my stomach, tiny nicks of pain from the wound in my side that mingled with a heat and intensity building in my stomach and between my legs. He slid the jogging bottoms down my legs, thrusting his fingers up inside me, taking me by surprise.

"You're soaking fucking wet, sweetheart," he mumbled, his face against me, his fingers plunging in and out.

He covered my clit with his mouth, his tongue swirling that sweet spot, fingers pumping and turning, hitting parts inside of me I didn't know existed, and I pushed myself against his face, grabbing a handful of hair and pulling his head into me as if I might suffocate him. He growled against my pussy, vibrations rippling

464

through me, his fingers thrusting faster, fucking me with his face, and his tongue and his fingers all at once until my body jolted sweet, hot blackness taking all control from me.

Cian rose to his feet, pushing his lips to mine, letting me taste my own pussy from his tongue.

"I've got something for you," Cian spoke, his voice low, almost hesitant.

I looked at him suspiciously as he rummaged inside the suit jacket he wore before pulling out and handing me a brown envelope.

"Well, open it then."

I pulled the paper out, skim reading the clunky, long-winded text on the formal-looking pages of the transfer document.

"What is this, Cian?"

"The yard. It's yours."

"How? You sold it?"

"I bought it back. Everything. The yard and the horses."

"So you've bought me a burnt down racing yard?"

Cian rolled his eyes.

"We. You. You can build it all back up. The horses are still there in the summer fields, waiting for you," there was a tension in his eyes, apprehension, but he continued, "Bobby told me that he had left his entire estate to you. If I hadn't taken it from him, the yard would have been yours. But it's yours now if you want it."

I turned the thick paper over in my hands. There were two boxes for signatures at the end of the document. One was signed by Cian O'Sullivan.

Cian continued, his voice quieter this time, as if unsure.

"I'm yours too, if you want it?"

"And what about Ireland? What about the business here?"

"The North of England is really profitable. There's a lot of room there for us with the Polish out of the picture. And Ireland is always nice for a holiday."

"And what about this?" I asked, placing my hands over my stomach.

Cian's hand covered mine.

"I never wanted to be a father. I never wanted to fall in love either. But love is selfish, it's blind, it's messy. Love is all kinds of fucked up. Like me and you. But it's all worth it. You are all worth it. As for our baby? I guess it's going to be as stubborn as its mother, and I can't wait to have someone else with no fucking discipline in this house."

He smiled, pulling me into him, his hands sliding up the back of my top, edging it over my head and sinking his teeth into my nipple.

"You're an arsehole, Cian O'Sullivan," I whispered as his tongue got to work and wetness gathered between my legs once more, "but I love you."

℘ The End ℘

Want More?

All the books in The Northern Sins Saga can be purchased here:
https://nikterry.link/thenorthernsinssaga

Keep up to date with new releases, get access to bonus scenes and exclusive giveaways by signing up to my newsletter:
https://nikterry.link/newsletter

Follow my Facebook page to learn more about me and join my reader group.
https://nikterry.link/facebook

About the Author

I can't remember a time I haven't written stories. I wrote my first short story collection at six years old and they went a lot like this:

Once upon a time there was a goat. The goat was good. The goat met a witch. The witch was bad.....

Well you get the idea, but the imagination, creativity and story structure was there, even when I'd barely learnt to read and write.

I then took to writing thrillers and fantasy series, none of which I have ever published but are sitting, patiently waiting to be given some attention at a later date.

My very first fascination with romance came from the absolute best series of my generation – Buffy the Vampire Slayer. How I loved bad-boy Spike and how angry I used to get with Buffy over some of her rubbish romantic choices (I only approved of Angel when he lost his soul). Then there was Cole and Phoebe in Charmed and later Bella, Edward and Jacob in Twilight (I was strictly team Jacob by the way – he was much more my type – I think you're getting the picture).

One day I stumbled into the steamy romance genre (before EL James made Romance so very sexy) and bought a book that looked like a fantasy story – which it was – but with extras. I remember reading it on the commute to work and hiding it in a newspaper because I was worried about what people would think if they read it over my shoulder, because that's what I always did to others. I also remember coming across that first scene totally not expecting it and turning bright red when I realised just what I was reading. But I quickly became hooked and I've read so many in this genre since, falling in love with the passion, action, and angst and the adrenaline rush of a hot scene.

Then, just before the Great Pandemic of 2020 (this will sound much more dramatic in ten years' time), I decided to see if I was capable or writing such scenes. It seemed I was, and my hubby was happy to 'sense check' them with me. Now, between us, we have released the first book in the Northern Sins Saga, set in the North East of England where we live with our two daughters, two cats and three ponies.

I'm really excited to get you all on board the steamy romance train with me because what a ride this is going to be!

Printed in Great Britain
by Amazon

87193273R00274